D1566705

Let Us Prey

LET US PREY

The Public Trial of Jimmy Swaggart

by Hunter Lundy

"The prophets prophesy falsely, and the priests bear rule
by their means; and my people love to have it so: and
what will ye do in the end thereof?"
—*The Book of the Prophet Jeremiah, 5:31*

Genesis Press, Inc.
Columbus, Mississippi

Genesis Press, Inc.
315 3rd Avenue North
Columbus, MS 39701

ISBN: 1-885478-70-4

Manufactured in the United States of America

First Edition

I would like to dedicate this book to Tomy Dee Frasier and his lovely wife, the late Julia Fredin Frasier–two people who demonstrated unconditional love for each other and who without a doubt made this country a better place to live. Tomy Dee Frasier, through his direction, leadership and wit, convinced me I had chosen the right profession. Hopefully, one day, I can say I was half the lawyer that Tomy Frasier was.

Also, I am grateful to my wife, Beth, who pushed me to complete this book, but who also inspired me as a young lawyer from Lake Charles, Louisiana, taking on the entire Bar Association of New Orleans. The letter Beth wrote to me on August 7, 1991, during the middle of the trial, has always been kept in a place of safekeeping. I periodically take it out and reread it and realize how much she loved me and prayed for me during this episode of my life.

• PROLOGUE •
THE DEVIL AND NEW ORLEANS

"O full of all subtlety and all mischief, thou child of the devil, thou enemy of all righteousness, wilt thou not cease to pervert the right ways of the Lord?"
—The Acts of the Apostles, 13:10

Possibly no street in the United States evokes the history of the city that surrounds it more than New Orleans' Canal Street. Among America's many classic streets—Wall Street, Beacon Hill, State Street, and even Hollywood Boulevard—Canal Street stands out. Visible even to the untrained eye is the mark of old New Orleans, old Louisiana, taking the word *old* in any way it can be defined.

Behind Canal, only a few blocks off the broad expanse of concrete and the weak attempts at modernity, is the French Quarter. Home to beggars and bards, confidence artists and crafty entrepreneurs, the Quarter has been called one of the most popular tourist attractions in the country. Even the musicians and the artisans gathered around the corners and squares to play their instruments or display their paintings fail to relieve the tawdry facade of a city whose greatness lies in a fog-shrouded past. Daytime visitors may wonder how an antique collection of wrought-iron-draped buildings with rotting thresholds stuffed with overpriced objets d'art, gaudy T-shirts, and cheap gag gifts could maintain such an appeal—but it does.

Nighttime visitors don't wonder at all. The blaring notes of hot jazz vie with strip-joint street hawkers, female impersonators, noisy night clubs, aromas of cajun cuisine–oysters and beer, whiskey and shrimp–the buzz of neon, and the enticing window displays of seminude dancers to create an atmosphere of decadent pleasures, of forbidden fruits, of sin.

By full dark on a Sunday, the seventh day of the ninth month of the year of Our Lord, 1986, the last trolley of the day was back in the barn.

1

Traffic was light, mostly made up of misdirected tourists seeking the Quarter's naughty blandishments or the correct turn into a hotel's parking garage.

It was a night for mischief and self-indulgence. It was a night to give somebody the devil.

In a small Canal Street Assembly of God church, the Reverend Tom Miller had just concluded his Sunday evening service. Although his was a small church—claiming just under a hundred regular members, it was part of a rapidly developing Assembly of God presence in Orleans Parish. It would never challenge the larger, more prestigious congregations in the suburbs, but that was never its mission. Its parishioners were largely reclaimed from the streets; they were generally poor, generally black, generally in need of God's guidance and God's love; mostly they were in need of jobs and education, of the courage to continue to avoid the needle, the bottle, the boneyard. Mostly, they needed hope just to keep on keeping on.

Providing that hope, Tom Miller believed, was the highest priority of his calling to do the work of the Lord.

The Reverend Tom Miller was hardly an impressive man. He was in his mid-forties and just over six foot in height, but his thinning hair and reserved manner made him seem somehow smaller, somehow less imposing than the more flamboyant ministers in the highly evangelistic, markedly aggressive Full Gospel Faith. Miller was a man of little formal education but much devotion. He took his work seriously, and he was good at it. He took his call to the pulpit seriously, and he had remained committed to that calling. Surrounded by the largest urban population of Roman Catholicism in the South, his ministry provided an almost stereotypical image of metropolitan missionary work.

Tom Miller was personally convinced of the correctness of his faith and of the Word of God as he interpreted it. He was regarded as a pleasant man, even by the nonbelievers in the neighborhood around the church. He was a highly motivated, if somewhat idealistic. Altogether, he was well-suited to the profession he followed. He was generally liked and respected.

After that Sunday evening service, after most of the sparse crowd had departed, Miller moved from his pulpit to the church lobby, where he was asked to do something that few contemporary men of the cloth of any faith had ever done. He was asked to perform an exorcism.

Called a deliverance in the parlance of Protestant fundamentalist churches, the casting out of demons and cleansing of the spirit of an individual is a prescribed part of a minister's duty. It was part of the resurrected Jesus Christ's instructions to the disciples and has been a major tenet and an accepted practice of Christian faith for twenty centuries since. Often accompanied with the "laying on of hands," exorcisms are used for the curing of dread diseases and the correction of many outward manifestations of the presence of Satan and his demons in the tortured soul of a sinner's handicaps. Exorcism of an evil spirit is a cornerstone of Christian faith.

But, in these more modern, perhaps more cynical times, most mainstream denominations have come to regard the ritual more as a metaphor than as a physical rite.

In the Assembly of God denomination, however, the ritual retains its early significance. It has often been part of public evangelistic services—especially revival services. But it was unusual for someone to request a private deliverance—a personal exorcism—especially from a little known and overworked innercity missionary, particularly when the individual making the request was not a regular parishioner, indeed was not even known to the minister in question. Some lifetime Assembly of God ministers—many with national stature within the church—have not once in thirty or forty years of service been asked to do such a thing even by well-established parishioners. Thus it was, to say the least, an unusual request that Sunday evening in Tom Miller's tiny church on Canal Street.

The request was made by a Hispanic woman known only as Theresa. She had with her a girl whom she introduced to Miller as Rosary Ortego. Rosary, the Reverend Miller was given to understand, was but fourteen years old, deaf and mute, and, Theresa informed Miller, very much in the grip of the devil.

In the company of his wife, Mary, a regular member of his congregation named Ruth Turner and Theresa, Miller proceeded with the deliverance. To his amazement, the girl began to speak not as a child might but in a variety of voices and tongues representing a variety of personalities. It was hideously frightening, threatening, most astounding.

To hear actual voices of the spirits was not, in and of itself, at all unusual to Miller's ear. The Assembly of God denomination expressly believes in "glossolalia," or "speaking in tongues" and in the physical manifestations of God and Satan in the world. But to hear these spirits identify themselves as actual people—people known to those witnessing the ritual—and to hear those words spoken by a deaf-mute was without a

3

doubt the most mysterious experience most ministers would ever hope to have.

The ceremony soon removed to the sanctuary itself, partly because Turner wanted more room, partly because Miller felt more comfortable within the innermost sanctum of the House of God. The church, according to Ruth Turner, filled with the "stink of the Devil." The odor became so profound that everyone retched and choked. But Miller was steadfast. The ritual continued, the voices continued, and the service progressed through the night.

As the exorcism continued, Reverend Miller was able to identify several of the spirits speaking through this deaf-mute's mouth. He was amazed, then horrified by what he was learning. The tortured girl writhed and moaned, screamed and spat, and the bizarre stench continued to grow as the voices continued; but by far the most shocking revelation that emerged from this all-night ceremony was when Rosary Ortego identified the most dominant of the articulating spirits as being none other than the Reverend Marvin Gorman.

The Reverend Gorman was well-known to Miller. Until very recently Gorman had been pastor of the First Assembly of God Church, one of the largest congregations in New Orleans. Although he had resigned quietly and somewhat mysteriously in July, Marvin Gorman remained the most distinguished and best respected man of God in the city.

Functioning at the height of his profession at the start of that summer, Marvin Gorman was one of the most powerful and influential of Assembly of God clergy; at that moment, he was home in bed, with his wife, most likely attempting to shove aside the problems in his life caused by recent developments in his career, but still dreaming of his imminent plans to further enlarge his personal power and evangelistic influence throughout Louisiana, indeed throughout the United States. In any event, he was blithely unaware that he had taken the form of a demon, speaking the words of Satan with the tongue of a teenaged deaf-mute.

Miller was stunned by the revelation that the demon in possession of Rosary Ortego was in fact this distinguished man of God, Marvin Gorman, a man he personally admired and had emulated. But he was convinced that the voice he heard was none other than that of Marvin Gorman. According to Miller and Turner, they were further astonished when the demon, still speaking in Gorman's voice, announced: "I'm going to destroy the Assembly of God and all you Christians."

There was no doubt in Ruth Turner's mind or in Tom Miller's mind that Rosary Ortego was possessed by an evil spirit.

Ultimately, the voices ceased, the stench dissipated, and the demons disappeared. The girl was delivered, "cleansed." Miller led the group in one more prayer. Ruth Turner piously vowed not to relate the words the girl had spoken in the voices of the demons, for to do so would be to repeat "the words of the devil." Such words were *ipso facto* untrue, and no Christian should repeat them. It was her belief that the entire episode should be kept secret.

Mary Miller, the Reverend Miller's loyal wife, however, was not convinced that what she had witnessed was genuine. She believed they had all been duped, hoaxed; but to what end, for what purpose she could not divine.

The Reverend Miller soon reported it to Jimmy Swaggart Ministries in Baton Rouge, and, for some reason, to another Assembly of God minister in New Orleans, The Reverend Michael Indest, as well as a group of ministers during a luncheon.

Rosary Ortego, accompanied by her companion, Theresa, swept out into the bustle of early morning Canal Street and disappeared into a sea of ordinarily sinful humanity.

Thus ended what was probably the longest night in the Reverend Tom Miller's ministerial career, if not his life. His holy mission was accomplished, the girl, he believed, was freed of her demonic tormentors, and that should have been an end to the matter.

It was only the beginning.

• PART ONE •

EAST OF EDEN

"The beauty of Israel is slain upon thy high places: how are the mighty fallen!"

—The Second Book of Samuel, 1:19

• CHAPTER ONE •
FROM THE MOUNTAIN TOP

> "And I say also unto thee, That thou art Peter, and upon this rock I will build my church; and the gates of hell shall not prevail against it."
> —*The Gospel According to St. Matthew, 16:18.*

In late April of 1986, I had just remarried. My wife, Beth, and her son, Johnny, joined me and my daughter, Tricia, in setting up house in my hometown of Lake Charles, Louisiana. We had just gone on our first family vacation, a trip to Steamboat Springs, Colorado, for which we had saved for months, and I was continuing to work at my legal practice.

The law was by no means my lifelong professional dream. I graduated from LaGrange High School in 1972, living my life for football up until that time. During my senior year at LaGrange I got a job and enjoyed the money so much that I bypassed college football and decided to attend the local university, McNeese State. While at McNeese I worked and majored in my fraternity, Kappa Alpha Order. In my sophomore year, I realized that I was not getting an education and that I missed football more than I expected, so I started looking for a school where I might be able to play. A cousin of mine in Jackson, Mississippi, told me I should walk on at Millsaps College and see if I could play. In 1974, I did just that and in the second week was awarded a scholarship.

I had been recruited by the Coast Guard Academy and talked to small colleges while in high school but I was never really big enough to play major college football. Millsaps was a good opportunity—a very academic-oriented school, enticing for a student athlete. At just a half inch short of six feet tall and a little more than 200 pounds, what I lacked in size and speed, I made up for in heart and determination.

The next two years of my life were quite enjoyable, with the 1975 football season of Millsaps still being recognized as having the most talent of any team in the history of the school. We were chosen to go to the NCAA playoffs and made it to the semifinals before losing to the ultimate national champions, Wittenberg University. I was chosen scholar-leader-athlete by the Central Mississippi chapter of the National Football Foundation and Hall of Fame in March 1976.

Scheduled to graduate in May, I was uncertain where my life was going. My Uncle Francis, a mover and shaker in the Mississippi political circles, suggested that I apply to Mississippi College School of Law, a new law school in Jackson. Although football had been my life through high school and the latter part of my college years, a career in coaching was not appealing to me. Thus, in the fall of 1976, two weeks after marrying my first wife—a girlfriend from Lake Charles, I started law school. I committed my life from that point on to a career that I would soon learn would be as competitive as the game of football. This competitive side of law really appealed to me. Once committed to law school, I worked hard and eventually became Editor-in-Chief of the Law Review and then graduated high enough in my class to secure a clerkship with United States District Judge Walter L. Nixon in Biloxi. My daughter, Tricia, was born 1979 while we were living in Biloxi.

It seems that during my entire life, I have experienced extraordinary challenges. Supposedly, I was too small to play offensive guard for any college football team but I not only played, I excelled and later became one of the few offensive line inductees into the Millsaps College Sports Hall of Fame. Like college, law school was probably for those who were a little bit smarter than me. However, I worked exceptionally hard to achieve academic recognition and succeeded in obtaining one of the most sought after law clerkships in Mississippi.

One day while Judge Nixon was away from the office, I was lounging in his office reading his *Louisiana Bar Journal* and read that a firm in Lake Charles was looking for an associate. I had already accepted employment in Jackson but it dawned on me that if I was ever going home, now was the chance. I was hired by the firm of Jones, Tete, Nolan, Hanchey, Swift and Spears and returned to Lake Charles in May 1981. I became the first Mississippi College School of Law graduate to practice west of the Mississippi River and within a short time, earned a reputation for aggressiveness, particularly in litigation. It seemed once again.that I was the underdog, and I strived hard to outwork everyone and make a name for myself. Within eighteen months, I became a partner, and I was proud of the fact that my counsel was often sought on particularly difficult cases and was well-regarded in the firm.

Less that two months after being admitted to the Louisiana Bar, in late 1981, I was in the courtroom trying cases. One of my first was in Acadia Parish, Louisiana, which involved defending Greyhound Bus Company in a slip-and-fall case. A woman claimed that she was standing in the aisle of the bus as it was traveling down Interstate 10 when the bus driver suddenly braked, causing her feet to slip out from underneath her and her to fall on her back. I argued to the court that her claim was not only contrary to the law of Louisiana but it was contrary to the laws of physics. Judge Bertrand agreed and dismissed the lawsuit.

Thus in April 1986, I was thirty-one years old, had won a few cases, and believed that I could take on the world. Little did I know that I was still green, naive, inexperienced, and a long way from having the strength to slay Goliath.

I was sitting in my office one day when I received a telephone call from Randy Roach, another Lake Charles attorney; Roach represented The American Bank of Commerce, the largest creditor of a local television station, KVHP, Channel 29, which was in receivership. Previously owned by a syndicate that included a former district attorney and a former Baptist minister, the station had gone under because of a small broadcast tower and lack of managers experienced in the communications industry. Roach told me that a mutual friend, Winfield Little, an attorney representing the management company serving as receiver to the station, had recommended that I be contacted about representing the Reverend Marvin Gorman from New Orleans.

Gorman, a popular televangelist, had made an offer to purchase the station and rescue it from its indebtedness to the American Bank of Commerce. Roach and Little agreed that Gorman would make an excellent choice as buyer for the station; but the legal details would be difficult to work out, as both the Federal Communications Commission and federal bank examiners would be scrutinizing the transaction. In a phrase, there would be a lot of court time and a good deal of legal footwork to prepare the deal for closing. To an ambitious young attorney, of course, this meant a lot of billed hours, which in turn meant a lot of bonus money from my firm, should I take the case.

At the time, I had never before represented a minister, certainly not a televangelist; indeed, I had never met one, and I had doubts about the wisdom of becoming involved. In the first place, I was skeptical that any single individual—particularly a preacher—could afford to buy a television station, so I asked Roach for references that could vouch for Gorman's background and financial resources. Roach suggested I call an attorney with the Jones, Walker firm in New Orleans and ask him about his past experiences with the Reverend Gorman.

From that inquiry, I learned that Reverend Gorman was an important and well-known Assemblies of God minister who was frequently involved in six- and seven-figure transactions; he also had a reputation for honest dealings and prompt payment of attorney's fees. Indeed, Jones, Walker's standard fees were almost twice as high on a per-hour rate as our firm's, and since it was a smart move to use local counsel to handle a local transaction of this nature, it looked like a bird's nest on the ground for us.

Even with those matters settled, I still had doubts as to my suitability to handle this matter, but Roach assured me that my religious background (Southern Baptist) and familiarity with the local court scene made me an ideal choice. With all of this in mind, I agreed to meet with the Reverend Gorman and do whatever legal work was required in connection with the purchase of the station.

That same day, I was told that the minister and one of his sons, Randy, and their pilot would be flying in to Lake Charles in Reverend Gorman's private King Air plane to attend the hearing. I was instantly impressed. I had heard about ministers with The World Wide Church of God who flew around in jets, but I knew of no local ministers who owned their own airplanes and commanded their own pilots. I picked up the party at Transit Aviation in Lake Charles and drove them to the hearing.

The Reverend Marvin Gorman was a well-groomed man who looked much younger than his fifty-four years, above average in height and solidly built. His brown hair was styled and very neat, worn in a straight-back style, allowing his facial features and soft brown eyes to stand out behind rose-tinted glasses. He also was well-dressed—he wore an Armani suit and what appeared to be custom-made Italian shoes. I noticed that his fingernails were immaculately manicured and cut a little longer than the average man's. He came across as a very sure but not particularly vain or arrogant individual, his appearance not at all unlike that of many successful business or professional men of about the same age. In short, he cut an imposing figure, one that suggested strength, charm, and personal charisma.

By contrast, Randy Gorman was balding, slender with completely different facial features. It was not until some time later that I learned that he was Gorman's adopted son from his wife, Virginia's, first marriage.

12

Energetic and enthusiastic, the Reverend Gorman greeted me robustly, as a friend might. I was taken with his tact and polite manner and also with his expert knowledge of the transaction we were undertaking on behalf of his ministry.

I was also impressed with how well-known he was. Like many people, particularly Southern Baptists, I paid scant attention to televangelism; truly, my closest experience with the entire world of television ministries centered more on parodies and comedians' remarks than on any serious study or observation. Like many people, what encounters I'd had with them came while "channel surfing" on late-night television; and, again like many people, I quickly moved past their broadcasts when I came across them. Prior to Roach's call to me, however, if I had ever heard of Marvin Gorman, I couldn't recall when or in what context. He was simply one of the figures who flicked across my TV screen, a mere name more than any sort of personal presence.

I soon discovered though, that Gorman was well-known in my hometown. While attending the first hearing, the Clerk of Court as well as other courthouse employees came over to greet Marvin Gorman in person, to shake his hand and exchange pleasantries with him. It was obvious that he enjoyed a wide popularity among many churchgoers, especially those from charismatic sects. I observed that several who approached him gave him the sort of deferential treatment usually reserved for sports figures, movie stars, recording artists, or famous politicians.

After numerous courtroom appearances by counsel, the judge finally approved the buy-sell agreement as well as the financing plan offered by Marvin Gorman Ministries, Inc. The closing of the deal was initially set for August 1986. I assumed my work was nearly done.

In early June, I asked Ray Guillory, my personal certified public accountant, ski buddy and close friend, to drive with me to New Orleans to visit Reverend Gorman. I wanted him to meet the head of the First Assembly of God Church of New Orleans, as well as Gorman's manager, his family, and other members of his staff. It was my hope that after the meeting, Gorman would ask Guillory to continue providing the accounting services for the television station after it was sold, but I also had grown curious about Gorman and his church. I wanted to see his operation for myself.

The assumptions I made during my initial association with Gorman were substantiated by the physical facilities I saw and by the facts

13

presented to me during my tour. The complex on Airline Highway consisted of a large building that contained a huge sanctuary, a school, administrative offices, as well as a television production studio. I discovered that The First Assembly of God of New Orleans had a congregation numbering in excess of five thousand members. Services were conducted five times on Sunday, once each on Monday, Wednesday, and Thursday nights; all were well attended. The parochial school enrolled more than five hundred students in kindergarten through the twelfth grade, and had established a presence both academically and athletically in the New Orleans community.

Clearly, Marvin Gorman Ministries was a force to be reckoned with, not only in Orleans Parish but also in the entire state and region. I could immediately see what value a television station would bring to Gorman's work and reputation. It was a wise move—a power play—but it also was the logical next step in the advancement of Gorman's non-profit corporation, Marvin Gorman Ministries.

During our meeting, Guillory and I learned that Marvin Gorman Ministries had not only signed an agreement to purchase Channel 29 in Lake Charles, the corporation also had signed an agreement to purchase the communications permit and facilities of Channel 11 in Houma, Louisiana, a matter being handled by another firm. This was a bit surprising to me, at first, but when I considered it further, it also made sense. It additionally impressed me with the depth of his backers' pockets. There was obviously big money involved here, much bigger money than I had imagined.

Gorman explained to us that his dream was to spread the Gospel from Mobile, Alabama, to Houston, Texas, from production facilities at his home in Metairie, Louisiana. The two television stations—with a satellite uplink from the church—would enable him to conduct Bible studies and talk shows from his home, spreading the Word of God across the Gulf Coast, then to the entire nation, and ultimately throughout the world. It was an ambitious prospect, but at that meeting, I became convinced that if anyone could do it, Marvin Gorman could.

After seeing the First Assembly of God production facilities and touring Channel 29 and knowing its capability, I was frankly in awe of the intelligence of Gorman and his support personnel. Their expertise and talents far exceeded the average pulpit ministries with which I was familiar from my Southern Baptist upbringing. Gorman's organization and complexity of operation matched his ambition and also matched easily any corporate client in my legal experience.

But at the same time, I harbored serious doubts as to whether Gorman was as interested in the "Great Commission"—his calling and his mission—as he was in the intricate workings of the Federal Communications Commission. As his attorney, though, I was committed to handling matters legal; I was content to allow matters spiritual to remain between Gorman and whomever he consulted on those issues.

Following this initial meeting and tour, we drove farther down Airline Highway to a shopping center where the First Assembly of God of New Orleans was building a new facility. This was located in a shopping center that had been purchased by Gorman's church. At one end of the shopping center, the church was building a new auditorium that would seat twenty-five hundred to three-thousand people, almost twice the number that could be accommodated at the older building. The shopping center parking lot would be ample for the congregation during the Sunday morning services, when most of the retail businesses would be closed, and even during the week, it would offer substantial parking for those involved with the education program of the church.

At first, I found it incongruous that a church would buy a shopping center and then build a church auditorium on one end of it, but then I realized that the remainder of the retail facilities would remain under lease and the First Assembly of God would be the beneficiary of the revenues.

We then visited Gorman's home in Metairie. Although by no means ostentatious, particularly from the outside, the interior of the house was well-appointed and approached opulence. There was no less than five-thousand square feet of living area, all well-designed for comfort. Gorman gave us a tour of the house, and by far the most impressive room was the master bedroom which doubled as his study. The room was created in a wing of its own, the result of a twenty-thousand dollar gift from someone in his congregation. It contained an enormous big-screen television, a large jacuzzi, and comfortable furniture. It was from here that Gorman planned to conduct his talk shows via satellite.

While walking through the kitchen, we were met by his wife Virginia Gorman, a pleasant woman in her early fifties with brown hair, hazel eyes, and an attractive figure. She greeted us with a pleasant handshake and a bright smile. Although she was not the sort of woman who would dominate a room either by virtue of her personality or good looks, she was a pretty woman and in many ways the very picture of a successful preacher's wife.

After this trip, during which we also met with the First Assembly of God's business manager, Carl Miller, I felt confident that Gorman would accept my recommendation of Gragson, Casiday & Guillory as the CPA firm to handle their dealings in Lake Charles. I'm also sure that Guillory's reaction to what we had seen and heard on our trip reflected my own. On the drive back to Lake Charles, he remarked and I agreed that neither of us had ever imagined that "God" was such a big business.

I was enjoying the prospects of representing a wealthy minister who had his own plane and would soon own a television station in Lake Charles. After all, Gorman had been referred to me personally so, at the time, this appeared to be a good plum for the firm.

• CHAPTER TWO •
THE BUSINESS OF GOD

"And when the day of Pentacost was fully come, they
were all with one accord in one place"
—*The Acts of the Apostles, 2:1.*

Perhaps the best organized and most unified of all the Pentecostalist
sects, the Assemblies of God was founded in Hot Springs, Arkansas, in
1914 as a spin-off group of the Holiness Movement. Governed by a
General Council and Presbytery, which formulates and administers
policies for its nearly eleven thousand congregations, the Assemblies of
God's faithful affirm baptism with the Holy Spirit, glossolalia, divine
healing, and charismatic evidence of God in daily life. They also embrace
the early Christian belief in Jesus Christ's imminent return to earth, when
He and His saints will reign over a long period of peace and harmony
based on righteousness.

The more than thirty thousand credentialed ministers of the
Assemblies of God are confirmed and supported first by District Councils
(loosely organized on the basis of states or general geographic regions),
which are, in turn, overseen by the General Council in Springfield,
Missouri. While matters of individual and independent church
organization remain in the hands of separate congregations, the councils
maintain a strict code of conduct and behavior for all member ministers,
most all of whom are ordained by the General Council.

Some observers have said that the Assemblies of God are growing at
such a fast pace that they will soon outstrip the Southern Baptists for
preeminence in terms of membership. Certainly their popularity,
particularly in rural areas, is observable in almost every community in the
South and Southwest. Although their *laissez-faire* organization lends
itself to independence from congregation to congregation, the church
itself has found that modern times sometimes call for modern measures.

17

Among these measures is a stricter and tighter governance of ministerial behavior and public image. Additionally, there have been observable movements toward tighter national organization and control of individual congregations, at least in terms of administration, especially in the case of churches that have exceeded their local boundaries to reach out to a regional or even national or world audience through the medium of television.

Doctrine, insofar as the General Council is concerned, remains a matter of faith, so long as the interpretations remain in the general perimeters of fundamentalism and charismatic dogma. However, as some churches become richer and more powerful within their communities, as they develop schools and other educational and social programs in an effort to appeal to the young, they find themselves more closely inspected by governmental and social powers, more subject to the kinds of controls that religious purists abhor.

Ecclesiastically, Assembly of God churches remain independent. But in a secular sense, the Assemblies of God, like almost every other denomination and sect, cannot avoid public and secular scrutiny. Increasingly, it seems, they cannot avoid public condemnation, either, particularly when their ministers misbehave or, as in the case of Marvin Gorman, find themselves engaged in a religious war with other ministers in the denomination. And this is especially true when that war is apparently fought over the issue of that most fascinating of human subjects, original sin.

Over the next six weeks I had no contact with Marvin Gorman. I called a couple of times to talk to him and was told he was out, and he returned none of my calls. I spoke with Randy Gorman to determine how everything was going. Although I had no inkling that there was anything wrong, I somehow instinctively wanted reassurance that all was in order for closing the television station deal in August. Without verbal prompting, Randy said that his father had been experiencing "some problems," but that they had nothing to do with the purchase of the television station, and he assured me there was no impediment to the purchase going forward as planned.

During the first week of August, I received a telephone call from Randy Roach, who asked if I had heard about my client's "problems." At first, I made no connection between his question and what Randy Gorman had mentioned in passing earlier, so I told him I hadn't heard a thing. Roach suggested that I meet him and Winfield Little at Gene Reddell's

18

office at American Bank of Commerce.

Gene Reddell was the Executive Vice President of the bank. At this point, savings and loans, banks, and other financial institutions were failing all across the South and Southwest. The Federal Savings Insurance Corporation was taking over billions of dollars in assets and debts, and the U.S. Congress was becoming involved as talk of a bailout was making headlines all over the country. Bank examiners were a common sight in any lending institution, and the economy was reflecting the dilemma by sliding into recession.

The American Bank of Commerce was no exception to this scrutiny. In the summer of 1986, all of its outstanding loans were being closely watched by federal regulators; one of those outstanding loans was that held by Channel 29. Reddell explained that it was extremely important that the bank recover its indebtedness from the television station, because if it didn't there was a serious threat that the federal government would take over the bank.

When we met in Reddell's office, Randy handed me a copy of a letter written by the Louisiana District Council of the Assemblies of God to a number of ministers statewide. The letter indicated that Marvin Gorman had resigned his church and had been dismissed by the Assemblies of God because of unspecified "moral conduct." The letter read as follows:

Dear Friend of the Gospel:

This letter is to inform you of action taken by the District Board on August 4, 1986, regarding Marvin E. Gorman.

On July 16, 1986, the superintendent and secretary-treasurer went to the Gorman residence in Metairie, along with Brother Carl Miller and Brother Daniel Flanagan of First Assembly of God in New Orleans. In our presence Brother Gorman confessed that he was guilty of conduct unbecoming to a minister and indiscretions involving morals. (See 1986-87 Yearbook, Page 46 of Bylaws, ARTICLE XI, Section 2, Paragraph A.) He then presented his fellowship card to the superintendent. After expressing our deepest sorrow and disappointment, and our love for Brother Gorman and his family, we had prayer with them and left.

19

With this type of violation there is only two possible decisions the Board could make: (1) dismissal or (2) two-year rehabilitation program. (See 1986-87 Yearbook, Pages 48, 49, 50 of the Bylaws, ARTICLE XI, Section 7, 8 and 9) Brother Gorman indicated to the superintendent and secretary-treasurer that he planned to continue his television ministry and pulpit ministry. Therefore a rehabilitation program would not be feasible. Final decision by the Board was for dismissal.

Please be reminded of your ethical responsibilities as outlined in the 1985 General Council Bylaws, ARTICLE VIII, Section 10, Page 139.

We trust that you will be in prayer for Brother Gorman and his family, and the many people affected by these circumstances.

In His love and grace,
Forrest H. Hall
Secretary-Treasurer

Apparently a local minister in the community had passed a copy of the letter to Judge Lyons, Winfield Little, and Randy Roach. At the time, I had no idea of anything of this nature being in Gorman's background. I suspected, though, that Gary Hardesty, whose investment group was competing for the station, might have somehow obtained a copy of the letter and passed it to the judge and other involved parties in a last-ditch attempt to derail the television station deal.

Regardless of how it came to the court, it was there, and it was distressing news, to say the least, although I was by no means certain that it was legitimate.

I immediately returned to my office and called Gorman. Again, he was not available, but my call was intercepted, again, by his son Randy. I informed Randy of the letter's contents and demanded an explanation on behalf of Channel 29's receiver and the bank. Randy again assured me that there was no problem at all. Implying that his father's troubles were more of a personal nature than anything else, he stated that Marvin Gorman Ministries intended to move forward with the purchase and suggested that we set up another meeting with the receiver, the bank's attorney, and any other interested parties.

I made the necessary arrangements, and during the second week of September that meeting was held in the conference room at the Jones,

Tete law firm in Lake Charles. Present at the meeting were Little, Reddell, myself, an attorney for the American Bank of Commerce, my law partner, Carl Hanchey, and Marvin and Randy Gorman. Gorman appeared no different from his first court hearing: confident, strong and self-assured. There was no suggestion that he was a man under stress who had just been caught with his pants down; on the contrary, he gave the impression of a very sound businessman who was altering his course slightly in order to accomplish his goals. He assured everyone that the deal would go through and that Marvin Gorman Ministries was still sound.

Everyone in the room was aware of the letter's contents, and I, for one, was eager to question him about it, but no one brought it up. Technically, it was not anyone's business, of course, so long as the enterprise he represented wasn't harmed, and it apparently was not.

Gorman stipulated that he had access to underlying financing, and while he did not elaborate or share details, he did insist that money would be forthcoming and that the deal would be completed. He did ask, however, that the closing date be postponed until October. This seemed like a reasonable request—particularly as there were no other buyers, especially cash buyers, in sight. The parties agreed and went back to the courthouse and filed for an extension of time.

Following that action, I held a private meeting with Gorman and one of my law partners, Greg Massey, to determine what, exactly, was the extent of Gorman's personal problems with the Assembly of God. In response to our questions, Gorman produced a statement purportedly written by the Louisiana District Council of the Assemblies of God. The statement read:

> *To Fellow Believers and Congregation of the First Assembly of God Church in New Orleans, Louisiana:*
>
> *On Sunday, July 20, 1986, your Board of Directors made a statement to the congregation in its three morning services explaining the basis for the resignation of Marvin E. Gorman as pastor. A continuation of comments, conflicting statements, and misleading explanations lead me to repeat and add to that first statement.*
>
> *The Louisiana District Council of the Assemblies of God, with the concurrence and agreement of the General offices of the*

Assemblies of God, makes the following declarative statement in cooperation with the First Assembly's Board of Directors, its interim pastoral committee, its pastoral staff, and its entire congregation:

This is no time for vengeful spirit, for a retalitory [sic] attitude, for vindictiveness, for pious self-righteousness, or for taking pleasure in another's suffering. At the same time it is necessary for me to speak out of the conviction of my heart in love. The love of Calvary cannot allow the Body of Christ to be led into error. Those who are spiritual leaders have accountability to God to preach the gospel, both by precept and by example. Leaders must put the welfare of the people under their influence and ministry ahead of their own interests. The manner in which members and supporters of First Assembly have been contacted directly and indirectly by Marvin E. Gorman demonstrates a disregard for ministerial ethics. Such conflict and the misleading message being given shows an absence of christian [sic] love. There has been a disregard for unity and harmony in the Body of Christ and the local assembly. Some, the responsibility for confusion, discord, and strife coming from some media messages and the personal contacts lies at the feet of Marvin E. Gorman and individuals coming to his defense, presumably out of ingnorance [sic] of the true facts. We find this tragically unscriptural, misleading, and detrimental to the spiritual well-being of all believers. Although it hurts me deeply to do so, I must inform you as a fellow believer, spiritual leader, and as an extremely close friend of Marvin E. Gorman over many years, I believe that your Board's statement on July 20, 1986, was completely true and accurate. In addition, more evidence has been presented to me and the executive offices of the Assembly of God that make it clear that the information spread by Marvin E. Gorman concerning his conduct has been incomplete and misleading. A local television broadcast was aired last week in which Marvin Gorman repeatedly stated that "most or 95% of what was being said about him was lies." He did not say who lied or what was lied about, and this simply causes confusion. To my knowledge, Marvin E. Gorman has no enemies in this district or in this church. All these men love Marvin E. Gorman and are praying for him to do the right thing. Established evidence and facts prove that Marvin E. Gorman engaged in multiple, immoral incidents over a period of years, which includes

*adultery, illicit affairs, and unscriptural lascivious conduct
with women who came to him for counsel. I have a statement
from a woman telling of his conduct with her this year, which
was unbecoming to a minister. We cannot minimize the
loathsomeness [sic] of sin or the horrendous consequences of
sin and the damage, hurt, and pain it can bring to individual,
family, church, community, or nation. Righteousness exalteth a
nation, but sin is a reproach to any people. Sin or transgression
must be faced up to, confessed, brought to heart-wrenching
repentance, turned from, renounced, put under the blood, and
forsaken. Sincere request for forgivenness [sic] should be
sought by the sinner from those personally sinned against. The
accountability for sin lies at the door of every human heart,
subject to every human will. No one puts a gun to our head to
make us sin...it is an act of our own free will. There is no excuse
that Satan trapped us, that we were seduced or ensnared. Such
excuses will be of no value at the judgment seat. Rather, every
man must give an account of himself for every deed done in the
body. You do not make excuse for sin. You acknowledge your
sinfulness and your sin. You do not parade your sin as a means
of self aggrandizement and gain by explaining it, justifying it,
or blaming its cause on someone else. It seems this is what has
been done by Marvin E. Gorman and for Marvin E. Gorman by
others. Statements have been made locally and nationally on
TV ministries reflecting on the judgment, action, and integrity
of your church board, congregation and your pastoral staff that
the Louisiana District Council and the General Council of the
Assemblies of God totally disagree with and oppose. A local
television station, a broadcast last week by Marvin E. Gorman,
gave some the impression that myself and other district
officials as well as some national officials of the Assemblies of
God had somehow endorsed or approved of his continued
ministry. Any such implications [sic] is erroneous unfounded,
and without permission. There are national ministries
recognized and endorsed by the Louisiana District Council and
the General Council of the Assemblies of God. Marvin Gorman
Ministries is not one of them now; in fact, it has never been one
of them. Speaking for the Louisiana District Council as District
Superintendent, I want to be crystal clear: Marvin Gorman
gave up his credentials, his ordination as a minister of the
gospel with the Assemblies of God. He did so voluntarily on
Wednesday, July 16, 1986. By his action he expressly chose not
to seek rehabilitation and restoration to the fellowship. This*

means he is not able to pastor an Assemblies of God church now nor in the future unless he repents and submits himself to the rehabilitation processes. If he expresses true repentance and submisson [sic] to the rehabilitation process prescribed by the constitution & bylaws of the General Council of the Assemblies of God and the Louisiana District Council, he can seek restoration and re-instatement. He has not taken any steps in this direction up to this point. The rehabilition [sic] process is provided to allow an erring brother, an elder, the opportunity to experience restorative grace as set foth [sic] in scripture.
Galatians 6:1...

> *'Brethren, if a man be overaken [sic] in a fault, ye which are spiritual, restore such an one in the spirit of meekness; considering thyself, lest thou also be tempted.'*

James 5:19 & 20...

> *'Brethren, if any of you do err from the truth, and one convert him; Let him know, that he which converteth the sinner from the error of his way shall save a soul from death, and shall hide a multitude of sins.'*

The question is asked, 'If God has forgiven, why can't man forgive?' The answer is, everyone I know connected with the matter has expressed love and forgiveness to Marvin Gorman. But an elder and minister of the gospel must be above reproach. If Brother Marvin Gorman fully confesses and repents, God will forgive him. And by the process of time and proven performance, Marvin Gorman can be restored. Let us continue to pray that this will take place.

Although what Gorman handed me and Massey was a photocopy and we could not tell if it had been altered in any way, it was obvious to both of us that the document was a transcribed statement of a presentation that had been given to the church and later mailed out to ministers around the state and possibly all over the country. We also agreed that the statement was outrageous on its face and the contents were unquestionably defamatory. I encouraged Gorman to file suit immediately and enthusiastically volunteered my services if he wished to pursue legal action.

Gorman demurred. He volunteered no details or background concerning the statement except to say that he was certain it had been authored by Jimmy Swaggart, perhaps the most powerful and best known

Assembly of God minister in the world, whose headquarters were in Baton Rouge. He said, that while he could not prove it, he was certain that the August 7 letter, which had created the stir among the parties involved in the television station deal, was at least heavily influenced by Swaggart if not actually authored by him.

Gorman was aware at that time that the Board of Directors of the First Assembly of God in New Orleans had met with Swaggart at his home in Baton Rouge in July, which meant they were behind the statement of July 20 pertaining to his resignation from his church. But he had no direct evidence of the authorship of either the August or the September letters. At that time, he made no statement regarding his admission or denial of any of the allegations in any of the letters.

• CHAPTER THREE •
GORMAN'S RESIGNATION

"Them that sin rebuke before all, that others also may fear."
—*The First Epistle of Paul the Apostle to Timothy, 5:20.*

One of the mysteries that bothered me about the entire Gorman case was Gorman's sudden resignation from his New Orleans church. The August letter and September letters had clearly been the product of one or more individuals who had set out to ruin his character and ministerial career by a gross process of defamation. He had made no statement to me concerning his guilt or innocence of any of the charges leveled against him in the September statement. At this point, he had not seen the Swaggart statement; he had only heard about it. He still believed, though, that Jimmy Swaggart was behind everything being said and published about him. Still, the allegations in the September statement were so outrageous and, to a great extent, unprovable even if they were true, that it seemed unreasonable for a man of Gorman's status and popularity merely to back away without a fight.

Nevertheless, that was precisely what Gorman did. He resigned from the First Assembly of God in New Orleans, which was the base of his financial power. Still, he had not sought my counsel concerning any possible legal action either against Swaggart or anyone else. I couldn't entirely fathom this, but I did not question it; it seemed to be a personal matter between Gorman and Swaggart, if not between Gorman and the Assembly of God. It wasn't until much later that I learned the details surrounding this unprecedented resignation of one of the South's best known and most beloved ministers.

On July 15, 1986, Gorman was confronted at his church by the Reverend David Savage, a young minister and Pastor of the Assembly of God Church in Kenner. Savage was an unassuming but relatively

26

handsome individual. In his late thirties, he had piercing blue eyes and brown hair worn in a stylish fashion. Savage and his wife, Lynda, an extremely attractive, blue-eyed blonde in her late twenties, had been friends of the Gormans for years; Marvin Gorman had many times counseled Lynda on personal matters, particularly with regard to marital problems she claimed to be having with David. Lynda also worked in the vault at the First Assembly of God Church of New Orleans.

That afternoon, Savage openly accused Gorman of having had an affair with Lynda. Gorman admitted to having sex with Lynda but did not discuss any of the details with David.

Savage informed Gorman that he would have to meet with another Assembly of God minister, Michael Indest, the pastor at the Lakeview Christian Center, a church attended by William (Bill) Treeby, who happened to be an attorney and board member of Jimmy Swaggart Ministries. Apparently, at the time, it was Savage's implication to Gorman that Indest would intervene in the matter and attempt to find a basis for forgiveness and mediation between the two ministers, Gorman and Savage.

Gorman agreed and accompanied Savage because he wanted to placate Savage. In the meeting, in front of Savage, Indest surprised Gorman by broadening the accusations, to allege that Gorman had had numerous sexual affairs over a period of years, not only with Lynda Savage, but also with several other women. Obviously, Indest's involvement at this point was more than just facilitating forgiveness.

Indest, a former wine merchant-turned minister, below average in height and stout, listened intently. He exhibited shock at all he was hearing from Savage and told Gorman that this was "too big for him to handle alone," that they would have to see Jimmy Swaggart and put the whole thing in front of him.

Already embarrassed, and without thinking about the consequences of admitting his sin with Lynda Savage, Gorman consented to meet with Swaggart as soon as it could be arranged. As it happened, that very night seemed to be the most convenient time.

But what Gorman—and possibly even Savage—did not know was that the evening's events had been carefully orchestrated. Swaggart, Treeby, and Indest had conversed over the telephone on July 11 and July 14 about the situation regarding Lynda Savage. Their planned confrontation of Gorman was no surprise to anyone except Gorman himself. Indeed, insofar as all present were concerned, Gorman's fate was sealed well in advance of the meeting at the Swaggart home on the night of July 15. All that remained was the formality of announcement–and judgment.

Neither Treeby nor Swaggart held any official position with the Assemblies of God, either on the district or national levels; although they did hold financial sway over the Louisiana District Council; and neither was empowered to impose discipline or take action against anyone not in their immediate employ, which Gorman wasn't. These men were obviously present for no other reason than to further a conspiracy.

Indest knew that Gorman had a close personal friendship with G. Raymond Carlson, Superintendent of the General Council of the Assemblies of God, as well as a good relationship with Cecil Janway, Superintendent of Louisiana District Council, and they felt that the only way they could force Gorman's resignation from the church was to go "outside the loop" and initiate a confrontation with Swaggart. This would avoid the niceties of a formal procedure from either the General or District Council, and it would also permit them—Indest, Treeby, and Swaggart—a free hand in dealing with Gorman's destruction. Although Gorman never claimed such, it is also possible that he believed his friendship with Swaggart would prevail in his favor and serve to keep the entire matter quiet and among these local ministers who, initially, put a serious but fraternal cast on the situation. Indeed, this would be Swaggart's printed assertion later on.

Nevertheless, at approximately 7:00 that same night, July 15, Treeby, Indest, Savage and Gorman drove to the Swaggart mansion on Highland Road in Baton Rouge, with Gorman and Savage riding together in one car, and Treeby and Indest following in another.

During a recent interview on CNN, which Gorman had seen, Swaggart had described his house as a "modest two-bedroom" home. Gorman was immediately struck by the grandiose furnishings of this modest abode when he entered the foyer. He had already marveled at the large swimming pool handsomely situated next to the home among twenty acres of well-manicured and extravagantly landscaped grounds, and the matching Lincoln Town Cars parked in the driveway had not escaped his notice either. Among other appointments in the "million dollar parsonage" was a large circular stairway with handrails leading to the second floor, an enormous living room complete with grand piano. The furniture and accessories were rich in appearance and comfort. Gorman and Virginia were proud of their New Orleans home, but

Swaggart's "two-bedroom" house was palatial, even when compared to the Governor's Mansion.

Upon entering the Swaggart mansion, Gorman and the rest were greeted by Swaggart's wife, Frances, who escorted him into Swaggart's study. This was positioned next to the stairwell and measured forty-by-twenty feet with a larger library than that found in most elementary schools. An executive desk with leather chair sat off to one side, and other posh, comfortable chairs and a sofa were positioned strategically around the room.

Swaggart, a robust and handsome individual of about six feet, two inches and two hundred-twenty pounds, rose to meet Gorman when he entered. He wore casual slacks and a sport shirt and seemed to be expecting them. Also present was Jim Rentz, Swaggart's assistant and right-hand man. Frances remained outside the room.

Once everyone was seated, with Gorman and Savage positioned somewhat deliberately on the sofa, Indest began the meeting by relating the accusations Savage had brought against Gorman. He also detailed a purported confession made by Gorman to Savage. He then turned the process of questioning over to Swaggart himself. Gorman was then severely interrogated in turn, not only by Jimmy Swaggart, but also by Rentz, Treeby and Indest, while Frances sat on the stairs outside the room eavesdropping.

Indest interrupted the questioning at one point and revealed to Gorman's shock and surprise that he had learned from Lynda Savage in a private personal confession that she had had an affair with Gorman beginning in 1978 and ending 1981. Gorman, assailed on all fronts, admitted to having the affair, but said, "it was not the way you describe it."

The "affair," such as it was, had taken place in December 1978. Gorman told them he received a telephone call from Lynda, who was in a motel room in New Orleans; she was threatening to kill herself. When he arrived he found her in a severely agitated and highly emotional state. According to Gorman, in a misguided attempt to comfort her, he succumbed to temptation, and he and Lynda had what amounted to a one-night stand, a single sexual encounter which, Gorman forever insisted, he deeply regretted.

Gorman's later account of the inquisition taking place that night in Swaggart's study, though, was that he was more or less forcibly seated right next to David Savage, so he was reluctant to say anything that would put Lynda Savage in an unfavorable light or make it appear that she had deliberately and for whatever reason lied to both her husband and to Indest about who had initiated the sex. So he offered no details. According to Gorman, Savage then told him that he was forgiven for the affair, and Gorman thought that would be the end of the matter.

When Gorman first entered Swaggart's study that night, he noticed a Bible was opened to First Timothy, Chapter 5, wherein the Apostle Paul discusses the manner of treatment of an elder who has sinned. The Apostle's prescriptions for punishment are severe, one might even say relentless. Therefore, Gorman should not have been surprised when Swaggart ignored Savage's statement of forgiveness and turned to the matter of the pending purchase of Channels 29 and 11 and Gorman's plans for a satellite uplink. Swaggart said it was a shame, but the deal could not possibly go through. He informed Gorman that he would have to tell the bonding company of his moral failure and then he would have no choice but to resign from his church.

Gorman was stunned, but before the shock of this statement wore off and outrage had a chance to replace it, he discovered that there was much more to come.

Indest now repeated the accusations he had made against Gorman earlier that day. He accused Gorman of encounters with numerous women extending over a number of years. Gorman denied every accusation; but Swaggart pretended to listen with growing outrage. He insisted that Gorman was through, not only as pastor of the First Assembly of God in New Orleans but also as an Assembly of God minister of any sort. Treeby, Indest, Savage, and Rentz concurred.

Gorman's career was over, and he had been judged: amen.

Gorman returned to his New Orleans home that night, shaken and contrite. He immediately confessed to Virginia his one-time sexual encounter with Lynda Savage. He did not discuss the details of the meeting with anyone else at the time because apparently, he did not think they needed to be discussed. He might be done with the First Assembly of God, but his personal faith, his personal calling remained intact. He had no intentions of relinquishing his entire commitment to God and to his faith on the basis of a bunch of trumped-up charges from the likes of Jimmy Swaggart and his minions.

Accordingly, on July 16, 1986, Gorman resigned his church and tendered his Assembly of God credentials to Cecil Janway, the Louisiana District Superintendent of the Assemblies of God and Gorman's longtime friend. For reasons that only Gorman could understand at the time, he had no desire to take any legal action or to fight against what was clearly a carefully constructed injustice.

The Board of Directors of the First Assembly of God met and requested that Gorman not appear before his church to present his resignation. They drafted a simple statement of their own, and that night it was read to Gorman's congregation at the First Assembly of God Church in New Orleans. The statement said that the Reverend Gorman had resigned, effective immediately. That was it. No explanation was offered, no comment made as to the cause.

But the situation was far from over. On July 17 and 18, Treeby and the board members of the First Assembly of God held numerous conversations and meetings about Gorman and the situation. On July 19, a second meeting was held at the Swaggart mansion wherein Swaggart told the Board of Directors of Gorman's church about Gorman's moral failure. The Board included two of Gorman's close personal friends, or those he thought to be his friends—Carl Miller, the business administrator for the church, and Allan McDonnel, whose construction company was building the new First Assembly facility in New Orleans. Treeby, Rentz, and Indest were also present at this meeting which turned out to be a second inquisition, one in which Marvin Gorman was tried and convicted all over again, this time, *in absentia*.

During this meeting, Swaggart accused Gorman of having a "lifestyle" of extramarital affairs dating back to the 1960s, when Gorman was a youth minister. He stated that a list had been compiled naming fifteen women with whom Gorman had had sex. Swaggart also stated that Gorman had "lined his pockets" with monies from the church and had mishandled church funds.

Those present listened carefully to Swaggart's charges and agreed that Gorman could not be permitted merely to resign quietly. A draft of a statement prepared by Treeby, McDonnel, Indest, Miller and Rentz was prepared at the mansion to be read to the congregation of the First Assembly of God of New Orleans.

On the night of July 19, McDonnel called Gorman at a Lake Charles hotel where he and his family were staying. In light of developments, Gorman was considering moving to Lake Charles to run Channel 29 directly from there. McDonnel read the prepared statement over the phone to Gorman; the draft included the following:

31

> *Some of what you have been hearing on television and reading in the newspaper is true; some of it is not true. We must let the truth and the light it brings make clear what is happening and what has happened.*
>
> *Brother Gorman resigned as pastor voluntarily when faced with the facts that he had been involved in two known immoral affairs involving different married women. One of these immoral affairs continued over three years. He stated that he had confessed these affairs to God and had received forgiveness. But he had never confessed them to the husband of one of these women and had lied about involvement in such affairs on several occasions.*

Gorman interrupted McDonnel and said the statement was a lie. McDonnel replied that it was going to be read anyway and hung up.

On July 20, the statement was read at a number of services at First Assembly of God in New Orleans. It was also distributed and read to the congregations of the Lakeview Christian Center—where Indest pastored and Treeby attended—and to Kenner Assembly of God, the church David Savage pastored and his wife, Lynda, attended.

On August 7, 1986, the Louisiana District Council circulated a letter to all Assembly of God ministers in the state, notifying them that Gorman had been dismissed from the Louisiana District Council of Assemblies of God. It was this letter that so alarmed Roach and Little and first jeopardized the television deal.

On August 14, the General Council of the Assemblies of God in Springfield, Missouri followed the Louisiana District Council's actions by dismissing Marvin Gorman from the church and circulating a letter announcing their decision around the nation.

Then, on August 20, Jimmy Swaggart drafted his own five-page statement about Gorman which he mailed around the country, reiterating his allegation of Marvin Gorman having a lifestyle of extramarital affairs and of being a liar. Swaggart's statement reads as follows:

STATEMENT FROM JIMMY SWAGGART
CONCERNING MARVIN GORMAN
There will be no names given concerning guilty parties or innocent victims related to the incidents set forth in this statement. The names are fairly well known and can be supplied upon request. To save embarrassment, no names

except those of witnesses will be used in this statement.

In 1981, Frances Swaggart began receiving telephone calls from a lady who attended Marvin Gorman's church. The lady involved has been and is a long time friend of ours. Her family is quite prominent in First Assembly.

Over a series of several weeks, this lady began to relate to Frances events leading into an immoral affair involving Marvin Gorman.

I personally questioned the lady very closely concerning these events and I feel that she was truthful in all accounts given.

This affair lasted approximately two years. Marvin Gorman would purchase gifts and give them to her. They would park on side roads or remote places for long periods of conversation. All of this was done with no chaperon nor anyone else being present.

The affair gradually evolved into "petting" and "kissing" and finally concluded in a motel room in approximately 1981.

"Petting" and "kissing" were involved in the motel experience. In the conversation that was included in the incident, the lady said that Marvin Gorman applied heavy pressure on her involving a sexual affair. His statement was, "I can cover it and no one will ever know." She states that she jumped up and ran out of the room. The following should be added to this scenario.

For several months before this situation was stopped, her husband (a former deacon at First Assembly), suspected something was going on, had the telephone tapped. He recorded many hours of conversation between his wife and Marvin Gorman over a period of several months. He is satisfied that his wife is telling the truth.

There seemed to be no adultery involved, even though Marvin Gorman pressured her greatly to engage in the same but, as stated, she ran out of the room.

A short time after her relating this incident to me by telephone, I saw Marvin in an airport terminal. I asked him to come ana

33

see me in Baton Rouge when he had some time. A few weeks later, he came to my office in Baton Rouge.

In the privacy of my office with only the two of us present, I confronted him with the information I have just stated.

He broke down, started to weep and admitted it had happened with one exception. He denied any effort to try to get her in bed. Of course, it must be understood that, according to her testimony, they were sitting on the bed at the time.

She vows vehemently that a strong effort was made by him to get in bed for a sexual affair.

As we discussed this in my office, I told him it would be hard to believe that any man would take a woman to a motel room, engage in "petting" and "kissing" and give no thought to going to bed with her.

I asked him if there had been other situations involving other women and he vowed that this was the only one. However, it must be understood that at this same time, he was, even then, having an affair with a second woman (an Assemblies of God pastor's wife). So, in effect, he lied to me.

I told him that I would not say anything to Brother Janway or Brother Zimmerman (then the General Superintendent) if I was assured that the matter would stop immediately. I felt I had a way to monitor the situation through the woman in question. He assured me the matter would end then and there and I feel it did end. However, it must be added once again, the affair with the other woman was even then going on and continued for nearly a year after this particular confrontation. (This was learned after the fact).

While at General Council in San Antonio, Bob Schmidgall, who was to become an Executive Presbyter at this particular Council called me.

He stated that Marvin Gorman had received a strong vote for the position of General Superintendent. The possibility definitely existed that Marvin would be elected Assistant General Superintendent. Brother Schmidgall said this.

"I have heard that you have some information respecting an immoral situation concerning Marvin Gorman. If you do, I need to know about it."

I hesitated and then went ahead and told him what I have related above. I never saw Brother Schmidgall after that and do not know what transpired. However, I do know that Marvin Gorman removed his name relative to this particular position but was re-elected as Executive Presbyter of the Assemblies of God.

On Thursday, July 10, 1986, Bill Treeby, a board member of Jimmy Swaggart Ministries and a member of the Lakeview Assembly of God Church in New Orleans came to my office on business concerning JSM.

In my office, he said to me, "There has been a problem in New Orleans. An Assemblies of God pastor's wife has committed adultery with an Assemblies of God pastor." Oddly enough, I did not ask him who it was and he did not, at that time, tell me.

The following Sunday morning I preached at Family Worship Center. Immediately after the service, we left to go to San Jose, Costa Rica to dedicate a church. Bill Treeby and his wife, Nancy, accompanied us. Bill had been involved in the Costa Rican work and wanted to see the church.

On the plane, he told us the names of the pastor's wife and the corresponding party. That party was Marvin Gorman, he said.

When we arrived in San Jose, Bill called his pastor, Mike Indest of Lakeview Assembly in New Orleans. I understand the following is what transpired respecting Mike Indest and Bill Treeby.

The woman in question (the second woman) came to Mike's home for counseling. These people had been long-time friends. I understand Mike's wife and children were present. At any rate, the woman confessed to Mike several immoral affairs, one of them involving Marvin Gorman.

I talked to Mike briefly on the phone from San Jose. The conversation basically included the events up to that particular time.

We returned to Baton Rouge from San Jose on Monday morning. I am told that some time on Tuesday afternoon, the pastor whose wife had committed the offense confronted Marvin Gorman in Marvin's office. After being informed that Mike Indest was a party to this knowledge, Marvin called Mike Indest. He asked if Mike would come to his office. I understand that Mike requested that Marvin come to his office instead. This was done.

At 5:30 P.M. that Tuesday afternoon (July 15, 1986) I was still at my office when Mike called to tell me that Marvin Gorman was in his, Mike's, office. Marvin was accompanied by David Savage. Mike said to me, "He has confessed everything." Mike said he wanted to come to my office. He said he did not feel qualified to deal with this situation any longer and it needed to be placed in someone else's hands.

I understand the reason he did not contact Brother Janway was because Brother Gorman asked him not to. At any rate, Mike requested that they come to Baton Rouge.

I acquiesced to this but requested that Bill Treeby be included because Mike, realizing the enormity of the situation, had confided in Bill from the very beginning. (Bill Treeby is an Attorney-at-Law with the prestigious legal firm of Stone, Pigman in New Orleans.)

They consented to this and arrived at my home in Baton Rouge around 8 P.M. Those at this meeting were myself, Jim Rentz, Bill Treeby, Mike Indest, Marvin Gorman, and David Savage. Mike Indest briefly related to me what had taken place.

I then turned to Marvin Gorman (we were in my study) and asked him if this was so. He said, "Yes."

He basically related the same thing Mike Indest had. The situation had continued for nearly four years. The names of motel were provided by the woman in question to Mike Indest and even some dates. Marvin admitted, in front of all those present, that this was true.

36

I then asked Marvin if there had been any other women involved. He assured me no other women were involved. I said to him, "Marvin, I believe there have been women involved all the time since you were D-CAP up until this present hour. Why don't you, at this moment, come clean about everything and make a total confession?"

He vehemently vowed that there were no others involved. Then I said this to him.

"Those are the same, identical words you told me when I talked to you about the first woman in 1981. You vowed then that there were no other women involved and at that very time you were involved with this particular woman. You lied to me then and I believe you are lying to me now."

He was forced to admit that he had lied back in 1981, but he again remonstrated that no other women were involved.

I asked him what he was going to do. The room became very heavy with silence. No one said anything. Marvin never answered.

I walked to my desk, picked up the Bible and turned to I Timothy 5:20. I told him to read it. He did so outloud. This particular passage relates to an elder who has sinned.

He, still, said nothing.

I, then, rephrased my question and asked, "What should you do?"

Once again the room became very heavy with silence and he still did not answer.

After a considerable period of time, I stated to him, "You are going to have to call Brother Carlson and Brother Janway."

He then pleaded to be given a period of time to get the finances of the church in order. He said, "Men will be in the church offices tomorrow relative to making a loan to the church of some $16 million. I must be allowed to get this loan in order."

I told him it would not be right for these men (whomever they were) to make a loan to a church without information of this magnitude being given to the lending agency. To carry forth with this would be tantamount to fraud.

Everyone in the room agreed with that. I further stated to him, "You must tell the lending agency about this change in the church. If they still want to loan the money, that is their business, but they must know about this."

No more was said concerning the loan. Marvin then said to me, "I will call Brother Carlson and Brother Janway, but first of all, I want to tell my family."

We were concerned for him; consequently, I had Jim Rentz drive his car back to New Orleans while Bill Treeby and Mike Indest went back in their car. I took Marvin and David Savage in my car.

On the way to New Orleans, Marvin asked about a woman who had worked for him and then had worked for us for a short time. He wanted to know if she had told me that they (she and Marvin Gorman) had had an affair. I told him she had not told me this. It is my personal belief that this was another case involving an immoral affair; however, I say this without proof.

We had had prayer together in my study and when we all arrived at David Savage's church in New Orleans, we had prayer together again and Marvin Gorman left.

This is the sum total, as best I can remember, of my involvement concerning the affairs in question respecting Marvin Gorman.

[signed]
Jimmy Swaggart

On August 29, Swaggart sent a personal letter to Gorman which stated, "Gorman, we love you, but I know you are lying. There have been other affairs." He blind carbon-copied a number of people around the country with this letter. The full text of his statement was later printed in *The Washington Post.*

On the same date, August 29, Bill Treeby met with Forrest Hall and Cecil Janway, the head officials of the Louisiana District Council of the Assemblies of God, at Jimmy Swaggart Ministries and prepared a draft of yet another statement about Gorman. This draft was taken to New Orleans, edited by members of the First Assembly of God Church, and was once again read to the First Assembly of God congregation in New Orleans by Janway on September 2, 1986.

Following this reading, Janway took the September 2 statement back to district offices in Alexandria, Louisiana and subsequently mailed it around the country to a number of ministers. Thus, the September 2 statement fell into many hands; it was read not only by people in the religious community, but also by many in the secular community and the media as well.

As if to metaphorically drive a stake in Gorman's heart, the final blow was delivered by Indest at a sectional meeting of the Assemblies of God ministry in a New Orleans restaurant on September 16. Sectional meetings were normal monthly gatherings of Assembly of God ministers and leading businessmen from the churches. They were generally designed to discuss community services and inter-congregational cooperative activities. At this meeting, however, Indest introduced the Reverend Tom Miller, who stunned everyone present by relating the details of an exorcism—or "deliverance"—he had performed on September 7 in the Canal Street Assembly of God Church.

Miller's account included the obnoxious odors and horrifying voices that accompanied the deliverance of a demonic presence from a girl identified as Rosary Ortego; he then shocked everyone by relating the words of Satan himself, spoken through Ortego's supposedly mute mouth in the familiar voice and cadences of no one other than the Reverend Marvin Gorman.

Many of those present were openly skeptical. Indeed the Reverend James Brown, who had taken Gorman's place at the First Assembly of God, stated that he wanted no part of this malarkey. But others present were at least unsure. The casting out of demons and exorcism of the spirit was a fundamental part of Pentecostalist doctrine, and Miller, simple and sincere as he was, seemed convinced that his holy experience had been genuine.

No one questioned at the time why Miller called Indest about the matter; nor did anyone present question Miller closely about the whereabouts of Rosary Ortego or her shady companion "Theresa." But

Indest noted that he and several people from his church came to the Canal Street Assembly of God and held a prayer service to cleanse the place following the spiritual warfare that had taken place there.

Regardless of the degree of credibility afforded the exorcism—or the other charges against Gorman—at the sectional meeting or throughout the entire community of the Assemblies of God churches, the die were cast. Marvin Gorman's career as a minister of that denomination was over.

In late fall of 1986, a default judgment was taken against Marvin Gorman for his inability to perform on the buy-sell agreement for Channel 29 in Lake Charles. I heard nothing from Gorman for several months. I assumed my professional association with him was over and that I would never hear from him again.

• CHAPTER FOUR •
THE ROAD TO JUSTICE

"I know thy works, and thy labor, and thy patience, and
how thou canst not bear them which are evil: and thou
hast tried them which say they are apostles, and are not,
and hast found them liars."
—The Revelation of St. John the Divine, 2:2

My mother was a schoolteacher in Lake Charles, Louisiana; my
father was a stevedore. I grew up there. After completing the Mississippi
College School of Law in Jackson and a two-year tenure as a law clerk
for United States District Judge Walter L. Nixon, it was a natural move
for me to return to my hometown to practice law in 1981. I had many
friends and business contacts in the area, I knew the region, and, mainly,
it was home.

Five years later, though, in July 1986, while still working on Marvin
Gorman's acquisition of Channel 29, I decided that my legal career was
stalled. I was at a crossroads though I had not yet traveled very far down
my chosen professional path. I had been with the Jones, Tete, Nolan,
Hanchey, Swift and Spears law firm for more than five years and felt I
had worked hard and had become a top producer in my short tenure as a
junior partner. It was a prestigious firm in both the city and the state and
I was gaining valuable experience, but I felt I had hit a kind of glass
ceiling beyond which I might not advance for years.

Basically, I was a maverick, wearing cowboy boots to work and not
conforming to the expected demeanor of an associate or younger partner.
I was very outspoken and on occasion, as my father used to say "let my
mouth overload my butt." My approach definitely grated on the nerves
of a couple of my senior partners. As Ken Spears used to say, when I
"drew my sword, it was never resheathed without blood on it."

For one thing, the firm's philosophy was that one had to be with them a long time before being made an equal partner. For another, bonus money was distributed by virtue of a special formula subject to the discretion of three management committee members. Thus, if one's personal politics were not in line with the management committee's, or if one merely was not well liked, then one's income potential—to say nothing of advancement—was handicapped.

My experience at Jones, Tete, had focused to a large extent on litigation. The firm, however, had a major practice in real estate and commercial law, which was the sort of matter that I had been called upon to handle for Marvin Gorman. My personal growth potential was contingent upon the growth of the firm; thus, by 1986, I often found myself handling the same sorts of cases as I was handling for Gorman. By this time, owing to a crunch in oil prices and investments nationwide, real estate and commercial legal business in Lake Charles was scarce; interest rates were high and rising, and the economy was depressed in Lake Charles and throughout Louisiana and the South; a recession was imminent. As a result, my potential for rapid advancement and higher earnings dropped even more. I found that my discontent grew with each depressing headline in the *Wall Street Journal*; without being fully aware of it, I was looking for a way out.

During my tenure at Jones, Tete, I had developed a friendship with one of my partners, David Dwight. Dwight was principally a real estate and commercial lawyer, but, like me, he was a junior partner and probably would be for a long time. In November 1986, just prior to the final disposition of the buy-sell agreement involving Gorman and KVHP Channel 29, Dwight had a disagreement with the senior partners at Jones, Tete and decided to withdraw and move back to his hometown of Covington, Louisiana, and set up his own private practice.

When I heard of this, I approached Dwight with a proposition: partnership. I had always envisioned starting my own law firm, and while I never expected it might occur so soon, I sensed that in conjunction with Dwight, a rare opportunity was available. Dwight agreed, and I immediately withdrew from Jones, Tete also. On December 5, 1986, David Dwight and I created the partnership of Lundy & Dwight and moved to the Lakeside Building in Lake Charles.

With Kristie Plumb, our only secretary, who also served as receptionist, runner, and bookkeeper; a couple of desks and a small office, we started afresh. Our beginning was modest, and I suspect we both shared the same anxieties. I must confess that I worried about whether cases of sufficient size would come our way; I didn't have to worry long. In January 1987, a cool winter afternoon, I received a phone call from an attorney in Tulsa, Oklahoma, who identified himself as Tomy Dee Frasier.

Frasier explained that he had been hired by the Reverend Marvin Gorman to consider prosecuting a defamation case against the Reverend Jimmy Swaggart. This came as something of a surprise to me, as only a few months before Gorman had been quite clear on the point that he not only did not wish to take any legal action against Swaggart—or anyone—but also that he did not personally believe in litigation to resolve such conflicts.

Nevertheless, Gorman had consulted with Frasier, who enjoyed a fine reputation as a Civil Rights attorney, to see if a legal action was warranted and feasible. Frasier said my name was on a list of attorneys Gorman sent him to consider as local counsel in Louisiana and that he had chosen me because Gorman spoke highly of me personally and of my work for him the previous year. A Louisiana counsel was needed because of a slight difference in court rules and procedure with which a local attorney would be familiar. Additionally, local counsel is beneficial in any case handled by an out-of-state lawyer because conferences are frequently called by the court on the spur of the moment and pleadings must be hand-delivered in emergency situations.

Frasier asked that I provide him a brief summary of Louisiana law as it applied to defamation, along with some personal references as to my suitability as local counsel.

Frasier then asked me how strong I was. I thought it was a strange request and wondered what, precisely, he had in mind. I replied that I was physically fit. He then explained that he was six feet, four inches tall, weighed over two hundred-twenty pounds, and was confined to a wheelchair. He would need assistance from time to time and that required physical strength. I assured him I could handle it, and we agreed to meet and discuss preliminaries with regard to a potential case.

A week later, I met Tomy Frasier face-to-face in Metairie, Louisiana, a suburb of New Orleans. We met at a complex of offices on Sanford Street, which had always served as primary headquarters for Marvin Gorman Ministries. Although he had managed some of the corporation's business out of offices at the First Assembly of God on Airline Highway, the majority of his telecasts, publications, and principal business functions were generated out of these offices.

Frasier flew down from Tulsa in his private plane. He was as big as he had described over the telephone. I met him at the airport and helped lift him from the plane into his wheelchair. Unquestionably, he weighed well over two hundred pounds. Though sixty-four years of age, he didn't look a day over fifty. He exhibited a youthful appearance, something that surprised me when I learned he had spent the last forty years in a wheelchair. His hair was dark but sported a touch of gray and his facial features were large and almost animated behind his glasses. He had a definite Oklahoma twang, but he was articulate and obviously well educated.

Not a man given to false formality, he greeted me that day in a pair of gray baggy slacks rather than a "lawyer suit" such as I anticipated. I noticed that alongside him in the wheelchair, he kept a navy blue Crown Royal pouch. This was unusual, to say the least. I later learned that is where he kept his wad of cash. I also found out that pouch was not just a souvenir; it was something he frequently replaced after consuming its contents, which he often referred to as the "nectar of the Gods."

As soon as he was seated in the wheelchair, I learned what a "pull-down" was. He grabbed the chair's armrests, picked up his body, and his partner, Steve Hickman pulled his pantlegs out of his crotch. This was something I would assist in doing many times over the next four years as I came to know, admire, and love this Okie lawyer, Thomas Dee Frasier—Tomy Dee.

Frasier had, I soon realized, a right to whatever eccentricities he affected. He was an impressive man with an impressive background. He had quit high school at sixteen, during World War II. He falsified records as to his age and enlisted in the United States Marines Corps . He served in the Pacific as a sharpshooter in his battalion.

When we met at the Marvin Gorman Ministries' office, Frasier was accompanied by Steve Hickman, with whom I also had spoken on the telephone. Hickman, Tomy Dee's law partner, was a young man with blond hair and a fair complexion. He looked to be about twenty years old, and I was immediately skeptical of his background and experience. But as it turned out, Hickman revealed himself to be a useful foil to Tomy Frasier in both personality and outward appearance.

Hickman was reared a Roman Catholic and came from a family of lawyers. His father had been an old drinking buddy of Frasier's years before. Hickman was converted to the Church of Jesus Christ of Latter-Day Saints—the Mormons—when he was very young, as a result of a visionary dream. A Brigham Young graduate, he was a practicing Mormon and very devout in his beliefs. He did not drink or swear and, according to Frasier, was a virgin until he was thirty-five and married his wife, Katherine. After finishing college, Hickman went to Sweden for two years to perform his Mormon missionary work and then returned to complete law school. He often took his deposition notes in Swedish so there was no hope of anybody being able to read his handwriting. He turned out to be one of the brightest lawyers with whom I have ever worked.

At Marvin Gorman Ministries' facilities, we met Rita Nugent, Gorman's secretary, and Beverly Bilbo, his daughter, we were introduced to Gorman's son, Randy, whom I, of course, already knew. We received a tour of Marvin Gorman Ministries, particularly the mailroom. I was most impressed to see the thousands and thousands of pieces of mail that Marvin Gorman Ministries was receiving. I was also impressed with their mail-out method's efficiency. The back of the complex contained a small studio where Gorman taped his television shows. It was modest in appearance compared to the facilities I had seen at the First Assembly of God, but I assumed it had been slapped together since his resignation and was more or less serviceable.

Gorman also looked a bit slapped together. This was the first time I had seen him since late October, and he appeared to have had a rough two or three months. In a word, he looked "aged." He also looked near exhaustion. Even so, he was as courteous and enthusiastically polite as ever. Fairly quickly, though, his role as host and boss of the operation gave way to Frasier's presence. I was keenly aware that the attorney from Tulsa would be calling the shots.

Following some brief conversation, Frasier, who was a chain-smoker, announced that he wanted to go outdoors in order not to offend the Gormans with his habit. He, Hickman, and I went out to the parking lot, where we began to discuss possible strategies. Frasier preferred to discuss strategic moves with his co-counsel outside the presence of the client, so we could then present a united front and consensus when we laid it out for Gorman. This was counter to my previous practice and experience, as I had always regarded the client as the boss, and while it seemed natural at the time, it would at a much later date become something of a point of contention between me and Frasier.

In any event, for the moment, Frasier wanted it clear that he was running the show and was the only boss any of us had, including Marvin

Gorman. We were all taking his instructions.

Gorman had previously prepared a narrative for each of us, and we had all studied it as well as several other documents. Some of these were authored by Jimmy Swaggart, others by the Louisiana District Council Assemblies of God, and still others came from the General Council Assemblies of God. These included the September 2, 1986, statement, which seemed to provide a basis for a lawsuit all by itself.

We knew a statement had been read to the First Assembly of God Church on July 20, 1986, after the First Assembly of God board members had met with Jimmy Swaggart on July 19. However, we did not have a copy of that statement at this juncture. We also understood that part of whatever was read on July 20 was encompassed in the September 2 statement. It would take a lawsuit and the discovery process for us to get our hands on the July 20 statement.

It was now clear that the Reverend Marvin Gorman—a man who flatly stated he did not believe in litigation—wanted to sue everyone in sight. He wanted to file against every board member of the First Assembly of God, every member of the Louisiana District Council of Assemblies of God, the General Council of Assemblies of God, and, of course, Jimmy Swaggart. He also wanted to file suit against everyone on the board of Jimmy Swaggart Ministries and all their relatives. It seemed to me that the only significant individuals omitted from his list of chosen targets were the mayor of New Orleans and the Governor of Louisiana. I wondered if they might not be added later.

Frasier's ambitions, on the other hand, were more modest and more practical. They also were more focused. Frasier wanted to sue only one person: Jimmy Swaggart. Frasier said he had watched Jimmy Swaggart for years, had studied him as his ministerial empire had grown, had seen his face on the covers of magazines and, of course, on television. It was, Frasier said, "a face of hate."

Frasier said there was nothing about Jimmy Swaggart—his face, his reputation, his personality, his work that indicated any love—of God or of man, of no one, in fact, but Jimmy Swaggart—and he wanted "a piece of Jimmy Swaggart's ass."

After returning to Lake Charles, I enlisted the services of Scott Bailey, an investigator who had assisted me on many occasions at Jones, Tete. Bailey was a former deputy sheriff for Calcasieu Parish, had worked in security for the Kroger Supermarket chain in West Virginia, and had now become a successful private investigator. Bailey was a tall, prematurely gray man in his late thirties. He had an affable and outgoing personality. He would later become the subject of a *Washington Post* article and a story run by *A Current Affair*, only to be nicknamed by Art Harris of CNN as "Magnum Poohyie." Bailey and I flew to Tulsa and visited with Frasier about what investigations needed to be conducted.

First of all, we decided we would need formal statements from every woman we believed to have been on Jimmy Swaggart's supposed list of those with whom Gorman had had sexual relations, or with every woman we believed to be on any other list, particularly one purported to have been compiled by the Board of Directors for the First Assembly of God. As Swaggart had also accused Gorman of having affairs with counselees from the church, we felt it was necessary for Bailey to take statements from these women just to see what they had to say. In addition, we wanted Bailey to dig up whatever he could find on Jimmy Swaggart that would put him in any sort of unfavorable light with his congregation or, we hoped, with the powers in the Assembly of God—and, of course, with a judge and jury.

Because Louisiana imposes a one-year statute of limitations for personal injuries, including defamation, a plaintiff has one year from the date of the action or offense to file suit or the right to do so will be lost. We believed we had more than ample time—until July 1987—to conduct our investigation and file our petition. But we wanted as many of our ducks to be in a row as possible beforehand. It was our hope to catch Swaggart unaware and off-guard.

After numerous debates, we decided that the suit would be filed in the Civil District Court for Orleans Parish in New Orleans. This was a calculated move. And it was my idea, based on demographic breakdowns.

In 1987, the City of New Orleans' population was more than fifty percent African-American. Gorman was widely known as a social reformer, particularly in the area of race relations. He had pastored the first integrated Assembly of God church in Louisiana and many of the social programs he sponsored were aimed to improve conditions in the black community. Moreover, at the time of Gorman's resignation, approximately thirty-five percent of his congregation was African-American. Furthermore, and possibly of greatest significance, sixty to seventy percent of Orleans Parish was made up of Roman Catholics, and Gorman's congregation consisted of many Catholic converts.

Jimmy Swaggart, on the other hand, was the largest employer in East Baton Rouge Parish, a district with more whites and Protestants than lived in the entire city of New Orleans. In short, Swaggart lived and worked and provided an economic base in the proximate middle of the "white flight" suburbs of Louisiana's capital city.

Swaggart also had always been outspoken against the Roman Catholic Church—which some ministers in the Assemblies of God characterized in their sermons as "The Whore of Babylon"—as well as Jews and even non-charismatic protestant faiths. Many throughout the entire country already considered Swaggart to be little more than an upstart redneck racist from Ferriday, Louisiana, an intolerant bigot and segregationist, a Southern cracker clown. This was, we came to find out, both an accurate characterization and, as well, a dangerous underestimation of this notorious televangelist.

Without a doubt, though, Gorman's best venue against Swaggart would be in predominantly black, predominantly Roman Catholic, and decidedly innercity, urban Orleans Parish.

The principal objection to this strategy centered on our role as Gorman's mouthpieces. Louisiana in general, and New Orleans in particular, constitute to some extent a closed society, as loyal to its own as it is brutal to outsiders. Although I was a Louisianian, I was not an Orleansian. Frasier and Hickman were most decidedly not; they weren't even Southerners, not insofar as Lousianians defined the term. Insofar as New Orleans would be concerned, we were all three outsiders.

And there was another consideration: as Gorman's attorneys, we would be taking on Jimmy Swaggart with all his wealth, his followers, and the powerful and well-established Assemblies of God before a judge, who, in all probability, was placed on the bench by the same lawyers who would defend Swaggart.

It was still a calculated decision to proceed against Swaggart in the vicinity of his own backyard, as it were. It was also a calculated risk. If we lost, Gorman would be out a great deal of money and his reputation would be ruined; if we won, though, the victory would be all the more decisive. For Frasier, it would be all the sweeter as well. We decided to take Jimmy Swaggart on his own turf and "to beard the lion in his den"; let the Devil take the hindmost.

• CHAPTER FIVE •
ACROSS THE WILDERNESS

"For we walk by faith, not by sight."
—The Second Epistle of Paul the Apostle to the
Corinthians, 5:7.

In the eyes of millions of the faithful, the Reverend Jimmy Swaggart always had God on his side. Ranked in the mid-1980s as one of the top five televangelists in the country by Neilson and Arbitron rating standards, Swaggart began with a humble Assembly of God church and built it into one of the largest and most successful media-supported ministries in the world.

From his Baton Rouge headquarters, Swaggart was guided and aided by his wife, Frances, and son Donnie, advised by the best attorneys and accountants money could buy, and surrounded by a tightly knit and loyal group of associates, all enhanced by the top technical consultants in the business. By 1986, Swaggart pastored an enormous and loyal flock of the faithful, most of whom were eager to open their hearts—and their pocketbooks—in response to his flamboyant, emotional preaching style, to his simple, fundamental, yet stridently unyielding interpretation of the Gospel.

Swaggart had taken advantage of the technological revolution in every possible way. His rapidly growing Assembly of God congregation had burst the bounds of its regional base and by now extended throughout the country. He was moving up the ladder of popularity with almost lightning speed. Like Billy Graham and Oral Roberts before him, his name became a household word, his face as familiar as any celebrity's in the country. He was on top of the world.

As was the case with many televangelists, Jimmy Lee Swaggart had humble origins, a poor educational background, and a sound proletarian image. Born in Ferriday, Louisiana, on March 15, 1935, just across the

Mississippi River from Natchez, he was reared in the Assemblies of God churches that his father built. Swaggart dropped out of school in the ninth grade to go to work; and in 1952, at the age of seventeen, he married Frances Orelia Anderson, who was then but fifteen, from the nearby community of Wisner.

From childhood, Swaggart was a fine vocalist and was often in demand as a church soloist. It was a talent that ran in the family: He was first cousin to both country music recording artist Mickey Gilley and "The Killer," Jerry Lee Lewis, possibly one of the most sensational (and scandalous) crossover recording artists of the 1960's and 1970's. Swaggart was close to both singing-star relatives and was publicly involved with Lewis when his May-December marriage to a 13-year-old child became a matter of international concern.

In the early 1960s, Swaggart moved from eastern Louisiana to Baton Rouge. He attended a small church there and began building a reputation as a fine singer of hymns. Soon, he was working as a singing evangelist, hitting the revival circuit, visiting churches all over the region, being well paid for his efforts. Soon, he added preaching to his repertoire, developing a popular "hell fire and damnation" style of oratory that suited his Assembly of God brothers and sisters perfectly. Swaggart was much in demand as a visiting evangelist; his popularity and income increased.

In 1970, Swaggart met Bill Treeby, an attorney practicing with the Stone, Pigman firm in New Orleans and, not incidentally, an Assembly of God minister himself. Immediately, Treeby recognized Swaggart's potential as a force in the denomination and began assisting him in several legal endeavors connected to Swaggart's growing evangelistic activities. Shortly, and with Treeby's help, Swaggart created the Jimmy Swaggart Evangelist Association and began expanding his road show.

By 1980, Swaggart decided he needed a home base. He started his own church, the Family Worship Center in Baton Rouge. It was originally a small, suburban congregation, but one with enormous potential for growth. He changed the name of Jimmy Swaggart Evangelist Association to Jimmy Swaggart Ministries, put most of his family on the payroll, and began solidifying his financial position. As Swaggart predicted, the small church grew rapidly, in part because Swaggart's popularity had made him a regional celebrity, and in part because his suburban location brought him a large and prosperous congregation.

The enterprise prospered. By 1985, Jimmy Swaggart Ministries occupied close to 200 acres of prime property on Bluebonnet Drive in

Baton Rouge and employed more than 2,000 people. More than 500 young men and women attended the recently opened Jimmy Swaggart Bible College and Jimmy Swaggart's television ministry was touted—inaccurately—as being the only worldwide television ministry. Swaggart also publicly held himself out to be the only evangelist "called by God" to deliver the message to the whole world.

Accordingly, he had moved into a huge mansion, which many thought resembled a castle, complete with a moat, and presided over his holdings in an almost feudal manner, handing down decisions and mandates like a king, anticipating that personal loyalty—and fear—would keep his barons—neighboring Assembly of God ministers—in line.

Swaggart's credibility and national status were bolstered by the fact that his organization ran operations in Canada, Europe, and Costa Rica. He and his entourage visited these far-flung ministries in a 727 jet provided by his company. By 1985, Swaggart was one of the most powerful and wealthiest televangelists in the country.

The success of Swaggart's ministry was measurable and visible in many ways, but nowhere was it more in evidence than in his financial investments and real-estate holdings. The "nickels and dimes of the faithful," so zealously sought by Swaggart during his evangelistic broadcasts, filled mailbags by the score on a daily basis; his headquarters received so much mail—more than 50,000 cards and letters per week—that it was given its own zip code by the United States Postal Service. Other donors came in person, and visitors had to have appointments months in advance.

By 1985, the ministry was televised in more than 145 countries, supported 564 missionaries, paid more than 1,400 employees and was involved with more than 2,000 TV stations and a like number of cable TV outlets. His programs generated more than $145 million in revenue annually, which included tuition from more than 500 students at his Baton Rouge Bible college. Every crusade with which he was involved reportedly cost more than $200,000. He was routinely watched and believed by millions, who also subscribed to *The Evangelist*, his personal magazine, and who regularly read his syndicated newspaper column in the national press. He boasted that he was taking in more than a half million dollars a day from the "nickels and dimes of the faithful." His company owned eleven buildings and was taking in more than $12 million a month by mid-1986.

Though he had only an eighth-grade education, Swaggart was sought by people outside his immediate sphere of influence as well. A frequent guest on talk shows and news programs, he was often invited by the secular media to comment on or give his opinion on matters of public interest, often issues that had nothing to do with his ministry or religion in general. Intelligent, well-educated, and sophisticated journalists and talk-show hosts deferred to him as if he were some sort of "grand pooh-bah," filled with wisdom and learning. It was at this point that he began making negative comments about his fellow televangelists around the country.

Never stingy with opinions, Swaggart freely expressed his criticisms of other successful televangelists and attempted to undermine their public images by attacking their sincerity, their commitment to their faith, even their personal morality. He matter-of-factly named the Reverend Robert Schuller as a preacher of "humanism," perhaps the greatest "bogeyman" of the charismatic movement. Oral Roberts was, in Swaggart's view, the "poor, dear brother perched up in the tower with God holding him hostage." Appearing on NBC's *Nightline*, Swaggart stated: "We have got a dear brother in Tulsa, Oklahoma, perched up in a tower telling people that if they don't send him money, God is going to kill him. . ."

Jim Bakker, whom Swaggart characterized as the minister "with the pompadour hairdo who preached from rollercoasters and waterslides," also felt the sting of Swaggart's comments: " . . . we have got this soap opera that is being carried out live down in North Carolina all under the name of God," he said. Later, speaking on a CNN broadcast, Swaggart characterized Bakker as "a cancer on the body of Christ that needs to be excised," and then lashed out at all the "pretty little boys with their hair done and their nails done, who call themselves preachers."

Swaggart also made negative comments about Pat Robertson and other ministers; but he tempered some of these in deference to their obvious political power and personal reputations. He made no recorded comments about Billy Graham. Whatever restraint he felt soon began to fade, though, as his personal power increased and his ego swelled.

Brash, unsophisticated, poorly educated, ill-mannered, and physically gross in appearance and demeanor, Swaggart liked to present himself as a "man of the people." Not even Oral Roberts in his early ministry ever appeared so crass and unobservant of tact and diplomacy as did Jimmy Swaggart in even routine appearances. But not since Billy Sunday, perhaps, has any single minister so rapidly captured the imagination and undying faith of so many people. Like Graham, he had an instinctive knowledge of how to manipulate media to serve his purpose; like Robert Tilton and other—by Swaggart's standards—lesser lights, he had an instinctive knowledge of what people wanted. And he gave it to them.

As was and is the case with so many televangelists, Swaggart adopted and made his own a particular "theme of sin." His favorite topic centered on sins of the flesh. He wrote article after article on pornography and how it was America's "darkest stain." In *Rape of a Nation*, he declared pornography to be an evil that did not merely arouse its victims but consumed them and described those who were addicted to it as being no different from drug addicts who constantly needed stronger doses to maintain the sinful habit.

He also vociferously attacked prostitution and those who sought the service of prostitutes. He campaigned for censorship of erotic or pornographic material—books, films, television programs—and railed against displays of pulchritude wherever he found it. He additionally opposed any type of psychological therapy or in-depth counseling, and he was frequently quoted as saying "psychology was of the devil." His repeated attacks on fellow ministers increasingly focused on their proclivity toward worldliness, particularly that part of the world having to do with illicit sex.

By the mid-1980s, Jimmy Swaggart had evolved from poor lay-preacher to powerful religious force. He was the antithesis of what most televangelists tried so hard to achieve in their public images. He was not slick like Jim Bakker nor smooth like Robert Tilton, not dignified like Robert Schuller nor paternal like Pat Robertson. He lacked the quiet sincerity of Jerry Fallwell and the simple dignity of Billy Graham.

Jimmy Swaggart was one of a kind. He reveled in his uniqueness, wallowed in his personal glory.

Swaggart also understood that the power of television in spreading the Word of God is connected to the nature of the medium itself. TV is merely a conduit, a device for communicating. Almost no one was turning technology and electronics to such advantage as effectively as was Jimmy Swaggart (speakers were strategically placed throughout the Baton Rouge complex, even in the restrooms, so Swaggart's sermons could be heard by everyone at all times); few were joining that technical prowess with a forceful personality that knew how to move masses to tears of anguish, cries of anger. By virtue of his national reputation, his national celebrity, Swaggart became known as a man who stood for faith, for integrity, for unyielding obedience to God's Revealed Word; and he stood for the South, ever a bastion of fundamentalism, ever a source of consistent and reliable money, particularly from the poor, the ignorant, the hopeless.

At his height of power, Jimmy Swaggart absolutely ruled a $145,000,000 empire, a monolithic testimony to God's power and the beneficence of unquestioning faith. It also was testimony to shrewd business practices and a canny ability to manipulate enormous numbers of people through the medium of television.

Is it any wonder that everyone, especially Swaggart, believed God was on his side? How could He not be?

But Swaggart was, in the final analysis, only a man, a fallible human being, subject to the same temptations and failings as any other mortal, and subject to the same fears and doubts about his position, however secure it seemed. Like heroes of classical tragedy, he lost sight of his own humanity, his own mortality, his own weakness. Swaggart forgot that having God on his side was not the same as *being* God; that fundamental lesson of Eden, so often the basis for Swaggart's sermons, was not completely learned by this popular preacher. Thus, Swaggart was not satisfied merely to be God's messenger; he was coming to see himself as God's Anointed: indefatigable, indomitable, infallible—bulletproof.

To achieve that—as David learned when he confronted King Saul—would require more than a divine confidence and an audience of more than eight million in the United States and five hundred million worldwide. What it would require was a concerted effort to eliminate the competition and to avoid the financial trap that had so deftly sprung on Oral Roberts and that he was preparing for others who stood between him and absolute domination of the nation's religious broadcast airways.

A mere audience share was not sufficient. Swaggart wanted it all. And, taking a page from the wisdom of football coaches all across the South, Swaggart understood that the best defense was always a good offense.

Hence, in the mid-1980s the Reverend Jimmy Swaggart placed his entire empire behind an active and carefully planned holy war against other tele-evangelists. Following the pattern of so many fundamentalists who, since the earliest days of Christianity had thrived on attacking what were often seen as perversions of faith, heresy, and intolerable sin, Swaggart turned his sanctimonious guns on his fellow fundamentalists.

Those he could not utterly destroy, he planned to reduce to a level of insignificance.

In mid-1986, Swaggart assumed the role of "policeman" of the Assemblies of God as well as the rest of the charismatic world. He proclaimed himself to be a reformer of the denomination as well as the sole spokesperson for God. His negative comments soon transformed themselves into a rampage against other popular Assembly of God ministers as well as ministers of other denominations, in particular those who pastored churches with large congregations and who had sizable television and radio ministries.

Understanding the ecclesiastical procedures of the church and the methods for internal judiciary they offered, he set his minions to work, making use of whatever he could to undermine his brethren's ministries.

One of his first direct attacks on a fellow minister came when Swaggart filed charges with the Assemblies of God against Karl Strader, a pastor of a 7,400 member congregation in Lakeland, Florida. A Swaggart Ministries official and close personal friend, Jim Rentz, publicly alleged that Strader had embraced the "Kingdom Age" teachings of Bishop Earl Paulk as well as the teachings of charismatic Bible Ministries of Oral Roberts. Paulk pastored a non-denominational church in Atlanta, Georgia that had a congregation of 10,000 or more, and his popularity in the Deep South was growing. By simultaneously linking Strader with Roberts and Paulk, Swaggart took down three men at once.

At the same time, Swaggart attacked Glen Cole, pastor of the Capitol City Christian Center in Sacramento, California, also an Executive Presbyter of the Assemblies of God. Cole had a congregation of almost 8,000 and a strong radio ministry. Rentz's charge against Cole was that he invited Robert Schuller to preach at his church, thereby spreading the anathema of humanism among the faithful. Two more fell before Swaggart's wrathful sword of fundamentalist righteousness.

When, in July 1986, Swaggart turned his guns on Marvin Gorman, his chief rival in his home state, he was basking in the light of these other successes. In rapid order, he was steadily diminishing if not destroying his competition, at least within the Assemblies of God; with Gorman out of the way, only one other significant charismatic remained before Swaggart could take on the national giants such as Pat Robinson or Jerry Fallwell. That was Jim Bakker and the powerful and popular PTL Network.

55

• CHAPTER SIX •
THE PREACHER AND THE LAWYER

"How then shall they call on him in whom they have not believed? and how shall they believe in him of whom they have not heard? and how shall they hear without a preacher?"
—*The Epistle of Paul the Apostle to the Romans, 10:14.*

Traditionally, Assembly of God churches, particularly following World War II, were tiny affairs, often setting up in storefronts, offices, even private homes, and other places where a handful could "gather in His name" for worship. Services were never lavish, never spectacular; they generally emphasized the sermon over other rituals and practices. Proselytization was a vital part of every ministry, but so was the sustenance of membership as a small congregation grew and, then, like a spider plant, sent tendrils of new life out in the form of other tiny churches which would in turn expand and reproduce.

Membership in the Assembly of God had, likewise, followed a traditional pattern. Few ministers were well-educated, and most of those who did hold higher degrees avoided secular (and "humanistic") scholarship in favor of seminary-style academics, generally centered in fundamentalist parochial colleges. Many, and for a while a majority, held degrees from correspondence schools; these sometimes lacked accreditation or even any semblance of real curricula, but were willing to exchange a degree certificate (Doctor of Divinity, for example) for a series of payments and, one would hope, successfully completed assignments.

From a fundamentalist standpoint, the study of theology or academic approaches to scripture was of no particular importance when measured against the personal revelation of God's will through prayer, devotion, and meditation. "Book learning," while a nice thing to have, was not a criterion for acquiring the title "Reverend" or even "pastor."

Tomy Dee Frasier's assessment that many Assembly of God parishioners worshipped their ministers more than their God was not far off the mark. The most important trait a minister of this highly charismatic faith could possess was charisma. Education, indeed, could be a hindrance.

A profile of Assembly of God members in the early 1950's would suggest that for the most part they were poorly educated or uneducated beyond middle school grades, were lower middleclass, and "working poor," largely rural and mostly white. Easily impressed by a reinforcement of traditional ideas, they were politically conservative and committed to a high sense of moral code. They embraced what would in later decades be called "family values," emphasizing a patriarchal domestic philosophy based on what was then called "old-fashioned" notions. Basically fundamentalist in their interpretation of both scripture and law, they applied their religious education, such as it was, directly to their lives, and in a manner reminiscent of the Puritans of Massachusetts Bay Colony they tied secular behavior to spiritual commitment.

At the same time, they were people eager to follow a powerful and exciting leader. It would never have occurred to any to question a minister's claim to have been "called" to preach, to pastor a church; and while some ministers stumbled or even fell in the course of their professional lives, a personal declaration of faith remained sufficient to qualify anyone, no matter how ill-educated or prepared for preaching, administration, or counseling. They were additionally committed to the concept of forgiveness, and personal atonement for the sincere confessor of wrongdoing. To their credit, for the most part, they professed to love the sinner but to hate the sin.

The problem came when the two were confused.

Like many Assembly of God ministers, Marvin Gorman lacked the benefits of advanced, formal education, though he had more than most. Gorman demonstrated, particularly when he was a youngster, a strong commitment toward bettering himself and his knowledge of theology, and he seemed to possess an instinctive ability to apply what he learned to his work for the maximum results in his ministerial career.

The youngest of six children, Gorman was born November 3, 1933, in Hampton, Arkansas. His father was an alcoholic, but his mother maintained high moral standards for the family; it was she who also promoted the sense of traditional religious values to her children. He graduated from Hampton High School, but his subsequent education came through courses taken from correspondence schools specializing in Bible studies and theology. By the time he completed the last of these, he was already an important minister of the Assembly of God—and he was only twenty years old.

Gorman's acknowledged conversion to Christianity took place when he was fifteen; a year later, he dedicated his life to the ministry; and two years later, he was pastor of his own small church in Hampton. After a year's work there, he resigned from the tiny, thirty-member congregation, and accepted the pastorate of a church in Callion, Arkansas, which had an enrollment of approximately ninety members. It was a major step up. Across the country, Assembly of God churches often had no more than twenty to fifty members. Taking over a ninety-member congregation was a coup for any minister, particularly one of Gorman's tender years.

At this point, Gorman's reputation began to grow. He attracted the notice of the Assemblies of God leadership and was named Area Representative for youth ministry, a vital position in a rapidly expanding denomination. He also began working as a traveling evangelist, preaching in numerous churches in the region. He was much in demand, and his popularity and financial status increased. He was rising quickly and surely toward the top of his calling, and many congregations were taken with the dynamics of this bright, young, handsome, well-spoken preacher.

In October 1955, Gorman married Virginia Adams, whom he met during his work with the youth ministry. Virginia was born in Banks, Arkansas, in 1935; she married shortly after she graduated from high school, but when she was merely nineteen, her husband drowned in an incident that she never discussed, leaving her a widow with an infant. (Frasier often joked that Marvin drowned Virginia's husband while conducting his baptism, so he could marry her; Virginia was [and is] an attractive woman.) A capable and intelligent individual, she went to work as a bank teller in El Dorado, Arkansas. In 1955, she attended a religious youth rally in El Dorado one night when Marvin was preaching. Marvin claimed that he looked up when Virginia walked in, and God spoke to him and said that she was going to be his wife. They began dating the next week and three-and-a-half months later they were married. Marvin adopted Virginia's child, Randy; they had two more children, Mark and Beverly.

Virginia continued her work in the bank while her young evangelist husband built his reputation and sought a more permanent and substantial position. It didn't take long. Less than a year after they were married, Gorman accepted the position of associate pastor of the First Assembly of God in Crowley, Louisiana. It was a major step up from the tiny congregations with which he had previously worked; as it turned out, it was a fortuitous decision. Within five weeks after he arrived in Crowley, the senior pastor, the Reverend D. W. Jolley, died of a heart attack, and Gorman was immediately elected to the position.

Over the next eighteen months, Gorman's work in the church won him the recognition of the Louisiana District Council of the Assemblies of God; they were impressed enough to elect him to serve as director of both the Youth Department and the Christian Education Department for the District. This meant another move. He and his new family relocated to the district's headquarters in Alexandria, Louisiana, where they remained for eight years.

As a handsome and energetic young man, Gorman took naturally to youth work. He had more education than many Assembly of God ministers and youth directors, so he was also advantaged in his work with Christian education.

His accomplishments mounted rapidly and during his tenure with the district offices he found himself in great demand, not merely on a regional but also on a national basis. He traveled all over the country to speak at major Assembly of God functions, and his advice and counsel were sought by many churches seeking to enlarge their youth ministry and to expand and improve their Christian education programs. Under his leadership, youth participation and enrollment in Assemblies of God grew enormously. Gorman evolved from a competent and able functionary in the church to a celebrity, one who had an instinct for organizing various outreach programs designed to attract and keep new members— particularly young members—faithful to their churches.

In 1965, the years of hard work and extended travel began to pay off in a more substantive way. By this time, he and Virginia were eager to settle down and find a permanent home away from the bureaucratic work in Alexandria.

Accordingly, he applied for and was elected as senior pastor of the First Assembly of God Church in New Orleans. On the surface, this did not appear to be a great honor or reward for his accomplishments on both regional and national levels. The First Assembly of God in New Orleans was a comparatively small congregation of only about a hundred members. Gorman, however, saw potential in the sin-rich fields of one of

America's most wide-open cities. He was the right man in the right church at the right time.

Gorman hit New Orleans precisely when a charismatic religious movement had a ripe opportunity to take hold. The Civil Rights struggle, which was growing to a crescendo in the late sixties, combined with other social unrest centered on an adult (and conservative Christian) distressing "counterculture" among the young to create an environment both hungry for reform and assistance (and assurance) from established religious forms.

Traditionally, Roman Catholics and Southern Baptists were prominent in Orleans Parish, with some good number of Methodists, Episcopalians, and Presbyterians as well; but there was a growing interest in charismatic movements, particularly those which reached out to the urban poor and socially discontented in the city.

Gorman went to work. He discovered that his personality and preaching style translated well through television, and he employed that medium as well as radio to begin to build a strong base in New Orleans and its environs. Within a short time, the humble hundred-member congregation of the First Assembly of God had grown to more than 5,000 members, and it prospered. Within a decade after his arrival, he was managing a budget of more than eight million dollars a year. His television ministry was now broadcast throughout the region, and he took steps to broaden it to encompass a national market. By the end of the seventies, his program was seen in all fifty states as well as in Canada on a daily basis.

As Gorman's personal reputation as a competent and valuable local minister grew along with his national reputation as a dynamic and effective televangelist, his professional status also elevated. In addition to his local ministry and television broadcasts, he found the time to serve on a number of boards and committees for the Louisiana District Council of the Assemblies of God, and he also was called on for service by the National Organization of the Assemblies of God, whose headquarters were in Springfield, Missouri. In 1981, he was elected as one of the eight nonresident Executive Presbyters for the Assemblies of God, one of the highest governing boards of the International Assemblies of God Ministries. His name was also being bandied about as a candidate for National Superintendent.

Marvin Gorman had arrived.

Joining the ranks of such well-known preachers as Jim Bakker, Jerry

Falwell, Robert Schuller, Pat Robertson, and, of course, Jimmy Swaggart, Gorman was rapidly making himself into a household name on a par with the best and brightest stars in America's religious pantheon. He seemed to be a tireless worker, an innovative and widely respected social reformer who was among the first in his city or even region to embrace a black constituency and welcome the integration of his congregation on Airline Highway in New Orleans. He also was instrumental in supporting young ministers and in establishing missionary-style churches in districts, which heretofore had no religious centers. One such church was the Canal Street Assembly of God.

By the mid-eighties, Gorman seemed poised to challenge Swaggart's burgeoning religious empire to the west. He was making moves that could be construed as challenging to Swaggart's monolithic organization. Among these moves was a deal he struck with Jim Bakker for a regular spot on the PTL Network's broadcasts. Bakker and Gorman were natural allies, both appealing strongly to younger viewers, and both centering their religious messages on "family values."

Indeed, Gorman's appeal to youth—always a strong part of his ministry—as well as to blacks, Hispanics, discontented and backsliding Roman Catholics, and also to those who found his apparent sincerity and high integrity appealing threatened to encroach on if not erode Swaggart's regional support base. It also, and not incidentally, bit deeply into Swaggart's ministry's earnings.

Swaggart was still king in the Assemblies of God realm, at least in Louisiana if not throughout the South, and Gorman openly admired him. But Gorman's own star was rising fast, and his move to expand his television ministry by purchasing bankrupt stations in Lake Charles and Houma, Louisiana, connecting them with his New Orleans studios and then broadcasting via a satellite uplink to the entire world had Swaggart worried. It was time, to borrow a phrase from Henry II when he complained of Thomas á Beckett, to stop "this troublesome priest" and show him that, in Louisiana and most of America, there was only room for one Assembly of God star: Jimmy Swaggart.

In many ways, Marvin Gorman's life formed a parallel line to Tomy Frasier's. Both came from more or less humble origins with only a smattering of education to bolster their ambitions. Both took risks in their younger years, and both followed a path of personal commitment and ambition that led them into sympathetic positions with the downtrodden and underdogs of society.

But apart from such abstract similarities, two men could not have been more different in temperament and personality. Their mutual traits—determination, a sense of moral right and wrong, and a strong sense of who they were and what they were about—might have been shared; but the elements which made them a most effective team in a defensive fight against the rogue king of fundamentalism—Jimmy Swaggart—are best defined through their differences.

Born in 1925 in Tulsa, Oklahoma, Tomy Dee Frasier, known to his friends as "Slim," left high school at age sixteen, used his height of six-four, lied about his age, and joined the United States Marine Corps. Over the next four years, he would develop a reputation as a gung-ho Leatherneck, fearless in the face of danger. He would accumulate twenty-seven months of combat service in the South Pacific and would win a Silver Star and two Purple Hearts.

He also would lose forever the use of his legs.

On Okinawa in 1945, Frasier volunteered to take the point in his unit's advance on a Japanese stronghold, which was protected by a ten-man machine-gun nest. The gun and its protective guard directly threatened his company and kept it pinned down, unable to attack the Japanese position. Although he was scheduled to rotate home in a few days, Frasier insisted on participating in a coin toss to determine who would provide a decoy to distract the gunners while a flanking assault was launched on the enemy position. Frasier lost the toss. Accordingly, he stood up, exposed himself, and thumbed his nose at the enemy. It was, in some ways, an adolescent gesture, but it was also typically defiant for a Marine who had gone through so much and who had nothing but contempt for his enemy. Anyway, Frasier was famous for doing it immediately before engaging in combat.

No sooner had Frasier completed his derisive display than two Japanese soldiers popped up from a "spider trap" pit just a few feet in front of him and opened fire. Frasier was quick. He killed both ambushers, but he also took a round in the chest near his left shoulder. Although this would not be the last time Tomy Dee Frasier would thumb his nose at his opponents, it was the last time he would ever stand up.

The war was over for Frasier. He was evacuated to the States and put in the care of Naval hospitals, where for a lengthy time he convalesced and healed and learned to use a wheelchair. While at the Corona Naval Hospital in 1946, he met Head Nurse, Lieutenant Julia Fraden, the daughter of a Presbyterian missionary.

According to Julia, Frasier was the main morale booster for the entire hospital. He proved so entertaining that the staff moved him from room to room to amuse the other veteran patients. His sense of humor, bright outlook, and unbridled enthusiasm for life was a grand tonic for the soldiers and sailors, many of whom suffered from crippling and disfiguring wounds.

Julia openly admired Frasier's courage and dedication to duty; and she also admired his acceptance of his own inevitable debilitation. They formed a tremendous bond—a bond for life—fell in love, and they were soon married.

In December 1946, the Marine Corps ordered Frasier back to active duty at the San Diego recruiting depot. By this time, Frasier had mastered his wheelchair, so he cheerfully obeyed and reported. The embarrassed officers realized their mistake as soon as they saw him; he was immediately discharged to a Veterans Hospital. Eight months later and just a few months after his marriage, the newlyweds moved back to Tulsa to be close to his mother and brother.

Frasier was no man to sit and idly contemplate the emptiness of a future as a handicapped war veteran. He soon took advantage of the G.I. Bill educational opportunities and enrolled at the Northeastern Oklahoma A&M College, then eventually transferred to the University of Arkansas in Fayetteville, where he later pursued a law degree. He returned to Tulsa to establish a practice and pursue a career after receiving his degree in 1951.

Frasier's personal endeavor proved an inspiration for many, particularly for his eight-year-old brother, who was born while Tomy was overseas. Jimmy grew up pushing Tomy's wheelchair and getting to know his long-absent brother; he later followed his brother's path to the practice of law. Today, Jimmy Frasier is regarded as one of the best trial lawyers in the State of Oklahoma and is his brother's law partner.

It came as no surprise to anyone who knew him that Tomy Frasier would become involved in politics. Almost as soon as he returned to his hometown, he ran for a number of offices and became a liberal force to reckon with in staunchly conservative Tulsa. In 1959 and 1960, Frasier worked with the JFK campaign; although the Roman Catholic and eastern liberal Kennedy did not do well in widely Protestant and traditionally right-wing Oklahoma, Frasier was still rewarded by the Senator from Massachusetts, now President, with an appointment as a regional solicitor for the Department of the Interior. The story was that Kennedy wrote a note to his assistant to give Tomy Dee Frasier any position he wanted.

As the sixties evolved, Frasier became an influential political force in his own right, but not without exciting controversy. One of his local political opponents, Attorney David Hale, assembled a grand jury to indict Frasier on two misdemeanor counts, one for criminal libel for calling Hale a "blubber ass," and another for extortion, alleging that Frasier led a scheme to shake down retirement home owners.

Frasier defended himself against the first charge through the media with the only legal weapon he ever completely trusted: the truth. But he also called into play another item from the Frasier arsenal: his sense of humor. Calling a news conference, he produced a yardstick and announced that truth was an absolute defense to libel. He stated that he would call the county attorney to the witness stand and would then measure the width of Hale's buttocks for the jury to evaluate.

After the indictments were issued, Hale had Frasier arrested. On the day of Frasier's arraignment, sixty-three attorneys appeared, each offering to defend Frasier, who ultimately won an acquittal on both counts at trial. The entire affair, particularly the easy acquittal, made Frasier a popular media figure and an even stronger political force in the community.

Frasier's legal practice centered on criminal law. He rapidly made a name for himself defending the accused felons in Oklahoma in the 1960s and 1970s, but he also handled controversial Civil Rights cases. He soon developed a reputation as a "bulldog reformer," one whose tenacity was tempered only by his ultimate goal of protecting the rights of the accused. His obvious physical impairment combined with his war record to lend credibility and emotional weight to many of his arguments. Tomy Frasier demanded the respect of his opponents, and he generally received it.

During the Vietnam era of the late 1960s, Frasier did an about-face, changing from a gung-ho Marine to peace activist. He stated that he had grown older, wiser, and that he learned to love people and realize God's beautiful gift of human life. He was an enthusiastic advocate for peace and antiwar demonstrator and was never afraid of putting himself on the line. He claimed that the greatest experience in his career was when he was arrested with Jane Fonda following a protest against U.S. involvement in the Vietnam.

Frasier was a brash and outspoken man, but he was never embarrassed to show his admiration and love for people of all backgrounds and all races. If a single word would fit his attitudes toward

64

humankind, it would probably be *tolerance* or perhaps *acceptance*. There was one exception: Throughout his life, he never forgave the Japanese. Whether his bitterness and disdain was centered completely in his own crippling wound, or whether it was an extension of his personal sacrifice that encompassed the whole useless slaughter of life and devastation that was World War II, he wouldn't say. But he was unable to tolerate Japanese people, refused to sit near them in a restaurant or to have direct, social commerce with them in any way. He usually hid his personal feelings about them well, but from time to time, it surfaced as a reminder of his deep personal pain.

At the same time, Frasier could be remarkably frank about his disability, and he never failed to demonstrate the strides he took to overcome it or used it as an excuse to avoid a fight. An avid gambler— and undeterred from games of chance by the fatal coin toss that cost him the use of his legs, Frasier continued to tempt fate at racetracks around the South; he also bet on football, basketball, and baseball games every chance he had, and was an enthusiastic poker player, although such gambling was not always without incident.

Frasier was with a buddy in a local club one night, when two out-of-towners came in and wanted to play poker. Frasier invited them to join him at a card table, and in short order had won all their money. The strangers were not pleased, and called Frasier a "sorry-assed crippled cheater." Frasier, who always wore gloves on his hands in order to work his wheelchair, took immediate offense at the insulting accusation. He immediately popped the offender on the jaw and knocked him to the floor. He then rolled his chair over and dumped himself out on top of his victim and, according to Frasier, "beat the living hell out of him." The next day, the other man from out of town came by Frasier's office to apologize and to assure the attorney that nothing would ever come of the incident; it was forgotten. Frasier replied with a laugh, "Well, this is probably the first time your friend ever had his ass kicked by a cripple."

By the mid 1980s, Tomy Dee Frasier was not only a formidable lawyer, he was also a formidable physical specimen. At the age of sixty-five, he had the great upper body strength of men a third his age. Although modest about his own abilities, Frasier swam thirty to forty minutes every day, lifting himself in and out of the pool by an overhead support and seating himself in his wheelchair. He routinely hoisted himself in and out of cars and bathtubs, and he never complained about any physical exertion that was within his limits of physical strength.

65

In one sense, he was a man driven by inner forces only he could understand. In another sense, he was inspired by a calling to what he saw as duty and professionalism that no one but he could define. And in that regard, he was very much like Marvin Gorman, indeed.

Frasier was not eager at first to take Marvin Gorman's case. Gorman had to make two trips to Tulsa to talk the attorney into considering it. But Gorman recognized something in Frasier, something almost everyone who knew the attorney from Tulsa took almost for granted. Frasier was a man of high integrity with a personal sense of who he was and what he was about. He disdained nonsense and had no toleration for phoniness. He was also a man committed to reason who had a profound determination to achieve set goals. In short, he was the perfect mouthpiece to represent Gorman in his defense of his name against an unwarranted attack by such a powerful and arrogant individual as Jimmy Swaggart.

Once committed, Frasier was completely on Gorman's side, and he brought to bear his complete life experience as he sought to provide Gorman with the soundest representation he could.

I'll never forget coming out of the depositions one day when the defendants were deposing Marvin Gorman. I remarked to Frasier that it appeared the defendants were trying to paint a picture that Gorman had counseled certain women whom he felt sorry for, and because he felt sorry for them, he offered them sex.

I said, "Tomy, it sounds to me like they're accusing Marvin Gorman of having sympathy sex with these women."

Tomy looked at me with a scowl and said, "Yeah, but it ain't true. If anyone knows about sympathy fucks, it's me, and the preacher's not guilty."

I was taken aback by Frasier's statement, by his direct and personal interpretation to an objective matter of legal determination. But the more I thought about it, the more I understood just how well he grasped the personalities involved and the painful circumstances surrounding the case of Marvin Gorman. And, moreover, I knew that he was right.

• PART TWO •

WAR IN HEAVEN

"Woe to thee that spoilest, and thou *wast* not spoiled; and dealest treacherously, and they dealt not treacherously with thee! when thou shalt cease to spoil, thou shalt be spoiled; *and* when thou shalt make an end to deal treacherously, they shall deal treacherously with thee."
—The Book of the Prophet Isaiah, 33:1

• CHAPTER SEVEN •
THE ONLY SHOW IN TOWN

"Then Paul said, I stand at Caesar's judgement seat,
where I ought to be judged . . . I appeal unto Caesar."
—Acts of the Apostles, 25: 7, 11.

At the outset of our agreement to handle the Gorman case, I believed
that we had plenty of time. The statute of limitations governing personal
injury suits in the State of Louisiana would not expire until July, and we
seemed to have the luxury of proceeding at a careful and studied pace as
we assembled our case.

Even so, we went to work right away. Our investigator, Scott Bailey,
began taking statements from a number of female church members of the
First Assembly of God in New Orleans. Almost all spoke highly of
Marvin Gorman, and it became apparent that finding character witnesses
to vouch for Gorman's general behavior would not be a problem.

At the same time, we began collecting rumors that had been spread
about Gorman throughout the church. Very quickly, we assembled a list
of names of women with whom Gorman supposedly had sexual relations
over the years. The rumors were curiously similar, regardless of our
source, something that made us suspicious right away that there was more
to this than a mere grapevine of gossip working throughout the
Assemblies of God in Louisiana. Specifics and particulars associated with
each name surfaced time after time, almost in the same language, no
matter how ludicrous the charge (one alleged sexual partner of Gorman's
was more than eighty years old); further, we were able to trace some of
them back through the rumor mill far enough to determine that Michael
Indest was spreading the word if not manufacturing the stories from
whole cloth himself. Each of the names, it was consistently suggested,
appeared on the supposed list Swaggart claimed to have when he met
with Gorman at his mansion on July 15, 1986.

Probably the most important statement taken during the entire investigation was a telephone-taped interview of Jane Talbot, one of the staff employees of First Assembly of God.

Talbot had provided Swaggart or his associates a written statement of complaint and accusation against Gorman to church officials after learning that Gorman had confessed to an act of adultery with Lynda Savage. Talbot claimed that Gorman had at one time touched her in inappropriate ways and had French-kissed her.

From the first, Gorman denied that he had ever made any advances toward Jane Talbot whatsoever. On the contrary, he claimed, she had once made an advance toward him. One day, Gorman stated, he was asleep on his office sofa behind a closed door. He awoke to find Talbot kissing him on the lips and grabbing his crotch. According to Gorman, he was outraged. He ordered Talbot from his office and subsequently moved her from the reception desk outside his office to another workstation located elsewhere in the church.

Although we had no copy of her original statement, which she supposedly made to church officials in August 1986, we believed anything Jane Talbot said was suspect. We learned that Talbot had been a personal devotee of Gorman's, what in religious circles is sometimes called a "frontpew admirer." She traveled from her home in Houma, almost an hour's drive, to attend Gorman's New Orleans services prior to being hired by the church.

If Gorman's version of events was accurate, then we concluded Talbot's motives for making a false statement to church officials were those of a "woman spurned" if not "scorned." She clearly was attracted to Gorman, possibly romantically enamored of him, but since he spurned her advances and was now admitting that he had a sexual encounter with another woman, Talbot became vengeful. It was also likely that under pressure, she might recant.

Indeed, she did. When Bailey taped his telephone interview with her, she reversed herself and denied that Gorman had ever had intercourse with her or made any sexual advances toward her at all. She would not go so far, however, as to discuss the reason why she might have made a false statement in the first place. In any event, her credibility would be very questionable should she testify.

The statement of Cheryl McConnel, another of Gorman's parishioners, also turned out to be important, and she would turn out to be a key defense witness at trial. Surprisingly, we learned that she had given

70

her statement to Carl Miller, the business manager for the First Assembly of God, but then later got it back and tore it up. We also had a copy of a letter that Cheryl McConnel had written Marvin and Virginia Gorman commending them on their service to the church and thanking them for all the love and concern they had extended to her through hard times. For this reason, we found it hard to believe that she would be a witness who would in any way hurt Gorman. But we were uncertain, for a number of Gorman's former close friends and admirers had turned on him after July 15.

Like Talbot, McConnel was a woman from whom church officials solicited a statement accusing Gorman of making sexual advances toward her. Also like Talbot, McConnel was a "front pew" devotee of Gorman's; her clear admiration for the minister was obvious to observers. McConnel was an extremely attractive and sincere individual whose testimony would be credible. We knew we would have to handle her carefully at trial.

In addition to tracking the women whose names were on the supposed list, Bailey traveled from South Florida to West Texas interviewing anyone who might have a tidbit of useful information about Jimmy Swaggart. Bailey also researched probate records in West Texas where Jimmy Swaggart Ministries had attempted to collect on several wills bequeathing large estates.

It soon became obvious that Bill Treeby, Swaggart's attorney, played hardball everywhere he went and was never shy when it came to acquiring money for Swaggart's enterprises. The probate records of the Ida Baugh and Zoe Vance estates in Texas, for example, had been sealed under a protective order during a controversy involving Jimmy Swaggart and Jimmy Swaggart Ministries. At least one of these probates involved allegations that Swaggart took advantage of an elderly woman on her deathbed in an attempt to persuade her to will the majority of her estate to Jimmy Swaggart Ministries. When the family contested the will, Treeby hired a battery of Texas lawyers who had the record sealed. What followed was a lengthy legal debate over the fortunes of the estate. We soon learned that the same approach to preserving the secrecy surrounding Swaggart's doings would be used in our case.

In the course of his work, Bailey interviewed several unique individuals, including a black woman named Jacklyn Warren, who was serving time in a penitentiary in West Texas for killing two people in the name of religion. Warren had apparently been hired by church officials as a house sitter or caretaker for an elderly couple who had made wills leaving their estate to Jimmy Swaggart Ministries. She was convicted of murdering the pair, although the terms of the will were not as suggested by Warren.

Additionally, Bailey, Frasier, and I each interviewed Ed Fields, the father of a young girl who had attended Jimmy Swaggart's Bible College. According to Fields, his daughter was raped by a student at Jimmy Swaggart Ministries, but Swaggart and the college administration covered up the crime. Swaggart, Fields asserted, felt that the incident involving his daughter was nothing more than a consensual sex act with "boys being boys." Since this woman was a Bible College student, Swaggart did not want to do anything about it. Instead, he more or less attacked the young lady and her family. Fields told his story to a number of magazines and appeared on *Geraldo* with a panel of individuals to vent his anger towards Jimmy Swaggart Ministries. Although all of these bizarre stories were interesting, much of the work was accomplished in vain. None of them would be deemed relevant to the trial.

Some good was coming of our efforts, but not in a way we anticipated or particularly welcomed. As we interviewed each of these individuals, either over the telephone or in person, others began to come forward, seeking us out to tell of even more vicious rumors about Gorman that had been and were still being spread by members of the staff of First Assembly of God Church. Once again, all roads led back to Michael Indest and other significant personalities within the Assembly of God. But the rumors also began to raise doubts in our mind as to the possible veracity of our client, or on the other hand, as to the extent of the conspiracy that was organized against him.

It seemed implausible that all this was taking place merely because a minister had "stumbled" in his moral demeanor, even more than once. Objectively speaking, the emerging scenario indicated either that Gorman was much more the philandering pastor than he or anyone in support of him was willing to admit, or that Swaggart and his minions were after far bigger fish than merely the making of an example through the public chastisement of one of their own.

Still, we stuck by our original precept, that Gorman was the target of a systematic and deliberate program of defamation, and we continued our process, attempting to be as thorough as possible. Very soon, though, events took a turn of their own and matters came into sharper focus.

On March 19, 1987, a report was released through the national news media that the Reverend Jim Bakker, one of the top five televangelists in the country, had been accused of having a sexual affair with one of his former church secretaries, Jessica Hahn, while they were in Florida on vacation. This was national news. Bakker and his wife, Tammye Faye, were the most popular religious couple on the air. Through their PTL ("Praise the Lord" or "People That Love") Network, they broadcast to millions of homes throughout the world on an almost continuous basis.

Born in 1940 in Muskegon, Michigan, Bakker was a tiny man with an outlandish pompadour, horn-rimmed glasses, and a naive manner. Fond of high-heeled shoes and white suits, he relied heavily on personal charm and the electronically enhanced deceptions possible through the magic of television to present himself as a person of physical presence.

Bakker and Tammye Faye, whose date of birth in International Falls, Minnesota, has been variously reported, formed a televangelical team. They worked together, on camera, to promote the faith of the Assemblies of God through a variety of programs orbiting around their world famous *PTL Club* program.

In contrast to the shorter and slighter Jim Bakker, Tammye Faye was a somewhat portly woman with exaggerated mannerisms; she was chiefly noted for her ability to weep on cue and then rapidly shift to a shrill laugh, which some technicians reported sent the sound meter dials well into the red if they were not prepared for instant adjustments. Her frilly, silly "Southern Belle" outfits were matched by trademark heavy eye makeup and wild, sometimes oddly colored (pink and blue highlights seemed common) coiffures and wigs. This outlandish husband-and-wife team somehow appealed to a wide television audience. After the founding of the PTL Network and launching of the *PTL Club* program in 1974, the Bakkers' programs were among the most lavishly produced, slickest examples of hard-sell glitz available on religious television.

They were also among the most lucrative.

Innocent-appearing or not, Bakker was no dummy. He and his silly sidekick wife had built an empire in the Carolinas. The Bakkers and PTL not only owned a television network, they also owned and operated a highly profitable modern theme and amusement park and a religious community in Fort Mill, South Carolina.

Emotionally charged and technically perfect, the Bakkers' teleministry carried the idea of selling salvation to new dimensions. One analyst observed that no more than five minutes passed on any PTL produced program when there was not an overt pitch for the viewing audience to send in money. The pitches were often subtle, merely on-screen scrolling words offering "counseling," books, pamphlets, or other materials in exchange for hard cash. But credit cards were also welcome, as were personal checks, pledges, money orders, almost anything negotiable. The Bakkers had turned the tradition of the offertory into a moneymaking science.

And they were popular. Apart from Jimmy Swaggart, Jim and Tammye Faye Bakker controlled the largest daily audience share enjoyed by any televangelist in the market.

And they lived well—too well in the opinion of many, including Jimmy Swaggart, who lived very well himself. Heritage U.S.A., the Bakker's celebrated amusement park and headquarters, was, in the eyes of one observer, "a sort of cross between Disneyland and a retirement village. All of the interiors in the main buildings were lavish, but truly tacky, the interior design complement to Tammye Faye's eye makeup. And the [attached] shopping mall was fairly bizarre, too, if you can imagine a Christian-oriented jewelry and makeup shop." If Bakker had set out to "out-Oral Roberts Oral Roberts," he succeeded; Heritage U.S.A. and the PTL were monuments to bad taste, and foolish excess.

What was of immediate interest to our legal team, though, was that Bakker's initial response to the allegations—a denial, naturally—suggested that he was a victim of a deliberate attempt to destroy his ministry, an attempt orchestrated by none other than Jimmy Swaggart.

This should have come as no surprise to us, for Swaggart had been hinting of sexual improprieties in the PTL Ministries for months. Apparently Swaggart had learned of Jessica Hahn's allegations against her employer, Jim Bakker, as early as the summer of 1986, about the same time he was attacking Gorman. Swaggart then used that information to attempt to blackmail Bakker to remove Marvin Gorman's programs from the PTL network in September 1986, following Gorman's resignation and expulsion from the Assembly of God's ministerial ranks. Bakker refused, or at least he demurred, telling Don Hardister, PTL's head of security, "If he gets Gorman, he'll get me next." Hardister subsequently stated that he was confused by Bakker's reaction, for if Bakker and PTL had nothing to hide, then they had nothing to fear. And insofar as he knew, there was nothing to hide.

Swaggart was furious when Bakker refused in September 1986 to fly to Baton Rouge and confer with him about Gorman's situation. Instead, Bakker sent the Reverend Richard Dortch, a top PTL administrator and one of Swaggart's longtime friends. Swaggart prevailed on Dortch to persuade Bakker to drop his support for Gorman, at least some of which had been solicited by Mark Gorman, Marvin's second son who himself was a minister, gospel singer, and a featured performer on PTL programs. Bakker continued to refuse both to become involved in Swaggart's move against Gorman and to withdraw his public support of Gorman's ministry.

The war escalated. Accusations and bitter recriminations flew from both camps, although Swaggart's verbal artillery won most of the press's attention. Calling Bakker "sissified," he attacked the theme park setting of the PTL ministry and stepped up the pace of the rumor mill about supposed improprieties in the PTL organization. Suggestions that Bakker was bisexual, if not homosexual, also emanated by way of rumor from Baton Rouge. Swaggart enlisted the services of John Ankerberg, a Tennessee evangelist, who publicly suggested that there were financial irregularities in PTL as well.

Bakker retaliated by canceling Swaggart's broadcasts on PTL, and Swaggart flew into a rage. To add fuel to the fire, Bakker was approached by Dwain Johnson, a musician who had worked for Jimmy Swaggart Ministries in the early 1980s, and who claimed that Swaggart had threatened to kill him after discovering that he had had an affair with Swaggart's daughter-in-law, Debbie. Johnson's wife claimed that Swaggart told her that Dwain had better leave town (Baton Rouge) or he would kill him. The accusations apparently were made during a lawsuit brought by the Johnsons against Jimmy Swaggart Ministries in an attempt to recover vacation and severance pay as well as royalties from Johnson's recordings, which were sold by Swaggart's company. Swaggart denied ever making any such threats.

The suit was settled for an undisclosed amount of money in 1983; however, the news of a possible sex scandal inside Jimmy Swaggart Ministries, one involving Swaggart's daughter-in-law herself, was too good for Bakker to ignore. He dug deep for more information, hopeful of finding something that could be used to fend off Swaggart's latest move, an attempted hostile takeover of PTL by Jimmy Swaggart Ministries.

By this time, it was March 1987, and it was clear that a lawsuit was being prepared by Gorman against Swaggart. In a deft move to distract attention away from himself and to finish, once and for all, Jim Bakker, Swaggart leaked the information about Bakker and Hahn to the *Charlotte Observer*; at once, Bakker and televangelism in general were ·in the national headlines.

Personally, I tended to believe Bakker was telling the truth, at least about Jessica Hahn. Released photographs of Hahn revealed her to be a very attractive and somewhat sophisticated woman with higher than average intelligence. It was hard to believe that she could have had even a temporary liaison with or any serious attraction to the diminutive and somewhat ridiculous Jim Bakker.

Among the accusations of excesses that would surface were charges that the Bakkers paid themselves huge salaries, lived in a stately mansion, drove luxury automobiles, and took lavish vacations at exotic resorts. It was during one such vacation that Jim Bakker allegedly seduced— "practically raped" was the rumor—Jessica Hahn.

Additional charges involved misappropriation of PTL funds, outright embezzlement, and tax evasion—a generally familiar scenario to anyone familiar with the Gorman case. Finally, it would be revealed that Tammye Faye had for years suffered from severe chemical dependency, which she had made no effort to break or, for that matter, to keep a particular secret from any of the PTL's inner circle.

In their usual eagerness to find a scandal whether there was one or not, reporters immediately confronted Jimmy Swaggart with questions about his possible involvement with the disclosure and/or accusations about Bakker's jaunt with Jessica Hahn, which allegedly took place in Florida in 1980, long before Bakker had arrived at the pinnacle of his success. At the same time, reporters asked Swaggart specific questions regarding his involvement in the downfall of Marvin Gorman. Because of comments Swaggart had made on national television regarding Jim Bakker running to some degree parallel to his published indictment of Gorman—at least in the choice of words and tone of accusation—there were obvious connections to be made.

The connections were more than obvious, however. Not only had Gorman's own television broadcasts been syndicated by PTL, but at the time of Gorman's resignation in 1986, Bakker made on-the-air comments in Gorman's defense and, as noted, refused to remove him from PTL program logs. At the time, Bakker indicated by both implication and direct statement that Jimmy Swaggart was the architect of Marvin Gorman's destruction.

Swaggart, not surprisingly, denied that there was any connection whatsoever. When confronted about his involvement in the disclosure of the Bakker-Hahn affair on CNN, in March 1987, Swaggart said he knew nothing about Marvin Gorman or his problems. At this point, of course, he had already written letters to church officials attacking Jim Bakker's defense of Gorman. Furthermore, he had met with Richard Dortch in Baton Rouge in September 1986 and threatened to disclose information about Jim Bakker if, in fact, the PTL Network did not remove Gorman's programs.

In any event, and regardless of connections or of Swaggart's involvement in the Bakker revelations, our timetable was advancing more rapidly than we had planned. In fact, on the very day Swaggart was interviewed by the press about the Bakker affair, I began drafting a petition, which for the next five years would become known as the $90 Million Lawsuit of Marvin Gorman.

I worked steadily on the petition from March 20 through 23. By now, I had access to copies of Swaggart's correspondence, the various statements from both the Louisiana District Council and the National Council of the Assemblies of God, and our own, as yet incomplete, investigative file compiled by Scott Bailey. Each day, I held discussions with both Gorman and Tomy Frasier and Steve Hickman to determine precisely what the contents of the petition should contain and about the wording.

Frasier indicated he wanted to file the suit on March 24 and presented me with that as a deadline. He arranged to come to New Orleans on that day and for Gorman to hold a press conference for the New Orleans media on that afternoon. Hence, he wanted to be sure the petition was filed and copies placed in the hands of the media prior to that time. The conference was to be held at the offices of Marvin Gorman Ministries in Metairie.

I worked all day, March 23, to produce a final draft of the petition, and I read it over the telephone to Gorman, who approved it. We were ready to file. At the time, my law office employed only two secretaries for both me and David Dwight, so I had to hire part time help for the workload I knew was about to come. Frances "Franki" Roll arrived shortly after five o'clock, when she left her regular job at Jones, Tete, and began preparing the final draft of the document. Thus, by 3:00 a.m. on March 24, 1987, we had a final draft and copies for all the defendants who would be served with it.

The petition, which was drafted on behalf of Marvin Gorman and Marvin Gorman Ministries, Inc., named as defendants Jimmy Swaggart, Jimmy Swaggart Ministries, the General Council of Assemblies of God, G. Raymond Carlson (General Superintendent of the General Council), the Louisiana District Council of Assemblies of God, Cecil Janway (Superintendent of the Louisiana District), the First Assembly of God Church of New Orleans, Lakeview Christian Center, Michael Indest, the Canal Street Assembly of God, and Tom Miller (the Exorcist).

Following my previous suggestion about naming as many individual defendants as possible, it was our hope that at least some if not most of those named would come forward seeking settlement. Or that their insurance companies would do so. This would not only help pay expenses for the legal process to come, it would also clear the way for us to go after the real villain of the piece, as we saw it, Jimmy Swaggart.

In the petition, Gorman asked for cash award in response to damages for defamation, invasion of privacy and intentional infliction of emotional distress. The demand for damages totaled $90 million. Because of the number of defendants and anticipated response of the press, we ran out of paper in the copy machine at about 2:00 A.M. and had to substitute bond typing paper to accumulate the requisite copies.

At 6:30 A.M. on Tuesday morning, March 24, I drove from Lake Charles to the Crescent City, a trip of about two hundred miles, where I picked up Randy Gorman at Marvin Gorman Ministries and drove him to the courthouse. Little did I know then that over the next four years, I would make several hundred trips and spend six months of my life in "the Big Easy."

By the time Randy and I returned from downtown, Frasier and Hickman had arrived from Tulsa. Frasier came with a prepared statement—a virtual script—for Gorman to read to the media. Frasier also laid out the format for the press conference. Gorman would read his statement, then reporters would be permitted to ask questions. Gorman would answer none of them. Instead, Frasier himself would conduct the interview portion of the press conference. In fact, for most of the remainder of the suit, Gorman was prohibited by Frasier from answering questions from the press. Frasier preferred to take his role as mouthpiece literally and to control what sound bites found their way into print and onto the six o'clock news.

Frasier lined up the entire Gorman family, with Marvin in front, reading the script to all present. In a brief, concise statement Gorman outlined the details of the suit and his reasons for bringing it. He then told the media that he knew he was going to be attacked by some of his "brothers in the church" for filing a lawsuit, as the New Testament specifically condemned anyone who would level a claim against a

Brother in Christ. However, Gorman went on, the Acts of the Apostles, 25:7 and 20 excused his actions. In that passage Paul appeals to Caesar after he could not be heard by the Pharisees, the principal ecclesiastical authority. Thus, his action had biblical authority behind it, biblical precedent to back it.

The Scripture Gorman cited implied by analogy that Gorman had attempted to resolve his differences with Jimmy Swaggart and the Assemblies of God through the prescribed ecclesiastical processes within the church itself, but he was not allowed to be heard. Thus, his only choice for relief and his only recourse to salvage his name and prevent further slander against him was to appeal to a modern-day Caesar, a secular court of law, specifically, the Civil District Court (CDC) of Orleans Parish, known by many lawyers in Louisiana as the "Black Hole," because jury verdicts in favor of plaintiffs coming out of this jurisdiction were the largest in the country and defendants were buried so deep in these judgments they could not get out.

After Gorman concluded his statement, the press was invited to interview Frasier, and the minister and his family stepped back, while Frasier moved forward to field questions.

I personally had never participated in any legal action that involved any sort of media involvement, but as I looked around the room, I realized that every newspaper in the state seemed to have a reporter there. In addition both the Baton Rouge and New Orleans television stations were represented. But the leader of the pack seemed to be one particular reporter, Bill Elder, a New Orleans television personality and news commentator from WWL-TV.

For weeks prior to the filing of the petition, Gorman and his sons had been receiving calls from Elder, who claimed that he had been informed of a number of accusations against Gorman. This was quite likely, of course, as Indest and others were not being at all stingy with the rumors touching on Gorman's alleged infidelities with "hundreds of women."

Elder said he was working on a story based on the accusations and he wanted Gorman's response. Following our instructions, Gorman steadfastly refused to discuss the matter with the reporter, but he told him that there would be a press conference at the appropriate time. Now was the time, and Elder wanted his questions answered.

As Frasier took center stage before the press, Hickman and I stood to the side to get away from the cameras. They rolled in close to the big man in the wheelchair; almost immediately, questions began to fly, and

Frasier began to respond.

One reporter led the way: "Is it true that Gorman has been unfaithful to Mrs. Gorman and had affairs with several women?"

Frasier held his finger up and said, "Gorman has been true to one woman all his life and the evidence will prove it."

I was shocked at this response as Gorman had already admitted a sexual indiscretion with Lynda Savage to us and in front of witnesses, including Michael Indest, David Savage, and Jimmy Swaggart. Much later, I learned that Frasier's words were carefully chosen and better expressed than they seemed.

Bill Elder now stepped forward and asked, "Is this anything similar to the Bakker downfall?"

Frasier responded simply: "It seems that the seed was planted in both camps approximately the same time."

Elder followed up quickly: "Well, just what is the purpose of the lawsuit?"

Frasier replied in his best Oklahoma twang, "To seek out the devil." Before the reporters could react to this answer, Frasier added, "We have a good idea where the devil resides: approximately seventy miles west of here, up on I-10, living in a mansion behind huge walls, surrounded by a moat." This coda brought laughter from the reporters, even Elder.

Frasier continued, "The only problem we see at this time is whether or not the devil is a 'he' or a 'she'." Once again the room filled with laughter, but Frasier kept a straight face through the entire press conference.

Hickman stood on the side of the room with a smile on his face. Obviously this was nothing new in his experience with Tomy Frasier.

Elder then asked, "What will you do if you catch the devil?"

Tomy replied, "Shake him like a dog shakes a rat in his mouth."

It was clear to everyone in the room that Tomy Frasier had no intention of handling the great Jimmy Swaggart with kid gloves.

Frasier's personal dislike of Swaggart seemed to grow each day and was, I believe, founded in Frasier's complete contempt for hypocrisy. He told me about the first time he came to New Orleans to visit Reverend Gorman in October 1986. Frasier made the trip by limousine from Tulsa; when he passed through Baton Rouge, he ordered the driver to take a detour off I-10 and tour around the campus and grounds of Jimmy Swaggart Ministries and the Bible College. No sooner was he spotted, than people flocked around his car offering assistance, directions, or help of any kind he might require. Obviously, Frasier recalled, they believed a "cripple in a limousine" had come to see Swaggart's home in hopes of receiving some particular favor from the great Reverend Jimmy. In return, of course, the grateful cripple might be good for a sizable donation.

The story always gave Frasier an opportunity to smile slyly at his deliberate deception of Swaggart's followers. But more important than the ruse he fostered was the opportunity it gave him to view the impressive structures and lavish surroundings—a veritable monument to Swaggart himself—the great man had built with the "nickels and dimes of the faithful."

By the time the press conference ended I was actively wondering what I had gotten myself into. I felt a need to go home and reread the "Canons of Ethics" to see if my co-counsel, Tomy Frasier, was following the rules of the game.

But it did not take long for me to realize that Gorman knew precisely what he was doing when he sought the representation of Tomy Frasier. Few attorneys knew the rules as well as Frasier did, and few were as willing as Frasier to bend them in the service of a client in whom he believed. Further, Frasier had learned years ago that even the most severely bent rule will often be overlooked by both the courts and the press when the bender is a decorated World War II veteran confined by his wounds to a wheelchair.

But Frasier had wisdom and practical experience behind him also, and Gorman was well aware of it.

Some years before, Frasier and Hickman had represented a young divorcée named Marianne Guinne from Collinsville, Oklahoma. Guinne filed suit against the Collinsville Church of Christ and all its elders for invasion of privacy and intentional infliction of emotional distress, damages which were precisely the same as those we had alleged against Jimmy Swaggart.

The cause of the action was that the elders of the Collinsville Church of Christ had publicly "shunned" or ostracized Guinne because she admitted to having a sexual relationship with the former mayor of the city. Even though she was a single woman and the mother of four children, and even though she resigned her membership in the church, the elders distributed a written statement about her sin to the congregation in Collinsville and in other Church of Christ congregations in the county. The purpose, Frasier argued, was not merely to chide but to punish.

Marianne Guinne's trial was highly publicized, and Frasier's counsel worked to gain her a favorable verdict not only for compensatory damages, but also for punitive damages against the church elders.

Thus, if I had already developed a sense that Frasier had been down this road before, there was a good reason.

After I returned home and recovered from the ordeal of the rushed filing and hectic press conference, I called Frasier to assess the situation. Jim Bakker's public disgrace and the attendant scandal were now dominating prime-time news magazine programs. It was in all the tabloids, both in the broadcast media and in supermarket checkout lines. Allegations were now emerging that Bakker had not only had an affair with Hahn, but that he had committed numerous other indiscretions. More to the interest of governmental agencies, however, were accusations that he had grossly misappropriated the funds of the PTL Network for his own enrichment.

Suddenly, Jim Bakker had become a household name in a way that he never dreamed, never wanted.

Frasier told me that the esteemed New York attorney, Roy Grutman, had called him and indicated he would be representing Jim Bakker. In an attempt, apparently, to impress the Tulsa attorney, Grutman told Frasier that he was placing the call from his Lear jet. Frasier, never one to be one-upped, replied that he was receiving the call on the "ass end of a mule."

Weeks later, I learned that Bakker had called Tomy Frasier before hiring Roy Grutman to represent him. Frasier, who was already committed to Gorman, told the famous televangelist that he was unavailable because he had a conflict of interest.

This was true, at least in the strict sense that if Swaggart was indeed behind the revelation of the Bakker affair, then the lines between the Bakker and the Gorman case would definitely cross. But I couldn't help but wonder why Frasier did not want to take on the Jim Bakker case. Bakker was a national figure, truly an international figure. His notoriety went far beyond Marvin Gorman's. The case would receive enormous publicity. For many lawyers, particularly those of Frasier's vintage age, such a case—win or lose—could be the crowning success of an entire career.

And, not incidentally, Bakker had money—enormous amounts of money—to spend on his defense. Gorman was very nearly broke.

As the facts unfolded, Frasier's decision to stay with Gorman proved true to form for this stubborn, independent man. He followed his gut instinct, which had always served him well. If he thought Bakker was a dead duck insofar as the more serious accusations of embezzlement and mismanagement of PTL funds was concerned or not, he never said. Instead, he told me, "Believe me, we don't want to be involved in the Jim Bakker scenario. When all the smoke clears, the Gorman/Swaggart case will be the only show in town." He ended the conversation with, "We got us a good one. Let's see it through."

Within a matter of weeks, all the defendants had filed exceptions for No Cause of Action and/or Lack of Subject Matter Jurisdiction, and Improper Cumulation of Actions. To some extent, these were delaying tactics, designed to provide time to prepare a defense. To a greater extent, however, they were much more than mere legal fancy footwork. They could spell real trouble in our suit.

Once again, largely because of the legacy of the Napoleonic Code and its influence on state law, there are subtle differences between Louisiana and other states. An exception, in the State of Louisiana, is similar to a motion elsewhere; both are defensive maneuvers designed to short-circuit a legal action in order to prevent it—or at least delay it—from reaching court.

The defendants' main exception asserted that the court lacked subject matter jurisdiction to hear this case because this was a church matter and did not fall under the jurisdiction of secular courts. Other defendants' counsel took a different tack and filed Exceptions of Improper Cumulation of Actions, arguing that there were numerous causes of action against numerous defendants, that they should not—indeed could not—all be tried in a single court action.

Unflustered by these arguments, we waited until we were served with all exceptions, then we amended our Petition to include Frances Swaggart, whom the press was calling "the steel magnolia," as well as all the insurance companies providing coverage to the named defendants.

This was, as I had earlier suggested to Frasier, a key strategic element of our case. Because Louisiana law provides that a victim of a tort can bring a direct action against the insurer of the tort-feasor, we could use this maneuver to try to defray the cost of Gorman's legal action by suggesting that some of the more minor named defendants might wish to settle for acceptable amounts before we ever went to trial. Further, such settlements would indicate to the main named defendants, namely Swaggart, that his defensive position might be eroding and could cause him to panic and make a move advantageous to our position. Additionally, the amendment to our original petition announced to a jury that there was plenty of insurance money to pay a judgment.

There are few reliable constants about juries, but one might be that almost to the man and woman, they dislike insurance companies almost as much as they dislike lawyers. And nobody likes a wealthy preacher.

In addition to adding defendants in the amended petition, we acted on our earlier feeling that there was more to this than simply a personal vendetta on the part of Jimmy Swaggart against Marvin Gorman because of a single moral indiscretion. The plethora of rumors we had uncovered, and our suspicions that Michael Indest was directly involved, suggested that we needed to broaden our approach.

Based on the July 20 statement and upon our knowledge that Indest, Treeby, and Swaggart had conferred about Gorman before the July 15 meeting, we therefore pled an allegation of conspiracy among the defendants, charging that they conspired to defame Marvin Gorman, invade his privacy, and to destroy the ministry of Marvin Gorman Ministries, thereby ruining Gorman's career and life's work. By alleging conspiracy among the multiple defendants, we answered the Exception for Improper Cumulation of Actions.

In other words, it takes more than one to make a conspiracy, and the more people involved, the larger and more sinister the plot against Gorman would seem to a jury. Further, if conspiracy is pled, then all the defendants have to be tried in one proceeding. This would thwart the Improper Cumulation of Actions exceptions. We hoped. At the time, this portion of our amendment was not much more than a counter-maneuver to neutralize an exception. Little did we suspect that the conspiracy would turn out to be the key to the whole case and a buzzword for the jury.

We propounded interrogatories or formal questions to all the defendants, then attempted to arrange to take their depositions; however, it was suggested by counsel for Jimmy Swaggart, and the judge agreed, that we wait to take depositions after the court had considered the exceptions, most especially the question of Subject Matter Jurisdiction.

The important consideration by the end of March, though, was that we were rolling, ready or not, toward a confrontation with Jimmy Swaggart and the entire structure of the Assemblies of God. "The only show in town" was about to begin.

• CHAPTER EIGHT •
THE HOUSE OF THE LORD

"Every kingdom divided against itself is brought to desolation; and a house *divided* against a house falleth."
—*The Gospel According to St. Luke, 11:17*

Although outward appearances suggest that Assemblies of God churches are crudely formatted and are chiefly made up of small, sometimes impoverished congregations led by ill-educated and poorly trained ministers, the denomination is in reality a well-organized, highly sophisticated ecclesiastical structure run by a well-educated and astute legal entity known as the General (sometimes "National") Council. Each church and each minister is technically autonomous from this governing body, capable of going its own way on a variety of matters; but most are tied directly, often through monetary support, to the central organization. Most, also, obey the General Council's directives and dictates—particularly those concerning doctrine and dogma—without question.

The General Council promulgates and passes its own Constitution and Bylaws, which are published and which are strictly adhered to by almost all Assembly of God congregations throughout the world.

Nationally, the Assemblies of God is made up of districts, each having its separate entity and purview. Most of these are designated by state names, although some are made up of combinations of several states, and some larger or more populous states have more than one district. Within each district, each church forms a separate legal entity governed by its deacons and boards of directors, which is part of the district; each district is, in turn, part of the General Council.

The General Council of Assemblies of God has four executive officers: the General Superintendent, the Assistant General Superintendent, General Secretary, and General Treasurer. There are presently thirteen Executive Presbyters chosen nationwide to serve on an

85

Executive Board of the General Council governing the Assemblies of God. At the time of Marvin Gorman's election to this Board, there were only eight Executive Presbyters, which is an indication of the rapid growth of the denomination during the past two decades. Additionally, there are General Presbyters making up a body of leaders, or delegates, who pass changes in the denomination's bylaws in a democratic manner similar to that used by a legislature or the Congress.

The voting constituency of the General Council is composed of all accredited members who are chosen by the assemblies or churches affiliated within the General Council; each church, regardless of size, is entitled to one delegate.

Under the "Constitution of the Assemblies of God," one article advances a statement representing the "Fundamental Truths" of their believers. Though similar in tone and content to the creeds and cofessions of other Protestant denominations, there are some telling differences, particularly with regard to biblical interpretation:

1. *That the scripture, both Old and New Testament, are verbally inspired of God and the revelation of God to man, the infallible or authoritative rule of faith and conduct;*

2. *The one true God has revealed himself as eternally self existed. "I am" the creator of heaven and earth and redeemer of men. That God has revealed himself as a body in the principles of a relationship and association as the trinity—the father, the son and the holy ghost;*

3. *The Lord Jesus Christ is the eternal Son of God;*

4. *That man was created good and upright for God said, "Let us make man in our image, and after our likeness." However, man, by voluntary transgression, fell and thereby incurred not only physical death but also spiritual death which is separation from God;*

5. *Man's only hope of redemption is through the shed blood of Christ, the Son of God through salvation;*

6. *Ordinances of the church include baptism in water and*

holy communion;

7. *All believers are entitled to and should ardently expect and earnestly seek the promise of the Father, the baptism of the Holy Ghost and fire according to command of our Lord Jesus Christ. This is known as the baptism in the Holy Ghost which distinguishes primarily pentecostal churches from most other Christian protestant religions;*

8. *The evidence of the baptism of the Holy Ghost is witnessed by the initial physical sign of speaking with other tongues as the spirit of God gives them utterance;*

9. *Sanctification is an act of separation from that which is evil and a dedication to God;*

10. *The Assemblies of God is made up of the church which is believed to be the body of Christ, the habitation of God through the spirit, with divine appointments for the fulfillment of the great commission. Each believer is born in the spirit and is an intrical [sic] part of the general assembly and church of the first born;*

11. *The ministry consists of the divinely called and scripturally ordained men and women who have been provided by the Lord for the three-fold purpose of leading the church and evangelization, worship, and building the body, the saints;*

12. *Assemblies believe that there is divine healing as an integral part of gospel deliverance from sickness;*

13. *The resurrection of those who have fallen asleep in Christ and their translation, together with those who are alive,remain, until the coming of the Lord, as the eminent blessed hope of the church;*

14. *There will be a millennial reign of Christ which includes the second coming of Christ by way of the rapture of the saints which is our blessed hope, followed by the visible return of Christ with his saints to reign on earth for one thousand years;*

15. *There will be a final judgment in which the wicked dead will be raised and judged according to their works. Whosoever is not found written in the Book of Life, together with the devil and his angels, the beast and the false prophet will be consigned to everlasting punishment;*

16. *There will be in accordance with God's promise a new heaven and a new earth wherein the righteous will dwell.*

The General Council of the Assemblies of God includes the membership of all "spiritually ordained" ministers holding accredited fellowship certificates and all other persons who are members of churches affiliated with the General Council and its district councils. Precisely what constitutes "ordination" of a minister is not clear through any Assembly of God documentation; however, the certification process is procedural and well-established. Ministers who fall into disfavor with the General Council or one of the district councils are not defrocked, in the sense that they are no longer regarded as being clerics; rather, they are decertified, meaning that they can no longer serve in a ministerial capacity for any Assembly of God church in any district.

The General Council has over the years promulgated rules for each district, as well as for each local church. And as a supplement to the "Constitution of the General Council," each district has its own bylaws and constitution formed principally using the governing documents of the General Council as a model.

Hence, according to the published rules governing the General Council and affiliated churches, no individual minister—neither Jimmy Swaggart nor anyone else—technically is in possession of more power, more influence than any other, even the lowliest pastor of the smallest congregation anywhere in the purview of the General Council.

In reality, however, in religion, just as in most other walks of modern life, money talks.

The articles of the "Constitution of the General Council of the Assemblies of God" also include provisions for discipline of a member, which may result in the dismissal, or decertification, of a minister against whom charges have been brought by other church members. The charges can be brought by almost anyone who is a member of an assembly or church, or they could be brought from outside the church—by a legal entity, such as the police, for example—and they are all liable to be heard by both the General Council and the appropriate district council.

If so deemed and desired by the charged individual, there can be a trial by a jury of peers through a procedure outlined in the Constitution; an appeals procedure is also provided. Prescribed punishments can range from the severe (shunning and ostracization) to the moderate (enforced resignation or outright firing) to the generous (recommendations for counseling or probationary observation). Rehabilitation procedures are provided for any minister who is found guilty and is dismissed but who wishes to seek forgiveness and appeals to church authority for reinstatement.

Overall, then, in spite of claims of individual church autonomy and independence from a centralized control, the organization and structure of the Assemblies of God is a complex and democratic but at the same time closely governed structure. It lends itself to a form of competent self-governance, which should prohibit the possibility that any single individual or even group of individuals could pervert the greater church's purpose to further his or his group's selfish ends.

Be that as it may, the fact remains that nowhere in the bylaws and the "Constitution of the Assemblies of God," and nowhere in "The Fundamental Truths" or tenets of faith is there a provision for punishment of anyone who brings false charges or lies about a member or a minister, who deliberately defames him, invades his privacy, and otherwise does him grievous injury in the name of preserving the integrity of the faith.

Once accused, a minister is automatically put into the position of proving his innocence; his accusers, however falsely inspired, selfishly motivated, or villainously aligned against him, risk no punishment from the church. In that sense, a trial within the Assembly of God structure could—if the matter were serious enough—come to resemble nothing more than the darkest hour of Christian justice: the Salem Witch Trials of the 1690s, or perhaps even the Spanish Inquisition of the sixteenth and seventeenth centuries. At best, it is a drumhead court, and at worst, a kangaroo court of judgment.

The verdict in such historical perversions of humane justice was almost always a foregone conclusion; the only decision to be made was the severity of the punishment. And the goal, always, was to preserve the church, even at the cost of the faith or the faithful.

On July 16, 1986, when Marvin Gorman chose resignation by giving up his credentials to Cecil Janway, Louisiana District Superintendent, he elected not to pursue a rehabilitation program with the church or to seek reinstatement. By doing so, he effectively cut himself off from any possibility of appeal or justice within the Assemblies of God's structure.

It was Gorman's belief—and for good reason—that Jimmy Swaggart and a group of men and women loyal to the Swaggart Ministries would be able to exert such pressure on both the Louisiana District Council and on the General Council itself that there was no possibility of a fair hearing within the ecclesiastical confines of the Assemblies of God. Like Paul facing the Pharisees, Gorman determined that he would have to be heard by an objective judge; hence he took his fight out of the cloistered confines of the General Council and, as he saw it, its Swaggart-influenced membership, and sought the justice and judgment of a secular court.

Gorman, who was an Executive Presbyter for many years and held many offices in the Louisiana District Council as well as in Arkansas, had been a General Presbyter, an Executive Presbyter, and had nearly been elected as General Superintendent. He was as familiar as anyone with the internal workings of the church's governing body, and he was also aware of the unique circumstances surrounding his treatment, both before and after his resignation. And yet in all his years as an Assembly of God minister and high church official, he had never heard of a condemning statement such as the July 20 and September 2 statements being written and read to the congregation of a church repeatedly, and certainly he had never heard of such a statement being mailed to ministers throughout the nation and abroad. It was, therefore, both logical and sensible for Gorman to seek a redress of his grievances in a secular court. Only there could he be certain that objectivity would be applied. Also, only there could he be certain that his judge and his jury would be completely free of direct influence of Jimmy Swaggart.

This was brought home early in the case once it proceeded to trial. The first deposition Gorman's legal team took was from Cecil Janway, a life-long friend of Gorman's and the man who so reluctantly accepted Gorman's resignation the previous summer.

Janway, a kind and elderly man, was a Louisiana District Superintendent and held much personal influence in the state's Assembly of God congregations. It was Gorman's hope that if we deposed Janway first, he would, for the sake of their friendship, tell the truth, reveal the conspiracy against his old friend, and the case could then be settled quickly and with no more fanfare or adverse publicity. Gorman was wrong.

During his deposition, which took place in December 1988, Janway immediately took the position that there was nothing wrong with the July 20 statement. He also claimed that he had authored the September 2 statement. Later, he would testify to the same thing under oath on the witness stand despite the fact that we had already put into evidence the July 20 statement and the September 2 statement and had demonstrated that they were written in the hand of Bill Treeby, attorney to Jimmy Swaggart.

But Janway was so kindhearted that it was hard to attack his credibility even in the face of an obvious lie. So eager was he to demonstrate to Swaggart that he was a team player, and to ensure his continuance on the board of directors of Jimmy Swaggart Ministries, that he betrayed his long-standing friendship with Gorman and, in effect, perjured himself to deflect blame from the other defendants, particularly Swaggart. It was a noble gesture, but a futile one. Clearly, Janway was under the influence of Jimmy Swaggart a great deal more than he was under the influence of any tenet of faith or Fundamental Truth of the Assembly of God.

In the course of our association, Tomy Frasier frequently called the Assemblies of God a cult and stated that the members tended to mistake worship of a man—a minister—for the worship of God. I questioned him about this often, and just as often I chastised him, fearing he would make such a statement to the press or in court. But as time went on and the facts unfolded in this case, I began to wonder what really did constitute a cult, and in what way a church which exerted such a tight control over the personal lives of its members differed from recognized cults.

Although I was no scholar of the Bible, as I studied the "Constitution of the Assemblies of God" and the bylaws, both as an attorney and as a professed Christian, the governing documents of the Assemblies of God seemed to me to be considerably less than scripturally based. This was a particularly curious observation, as the Assemblies of God were nothing if they were not adherents of a strict, fundamentalist interpretation of the

Holy Bible, particularly of the King James Version, which televangelists, especially, were fond of citing as justification for almost all their activities.

But the key issue was the question of ecclesiastical procedures within the Assemblies of God regarding judgment and punishment of wrong-doing. The prescribed penalties that could be meted out seemed entirely too severe for the "crimes" they matched. Of particular interest to me were provisions for shunning and ostracization, a process called disfellowshipping by everyone connected with the church, particularly by other Assembly of God ministers.

Marvin Gorman had friends all over the country who were certified Assembly of God ministers. Once he resigned his credentials, these pastors were prohibited from having any sort of fellowship with him or from assisting him in any way. Anyone who violated this prohibition could have charges brought against him and could, himself, be disfellowshipped.

My Southern Baptist faith taught me that the foundation stone of the House of the Lord was love, and the foundation of love was in forgiveness. No lesson is more severely impressed on a Baptist youth, perhaps, than the straightforward prose of The Gospel According to St. John, 3:16:

> For God so loved the world, that he gave his only
> begotten Son, that whosoever believeth in him should not
> perish, but have everlasting life.

This passage, which every Baptist Sunday School student memorizes almost before he or she can read, is dramatically reinforced by Jesus' forgiveness of those who crucified him.

To me, personally, and to many other Christians, I believe, the love and forgiveness that comes from love was both the sum and total meaning behind the ministry of Jesus of Nazareth, the most important philosophical tenant of The New Testament. In a phrase: To love is to forgive; to forgive is to be divine.

How any Christian denomination could promulgate rules that required ostracizing or shunning one of their number—particularly a minister of the Gospel—simply because he proved himself fallible, human, and tempted by sin, baffled me. But such a severity went to the heart of the theological basis for the Assemblies of God, and it seemed to undermine any notion I might ever have had of their sincere commitment to the teachings of the Gospel.

92

Fortunately for Gorman, many among the ministry of the Assembly of God did not completely adhere to the man-made bylaws of the church and took a higher and, in my view, more Christian if not more charitable approach toward their disgraced colleague. One of these, of course, was Jim Bakker, who paid the price for his fealty to his friend and brother minister.

But apart from Bakker and his revealed taint, other ministerial allies quickly appeared to offer support for Gorman's fight against injustice. One of these was the Reverend Gene Jackson from Tennessee, who was willing to risk punishment by the church to reach out to his friend and fellow minister. Jackson perceived political motives behind Gorman's ruination, particularly as they touched on Jimmy Swaggart. He knew that Swaggart's enormous monetary contributions to foreign missions and other programs sponsored by both the Louisiana District Council and the General Council had done more than merely endear him to the church's leadership; they had made him the goose that laid the golden egg, and no one was eager to slay that source of riches.

In a sense, the General Council and its officers were under Swaggart's control, for they recognized that failing to bow to his wishes could cut them off from one of the single most lucrative financial sources the entire world organization had.

But other ministers also came forward to support Gorman: Glen Cole, an Executive Presbyter with a large and successful ministry, was himself targeted by Swaggart, and Karl Strader, of Lakelyn, Florida, who had previously run afoul of Jim Rentz over a matter of theology, and who was also on Swaggart's hit list. Each of these ministers believed that Swaggart's attacks on his fellow clergymen, although publicly premised on theology and church discipline, were actually based on jealousy. They and other ministers lent moral and spiritual support to Gorman, something that sustained him through the long and arduous process of the legal battle.

When I first looked into the history of the Assemblies of God, my impression was the common one shared by most of the public. I believed it was a large denomination made up of ignorant, unsophisticated and naive rubes and crackers, virtual dupes who allowed themselves to be led by dynamic and charismatic but poorly educated leaders who tended to confuse personal power with spiritual grace. I believed the denomination appealed to and preyed on the hopeless, the helpless, and the spiritually bankrupt, offering them the illusion of salvation in exchange for their

93

dollars and donations.

Such a picture, indeed, was an accurate reflection of the denomination as recently as a few decades ago. And in some instances, it has not changed. However, it wasn't long before I realized that the present-day Assemblies of God, regardless of local church appearances, were led and directed by highly skilled, capable, intelligent, and learned individuals, whose shrewdness and political acumen was matched by their outward show of personal integrity. Among these were Dr. Richard Dobbins, Dr. Richard Dortch, Glen Coles, and many other able and well-educated directors of the denomination's affairs.

On one level, Frasier might have been accurate in his regard of this highly charismatic, fundamentalist group as being more cult than church with more mountebanks than ministers among its leaders. Certainly their strict demands of adherence to a prescribed behavioral code and attention to the control of the personal lives of their members, particularly their subordinate leaders and ministers, was matched by one of the strictest organizational structures of any organized group in the United States.

But at the same time and on another level, their openness, high visibility, and willingness to share their religious doctrine with any who wanted to know it indicated that they were in no way similar to Branch Davidians or the hundreds who followed Jim Jones to tragic death in Georgetown. Nor were they like the Mormons or other societal-based faiths. They weren't "snake handlers" or "holy rollers," weren't occultists or mystics in any unconventional way. The Assemblies of God were, outwardly and inwardly, made up of sincere, devout, and committed Christians, interpreting God's Word by their own lights, and enforcing their rules in what they saw as the best interest of their faith and the intentions of God.

It was soon obvious to me that Frasier's cult argument just could not hold for this denomination. And in a way, that was disappointing. For attacking a cult is easy; attacking a faith is a much more difficult proposition, one that tends to make a sincere Christian often wonder just which side God is on.

• CHAPTER NINE •
CAVIAR AND CRAWFISH PIE

"And the veil of the temple was rent in twain from top to bottom."
—*The Gospel According to St. Mark, 15:38.*

After filing the suit and making initial appearances in the courtroom, Frasier and I began to have second thoughts about our decision to file the suit in New Orleans. At the outset, this had seemed wise for demographic and political reasons, but now, we began to worry about the possibility that Gorman might not receive a fair trial in that city.

At the center of our concern was the realization that we were not only up against one of the most powerful ministers in the state, the South, or even the nation, we were also taking on what amounted to the entire Bar Association of New Orleans. The "silk stocking" legal firm of Stone, Pigman, Walther, Wittmann & Hutchinson, was lead counsel for Jimmy Swaggart, with Phil Wittmann, one of the senior partners, serving as the spokesperson. In most New Orleans courts, Whittmann was regarded as a legal counterpart to E. F. Hutton: when he spoke, everyone listened.

Peter Feringa, with Chaffé, McCall, Phillips, Toler, and Sarpy, another large exclusive and expensive firm, was lead counsel for Michael Indest and his church. Jerry Weigel at the Jones, Walker firm was lead counsel for the General Council of Assemblies of God; Wood Brown and Frank Accordo of the Montgomery, Barnett, Brown, Read, Hammond & Mintz firm were representing the First Assembly of God of New Orleans. Ross Buckley was lead counsel for State Farm Insurance Company and its insured, William Treeby; and Larry Mann of Leake & Anderson represented the Reverend Tom Miller and Canal Street Assembly of God. Lee Butler, with Adams and Reese, represented the Federal Insurance Company, the carrier for the officers and directors of Jimmy Swaggart Ministries. There were many others.

95

This was quite a show of New Orleans' finest legal prowess, and while there were a number of other lawyers representing other defendants, we believed that these high profile firms and their talented attorneys would be those most likely to give us trouble. We were right.

In most lawsuits, opposing counsels attempt to maintain at least a pretense of collegiality. This extends from the courtroom where such pat phrases as "the learned counsel" and "my distinguished colleague," are often bandied about during arguments and debates, to more private confrontations such as the taking of depositions and exchanging of briefs. Although such epithets are often laced with inflected irony, a more or less friendly and mutually respectful attitude among opposing counsel actually is more real than might be apparent. This provides an avenue for settlement; it also insulates attorneys from the emotional extremes that often arise in a trial, particularly in cases involving personal injury. In a sense, a carefully maintained cordiality objectifies the process, leaves lines of communications open, and maintains a high standard of professional, ethical behavior that sometimes seems strange to overwrought and angry parties who are at odds in the matter being adjudicated.

Sometimes, it seems, clients would prefer to dispense with the entire court process and merely let their lawyers slug it out in a ring, bare-knuckled, no holds barred. Sometimes, that method of deciding cases might be preferred by the attorneys as well. It certainly would be easier from the standpoint of stress and worry, to say nothing of risked expenses.

Because our legal team was already handicapped by being labeled outsiders by this collection of well-established New Orleans' firms, we knew we would have difficulty establishing immediate rapport and respect with our opponents. Additionally, I was regarded as a country lawyer from the comparatively small town of Lake Charles, and Frasier and Hickman were both from the often (in Louisiana) denigrated state of Oklahoma and were also regarded as being small-town lawyers (Tulsa *is* smaller than New Orleans, after all.). In short, we were not readily accepted as peers among equals by these prestigious Crescent City attorneys. In fact, the comment was made that Gorman had chosen a "redneck and an Okie" to represent him against the silk stocking legal crowd of New Orleans. It was champagne and caviar versus crawfish pie and chicken-fried steak, and oddsmakers in the city were not giving the "country lawyer and a cripple" much of a chance.

But a third factor, which ultimately, I think, turned out to provide us with an ironic advantage, was that Tomy Frasier's personal manner was clearly not in line with the more conservative and sometimes stuffy propriety observed by the "tea and crumpet" lawyers we faced.

Sometimes reminiscent of Spencer Tracy in the classic trial film *Inherit the Wind*, Frasier was given to mouthing original and sometimes folksy homilies, bromides, analogies and similes that caught everyone, including me, off guard. He gave the impression of being something of a hotheaded lawyer, shooting from the hip and careless of his words. Although the phrase was not yet in vogue, he was most decidedly *not* "politically correct"; sometimes it seemed that he went out of his way to offend people, even people he liked.

It was only afterward that it became apparent how calculated and precise Frasier could be in his statements. He knew how to "play to the back row," as professional stage actors say. He could demonstrate anger, satire, sarcasm, outrage, and indignation with equal conviction; he knew how to hold the attention of the press, the judge, and, of course, a jury.

Frasier's years of experience in trial law, often defending unpopular people involved in unpopular issues, had given him this sense of how to work an audience, whoever they might be, and how to bring them around to his way of thinking by combining rhetorical, emotional, and ethical appeals—the classic Aristotelian elements of persuasive argument—to advantage. In some ways, although he would have been loathe to admit it, he shared traits with the most flamboyant and outlandish televangelists on the air. He could motivate a crowd, move them to tears or laughter, and put them squarely in line with his point of view, and, most importantly, make them believe in him.

Accordingly, in spite of his physical handicap—which he also played to advantage (He disdained the word *handicapped,* preferring *cripple* to emphasize his condition.) while emphasizing his ability to overcome it—and his sometimes rustic manner, he made an excellent match for the highly sophisticated and self-confident attorneys we faced before the New Orleans bar.

However, evidence surfaced early that this case would not be fought on completely polite terms. Several among the defense counsel were openly appalled by Frasier's manner, his candor, and his sometimes pointed use of verbal irony. Before the case was concluded, we would be fighting down and dirty, pulling out all the stops. We never got bare-knuckled, but at times, it felt as if we were close to it.

Examples of this became apparent to me very quickly in our

97

relationship with opposing counsel. In the deposition of the Reverend Cecil Janway, for example, Janway's attorney Jim Murphy made a comment to Gorman which Frasier considered to be insulting. Rather than merely point out his exception to Murphy's statement, Frasier took the offensive. He screamed at Murphy and dressed him down so severely that for the next three years, Murphy only appeared personally a few times during depositions.

Later, during the Swaggart deposition, Denise Pilié, one of Swaggart's counsels, handed me some documents. As I was preoccupied with questioning Swaggart, I passed the documents to Frasier and Gorman to review while I continued to take the deposition. A few moments later, Phil Whittmann asked that the papers be returned for the assignment of a particular number for clarity, a process known as "bates-stamping." We returned them, at which point, Wittmann reviewed them. Alarmed, he whispered something to Pilié, who then announced that they were not going to produce those particular documents because they were not discoverable, although they had already been officially produced as evidence in the deposition process and technically could not be withdrawn.

Later, Gorman said these were smoking gun documents, which would have hanged Swaggart and the other defendants. Whittmann obviously recognized this and caught Pilie's error in turning them over. Unfortunately, I was in charge of questioning Swaggart, I did not see the documents. Frasier, though, had seen them, and he was incensed by this breach of decorum if not the rules of discovery governing such matters. He was also eager to communicate his displeasure to Wittmann and Pilié.

In the final analysis, it turned out not to matter. Gorman's network of friends and loyal supporters within the Assembly of God organization came forth and provided us with virtually every document we were unable to obtain through the discovery process.

But Frasier's rancor over the incident did not abate. Possibly, he regarded it as more than a mere breach of legal etiquette and procedure. He may well have seen it as an attempt to emphasize Whittmann's and Pilié's feelings that they were more sophisticated than we were and were superior to us. He refused to forget about it.

For the next several weeks Frasier refused to speak to Pilié. If she addressed him, even casually, he ignored her. Finally, Pilié asked Frasier in front of twenty or more lawyers if there was a problem between them, and Frasier told her he did not wish "to speak to a liar."

This raised Pilié's ire. She and Frasier engaged in a personal exchange of sarcastic remarks and insults that went on for a full fifteen minutes. Eventually, Frasier told her, "Listen, young lady, dragons have been slain before." This brought forth laughter from all present and stopped the argument—for the time being. But it was only one skirmish in a long battle of personalities that would escalate and expand as the case went forward.

Bitterness among the parties was obvious from the earliest meetings; in some cases, it grew to monstrous proportions. At the bottom of such feelings, of course, were the personal relationships Gorman had had with many of the defendants and their associates. But there were also individuals who felt personally betrayed by one side or the other, and whose interest in the case seemed always to be emotionally based.

Allan McDonnel, who had been the Chairman of the Board of the First Assembly of God and supposedly Gorman's best friend in New Orleans, became the most acrimonious individual in the whole case. McDonnel and his wife seemed to feel that Gorman had somehow harmed them personally; they both helped lead the crusade to ruin their former friend.

McDonnel, a construction contractor, attended almost every deposition in the case, regardless of where it was located. I often wondered how he could keep his business going and earn a living when he was traveling hundreds of miles across the country and spending long and tedious hours listening to depositions. Michael Indest did the same thing. It seemed the two men followed the lawyers around; in between depositions, they would go out to the halls and lobbies and attempt to preach to Gorman, or they made loud, sarcastic remarks about him, witnesses favorable to him, or about the legal team. As the process progressed, we found it worthwhile to keep a close eye on their activities.

Indest's motive for wanting to ruin Gorman, even at this point, was not entirely clear. But McDonnel had a more specific interest in Gorman's downfall. He was the general contractor on the ten million dollar ongoing construction project at the First Assembly of God, a project Gorman initiated and was overseeing at the time of his forced resignation. Gorman had actually handpicked McDonnel to build the new church and surrounding complex. Because of his televangelism and large reputation in New Orleans and southeastern Louisiana, Gorman had been able to raise sufficient funds—either in cash or through pledges—to support the project and begin work. But when Gorman left the First Assembly of

God, funding for the project sharply declined.

As Frasier put it, the "milk" began to dry up. Frasier frequently questioned the intelligence of the people who cut off the "big tit that fed the milk tusk" and saw such a lack of common sense as further evidence that the Assemblies of God were, in actuality, a cult.

Even so, it was apparent that Gorman's personality had a great deal to do with the influx of funds. Since his resignation, the First Assembly of God had fallen into some financial difficulties. It was clear even to outside observers that only a matter of time remained before the church could no longer meet its financial obligations on the building project, and McDonnel was on the hook for a great deal of money.

Eventually the project failed, and McDonnel was subsequently sued by many individuals. He continued to drive his Porsche, however, and showed no outward signs of serious financial difficulty.

In spite of the problems presented by friction between our legal team and the high profile firms representing the defendants, though, I decided that our course during the process of discovery was right. My mail increased dramatically, much of it supporting Gorman and our actions on his behalf.

I also received a great deal of hate mail from anonymous enemies of Marvin Gorman. This was something I never anticipated. Some was humorous, but some was disgusting, even frightening in a way. These always came to my post office box and were addressed either by typewriter or with cut-out letters assembled from magazines or newspapers and pasted on an envelope with no return address. More often than not, they carried a religious theme—sort of.

One greeting card I received pictured "the church lady" on the front saying, "Jesus loves you," with the inside of the card reading, "but the rest of us think you're a son of a bitch." The front of another card pictured an old woman regurgitating at the dinner table with the inside joke, "Your name came up during supper."

It was natural to speculate on who might have been sending such anonymous "fan mail." I often wondered if any of it came from McDonnel or Indest or even possibly from Denise Pilié, so capably had she demonstrated her capacity for vitriolic remark in her exchanges with Frasier. Kristie Plumb, my paralegal, speculated that all of it might have come from Frasier, sort of a motivational tactic from a "left-handed cheerleader."

To some extent, I was somewhat flattered that someone—anyone—

would take the time to go out, purchase these cards, and send them to me; but I also knew that these individuals were attempting to unnerve me and to thwart my pursuit of a successful verdict in this case.

My wife, Beth, and I also received frequent late night and early morning heavy phone calls from a breather. We considered changing to an unlisted telephone number, but ultimately I decided against it. To do so would be a sign that I could be intimidated, and I had no intention of giving in to anonymous threats and innuendos, however much I needed my sleep.

In the spring and summer of 1987, though, our direct problems with the defendants' attorneys lay further in the future than we imagined. So did the process of discovery and the taking of depositions. Before we could go forward with a trial, we had to make our way through a process of preliminary hearings, which would hear the exceptions of the counsel for the defense.

The defendants' attorneys pulled out all the stops in an effort to quash the suit before it could get to trial. And they very nearly succeeded. The exception for Lack of Subject Matter Jurisdiction was formally filed in April 1987, and hearings on the issue commenced.

The defendants argued that the conduct of the First Assembly of God, the Louisiana District and the General Council, as well as the statements made by Jimmy Swaggart and others, were in furtherance of the bylaws and "Constitution of the Assemblies of God" and were in accordance with the Assembly of God tenets of faith. The court, then, should be prohibited from reviewing those doctrines under the First Amendment of the Constitution.

In short, they argued that the causes of this action fell under the (supposed) constitutional provision for a separation of church and state; hence, no civil court had a right to interfere or adjudicate a purely doctrinal, purely church matter.

We had anticipated this move and recognized that on the face of it the entire argument was absurd. Our counter argument was, first, that the law did not allow any religion or denomination to commit tortious acts on its parishioners or ministers, and that there was nothing in the governing documents of the Assembly of God which condoned or permitted such conduct as represented by the public statements published and made about Gorman.

Secondly, we argued, even if such provisions were in the church's doctrine, the statements and other actions against Gorman were still tortious, hence were a violation of civil law, for which a remedy could be found through the judgment of a civil court.

We did not wish, at this point at least, to broach the issue of the wording of the First Amendment concerning the freedom of religion. (It was highly doubtful that any district court would entertain a constitutional argument of that magnitude at this juncture.) For the moment, we preferred to argue the more specific issue as to whether the court had jurisdiction in a lawsuit of one citizen against another—or a group of others—who for reasons of their own (religious or otherwise) had defamed his character and attempted to destroy his life's work.

While we prepared these arguments, Frasier tried to learn what he could about His Honor, Richard Ganucheau, the judge assigned to the case. The Ganucheau name was an old one in New Orleans, and the judge's cousin was the clerk for the United States Court of Appeals for the Fifth Circuit. Furthermore, the judge's former wife was an attorney in New Orleans; unfortunately, his present wife, Donna, an attractive blonde some fifteen years junior to her husband, was also his minute clerk. She let the attorneys know up front who was running the show. It was obvious from the beginning of the motion hearings that Judge Ganucheau was going to be involved in "all aspects of the case."

Ganucheau, who appeared to be in his late forties, stood approximately five feet, ten inches tall, of medium build with dark hair. He had a reputation for being a plaintiff's judge, which should have been to our benefit. I was extremely concerned nevertheless. State court judges are frequently elected on money raised by lawyers, and in all probability, all the law firms we opposed in this trial had contributed at one time or another to Ganucheau's campaigns. This made us more the outsiders than ever.

My concerns were magnified when Ganucheau accepted defense counsel's argument that the plaintiffs should come forth and post a cost bond on behalf of all the defendants. This motion was filed and heard during a deposition being taken at Stone, Pigman. In a telephone conversation, Judge Ganucheau agreed, as a courtesy to counsel, to come over to the Stone, Pigman office and hear the motion, rather than require all counsel to appear at the courthouse. This was the most unusual proceeding I had ever witnessed; I had never seen a judge go to a lawyer's office to conduct a hearing.

Not surprisingly, he sustained the motion and required that we post a $125,000 cost bond to secure the defendants that in the event the plaintiffs did not prevail in the case, we would be able to pay the defendants' costs.

Although I was confident that Frasier's heart was in this case and he would put up the necessary money to secure the $125,000 cost bond, I also knew that the ruling was contrary to the law and certainly an obstacle to our moving forward. Accordingly, we presented writs to the Fourth Circuit Court of Appeals and had Ganucheau's ruling overturned. The matter was remanded with an order by the Fourth Circuit requiring us to post a cost bond of $20,000. Frasier and I then each put up cash and a bank issued a letter of credit to the Clerk of Court in our favor for the cost bond.

After this ruling, however, I became quite concerned that this case might never go to trial.

From Scott Bailey's investigation of Jimmy Swaggart Ministries' attempts to secure funds through probate action in Texas, we already knew that one of the strategic ploys we could expect was a move by Swaggart's lawyers to seal the records of the case whether it went to trial or not. Predictably then, in May, before the court ever heard the defense's Exception for Lack of Subject Matter Jurisdiction, the defendants filed a Motion for Protective Order. What did surprise me was that they also asked the judge to prohibit the public from attending any of the hearings.

I had never been involved in a case where one party had moved to close the entire proceedings to the public. The most surprising thing about it was that Swaggart was a public figure, the Assemblies of God was a public church. To prevent the public from witnessing the trial, even through the eyes of the press, seemed to be a virtual admission of wrong-doing. It also was a clear indication that Swaggart feared publicity over proceedings he could not control. Swaggart always liked to play his cards close to his vest; and he preferred his games to be private. This motion served to redouble our determination to expose Swaggart's darker deeds to the light of day.

In forming the exception, Phil Wittmann, speaking on behalf of all the defendants, also asserted that there were many "innocent" women involved who had been taken advantage of by Marvin Gorman. In order for the defendants to properly defend this litigation, he argued, these "innocent" women would have to be protected. According to Wittmann, witnesses who might provide specific testimony that they had been sexually involved with Gorman would be reluctant to come forward unless they were assured that their privacy was protected, their identities kept secret.

Frasier immediately responded that the claim of a need for protection was ridiculous, to say nothing of unnecessary. The only women involved were Lynda Savage, with whom Gorman admitted having an act of intercourse, and Lynette Goux, another woman whom Gorman admitted having kissed and hugged in a sexual way.

At this point, the defendants received help from a most unlikely source: the attorney for the firm that represented the *Times Picayune*. From the first, but especially since the Bakker revelations and ongoing sensation surrounding PTL, we assumed with the press would want to keep everything in the open, and that they would be aligned with us in opposing the motion to close the proceedings to the public.

However, Jack Weiss, who at that time was a partner in the Phelps, Dunbar law firm, was able to get Judge Ganucheau's attention and compromised our position. Weiss was regarded as a "First Amendment Guru" because he had represented the media, particularly the Louisiana Press Association; so it came as more than a mild shock to find him supporting a motion of secrecy involving high profile, extremely newsworthy individuals involved in a case that had curious parallels and connections to the Bakker case, which was at this point still making national headlines.

Judge Ganucheau took us into his chambers to discuss the matter privately, or as Frasier put it "to cop a plea." It became clear that His Honor was disposed to grant the Protective Order and ensure the secrecy of the proceedings.

Frasier became more than a little excited and told the judge that a protective order such as this would give the world the impression that Marvin Gorman had lifted more skirts than "Indians had tepees." Judge Ganucheau admired Frasier's analogy, but when we went back to court and on the record, he stated that if the parties could not work out a mutually satisfactory protective order, he would enter his own, which would please no one.

In our view, Jack Weiss dealt the public a disservice in arguing in favor of a restrictive protective order. His premise was that he was protecting "innocent" witnesses from embarrassment and scandal; but in fact, he was protecting Jimmy Swaggart from exposure, regardless of how the trial might turn out.

(Actually, as the case progressed, we learned that Jack Weiss had left the Phelps, Dunbar firm to become a partner in Stone, Pigman. As Stone,

Pigman had the reputation for charging clients about one hundred dollars an hour more than other firms, this was obviously a lucrative step for him. As a part of his move, though, the *Times Picayune* became a client of Stone, Pigman.

Although I had nothing concrete to base my opinion on, I believed that Swaggart and Treeby had cut a deal to bring Jack Weiss and the *Times Picayune* to their side so they could help control the press during the lawsuit.

This may not have been the case, but Weiss's position on the secrecy motion and his subsequent move to a Stone, Pigman partnership was completely out of character for a man with "fourth estate" ties. And, given the traditional role of the press in such matters, it is the only reasonable explanation that presents itself.)

Finally, the court decided that information gathered during the course of discovery could not be made public; it could only be used for trial. However, the court also held that any hearings and the ultimate trial itself would be public, meaning that it would be up to us to expose to the public the depths of the conspiracy against Gorman through direct testimony, cross-examination, and the introduction of documented evidence. This was a less than perfect situation but it was acceptable, since we planned to do that anyway.

At this juncture, one point was obvious: There could not be a quiet settlement of this case. For the truth to be known in this case, it was going to take a full trial, full public disclosure. Otherwise, the information gathered during discovery would never be made public. Additionally, it would be most difficult to publicize any other information we gathered during our investigation without the advantage of the rules of evidence to help us get it out. Finally, without the public revelation of testimony, through examination and cross-examination of witnesses, the lies told about Gorman would always carry the potential impact of truth.

With our help, Gorman had to bring his accusers before the public bar as much as before the state bar; there was no other way he could achieve justice. Money was not the issue—I don't think it ever was for Gorman; nor was revenge important to him; the issue that mattered, the only issue that motivated him to put aside his distaste for litigation, was the truth.

In some lawsuits, the press does play an active role; though actually, in most lawsuits, the press plays almost no role at all beyond the pedestrian reportage of court proceedings, often relegated to newspapers' back pages, next to the TV logs and obituaries. Thus, lawyers tend to ignore whatever is printed about a case, about their clients, unless, of course, it is defamatory or libelous.

But in this case, a very popular pastor and television personality in the New Orleans community was defending his public reputation and status in that same community. He was also taking on a well-known national public figure, who was virtually worshiped by millions of people, who had the ear of America. Favorable press was vital to combat the lies that had already been told about Gorman, and a continuing good relationship with the "fourth estate" would be necessary to combat the potential damage that might be inflicted by the powerful defendants' statements, both in and out of court.

Whether Marvin Gorman would emerge in the public eye as "more sinned against than sinning" would rest, ultimately, less in the verdict of a jury than in the opinion of the press. That, more than anything, made this case a frightening and to some extent depressing proposition.

• CHAPTER TEN •
THE TRUTH

"Thou shalt not bear false witness against thy neighbor."
—*The Second Book of Moses, Called Exodus, 20:16*

Among the laws, statutes, rules, and codes governing the process of jurisprudence there is a singular item known as "attorney-client privilege." Basically, this precept is designed to prevent any client of any attorney from incriminating himself or herself by revealing to a retained counsel his or her involvement in a crime.

In a broader sense, though, the attorney-client privilege allows a lawyer to protect anything revealed in confidence by a client. Not only is the attorney protected from coercion by anyone—including and especially the court and its officers—seeking to know what a client might have revealed, confessed, or admitted, but he also is prohibited from revealing anything a client tells him without the client's permission.

This system enables a trial lawyer to prepare a competent defense based on all the relevant facts, even when such facts may never be revealed in court. But it has obvious pitfalls. In criminal law, for example, every attorney risks learning of some heinous crime committed by his client, then being unable to report it; or, he may find himself in the difficult position of pleading a client not guilty when he knows by the client's own admission that he is, in fact, the perpetrator. In civil law, an attorney can face more subtle moral dilemmas, such as entering court to sue for damages based on facts which, through client revelation, the attorney knows to be untrue.

It is this subtlety that can give a lawyer ulcers. Balancing a decision of whether or not to continue to represent a client and argue before a judge and a jury for the "plaintiff's truth" or the "defendant's truth" rather than the "true truth" may be one of the most difficult decisions a trial lawyer ever has to make.

107

Of course, no lawyer is bound to a client forever or even for any longer than the attorney feels comfortable with the client's truthfulness. He can always resign a case if he feels he cannot in good conscience provide both an adequate and vigorous defense, or if he merely feels his client is lying. In extreme cases where the "true truth" is clearly at odds with the "plaintiff's truth" or the "defendant's truth," such decisions are easy. But in between such clear-cut extremes lies a veritable minefield of possibilities, varying degrees of equivocation, rationalization, justification, and, in matters of civil suits for damages, varying amounts of monetary reward.

All of these can have a bearing on an attorney's discovery of or even willingness to admit the "true truth," even to himself.

Thus, "attorney-client privilege" is a two-edged sword, one which can slice through the truth by arming a counsel with all the facts needed for a case, or one which can bounce back and do irreparable harm to an attorney's career. It's never a sure thing.

In the case of *Marvin Gorman vs Jimmy Swaggart et al.* I had some advantage from the outset. Because of my professional association with Gorman from the previous transaction involving Gorman's attempt to purchase Channel 29 in the summer and fall of 1986, I already knew him and believed I had a close sense of his nature and character. Further, I knew members of Marvin Gorman Ministries, most especially those members of his immediate family who worked closely with him.

At the same time, I had misgivings about specific events that took place during that previous association. One in particular was a trip I made to the federal penitentiary in Springfield, Missouri with Marvin to see William Church aka Aaron Stanvanzellus. Church, who purported to have control of millions of dollars in a nonprofit organization, had convinced Gorman that the Lord had changed the error of his ways, causing Church to want to donate a portion of the foundation to Marvin Gorman Ministries. Church turned out to be a fraud who sought the favor of ministers in an attempt to obtain an early release from prison.

I excused this sample of marginal criminality on the part of Gorman's supporters on the grounds that at that juncture, Gorman was desperate to keep the television station deal alive. And, besides, he had committed no crime, no indiscretion really, himself. I could not hold him personally responsible for the actions of those who pretended to support him and may have, in actuality, been more misguided than malfeasant.

Thus, when we began working to bring a damages suit for

defamation of Gorman's character, I felt I had a fairly good sense of whether or not any of the charges alleged by Swaggart and others were true. In conversations with Randy Gorman and others close to Marvin the previous year, I had been steadily assured that in spite of Gorman's resignation, there was no serious breach of propriety on Gorman's part; and I was also assured that the rumors being spread by word-of-mouth and published documents about Gorman's sexual activities were also false.

At the point when we filed our petition on Gorman's behalf, then, I was about eighty percent sure that what he told us about his relationship to women in his church was true. Even so, the twenty percent of uncertainty remained, and Gorman had never spoken to me or to anyone I knew under oath.

A good lawyer, I always believed, should maintain a degree of skepticism about anything he is told, by a client or anyone else. So I had doubts, in short—small ones, but doubts nonetheless.

Frasier and Hickman had large ones, and they spoke of them frequently. In order for us to prepare a case that would reveal the "true truth," not merely the "plaintiff's truth," it was vital that Gorman tell us, formally and under oath, what his version of the truth was; it was also important that we believe him.

We agreed that it would fall to me to prepare Gorman for trial. As a standard part of readying any client who might be required to testify—and we planned all along for Gorman to testify—it was standard procedure to rehearse both the deposition and cross-examination so a client would know what to expect when the real thing took place.

Therefore, in the early summer of 1987, I spent a Saturday videotaping a rehearsal session with Gorman. The format was that of a "mock depositio" complete with cross-examination. I assumed the role of an attorney for the defense in an effort to prepare Gorman for the event during which he would be closely questioned on every point by defense counsel.

During this ten-hour session, I considered every possible position and point of attack that would be later taken by Peter Feringa with the law firm of Chaffé, McCall, counsel for Indest. The attorneys I deemed to be the sharpest—and the meanest—in the defense counsel pack. I knew they would pull no punches with Gorman, that they would go for the throat and try to quash the lawsuit through their examination of a man toward whom they felt superior in every way: sophistication, education, and world view.

To my amazement, Gorman fell into the part completely. Often witnesses undergoing this rehearsal process are unable to act in a way that is genuine. They merely go through the motions, knowing as they do that their lawyers are merely playing devil's advocate, and that the real thing is yet to come. It is difficult for a practice session such as this to approximate the real thing without the complete willing suspension of disbelief required of the potential witness. Gorman was a natural. He ignored the camera's intrusive eye and assumed the role of a deposing witness facing a hostile and probing examiner.

Given my twenty percent of doubt, I suppose that's precisely what I was.

During this ten-hour session, Gorman displayed every conceivable reaction—anger, sadness, joy, humiliation, embarrassment, and anguish—in the human emotional spectrum. He wept, sobbed, laughed, and scoffed at my questions. It was truly an amazing display of one man's potential for feeling and depth of genuine self-examination and for exhibiting authentic range of emotional response.

Beginning at eight o'clock in the morning, I started by belittling and berating him both as a person and as a minister, then shifted to asking him some of the most intimate and potentially demeaning questions that could ever be asked of a witness. I began with his birth and humble upbringing, then brought him up to the present date, covered his admittedly modest education, his work history, his personal life. I then asked him to tell me about every woman with whom he had ever had sex.

Gorman balked at this point. It was not a subject he wanted to discuss at all, but I advised him that if he wished to go forward with his lawsuit, he had to prepare himself to answer such questions and more intimate personal queries as well. I explained that his sexual history, licit or otherwise, was at the center of his case. The jury would want to know, and any evasiveness on his part would be construed as an attempt to hide the truth.

Gorman then admitted that before he became a Christian, he had had sexual relationships with two women whose names he would never reveal. Given the remarkably young age at which he converted and received "the call" to the ministry, I found this both surprising and remarkably credible.

After becoming a Christian, he went on, the only woman with whom he had ever engaged in sexual relations was his wife.

Except for Lynda Savage, of course.

I pointed out that he had already confessed to having had sex with Savage, and Gorman admitted that he had the one incident of intercourse with Lynda Savage in late December 1978. The story he told me that Saturday was the same one he stuck to throughout his actual depositions and at the trial; by virtue of its consistency in detail and because of the forcefulness with which he told it, I was convinced it was a true and accurate version of events.

Gorman stated that in 1978, he began counseling Lynda Savage at the request of her husband, David, the pastor of the Kenner Assembly of God Church. Gorman had been friends with Savage for some time, had helped him begin his ministry, and had been concerned for the couple's marriage. He did not reveal the exact nature of their marital problems, only that they were unhappy, and that David was concerned that their future as a married couple was in jeopardy.

During the counseling sessions, Lynda Savage confessed her extramarital relations to Gorman. She was also extremely depressed, according to Gorman, and indicated that she might not be able to go on with life.

On December 28, 1978, Savage called Gorman at his office and said she was alone in a motel room and was thinking about committing suicide. Gorman asked her for the name and address of the motel and immediately rushed to her. When he arrived, he found the door unlocked and slightly open. He stepped into the room and saw Lynda sitting on the edge of the bed with a robe over her shoulders. Across the room on a desk was a bottle of spilled pills.

Gorman rushed to her and sat down. She pulled back the robe, revealing that she was naked underneath. She turned to him and hugged him, and they began to hug and kiss, when one thing led to another and soon they were reclining on the bed.

According to Gorman, he never disrobed but merely unzipped his pants and began to have sexual intercourse with her. During the act, he was suddenly overcome with guilt, lost his erection, stood up, zipped his pants, and begged Savage's forgiveness. He told her that what they were doing was wrong and stated that he was leaving. So he did.

Gorman indicated that he never experienced a climax during his physical contact with Lynda Savage or while he was in the motel room. He left the room shaken and shocked by his own behavior. He bore this sin and guilt for a long time. According to Gorman, he immediately asked

111

God for forgiveness and the sin, in his opinion, was "under the blood of Jesus" and did not have to be confessed to anyone else.

Following the incident, Gorman said he received numerous other phone calls from Lynda Savage demanding that he meet her and have sex with her. She also asked him to meet her on the pretext of counseling her against killing herself. He stated that twice he met her—again at motels—for this purpose, and in each instance, she greeted him while dressed in sparse clothing, attempting to entice him into a sexual encounter. Each time, Gorman rebuked her and asked her to forget what happened, to repent, and go on with her life with her husband. It was only after the third time he met her that he told her he would never come to her call again, and as far as her threats of suicide or threats of revealing the incident to anyone, she could do so according to her own conscience.

This was Gorman's story, and he was sticking to it. After learning more about Lynda Savage and her other activities, I came fully to believe it.

During this session, Gorman also revealed that in the course of his life he had had two audible conversations with God. I questioned him closely on this point because of my own cynicism and because I was intently aware of the skeptical eyes that would be watching Gorman throughout this lawsuit. Nothing I asked could shake him from his determination that his experiences were real. He stated that he received his calling from God one day while driving a tractor on a small farm in South Arkansas. He heard a voice from the woods and understood it was God talking to him, calling him to preach the Gospel.

As a Christian and a Southern Baptist, I believe in the power of prayer; I believe in the Age of Miracles and the Holy Bible; however, like most Christians, I had never heard God speak audibly, and I have serious doubts that anyone ever does. But that morning in his office, Marvin Gorman convinced me that he had indeed heard God speak.

Of course, the important *legal* point here was not whether God actually spoke audibly to Marvin Gorman. The important point was whether Gorman *believed* beyond the shadow of a doubt that God had spoken to him. I was convinced that he had.

Another reason this discussion concerning Gorman's perceived relationship with God was significant was that I was looking for elements that distinguished Gorman from Jimmy Swaggart. Swaggart had from his pulpit claimed many, many times that he had frequent and numerous conversations with God. Swaggart once stated that God physically locked him in his car and spoke to him, telling him that he, Jimmy Swaggart, was the only evangelist called to spread the Gospel to the world. There was no doubt in my mind that Swaggart believed that.

And, of course, up in Tulsa, Oral Roberts was proclaiming that he and God were having regular chitchats, during which the Deity revealed, more or less, that He was holding the great televangelist for ransom if he couldn't raise the funds necessary to keep the City of Faith open for business.

Swaggart's and Roberts's veracity was not the issue, though. What was the issue was Marvin Gorman's conviction, his credibility in comparison to these other oracles.

I left this point then and returned to the matter of Lynda Savage and her liaison with Gorman. Specific questions were necessary. I asked: Did he undress her, pull down her panties? Did he have oral sex with her? In what manner had he ever fondled her? I continued through a virtually pornographic litany of suggested sexual acts, trying to phrase each one in a way that suggested that she had sworn he had done all these things and more.

For Gorman, this was the most unpleasant part of the interview. He responded to each question with a negative answer and often became quite angry, which indicated that we would have to do a lot of work before he would be ready for his deposition. It is vital for a witness facing a hostile examination to maintain his composure, his cool, especially when the questions touch on sensitive areas.

I then turned to the list of other women who had made statements or had been named in rumors spread by Swaggart, Indest, and others: Jane Talbot, Cheryl McConnell, Lynette Goux, and others Gorman had allegedly taken advantage of or with whom he had allegedly had sexual relationships.

Again, I was specific and graphic, and again this sequence of questions was painful for Gorman, but again he sustained his denial in a convincing fashion. My twenty percent of doubt measurably reduced. I was at last as convinced as any lawyer can be that my client was telling the "true truth," or at least, that the legal team could stand solidly behind a presentation of the "plaintiff's truth."

In the course of that interview, we also covered the allegations of malfeasance and mismanagement of funds of the First Assembly of God. Again, Gorman's responses were clear and concisely negative, convincing me that any charges of financial impropriety were nothing

113

more than decoys designed to lure in the press and permit Gorman's enemies a conduit through which they could introduce more damaging and unfounded statements about his personal deportment. There was ample precedent for this, for already the Bakker-Hahn affair had taken a back page to more serious—and criminal—allegations of income tax evasion and fraud on the part of the diminutive CEO of PTL.

The most amazing revelation during this interview, though, was Gorman's acumen and knowledge of a vast array of subjects. He was far more sophisticated and worldly than he might first appear; and, to contradict any lingering doubts I may have had, he proved he had a strong sense of when he was being deceived or flimflammed. He was not only well versed in theology and biblical studies, he also had a profound sense of business. He was a capable accountant, a canny marketer and product packager, and a shrewd salesman all rolled into one. For a man with limited education, he demonstrated a high level of understanding of the world of business and finance as well as the nature of human psychology; at the same time, he was street smart and had a great store of common sense.

He also had a temper, and he wasn't shy about revealing it. But in spite of that one potential problem, I knew we had a client who was smart enough to present his whole case to a jury. And, more important, I knew we had one who utterly believed that the plaintiff's version of the truth was the "true truth."

Very soon after our rehearsal for deposition, however, the possibility arose that a deposition or cross-examination of Marvin Gorman would never take place. Indeed, the possibility arose that the trial would never occur.

We had been encouraged by the proceedings thus far. Our investigation was moving along briskly, and we had won major victories on the issue of protection. In late May 1987, the court denied the defense's exceptions for Improper Cumulation and failure to state a cause of action. It was our belief that we would move easily past the final obstacle, the Exception for Lack of Subject Matter Jurisdiction, and would be going to trial soon.

On June 8, 1987, though, Judge Ganucheau sustained the defendants' exceptions for No Cause of Action and Lack of Subject Matter Jurisdiction. His Honor accepted defense counsels' argument that the statements made about Gorman and Gorman's conduct were nothing more than a form of ecclesiastical process—church discipline, in other words. The judge held that Gorman, as a former minister of the church, could not use a court of law to contest this discipline or circumvent his punishment. By analogy, Ganucheau explained, a serviceman could not resign the army to avoid a court martial. The judge then dismissed the case with prejudice, meaning that the case could not be brought again and was final, unless we could overturn it on appeal.

To say the least, Frasier, Hickman, and I were stunned. We could not believe Ganucheau made this ruling, especially since we were not allowed to conduct any discovery before having to argue these motions. Thus, Ganucheau accepted at face value defense attorney's arguments and made his ruling accordingly.

The entire decision smelled of an inside move, one that was doubtless predicated on Ganucheau's connections in the New Orleans' legal community. Ganucheau was making us aware that even though we were winning the battles, he was the one who controlled the war. As we received the ruling, the smugness of defense counsel was obvious. Another New Orleans lawyer observing the situation summed it up another way: In New Orleans, he noted, "Justice was for 'just us.' "

I was profoundly disappointed by the ruling, but I knew that Frasier would not retreat quietly, and I was right. Discussions about how to formulate an appeal began immediately, and I understood that the work involved in that process would largely be mine.

Appeals take time, and in a way, I was pleased by that fact. I was half of a two-man law practice, which was hardly off the ground, and the majority of my time and energy was going to a case that was not paying me. The time involved to research and write the appeal would afford me an opportunity to try to make a living for a while.

I also knew that I would need help in formulating such a complicated appeal. Accordingly, I recruited my younger brother, Matt, who was in law school at LSU, to assist me in preparing the brief. Matt attacked the chore with enthusiasm, working hard on a draft that would assure us of an overturning of Ganucheau's ruling and put the lawsuit back on track. The research required was daunting. He would have to read virtually every pertinent case concerning religion and the state ever tried in the United States.

Working closely with Hickman and myself, Matt finally put together an excellent brief, which we filed in the Fourth Circuit Court of Appeals on October 21, 1987. Oral arguments were set for March 1988.

Matt's work proved fruitful for him in other ways besides the practical experience involved. Some of the language regarding the defamation of a corporation which he developed in composing the appeal would later become law in Louisiana.

In the meantime, Frasier's wisdom about refusing to become involved in the Bakker scandal was verified. With his legal troubles and his expenses mounting, Bakker enlisted the help of Jerry Fallwell, from Lynchburg, Virginia, to be caretaker of the huge PTL enterprise. Fallwell, however, proved to be less than encouraging in his actions. He banished Bakker from the PTL, and very soon, Bakker was on his way to prison and eventual divorce from Tammye Faye. The PTL was on its way to bankruptcy, and Jimmy Swaggart had won a major victory in the world of televangelism. All that stood between him and complete domination of fundamentalist religion, it seemed, was Marvin Gorman and his team of outside legal advisors. And we were trying to recover lost ground.

Once the appeal was filed, there was really nothing more we could do for the time being. We advised our client of our action and asked that he be patient. We were fairly confident that we would have our day in court.

Thus, from August 1987 until midnight, February 18, 1988, I did not hear a word from Marvin Gorman, and I turned my attention to my own much neglected practice and career.

• PART THREE •
THE WHORES OF BABYLON

"Jesus wept."
—The Gospel According to St. John, 11:35

• CHAPTER ELEVEN •
"THE DEVIL MADE ME DO IT"

"And behold, there met him a woman with the attire of a
harlot, and subtle of heart."
—The Proverbs, 7:10

In the fall of 1987, while we all awaited word on our appeal brief,
events once more took a direction of their own, and our case became
more complicated than we ever imagined it would. It also moved in the
public's eye from merely a state and regional affair to a sensational
national media event. That seemed appropriate, in a way, as the ministers
involved were creatures of the media, particularly of television; but for a
small town lawyer from Lake Charles, it was something of a shock. It
likely was a shock for Jimmy Swaggart as well.

When the events began to unfold, though, I was blissfully unaware
of them; I sometimes wonder how I would have reacted had I known what
was going on "down the Mississippi in New Orleans."

Randy Gorman held a commission with the Jefferson Parish
Sheriff's Department as a deputy. The appointment was largely a political
favor from Harry Lee, Jefferson Parish Sheriff, to Marvin Gorman. Lee,
a physically imposing man of Chinese descent, had been a United States
magistrate. He then became one of the most powerful sheriffs in the State
of Louisiana. Louisiana sheriffs have enormous leeway in choosing their
deputies, many of whom are unpaid volunteers but who have full law
enforcement powers within the sheriff's office's jurisdiction. Lee
sometimes attended Gorman's church; he thought well of the minister and
gave Randy a badge as a favor.

In the early fall of 1986, when his father's troubles with Jimmy
Swaggart were first unfolding, Randy overheard several rumors around
the sheriff's department that someone resembling Jimmy Swaggart had
been seen frequenting the Travel Inn motel on Airline Highway in New

119

Orleans. The only reason anyone would be cruising Airline Highway, Randy knew, was to look for either drugs or sex. He was intrigued and decided to investigate.

The Travel Inn motel was one of the many notorious hostelries in The Big Easy. It fell into line with numerous seedy motels lining Airline Highway, all of which in recent years had enjoyed a decline in reputation. Over time, it had become a regular rendezvous for what in the parlance of the city were called "nooners": people wishing to meet in secrecy for a brief, private, and usually illicit sexual assignation. Additionally, several prostitutes were regularly using rooms there to run their illegal trade with sometimes high-profile clientele who would rather not be seen soliciting their favors in public.

The Travel Inn was, again colloquially, widely known to be a "no-tell motel," not a respectable place of business. In the event that anyone doubted this, a sign in the office's window proclaimed in large letters that "No Refunds" would be given after fifteen minutes. A large billboard nearby proclaimed, "Your Eternity is at Stake!"

Randy made inquiries and soon learned that one of the regulars at the motel, Debra Arleen Murphree, a known prostitute with arrests and convictions for solicitation and "crimes against nature," had a customer named "Billy" who was rumored not merely to resemble but actually to be the Reverend Jimmy Swaggart. This was the cause of a great deal of ironic laughter and ribald jokes both around the sheriff's department and among Murphree's sister working girls as well. Posing as a john, Randy located Murphree to find out if the rumors were true.

After visits by Randy, Murphree told Randy that her regular customer named Billy drove a white or tan Lincoln and made several visits each month to New Orleans to see her. She also said that she was sure he was Jimmy Swaggart. In a way she seemed proud of it. Randy asked her to write down Billy's license tag number, and gave her his beeper number. He told her to call the number and to enter all sevens to alert him that it was she, and he offered to pay her for providing the information.

Randy claimed that she did indeed call him and that he traced the license number back to Jimmy Swaggart Ministries and that he arranged for her to call him the next time Billy dropped by for a visit.

According to Murphree, however, she never called Randy. She claimed she threw his numbers away. Although she would say at one point that she was completely unaware that she was under surveillance, she later stated that Randy increased the frequency of his visits to her room at the Travel Inn and called her or stopped by every afternoon to see if she had heard from Billy.

She often spotted Randy sitting in his car across from the motel and decided he was staking her out, a feeling that was reinforced when he followed her across town to a motel on the Chef Menteur Highway, where she resided with her boyfriend. Eventually, she decided he was setting her up for an arrest, not knowing that he was merely a drugstore deputy.

Even so, she later declared, Randy was persistent. She said he asked her to go out with him on more conventional dates, to accompany him to Baton Rouge for drinks and dinner, trying to win her trust. Murphree stated that she refused, that she didn't mix "business with pleasure," and besides, she was nervous because all Randy seemed to want her to do was talk about "Billy," who he was now convinced was Jimmy Swaggart.

This situation continued, off and on, for months. Randy made his presence at the Travel Inn one which most of the working girls there took for granted. In the meantime, he heard rumors of Swaggart's association with other prostitutes in the district, a junkie named "Liz," and a woman in her late thirties named Peggy Carriere, who would later claim in a press interview that Swaggart had propositioned her on a street corner. Murphree knew neither of these women, and neither was forthcoming to Randy or anyone else involved in the Gorman-Swaggart case.

Randy also heard that several pimps in the area had been approached by Swaggart, but none of these could be identified or located for later questioning. Randy believed his best shot was with Murphree, who worked without a pimp, and he stuck to her like glue. Sooner or later, he felt assured, Billy would show up and he would have the goods on Swaggart once and for all.

Born in 1960, Debra Murphree was the picture of the stereotypical veteran New Orleans prostitute. Standing five feet, six inches or so, she looked ten years older than her actual age. She weighed about one hundred fifty pounds, was thickly built in the waist and thighs, and had sagging breasts and short, stubby fingers. She exhibited broad, harsh, severe features and dark eyes beneath a tangle of unruly black hair. She almost never smiled and when she did, she kept her lips closed, hiding her uneven teeth. In sum, she was a decidedly unattractive individual, described by many as being ugly or gross. She had two crude tattoos, one on each arm. On her left, her name was spelled out in primitive letters, and on the right she had a small cross flanked by two dots.

Born in Princeton, Indiana, she grew up in Patoka, dropped out of high school in the tenth grade, moved to Illinois and married a boy with whom she had run away. She was not pregnant but thought she was in love. The marriage was short-lived, but produced three children who were left with her parents. She worked briefly in a nursing home and a Pizza Hut before divorcing her husband and returning to Patoka. From there, she met another man who took her to Indianapolis, and soon she left him and was working as a professional prostitute in Nashville, Tennessee.

She claimed that she came to prostitution gradually, after competing in several wet T-shirt contests and working for an escort service in Nashville. She said the money was good and she was developing a taste for marijuana and cocaine. After a while, she moved out on her own and began freelancing, hustling tricks out of downtown Nashville hotels where she was arrested and cited for prostitution. Shortly thereafter, she fell in love with a drug dealer, who took her to Tampa, Florida. There, she was again arrested for soliciting, and she did time in the county jail.

She and her boyfriend then relocated to New Orleans, where they took up residence, first at the Bellaire Hotel, then at the Monte Carlo on Chef Menteur Highway, directly across from the New Orleans Baptist Theological Seminary.

To ply her trade, Murphree kept a room at the Travel Inn, which was operated by an Oriental couple who she believed also ran other brothel-motels on Airline Highway. She decorated the room with numerous personal items, including photographs of her children. She bused back and forth to work and often spent entire days walking the sidewalks up and down the street or sitting out in front of her room, waiting for business.

On October 17, 1987, just after 2:00 P.M., Murphree peeked out her room's window and saw "Billy" cruising the parking lot, his usual custom before making contact with her. Business had been slow that day, as the police had been particularly active in the area earlier in the week. She had been napping and watching television, when she looked outside and saw "Billy's" Lincoln.

Ordinarily, when she was free, she would sit outside or open her door or window as a signal that he could stop and come in. This time, though, she went out and met him on the corner, and he pulled up and asked if there were cops around. She said they had been around for a few days, but that things had apparently cooled off, so he parked several spaces down from her room and followed her inside.

Randy Gorman and Garland Bilbo, Marvin Gorman's son and son-in-law, photograph Swaggart as he enters the room of Deborah Murphree, a known prostitute, at the Travel Inn on Airline Highway in New Orleans on October 17, 1987.

Swaggart and Murphree exit Room No. 7 when Murphree fears she is being set up by the police.

Swaggart discovers a flat tire on his Lincoln Towncar. Bilbo cut the valve stem in order to prevent Swaggart from leaving the motel before Marvin Gorman could arrive.

Marvin Gorman's Oldsmobile Cutlass pulls into the Travel Inn parking lot next to Swaggart's car as Swaggart attempts to change the flat tire.

Gorman questions Swaggart as to why he is at the motel.

Gorman and Swaggart talk in Gorman's car after leaving the motel.

New Orleans, July 16th, Evangelist Jimmy Swaggart and his wife, Frances, arrive at Civil Court in New Orleans

New Orleans, Sept. 13th, Evangelist Marvin Gorman and wife, Virgina, leave Civil District Court with their attorney, Hunter Lundy, right.

According to Randy, he and his brother-in-law, Garland Bilbo, were working the stakeout of the Travel Inn that day, focusing as always on Murphree's Room, number 7. As was their custom, they were taking photographs of all the men coming and going. They snapped shots of six or seven men who came by earlier to sample Murphree's wares. To their surprise, they recognized several prominent New Orleans personalities. Then, after a while, they saw a Lincoln circle the parking lot.

They immediately began taking photographs of the car, trying to obtain a clear shot of the driver. After two passes, the Lincoln pulled up in front of Travel Inn's Room number 7 and parked, and Jimmy Swaggart himself emerged. He wore a gray sweatsuit and a red bandana, but there was no question that it was Swaggart.

Randy and Bilbo snapped away and took a number of shots of Swaggart going up to the room, being escorted inside by Debra Murphree, known prostitute, operating in her customary place of business.

This was an uncommon piece of good luck. It was incredible to see a man who had spent a lifetime preaching against fornication, adultery, pedophilia, perversion, and sins of the flesh passing through the doorway of a known bordello, with a prostitute. Randy raced to a telephone and called his father and advised him to come immediately to the Travel Inn Motel.

The Reverend Gorman was some distance away, and Randy feared his father would not reach the Travel Inn in time to catch Swaggart "in the act," as it were. At this point, though, his and Murphree's stories begin to differ.

Randy recalled that he called the Travel Inn and asked the manager to ring Room number 7. When Murphree answered the phone, he instructed her to keep "Billy" occupied for as long as she could and she agreed.

Murphree's version of events is that once inside the room, she heard a car door slam, and she looked out the window. It was then that she spotted Randy, who she referred to only as The Cop, leaving his car and running into Room number 12 as if he didn't wish to be seen. She then told "Billy" to stay still and she looked out again. She now feared that she was being set up, and that she was about to be arrested, so she suggested that "Billy" leave.

"Billy" then asked her to meet him at Popeye's Fried Chicken down the highway, presumably to continue their assignation at another location, but she refused. She was convinced that this was a setup, and she asked him to go outside with her and to hang around a few minutes and talk as a sign that they hadn't been doing anything wrong.

Bilbo, in the meantime, having seen Murphree peeking out, was fearful that Swaggart would make his getaway before Marvin Gorman could arrive. He went to Swaggart's Lincoln and cut the valve stem on one of the car's tires. Swaggart, apparently anxious because of the telephone call or Murphree's behavior, decided to leave immediately. He took the twenty dollars he had placed on the desk for her services, and hurriedly left the room, jumped into his car, and started to back out.

He only drove a few feet, though, when he discovered the flat. He stopped in front of Room number 6 and immediately set to work trying to change the tire, but he was in such a hurry and was so nervous that he initially placed the spare on backward. Murphree, in the meantime, came out and sat on the curb and talked to him, while she watched a blue car circle the parking lot and pull in. Certain it was a policeman, she began reminding "Billy" to swear that they had done nothing that afternoon for which she could be arrested. At this point, she stated, she also spied a telephoto lens peering from behind the curtain in the window of Room number 12, and she got up and raced back into her own room, leaving the door open just wide enough to hear.

While Swaggart worked rapidly to change his tire, the man in the blue car, a Oldsmobile Cutlass, pulled up and parked. He wore a baseball cap and grubby clothes, lest he be recognized, and he got out and walked up behind Swaggart and asked, "Jimmy, what do you think you're doing?" Swaggart looked up, and his worst fears were realized: Marvin Gorman.

Swaggart stood and tried to put the best face on things as he could. He stuck out his hand to shake Gorman's and asked, "Well Marvin, what are *you* doing here?"

Gorman refused to take Swaggart's hand, but only replied, "Jimmy, the *real* question is what are you doing here?" He indicated the Travel Inn and its obvious connotation in the world of prostitution and nefarious behavior.

Swaggart replied, "Well, I'm changing a flat, Marvin."

Gorman looked at Swaggart and, indicating Room number 7, said, "No Jimmy, what are you doing *here?*"

Swaggart did not answer but returned to changing his tire. Meanwhile, Randy and Bilbo continued to take photographs of the apparent chance meeting. Murphree watched from her door and heard Gorman, whom she neither recognized nor knew, tell "Billy" that he was in "serious [or deep] trouble."

Finally, Swaggart completed his chore, then asked Gorman if they could go somewhere to talk, away from the motel. Gorman agreed. They entered their respective cars and drove down the road, stopping at a shopping center parking lot, where they sat in Gorman's car and talked for two hours.

Murphree then saw Randy dressed in jeans and a baseball cap, cameras dangling from straps around his neck, race out of Room number 12, enter his own car and leave. She felt she knew what had happened, but at the same time, she didn't. Six weeks later, she decided that it was best for her to leave New Orleans, so she departed once again for Florida, where she took up residence in West Palm Beach, and began plying her trade.

In the car, Gorman and Swaggart talked the incident out. Gorman said later that Swaggart made no attempt to hide what he had been doing but confessed that he had a lifelong weakness for prostitutes and had consorted with them since he was a teenager. He stated he had frequently engaged the services of prostitutes in cities where he traveled. Then he said he truly needed help.

Gorman responded by telling Swaggart that even though Swaggart had lied about him, he still loved him and wanted to help him get the help he needed, if he could, if Swaggart would let him.

Swaggart seemed grateful and relieved. He asked if Gorman would follow him back to Baton Rouge, so he could confront his wife, Frances, tell her what happened, ask her forgiveness. Gorman agreed. With Swaggart in the lead, they took off up Interstate 10 heading west, but Swaggart soon changed his mind or, perhaps, the panic of being found out and the accompanying guilt wore off.

About two miles past the New Orleans city limits, Swaggart pulled over, then walked back to Gorman's car and said he thought he had better talk to Frances alone. He stated he would call Gorman later; having no choice, Marvin turned back to New Orleans, leaving Swaggart to proceed on his own.

The next morning, October 18, Gorman received a telephone call from Jimmy and Frances Swaggart asking for a meeting at the Sheraton Hotel in Kenner, Louisiana, to discuss the matter. Gorman agreed, but he was not a fool. He bore no trust for either Frances or Jimmy Swaggart, and he suspected Frances's complicity in the conspiracy against him was much larger than had been first apparent. On the way to the meeting, therefore, Gorman picked up Marty Simone, an attorney and a friend of his as well as a member of Gorman's church, who would act as Gorman's witness at the meeting.

When the Swaggarts showed up, Frances seemed nearly hysterical and kept asking Marvin what he intended to do about the situation. To Gorman, she seemed to be more concerned with the fact of Jimmy's being found out than with the particulars of his adventures with a prostitute. Her principal concern, as it turned out, was to learn if there was any chance that Gorman was planning to drop his appeal of the lawsuit and to find out what it would take to make him do so.

Gorman replied that he was not there to discuss the lawsuit, but thought he had been called to help the Swaggarts deal with this serious crisis in their personal lives.

Swaggart proved to be more astute than his wife. He seemed to understand just how strong the hand was Gorman now held in their game of personal reputations. In the course of the conversation that followed he admitted that he deliberately lied about Gorman and that he had written letters damning Gorman's reputation. He said he was deeply sorry about it. He said he now wanted to rectify that wrong by publishing an article retracting all his statements and confessing his lies in his magazine, *The Evangelist*, the same magazine where he had published some of his lies to begin with.

Frances interrupted. She asked what Gorman was prepared to do about the lawsuit if Jimmy did these things. Gorman told them he was not there to discuss the lawsuit. He added that he also wanted Swaggart, and Frances, too, to understand that he loved them and would be praying for them. He wanted them to love him and for Jimmy to get some help with his sexual problem. The meeting concluded cordially and with the understanding that Swaggart would begin working on the retraction at once and that he would get back in touch with Gorman about that and the other matters.

On the following day, Gorman received another telephone call from Swaggart, this time inviting Gorman and his family to dine with the Swaggart family in Baton Rouge. Gorman accepted, and on October 23, Gorman, his wife, Virginia, and children Randy, Mark, and Beverly Gorman Bilbo all drove to the Louisiana capital and had dinner with Jimmy, Frances, and Donnie Swaggart at the Country Club of Louisiana,

126

right across the street from Swaggart's palatial estate. During the dinner party, Swaggart offered Gorman a job with Jimmy Swaggart Ministries, stating he would like Gorman to come to Baton Rouge, be on his television program, and work for him permanently.

Somewhat taken aback by the offer, Gorman refused, stating that was not his aim or intention. He indicated that at some point he might agree to appear on television with Swaggart in some capacity or other, but this was not the proper time for such a thing. Again, Frances insisted that he drop his appeal to the fourth Circuit, but everyone present finally agreed that the evening was not to be spoiled by discussing such matters. Curiously, though, in the course of the evening, Donnie Swaggart brought up the September 2 statement and admitted knowledge that his father had helped author it.

By the end of the dinner, Gorman felt confident that Swaggart would publish his retractions and admit that he had lied about Gorman. In return, Gorman implied his willingness to keep silent about the Travel Inn and Debra Murphree. Although Gorman was not so disposed at the time, it appeared that at the least Swaggart was prepared to put things right either by hiring Gorman to work for him or to assist him in other specified ways. The families parted amicably, and Gorman was assured that in the course of the coming weeks, everything would be resolved and the entire affair would be allowed to die a quiet death without further expense or unpleasantness.

For the love of heaven, was he ever wrong!

Although Gorman did not confide any of these events to me or Tomy Frasier or to anyone outside his immediate family, he launched a series of discussions with Swaggart over the next several months. In effect, he was playing lawyer. Actually more negotiation than discussion, the point of the exchange was to secure Swaggart's published retraction in exchange for Gorman's silence about the Travel Inn escapade. Swaggart kept promising action, but he also kept stalling, and negotiations continued from the end of October until mid-February 1988, when it finally became clear to Gorman that Swaggart would renege, that he would never retract or back down.

Swaggart went overseas following the holidays. He returned in February from a revival crusade in Africa when Gorman heard several rumors that Swaggart might be planning to pull out of the Assemblies of God altogether. This was disturbing, for Gorman's principal interest was in forcing Swaggart to recant his lies and published defamations within the church itself. If Swaggart resigned from the church or separated himself from it, any recantation or retraction would be virtually meaningless to the governing body or membership of the Assemblies of God. Further, it would remove Swaggart from the church's jurisdiction, meaning that there would be no way to control his sniping at Gorman from the safety of an altogether new denomination.

Throughout this entire time, Gorman had kept his part of the bargain and had maintained his silence about Swaggart's adventures on Airline Highway; now he was reconsidering his position. He had no desire to blackmail Swaggart, but he did feel that Swaggart owed him the published truth in exchange for keeping the Debra Murphree affair quiet.

After a brief flurry of overtly social contacts, which ended in November 1987, the Swaggarts ceased calling the Gormans, stopped inviting them to join them for get-togethers. There also were no more overtures for meetings to discuss the matter, no more assurances of employment and restoration of Gorman to his former status. All conversations were being generated from Gorman's end, and negotiations were stalled on empty promises of future action that were becoming less and less specific.

Obviously, Gorman finally concluded, Swaggart believed that if Gorman came forward at this late date with his tale of prostitutes and motels on Airline Highway, no one would believe him. It would appear that Gorman made the entire episode up in an effort to blackmail Swaggart into publishing a retraction, or that it was manufactured out of a sense of revenge for Swaggart's published statements about Gorman's own sexual affairs. Who would believe anything Gorman said?

Swaggart's confidence was building as time passed. But what Swaggart did not know was that Gorman had photographs. And he was prepared to publish them.

During the second week of February 1988, Gorman called an old friend, the Reverend Gene Jackson in Tennessee. Jackson had maintained lines of communication with Gorman in defiance of church policy, and their friendship was strong and genuine. After Marvin told Jackson about discovering Swaggart's Airline Highway liaison with Debra Murphree, Jackson urged him to come forward with the information, not to a public forum, but rather to the highest of the church's official leadership. He also agreed to arrange the meeting.

Accordingly, Gorman agreed to meet with several Executive Presbyters of the General Council of the Assemblies of God in

Springfield. He flew to Memphis, where the General Council provided its private jet and transported him to Springfield, Missouri. What these presbyters anticipated in this meeting with Gorman is not known, but it is doubtful that they imagined they would spend that cold February night being confronted with irrefutable evidence of the fall from grace of one of the most celebrated evangelists, especially one whose recent career had been marked by his condemnation of his brethren for committing adultery.

It was doubtless an enormous bombshell. Not only could this mean an end to Jimmy Swaggart and his rich contributions to the entire Assemblies of God structure, it could also spell disaster to the integrity of the entire denomination. It was essential that it be kept quiet, which meant that it was essential that Gorman be brought back into the fold as quickly and quietly as possible.

All discussions and also a set of the photographs that were given to the General Council of Assemblies of God were to remain secret until the appropriate action could be taken through the Louisiana District Council. Gorman was sworn to confidentiality by the General Council. They then flew him to New York City for a scheduled church conference where the General Superintendent was present, with the understanding that the information discussed in Springfield would remain within the confines of the church's leadership. The implication seemed to be that Gorman was well on the way to reputation recovery, at least within the church. But once the genie was "out of the bottle," it was going to prove impossible to force him back in.

No sooner had Gorman left for New York, in fact, than the word was out; such a scandal was just too large, too juicy to keep secret. The gossip mill within the Assemblies of God itself spread the news that Jimmy Swaggart had been caught consorting with a common prostitute. There were apparently no secrets within the Assembly of God ministry, not even on the executive level. "We're not use to dealing with prostitutes and these kinds of things," one officer told the press. By the time Gorman checked into his hotel room in Manhattan, his phone was ringing.

But throughout this entire series of events, none of Gorman's attorneys were aware of a thing touching on their client or on our case. I was completely in the dark!

On February 18 at approximately 1:00 A.M., my wife Beth and I were awakened from a deep sleep by the telephone. To my surprise, it was Randy Gorman. I had not spoken to the Gormans in months—since the case had been appealed—I was awaiting oral argument in appeals court. The Gormans were the last thing on my mind. In fact, I was on the eve of a four-day skiing vacation to Breckenridge, Colorado, with friends. What Randy told me, though, came as a colder shock than any down hill spill.

Randy began by relating events that had occurred during the past six months, including his surveillance shots of Swaggart at the Travel Inn on Airline Highway and the confrontation between his father and Swaggart. He told me of Gorman's attempted negotiations and about how he had approached the General Council. He then said Gorman was holed up in a hotel room in New York and desperately needed legal advice. Rumors were flying, and the press was already on the prowl.

I was more than a little annoyed that Gorman had not informed us of the situation, but I held my temper and called Tomy Frasier, waking him up as well. Frasier was excited. We agreed to muzzle Gorman. I called him in New York and insisted that he not speak to the press until we could regroup in New Orleans and form a plan.

Thinking that it would take a week or longer before the media storm hit, I went ahead with my vacation plans and flew to Breckenridge, leaving my number there with my wife and secretary. No sooner had I arrived, though, than I was called to the telephone. My skiing buddies could not believe (and neither could I) that I was actually talking with Ted Koppel and Charles Gibson, or that I was turning down opportunities to appear immediately on *Nightline* and *The Geraldo Rivera Show*, among other nationally syndicated television news, magazine, and talk shows.

I got very little skiing done. When I wasn't talking to the press or TV personalities, I was on the telephone with Frasier, trying to figure out the best way to approach the problem and serve our client's best interest. The press was on Gorman's doorstep, and everyone wanted an exclusive interview.

Frasier and I decided that our best strategy would be to make one television appearance and to be selective about it, and to keep Gorman as much out of the center ring of the media circus as possible. Thus, he suggested that I should appear on *Good Morning America* along with Gorman, so he could make a brief statement about catching Swaggart with a hooker on Airline Highway and Gorman's subsequent conversations with Swaggart about his published lies.

Frasier's notion was that *Good Morning America* offered a national network news format that lent itself to brief but incisive interviews rather than sensational sound bites to boost ratings or make its hosts or anchors look good. It was not tabloid TV, meaning that it had a reputation for integrity, and they reached a huge audience. Also, because of its format, there would not be time to go in depth on the air and pin Gorman down on specifics about his own case that he might not feel comfortable discussing. Finally, because of the network's links, we could conduct the interview from a local studio rather than having to fly to New York or Los Angeles and brave the national press on their own turf.

In the meantime, Swaggart also had wind of the rumors and he decided to preempt any action that would embarrass him. Understanding now that there was hard evidence of his liaisons with Debra Murphree, he seized the moment and made his famous, emotional "I Have Sinned" speech on February 21, 1988, from his Baton Rouge church, the Family Worship Center.

Swaggart was in rare form, even for him. He cannily admitted to an unspecified sin and begged his congregation's, his wife's, his family's, and, of course, almost as an afterthought, God's forgiveness. He proclaimed, "My sin was done in secret, but God has said to me, 'I will do what I do before the whole world.' " He declared to the more than 8,000 worshippers at his Baton Rouge church, "I don't plan to whitewash my sin. I don't call it a 'mistake.' I call it a 'sin'. . . . I have no one to blame but myself."

It was a dramatic performance, even for Swaggart, replete with tears of anguish and the rending of his clothing and hair. It was also slyly conceived. He admitted nothing concrete and avoided specifics so adroitly that no one could think he was doing anything but offering a spontaneous confession of general but serious human failing. Thousands flocked to his "naked platform" to embrace him in a giant communal hug; women screamed and swooned; men tore their shirts open and bared their chests, as if willing to accept God's punishment in Swaggart's place. The entire event was televised worldwide; it was a virtuoso performance, worthy of the greatest thespians in theatrical history. And it was utterly convincing.

Of course, only a handful of people knew the specifics. And almost no one understood that he had nearly six months to plan this famous confession.

At the conclusion of his performance, Swaggart announced that to atone for his sin—and with the agreement of the officers of the Louisiana District Council—he would step down from the pulpit for three months and allow someone else to preach in his place. Frances stepped forward

131

as his emissary. His congregation at home and abroad was stunned by such magnanimity, such humility, such contrite behavior. Almost immediately support for his integrity and honesty began pouring into Jimmy Swaggart Ministries. Many people offered extra gifts in support of his obvious sacrifice. Rumor had it that Swaggart took in more money from that single broadcast than he made in an average three-month period.

No one seemed to consider that less than two years before, the Reverend Marvin Gorman was summarily dismissed from the Louisiana District Council of Assemblies of God for failing to agree to enter a two-year rehabilitation program. The previous year, Jim Bakker had also been decertified and turned out of his ministry because he failed to answer charges of sexual misconduct, misappropriation of funds, and alleged homosexual or bisexual activities. Gorman was bankrupt; Bakker was in jail, or would be soon. Swaggart, however, who had been undeniably soliciting the favors of a professional whore, was going to step out of the pulpit for only a few months, was entering no rehabilitation program, seeking no counseling, and sacrificing no part of his holdings or position within the church. But he had the Louisiana District Council's blessing. Of course, a $145 million ministry was nothing to dismiss casually; two of the Louisiana District officials were also members of Jimmy Swaggart Ministries' Board of Directors, and every one of them knew how to read a bottom line.

The General Council of Assemblies of God refused to accept the Louisiana District's punishment, though. It seemed possible that the great Jimmy Swaggart was on shakier ground than he himself realized.

Re-enter Debra Murphree. The stories vary, but either someone had run down Debra Murphree in West Palm Beach and persuaded her to come into the public light, or, as she claimed, on February 21, she was watching television when the man she knew as "Billy" appeared weeping on the screen. At last, she said, it all became clear to her. She now was as frightened as she was excited by her role in Swaggart's revelation.

She immediately returned to New Orleans and engaged an attorney, Warren Pickle. She gave an interview to New Orleans television station, WVUE, which also had copies of more than two hundred photographs of Swaggart and other prominent New Orleans men frequenting the Travel Inn. The genie was now completely out of the bottle, and, as another New Orleans minister would say later, the genie had hairy armpits and tattoos.

While all this was happening, I was concluding my ski trip, which had turned into a rather awkward working vacation. Along with my friends, I was in the Denver airport on my way home. One of our group, Karla Manuel, went into the gift shop for a magazine. She came out quickly and announced, "Hunter, your picture is in *People* magazine." We all laughed and thought she was joking; she wasn't. Right on the cover of *People* was Jimmy Swaggart's tear-stained face telling the world that he had sinned. The article in the magazine had photographs of Marvin, Tomy Frasier, and me taken at the courthouse during our arguments on the exceptions filed in Orleans Parish prior to the case's dismissal by Judge Ganucheau in June.

Now, we were national news, yet our case was still a long way from trial, indeed might never get to trial. And the conflict between Jimmy Swaggart and Marvin Gorman was only entering a new and much more intense phase.

Unbeknownst to everyone but me, Tomy Frasier had had a massive heart attack and I would soon become lead counsel in a case that would be considered a lawyer's dream. Although Jimmy, Tomy's brother, was concerned as to whether a thirty-three-year-old lawyer could take the lead in a case that would probably make history, I told him "Don't worry about the mule; just load the wagon."

• CHAPTER TWELVE •
THE LOUDEST MAILMAN IN TOWN

"Watch ye and pray, lest ye enter in to temptation. The
spirit truly *is* ready, but the flesh *is* weak."
—The Gospel According to St. Mark, 14:38

When I returned from Colorado, fresh from learning about the
Swaggart affair, we were only three weeks away from oral argument in
the Fourth Circuit Court of Appeals. We were also headline news. My
wife, Beth, and I drove to New Orleans, where the ABC affiliate's
limousine picked us up at the Hotel Intercontinental at 6:00 A.M. and
drove us to the television station for the morning show.

Upon arrival, Marvin and I were put on camera and had brief
conversations with Charles Gibson in New York before going on the air.
Of course, we could see the television monitors and could hear Charles
Gibson's voice in the headsets. Following preliminary introductions,
Gibson noted that Gorman had caught Swaggart on Airline Highway with
a known prostitute. He asked Gorman to outline briefly how it transpired,
what he saw and conversations he had with Swaggart.

Frasier and I had previously coached Gorman on his choice of
words. Gorman responded to Gibson's questions by indicating that
Swaggart had "wronged him" and that he wanted Swaggart to admit it.
(This was not mine or Tomy's choice of words.) He looked directly into
the camera and told Jimmy Swaggart that he forgave him and wanted
Swaggart to publish a retraction and to merely love him and get some
help.

I might have said a total of two sentences. It didn't matter, the small-
town lawyer was on national television. We were a media spectacle.

Back in Tulsa, Frasier was loving it. He was giving interviews to
anyone who wanted one; at the same time, he was reveling in information
about the Swaggart scandal.

In Lake Charles, my mother was getting calls from her friends all over the country who had seen me on television. She was very proud of her "Hunter boy."

In the meantime and in a more serious vein, my brother, Matt, had put in some long, hard hours preparing the appeal brief. Judge Ganucheau had ruled in May 1987 that one could not defame a corporation, but Matt made an argument that Gorman's name was inextricably tied to Marvin Gorman Ministries; therefore, if Marvin Gorman was defamed, his ministry was defamed as well. We believed that this, combined with Matt's other hard work, would win the appeal and send the case to trial.

The arguments were set for March 5, 1988, in New Orleans. Our strategy was for me to argue the appeal; meanwhile, Frasier would handle the media. This was, as of course, his long suit.

Because Gorman had declared bankruptcy since filing the suit, we anticipated defense counsel would initiate some kind of procedural tactic at the Fourth Circuit Court by moving that Gorman no longer had the Cause of Action, but that it belonged to the Trustee in Bankruptcy. As anticipated, immediately before we were able to begin our argument, Peter Feringa, counsel for Michael Indest, asserted that we were not the proper party. In response, we called David Adler, the Trustee in Bankruptcy, who confirmed that he had retained us to prosecute the case on behalf of the estate. We then noted that a motion to Substitute Party Plaintiffs was soon to follow.

The court ordered leave for us to file the motion to Substitute Party Plaintiffs within ten days; at that point, arguments finally began.

The Fourth Circuit Court of Appeals judiciary panel consisted of Judge Philip Ciaccio, Judge William Byrnes and Judge Steven Plotkin. Ciaccio and Byrnes had been on the court much longer than Plotkin, but Plotkin was regarded as both progressive and assertive. Furthermore, he was host, or soon to be host, of a television show on the law in the New Orleans area and was very popular as well as "media astute."

Judge Plotkin asked most of the questions from the bench. This indicated that the panel was cogently aware of what had recently surfaced in the news touching on Jimmy Swaggart and Jim Bakker. Even though it was not necessarily relevant to the issues of the case, the entire panel was also aware of the general sensitivity of the issues that were central to *Marvin Gorman vs Jimmy Swaggart et al.* This was, in a phrase, a *cause célèbre*, a matter of national news, national interest, possibly national legal importance as well. There was a sense that we might be breaking new legal ground, establishing a precedent for future cases involving internal disputes of religious organizations.

Following an oral argument during which the judges were unusually vocal for a procedure of this kind, we adjourned to await the decision. In the courthouse's hallways, Frasier took over. Reporters from every network—CNN, ABC, CBS, NBC, BBC—as well as all the print tabloids—*The National Enquirer, The Star*, and every major news and popular magazine were present, shouting questions, demanding responses. We were celebrities, and Frasier was center stage.

The man in the wheelchair remained cool—and witty. One reporter asked, "Mr. Frasier, what do you think about Jimmy Swaggart being caught with the prostitute on Airline Highway?" His response was, "Frances is so jealous." Laughter erupted through the hallways. Frasier went on, however, to say, "Frances need not worry because Jimmy was very sanitary . . . he wore rubber—gloves." Frasier knew how to master a media ceremony. His inflections and ironic statements, which seemed to say nothing substantive, communicated a great deal to the reading and viewing public and kept public opinion on our client's side for the time being, anyway.

Actually, we were prepared to go on the offensive and use Swaggart's hypocrisy as a major point in our arguments if necessary. On March 6, our private investigator, Scott Bailey, had videotaped a sworn statement from Debra Murphree, which turned out to be most revealing about Swaggart's personal proclivities and secret behavior. As it turned out, Swaggart's associations with Murphree were far from those of a typical john seeking sexual gratification from a typical hooker. But then, nothing about Jimmy Swaggart had ever been typical. In many ways, what Murphree had to say about Swaggart was a shock, even to Frasier, who possibly thought less of Jimmy Swaggart than of any living soul.

Murphree told Bailey, and later confirmed her story in press interviews, that she was first approached by Swaggart in 1986, although she was unable to remember the specific month. He was driving a tan Lincoln Town Car and was wearing a jogging suit, or possibly some other form of baggy trousers, with a seam cut open in the crotch. She remembered also that he didn't wear socks and covered his crotch with a handkerchief.

She was working a corner on Airline Highway in front of the Starlight Hotel, down the street from the Travel Inn, with a friend named Felicia Parker, aka Felicia Smith, but her friend had departed when

Swaggart pulled up. He rolled down a window and motioned for Murphree to come to the car. He asked if she was a policewoman working undercover; to prove she was not, she raised her blouse and exposed her breasts. She verified that he wasn't a policeman when he began fondling himself. She asked if he wanted a "date."

He offered her ten dollars, which Murphree declined. She normally charged that much for mutual fondling or manipulation, fifteen to sixteen for oral sex, and twenty for an all-night assignation. He replied that all he wanted to do was look at her naked breasts and masturbate while driving around. She insisted on her price, and he finally agreed; she entered the car, and they drove around for about fifteen minutes until he ejaculated, then let her out. So it began.

Over the next several weeks, he saw her infrequently, each time asking for the same procedure, paying the same price. Each session lasted for about fifteen or twenty minutes, whereon he would reach climax, then take her back to the motel. Soon, he began asking her to open her pants and expose her crotch, then to remove them and ride with her legs spread open. Murphree refused, noting that it was too dangerous, that if they were stopped she wouldn't have time to dress. She suggested they go to her room at the Travel Inn. He refused.

The liaison continued and adopted a frequency of about two to three times a month. Every time, the routine would be the same. He would meet her in front of the Starlight, pick her up, pay her, and they would ride around with her exposing her breasts or pubic area, him masturbating to climax. Once, he asked her to take off all her clothes and jump out in front of people so he could see their reactions; she refused and again suggested they go to her room.

She claimed that from the outset she knew he looked familiar, but she wasn't certain where she had seen him before. She asked him casually about his name, but he insisted that he was called "Billy" and would say no more. It wasn't until one or two of her girlfriends suggested his true identity that she began to believe that he was indeed the famous televangelist from Baton Rouge.

Finally, she persuaded him that going to her room was safer than the fifteen- to twenty-minute rides they were taking around that part of town. Again, he haggled over price, but she stuck to her twenty-dollar fee, and they began meeting regularly in the room. There, the routine changed only slightly, at least at first.

Initially, he asked her to pose in various ways while he watched and masturbated. Each time, she said, he was dressed in the same way—jogging suit, T-shirt, headband, sneakers with no socks—and most of the crotches were slit open to expose his penis. From time to time, he would drop his pants to his knees or ankles, but he never completely disrobed; she never saw him without a shirt.

Primarily, his interest was in looking at her in various revealing and, apparently to him, seductive poses. A particular favorite, Murphree claimed, was for her to climb onto the bed on her hands and knees, her buttocks facing him, and her underwear pulled tightly up inside her anal and vaginal areas, exposing her vaginal lips. He asked her to wear short shorts, with the cheeks of her buttocks hanging down, or to pose wearing a short skirt with no underclothing while he lay beneath her and looked up. He sometimes wanted her to stand in provocative ways with her underwear pulled up tight into her "crack," as she defined it. He liked to "peek," she said, to observe her as if she was unaware of being watched.

He asked her to masturbate also, and to "play with herself." At first, he almost never touched her, though occasionally when she was in the "doggie-style position," he would approach her and put a hand on her buttock, commenting that she "turned him on."

Most often, he used a handkerchief or a condom while he worked on himself. After a few months, he began asking her to manipulate him and bring him nearly to climax, but he preferred to finish himself. She claimed he never took very long to achieve an orgasm; once done, he was eager to leave. She also noted that he was cheap, that he never tipped and often complained about the twenty-dollar price of her services.

After several of these meetings, which on average took place twice a month, he asked her for oral sex. She obliged him for the same price, and he asked her to make her mouth "real tight," as if she were a virgin and he was experiencing sex with a young girl. Again, he wore the condom, and again, he preferred to achieve climax on his own, withdrawing from her mouth at the last moment. He discarded the condom as soon as he finished. If he used a handkerchief, he usually took it with him.

Another time, he asked if he could enter her for "a few seconds." She agreed and said that he made a partial penetration of her vagina for about ten or twenty seconds before withdrawing and completing his orgasm himself. Apart from this one time, Murphree recalled, he never touched her sexual organs.

He bragged often that he had to be away on business, but he

sometimes called her, presumably long-distance, and asked her to speak to him in an erotic way to excite him so he could masturbate. Even though he offered to pay her for this service, she always refused. She noted that except to tell her how much she excited him, he never talked much to her during one of their "dates," but preferred only to direct her posturing and posing, suggesting different things for her to do.

After nearly a year of their association, he took an interest in Murphree's daughter.

From time to time, Swaggart had implied that he was seeing or had seen another woman who involved a young child in their sexual affairs and that she also had a daughter. He had seen photographs of Murphree's nine-year-old child, and he began asking a lot of questions about her. He wanted to know if she was as pretty as her picture indicated, if she had developed breasts yet, and if she had hair "down there." Murphree answered his questions and tried to change the subject. Finally, he broached the possibility of involving the youngster in some way with them.

Murphree flatly refused to discuss this, but Swaggart pressed the point. He suggested he could pose as a photographer until the girl was comfortable, even take some pictures of them together; then, possibly, in time, she might watch Murphree and him having intercourse. Murphree still refused and asked him not to even mention her daughter. Swaggart then changed direction and asked if Murphree would be willing to have sex with another woman while he watched. Murphree had done this for money in the past and was willing, but she was too new to New Orleans to know of any ready partners. He urged her to find someone, but she put him off with the excuse that she wouldn't just do that with anyone off the street and she hadn't found a suitable mate for the display.

On another occasion, she used a dildo—a rubber penis—as a prop, which seemed to please Swaggart. He also asked her to strike more and different poses, and again brought up the subject of her daughter. Again, she refused to discuss any involvement of her child, who was still residing with Murphree's parents in Indiana, but she sensed that he would not let the matter drop for good.

After a number of months passed, she and Swaggart fell into a routine. She would wait for him, signal her availability either by being outside or having her door or curtains open. He would arrive, wearing the same clothes, particularly the headband, his hair mussed. He pulled through the parking lot, checked to see if she was free, then would park, enter the room, put his twenty dollars on the table, and they would begin. Once he finished, he was gone. It was, Murphree asserted, easy money for a woman in her profession. Swaggart always used a condom and hardly wanted to touch her or have her touch him.

By spring or summer 1987, she became convinced that "Billy" was indeed Jimmy Swaggart. Her suspicions were verified not only by other prostitutes who had seen him around the Travel Inn, but also by her observation of him on television. Under the television lights, in makeup, and wearing a dress suit, he appeared quite different from the sad, nearly silent man masturbating in a chair across from her bed. But he had a certain twitch or tic around his mouth and other recognizable traits.

In a way, it provided special status for her to brag about being the trick of the famous minister; but it was in that same way, that same desire for status, that Murphree came to Randy Gorman's attention. And it was that same desire for status that finally led her to reveal to Gorman that one of her regular johns was none other than the Reverend Jimmy Swaggart.

Debra Murphree's statements to Scott Bailey seemed devastating on their face. Moreover, there was no doubt in Bailey's mind that she was the same woman photographed with Swaggart by Randy Gorman outside Room number 7 of the Travel Inn, though she had lost weight and begun to wear her hair differently; she showed Bailey her tattoos, which were clearly visible in the pictures, and which Bailey believed were "as good as fingerprints."

More to the point of our interest, Murphree revealed Swaggart to be at the least a deeply disturbed man, a voyeur, a potential pedophile, as well as a man who happily paid for the services of a working hooker. But there were problems, as well. One was her credibility. She was, after all, a convicted criminal with a shady past and a record of drug abuse.

She was also a working prostitute, one who seemed eager to share her story of what she did for Jimmy Swaggart with the world. She gave interviews to television stations and tabloid magazines; and she also contracted with *Penthouse,* not only to tell her story for publication, but also to do a lavish and somewhat grotesque photo spread in the July 1988, issue. In the pages of that magazine, she appeared completely nude and graphically demonstrated the poses Swaggart asked her to strike. She also illustrated in close-up anatomical detail how she wore her underwear pulled up tight and used the dildo and her fingers on her sexual organs to excite him to climax. The grainy photographs captured the gross crudity of this association and its surroundings.

While neither Bailey nor any of the legal team had any doubt that Murphree was telling the truth, we were also aware that her role in the scandal provided her with an opportunity to make more money than she was accustomed to earning from her regular, albeit illegal trade. She also was defensive. Her ex-husband was suing for custody of her children as a result of learning of her role in the Swaggart saga; and she flatly refused, through her attorney, to meet with presbyters from the National Council of the Assemblies of God. The last thing she apparently wanted was to become a player in the Swaggart-Gorman scandal.

Even so, Murphree was going to prove slippery as a witness if we were to try to use her testimony against Swaggart. Thus, it came as a welcome but shocking revelation that she was by no means the only woman Swaggart had been seeing during the same period and from whom he was demanding the same sorts of bizarre sexual displays. Indeed, the strangest twist in the case came when Scott Bailey was contacted by a woman named Catherine Kampen who had a similarly disturbing but quite different story to tell.

One of Swaggart's favorite illustrations of his own devotion and piety, was to state during his sermons that he took trips to New Orleans to walk along the levee and "talk with God." He characterized such day-trips as an opportunity for spiritual renewal and an opportunity to secret himself from the trials and demands of his ministry and public life. Much of this, we knew, was accurate. He did go to New Orleans, and he did seek a "secret escape" from his usual habits and routines. But whether he was walking on the levee and talking to God or cruising Airline Highway and prowling for sexual deviance was a question only Swaggart and the women he met could answer.

Catherine Mary Kampen claimed that she became one of those women. She was by no means a prostitute, and she was not ignorant, but street-wise tough. She was, however, something of a professional exhibitionist. A New Orleans housewife married to Ralph Kampen, she had worked as a legal secretary for New Orleans lawyer William Slaughter before taking up the occupation of delivering singing telegrams, strip-o-grams, and belly dancing telegrams under contract for a legitimate and respectable New Orleans service.

Born in 1950 in New Orleans, Kampen was an exceptionally pretty, blond-haired, blue-eyed woman who stood about five-feet-four inches tall and weighed about 100 pounds. She had a well-proportioned figure, and in spite of a penchant for heavy makeup and bad permanents, was well within the range of looks that most men would describe as attractive. Reared a Roman Catholic and still practicing her faith, she and her husband had been married for sixteen years and had a thirteen-year-old daughter who attended a Catholic parochial school.

Kampen never finished high school and suffered from poor self-esteem; even so, she was articulate and well-spoken. In many ways, she was almost the perfect picture of the modern working-class woman. Her only police record was an arrest for shoplifting when she was about twenty, a time when she and her husband were in serious financial straits, plus another arrest for the same charge some three or four years before she met with Bailey.

Her work with the telegram agency involved her going to private homes, parties and restaurants, performing for a particular individual or small group. She ordinarily would carry a tape recorder with music and would appear in one of several costumes—a maid, a nurse, etc.—and would strip to the music down to a bikini. Sometimes, she worked topless but with pasties, round pieces of fabric, sometimes decorated with sequins or tassels and attached with spirit gum to her nipples.

She had been brought into the business by a friend who pointed out how good the money was. Kampen insisted that hers was always a "no touch" performance and that she had never been exposed to any untoward sexual behavior by any of the men she had entertained.

"There's no sleaze," she assured Bailey in her sworn statement. "My boss is very strict about such things. He wouldn't allow it. I wouldn't do it, and he wouldn't allow me to."

For Kampen, her job was a fun way to make enough money to keep her daughter enrolled in expensive private schools; and, she admitted, she liked it and was a little proud of how good she was at it. She noted that she drew a number of calls for repeat business.

Life was not entirely good for Kampen, however. She and her husband had frequent marital problems, money problems, and on one fateful summer day, her cat died.

It was mid-afternoon in late July 1987, when Kampen stopped for gasoline at a Shell station at the corner of Airline Highway and Shrewsberry Road. She was upset over the death of her pet, a purebred Persian, which was a final straw in a series of personal problems that seemed unending. It was a steamy, sultry day, Kampen, hot, depressed, and agitated, was fighting the urge to sob openly while she pumped her gas and distractedly observed the traffic passing around her.

142

She noticed a man in a car she described as a "pimpmobile" stopped in the service-station parking area, looking at her. He made a pass, then returned. She was watching him, not the business at hand, and gasoline suddenly backsplashed all over her. That was it. She broke into tears, became hysterical in reaction to this further blow to her self-esteem. She collected herself as best she could, then went in to pay for the gas. As she came out, her beeper went off, and she pulled her car to a pay telephone on the service station's parking lot, got out, and made her call.

The man in the pimpmobile pulled up next to her and slid his window down. He asked if anything was wrong and if he could be of any help. Even though he struck her as being familiar, she didn't recognize him, and she tried to ignore him. He insisted, though, telling her she looked distressed, as if she needed help, as if she was a person who could use some counseling.

Still trying to extricate herself diplomatically from the unwanted attention, Kampen continued with her call, but he kept saying that she was obviously having difficulties "coping" with her problems and suggested that he could help. He asked her what she did for a living, and she told him she did singing and striptease telegrams. He seemed delighted and said that he would like to see one sometime, that he had never had the pleasure of such a performance. She went to her car and found a business card for him, suggested he give her a call if he wanted to order a telegram.

He accepted the card, then returned to his theme that she looked like she needed help. She finally explained that her cat had just died, that she had numerous personal problems, and that the mood she was in, she hoped, was temporary. He replied that he still thought he could help her and suggested that they get together "to talk."

At this point she recognized who he was and asked if he was Jimmy Swaggart. He acknowledged that he was, indeed, the minister from Baton Rouge, then he offered again to help her. Kampen was flattered. "I was so touched that this man who had so much wanted to help me. I'm nobody," she told Bailey.

They talked generally about some of her problems, and Swaggart asked for her home telephone number. She was reluctant at first to give it to him, but then she remembered that he was a minister and was therefore "safe," so she wrote it down for him, and they parted after another brief flurry of offers of counseling and personal help. She didn't expect ever to hear from him again.

143

In two days, though, he called her. He again offered help in a counseling vein and suggested that he come to her home. She countered with an offer to meet him for coffee in a restaurant, but he demurred. He said he was so much in the public eye that if he were seen counseling someone, everyone would be harassing him for personal help. He asked her to pick him up at the Lakeside Shopping Center, then to drive him back to her home on Jefferson Highway. For some reason she never understood, she agreed.

After she picked him up near the Cinema at Lakeside Shopping Center, he began preaching to her about God's love and His plan for her life. Kampen found this somewhat obnoxious. It went against the grain of her Catholic upbringing, and she resigned herself to the fact that the "counseling" Swaggart was offering was really only proselytizing in disguise. Suddenly, though, he shifted directions and asked about her occupation, suggesting that if her husband loved and cared about her, he surely wouldn't allow her to do such a thing for a living.

This angered Kampen, who saw such an assertion as audacious; she assured him that her husband did indeed love her, then told him that her ambition was to open a flower shop as soon as the economy seemed right. He was delighted with the prospect and offered to help her—an offer he would return to many times. The first meeting, then, passed without further incident, and she acknowledged that she felt better about things. It was possible, she thought, that she needed the kind of counseling he could provide. She returned him to his car at the Lakeside Shopping Center.

A few days later, Swaggart called again, but Kampen was busy, so he arranged for her to pick him up on another day, later in the week, this time at the James Business Park on Airline Highway. This was a considerable distance from Kampen's home, and she was reluctant to drive all that way; on the other hand, she acknowledged that "therapy was therapy," and Swaggart was apparently willing to provide expert counseling to her for free.

This time, Swaggart was driving a small, imported car and was wearing a jogging suit with a polo shirt. His hair was messed up, pulled down into his eyes. She picked him up, noted how long the drive was back and forth, but still took him to her home, where he accepted a glass of ice water and assured her that what he had to offer her was worthwhile. Kampen recalled that she told him she wasn't sure how much good he could do her, but he argued that he was sure he could help her, and that by doing so she could help him.

He was very convincing, she remembered, and argumentative. "Everything I said, everything I did, he had a line to go against it. He had something in his mind and something in his heart that would say, 'Oh well, I'm right. She's wrong.' Whatever I did." He countered every statement she made, it seemed, with one of his own, suggested that she was not smart enough to think for herself, that he would have to guide her in every decision.

During this visit, Swaggart asked her to do a telegram for him, but because her daughter was waiting for her, she didn't have time. He said she should do one for him next time, and she tentatively agreed.

The next meeting took place about a week later. She picked him up in the same place. He was dressed in the same way, only this time, he'd added a headband to his wardrobe. When they reached her house, she said he asked again for her to do a strip-o-gram for him. She was a bit unnerved by the request, as she had never done a private performance for a single individual, but he argued that by complying, she could help him "preach his ministry better." She recalled that he said, "We can both help each other."

He continued to insist that she perform, so she changed into her French Maid outfit, turned on her music, and did her routine while Swaggart sat "like a king" on her sofa, smiling, and apparently enjoying himself while she stripped down to her rhinestone studded bikini and teased him with a feather duster. When she finished, he said it was "great," but that she shouldn't be doing such a thing for strangers, that it was not a good thing to do. Then he launched into a kind of homily or sermon, and she tuned him out.

As their conversation continued, he again offered to help her out with her ambitions to open a shop of her own; and Kampen, well aware of his wealth and his many contacts in the city, began to hope that this might be a real possibility. None of his promises were concrete, however. Instead, he continued to assert that she could help him in return. She said she was thinking, *Yeah, right* when he went on and on about how much he needed her help, as well. She couldn't imagine that she had a thing to offer a man like Jimmy Swaggart.

Seeing how dubious she was about his bid for help, he revealed that the root of his personal problems was that his wife, Frances, didn't love him, that instead, she preferred women. This caught Kampen completely off guard. She challenged him that he couldn't be sure; he said he was,

145

that there was a woman in his congregation who was his wife's lover. He was nearly in tears when he told her this, she recalled, and she had no doubt that he believed it was true.

"I felt kind of bad," she told Bailey. "The man looked so pathetic. When he looked at me while he was saying it, I looked him in the eyes and I knew that man wasn't lying. A man is not going to admit something like that unless it's really true because that's a blow to his ego. A woman with another man is a blow, but a man can tolerate that. But a woman with another woman. . .How can you compete with something like that?"

Swaggart collected himself, she recalled, then informed her that the next time she did a strip-o-gram for him, she was to take more off, that she would expose her breasts to him. She had told him she worked topless with pasties for some jobs, but after he questioned her about how the pasties worked, he said that was too painful a thing for her to do for him, and she should leave them off and strip without them. Then, he added, "I'm going to see you reach your goal of what you want to do."

Kampen thought about it and decided that she could parade around in front of him without causing any harm, especially if it would cause him to help her reach her goal—the flower shop—and she more or less agreed. After a few days, though, she had second thoughts, and when he called she said she couldn't see him. He replied, "When I need to see you, I expect you to be able to see me." He was quite stern about it, she recalled.

A week later, he called again. This time she went to James Business Park to pick him up, and he immediately told her he wanted her to strip and expose her "bust." She said she felt "degraded," but when they reached her house, he became more insistent than ever. She finally agreed and suggested several outfits, including a "Dolly Parton" and her belly dancing outfit. But what intrigued Swaggart was her leather outfit, which came with handcuffs and a small, faux whip as an accessory. He asked her if she was going to take off her top, and she said she would. He then asked her if she would remove her bottom; she refused.

He insisted that it was all necessary to "help" him, and assured her that she could quickly cover herself with a towel. "Look," he told her. "I'm trying to help you with everything. You have to help me too."

Kampen said she had no idea what came over her. She felt as if she was in his power, somehow, she recalled. "I don't know what made me say okay. I just said, 'What the hell.' It was like I didn't—I didn't have control over myself."

She tied him up, handcuffed him, then went into her routine: dancing, teasing him with the whip, stripping. "I wasn't paying attention," she said. "I'm dancing around, and I do all these stupid acrobatics and kicking my legs. I had just taken off my bottoms and reached for—I think it was a towel I had put down, a towel or something. It might have been my little robe. I reached for something to put over me, and I turned around and the son of a gun was masturbating. He had his pants down to his knees, and he was masturbating."

Kampen stopped her act immediately and asked him what he thought he was doing. But before she could finish her question, he finished. "Nobody's ever done that in front of me," she said. "All the telegrams I've done in my life, nobody's—I mean, they might have thought about doing it, but they didn't actually come out and do it."

She was embarrassed, outraged. She told him she wished he hadn't done that, but he replied, "I told you you have to help me. This helps me. You're the only person who can help me with this. And I want to make things nice for you, too. You deserve it. God wants you to have it. God loves you."

She argued that he embarrassed her, shamed her, but he replied that it was necessary and she shouldn't feel that way. "Sometimes," he said, "the only way to help people is by letting them help themselves. And you—you by doing what you do, you allow me to help me and in turn, I'll help you."

Kampen recalled that she was upset, confused. "How in the hell can you argue with that?" she asked Bailey. "How can you argue with a man who talks in circles?" She thought Swaggart was "sick" or "confused or something's wrong," but she felt terribly sorry for him, and she was unable to refuse him any request.

Over the next several weeks, their routine continued and escalated in terms of sexual play. She wore her leather outfit, used her whip and handcuffs to tease him, and he masturbated into a handkerchief or a condom he brought zipped in a pocket of his jogging suit. Eventually, he asked her to lay him over a chair and whip his buttocks while he masturbated. He would say, "Harder, harder. Beat me harder." Then, when he finished, he would tell her it was "wonderful," but that next time, she needed to beat him harder. "You have to tell me I'm scum," he said. "I'm no good. I need to be beaten."

Their meetings continued, following the same pattern. Each time, she drove to James Business Park to pick him up, complained about the

147

distance and the cost of gasoline, but he never offered her any money, any help with expenses for the trip. He only wanted to sit on her sofa "like a king on his throne," she said, and watch her perform or have her punish him with her faux whip.

One afternoon, a friend of hers, Chris Christopher, a car salesman, dropped by while Swaggart was there. She refused to let him in, but he spied Swaggart in the room and recognized him. Later, Kampen's husband, Ralph, came home unexpectedly to change clothes and found Swaggart sitting regally on the sofa. He was angered, although he was aware his wife was receiving counseling from the minister. He sensed that something else was going on, though, and ordered her never to bring him home again.

She did anyway. She felt powerless to refuse Swaggart. He never asked to have intercourse with her. But he did ask that she manipulate him from time to time, bring him to climax using her hand. He also began asking her to pose in different ways and to masturbate for him while he watched. She had a glass-topped coffee table, and he asked her to put on a skirt with no underwear and to dance on the table while he lay on the floor and stared up at her. As in almost everything else he asked, she complied.

He continued to tell her of his troubles, which played sharply on her sympathies for him. He maintained that his wife was a lesbian and that she had no interest in him sexually at all. He also said his mother was a horrible memory in his life, and he frequently spoke of his cousin, Jerry Lee Lewis, in tones that suggested that there was bitterness between them. In time, Kampen determined that Swaggart's problems, he believed, were rooted in a rotten childhood and only extended to his marriage to Frances, whose name he was now openly using.

When she pushed him to reveal specifics concerning his problems, though, he lashed out at her, telling her she had no idea of the problems in his life, that she couldn't help him, and that he didn't want to discuss it.

He then began to "step over the line" and to ask Kampen about her daughter. He had, of course, seen photographs of Kampen's teenaged daughter in the house, and he admired her beauty often. She remembered, "The first time he mentioned my daughter, he—sick son of a bitch—he told me, he said he wanted to meet her. And I said, 'Well, you know, I don't think—I really don't think that would be wise.' " He seemed surprised at her reaction, protested that her daughter was "so beautiful," and that he would "love to see the both of you together." He was "the loudest mailman in town," Kampen told Bailey.

She told him he was "crazy" and "sick," but he kept returning to the question, saying that he wanted to watch her have sex with her daughter. "It's about time she knew about sex," she remembered him saying. She told him she was too young even to date, let alone to have sex, but he replied, "Yeah, but wouldn't it be nice if we were to, you know, to teach her?" Her fury in response to this suggestion did not dissuade him from pressing the topic or from bringing it up time after time. He said he wanted to watch them have sex together, and he wanted to have sex with Kampen's daughter as well.

From time to time, he would call, Kampen said, when he knew that her daughter would be home. He would tell her he had seen her picture, that she was as beautiful as her mother, and that he wanted to meet her. This frightened Kampen more than anything else, and she was determined to shield" her daughter from Swaggart at all costs.

About this same time, he began asking Kampen if she would be willing to have sex with another woman while he watched. He claimed there was a girl he knew—most likely, Debra Murphree—who might be willing to participate. This took place about the same time he was exhorting Murphree to locate a partner for the same thing. Kampen flatly refused, telling him that such a thing would be "against God's law." He replied, "Not if you're only playing. If it's not real. If it's an act. You act, don't you?" She still refused, even when he offered again to introduce her to this girl he knew.

He also asked if she would talk to her husband about allowing him to watch while they made love. This proposition Kampen found both absurd and dangerous. She could only imagine her husband's rage if he had an inkling of what was really going on during her counselling sessions with the great Jimmy Swaggart. She could not imagine his reaction if she asked him to make love to her while Swaggart watched.

Sometime in November, after his affair with Debra Murphree had been discovered by Gorman, Swaggart brought what Kampen believed was a homemade dildo to her. "Never seen anything like it before and I don't think I'll ever see anything like it again," she told Bailey. "This very crude rubber-looking penis complete with testicles, and he wanted me to use it."

She told him that was impossible, that it was too big, but he angrily insisted, suggested she use it with Vaseline. She still said no. "He got loud," she recalled, "and he'd tell me, 'Do as I tell you to do. I want you to do this. You're doing it for me. Don't you understand?' I always felt real stupid around him, real—very subservient. And—like I was being dominated." He tried to insert the dildo into her himself, but it was too painful for Kampen to endure.

He also asked her to use other devices—a hairbrush, for example—on herself, and he asked to "have sex with her breasts," another request she refused.

As time passed and Swaggart's demands increased, Kampen became more and more upset with herself for giving in to the minister's desires. "I did things with him I had never done with my husband," she said. She felt guilty when she was away from Swaggart, would resolve not to acquiesce when he called, but when she heard his voice on the telephone, she discovered she was powerless to resist him. "It was like I was in this crazy little dream state, and I couldn't get out of it, and I didn't know how to—I was like Alice in Wonderland, and every door I opened, there was this new crazy thing he wanted me to do."

His instructions on how she should manipulate him and herself became more and more intricate, more weird. He came to orgasm quickly, she recalled, and seemed self-conscious about the small size of his penis. He also asked her to perform oral sex on him, but she claimed that she had broken her jaw in an accident when she was younger, and she was unable to open her mouth wide enough to accept him.

In late December or early January, Kampen could not recall, things were reaching a crisis stage. She was losing weight and found herself unable to sleep or eat properly. She lived in terror of his calls, but still was unable to resist his demand that she come collect him and bring him to her home for another "session."

She remembered that in October, his behavior began to change. When she commented on it, actually as a protest to one of his more extravagant demands, he told her, "You don't have any idea what's happening in my life. I'm going through hell right now, and I've got problems of my own." She couldn't imagine a man as rich and powerful as Swaggart having problems at all, let alone anything she could help him resolve.

One afternoon—their meetings always took place in the middle of the day, while her husband was at work, her daughter at school—Swaggart went into her bathroom and asked if the shower massage worked. She said it did. He then asked her to give him "golden shower," a deviant masochistic practice in which one partner urinates on the other.

She flatly refused. He pressed her, but she continued to refuse. "I told him I would not do that, that it was so far beneath me, and I couldn't understand why anybody would want that done to them."

He was enraged, she remembered: " 'You know why I tell you what I want you to do, you got to do it. You don't question me.' He grabbed me by a shoulder and he started—he was shaking me. I felt like a rag doll." She said she was sore afterwards.

Then, as suddenly as he started, he stopped. She told him he hurt her, and he replied that he was "so sorry." She said, "He just looked like this miserable, sad little kid. I always thought that about him. He always reminded me of a miserable, sad little boy."

He settled for watching her use the shower massage on herself, which she agreed to do in order to turn his resolve away from what she regarded as his disgusting and totally degrading request.

There were other demands she would not agree to. Others, she went along with. The "guaranteed piasta resistance," as she called it, came when he asked her to expose herself in public:

> He had been asking me from the fourth time he saw me to take off my clothes after we got on the river levee. He wanted me to go up on the river levee, take off my clothes, run around in front of the car. He would get in the driver's seat—nobody's going to believe—he would get in the driver's seat—and I thought this was really insane—and pretend like he was going to hit me, but the car wasn't even on. The ignition wasn't even on. He would just get in and pretend like he was going to hit me, and then wanted to know what it felt like if somebody was coming towards me, going to run over me.

Kampen stated she did this twice, but then the weather turned chilly, and she begged off.

A week after the golden shower incident, he called her again. She was recovering from an accident in a light fixture store; a lamp had fallen on her head, given her a concussion, and broken nose. He told her she needed to see him "for some healing," but she replied that her husband, fearful that she would try to drive in her condition, had taken away her car keys. She recalled:

> He said, "I said I want you to pick me up. Don't you understand?" It was almost like the devil would—one

151

day—one minute, he was just as sweet with honey dripping. The next minute it was like the Exorcist. And that's what I felt like over the phone. Like he was, "Don't you understand? You have to pick me up. Don't you— Don't you dare tell me no."

She was furious with him, and she felt herself breaking free, at last, from his control. She called him an "asshole" and hung up on him. She figured, given their history together, that he "probably enjoyed it when I called him that." She never heard from him again.

Not directly.

She began to reassess the experience she'd had with Swaggart and to realize how he had used her. She now believed she was in greater need of counseling than ever, and his offers of financial help never materialized. He even refused at one point to put gasoline in her car when she was returning him to James Business Park and the tank was nearly empty. "You've got credit cards," he told her. "Use them."

His tantalizing suggestions that he would help her were, as she put it, "something he used like a toy, like a tool to hurt me and keep me dangling like I was some sort of little puppet." But she was quick to add that she was also culpable for buying into the entire kinky sex routine. She acknowledged that she had the money to open a shop on her own, that what she truly sought from him was the moral support. Instead, he made her feel less secure than ever, more degraded and lacking in self-esteem. But she continued with it anyway.

She noted that she and her husband were having marital problems in the first place, and, not surprisingly, these were multiplying as her involvement with Swaggart deepened. She found that in spite of the aggravation he caused her, he provided her with a much needed emotional outlet. In short, he made her feel wanted, needed, and constantly reassured her that she was helping him, and could help him even more.

Overall, she stated that between July 1987 and January 1988, she met with Swaggart just under a dozen times. After it was over, she presumed it would be forgotten, but then in the spring, about the time that Gorman's photographs revealed Swaggart's involvement with Debra Murphree, she began receiving threatening telephone calls.

The first one came in March. A voice Kampen described as "genteel" and "southern gentlemanly" warned her on the telephone that she'd "better leave Jimmy alone. You better never say anything about Jimmy." She asked who was speaking, but the reply was, "Never mind. You just keep your mouth shut about Jimmy." She asked why Swaggart didn't speak to her himself, but the caller hung up.

More calls followed. One that especially scared Kampen informed her, "If you say anything or do anything you'll regret it. If you say anything about Jimmy. Because we'll burn you in your house. We'll burn your house down around you." Another call followed, and this time, her husband picked up at the same time she did. The voice said, "You'd better leave Jimmy alone or you're dead." Her husband was incensed, but she had not had contact with Swaggart since January.

Then, in April, about a week before she spoke to Bailey, a final call came. This time, the message was the same, that if she talked about Swaggart she was "dead," but Kampen was fed up. She said she replied, "Can you please repeat that because I want to make sure that my tape recorder got every word of it so I can take it to the police." The caller hung up immediately.

She sought help from the telephone company, but they were unable to do much without legal authorization for a wire tap. She was fearful of going to the police, so she sought the advice of Chris Christopher, the only person other than her husband, who was aware of her connection to Jimmy Swaggart. She told him the entire story. Christopher suggested she consult an attorney, and the lawyer he suggested was none other than Warren Pickle, who also represented Debra Murphree.

By sheer coincidence, or so it would appear, Pickle had bought a car from the same lot where Christopher worked. Because of the press stories about Murphree and Swaggart, Christopher was aware of Pickle's position with Murphree, and he urged Kampen to call him. She did, and Pickle led him to us and ultimately to the videotaped interview with Scott Bailey.

There was no question that Catherine Kampen's sworn statement held dynamite—if it was true. The question in our minds, as legal counsel for Gorman, though, was her veracity. The connection with Pickle via Christopher was almost too convenient; also, there was a question of why this fairly normal-appearing working mother and housewife would come forward on her own, jeopardizing her marital situation even more so by confessing to such a series of bizarre sex acts with a total stranger. There was the matter of the threatening telephone calls, of course; but the entire situation just did not feel entirely solid.

Further, I had trouble believing that she was such a shrinking violet in the entire affair, that she did not willingly engage in Swaggart's sexual games, and she may even have suggested variations herself. It was too much to accept that even a man of Swaggart's known charisma and personal power could charm anyone so completely, could effectively brainwash" a woman into doing almost everything he commanded. That, however, was Kampen's story, and she was sticking to it.

On the other hand, parallels between Murphree's reports of Swaggart's demands of her and what Kampen said he asked her to do were too close to ignore. The method he used to find satisfaction, a combination of voyeurism and self-abuse with suggestive poses and requests to observe women making love to other women, were quite specific. The requests he made for the women to involve their daughters in a pedophilic display or relationship also were identical, and he had persuaded Kampen to perform several stunts—the public exposure, for example—that Murphree said she refused to do for him. Moreover, there were the devices and particulars of Swaggart's involvement with both women: the dildos, condoms, lack of desire for normal intercourse, insistence on self-manipulation to climax, and so forth.

Kampen was either a very clever liar, or she was telling the absolute truth. Basically, it was her word against Swaggart's, but she had nothing to gain by telling her story, and she apparently had a great deal to lose. She did give a press interview or two, but unlike Murphree, who was shamelessly exposing herself in the pages of a men's magazine, Kampen didn't seem to want anything in return for her story except to be left alone. By and large, her principal interest was in seeking protection by going on record through a sworn statement and making it clear that she had been sexually involved with Jimmy Swaggart.

More to the point of our case than the sexual games and acts Swaggart demanded of Kampen, though, was her statement that he approached her under the pretext of offering Christian counsel and charitable help. That he used his personal position and his professional office as a method of seducing an emotionally overwrought and somewhat insecure individual who clearly needed solace and support was a more damning indictment than anything that might be revealed about rubber penises and golden showers.

Bailey made videotapes of statements from both women, and we hoped to use them, if not in the appeals process at least in the course of the trial in order to demonstrate Swaggart's hypocrisy and his arrogance. Unfortunately, the court felt differently and ruled that Jimmy Swaggart's sexual conduct was irrelevant to Marvin Gorman's suit for defamation, invasion of privacy, and intentional infliction of emotional distress; thus, the details of Swaggart's secret life with these two women, particularly with Kampen, were never made public.

However, the information did ultimately lead to some sensational newspaper headlines, particularly the following summer when the General Council of the Assembly of God did act and overruled the District Council's decision merely to punish Swaggart by restricting him from his pulpit until May 22.

After viewing Murphree's videotaped interview and listening to Frances Swaggart pronounce from her husband's naked platform that he would return on that date "come hell or high water," the thirteen Executive Presbyters slapped him with a full year's suspension from preaching and demanded that he enter a two-year rehabilitation program. Swaggart refused; and in April 1988, the General Council withdrew his credentials as an Assembly of God minister.

Swaggart, who had publicly accused Gorman of being unfit for the ministry and forced his resignation and decertification nearly two years before, preempted their move by announcing that he had already resigned from the Assemblies of God earlier—variously reporting the occurrence as having taken place in December, January, or February, then, following the District Council's announcement, he told a reporter that the church was "cutting off its nose to spite its face."

In spite of his obvious hypocrisy, of the public exposure of his involvement with a whore on Airline Highway, information brought to the General Council by Gorman, though, the District Council made no move to restore Gorman's name or his credentials. Rocked by wave after wave of scandal on a scale none of them ever imagined possible, the elder statesmen of the church were eager to disassociate themselves from the taint brought to the public eye by a man who was, only a few months before, their most celebrated apostle.

• CHAPTER THIRTEEN •
THE ARROGANCE OF PRIDE

"And I will punish the world for *their* evil, and the wicked for their iniquity; and I will cause the arrogancy of the proud to cease, and will lay low the haughtiness of the terrible."

—The Book of the Prophet Isaiah, 13:11

The few weeks following our appeals argument passed very slowly. I anxiously awaited the court's decision, which we hoped would place us back into trial court. Gorman remained quiet and hardly communicated with any of us; finally, on a Friday afternoon during the first week of May, he called to say the decision had been rendered. I immediately chartered a plane, flew to New Orleans, and picked up the opinion.

To my elation, Judge Ganucheau's ruling was reversed. The case was remanded for trial. There was still a cloud hanging over our fortunes, however. The opinion was entirely favorable in the sense that the appeals court found that the issues should be tried, and the three-judge panel additionally found that we had stated a Cause of Action over which the civil court *did* have jurisdiction; but there also was some language in the appeals court's opinion we knew once again might create a problem before the case was over. This language again dealt with the question of jurisdiction, but we were thrilled that we would get our day in court; Marvin Gorman was extremely happy.

In an Action for Defamation the burden on plaintiff counsel is to prove first that the defendants have made statements to third parties which are by definition, defamatory. Those statements—whether written or spoken—have to contain words that would place their subject in a position of ridicule or else would imply defamatory meaning, hence inflicting damage or injury on the subject. Our goal, then, was to prove that while Marvin Gorman had indeed committed a single act of

156

adultery—and had admitted the same—that Jimmy Swaggart and his followers had made public and private statements accusing Gorman of sleeping with dozens, even hundreds of women, many of whom came to him seeking counsel or solace for matters spiritual.

Additionally, we asserted, Swaggart had falsely accused Gorman of misappropriating funds from his church, fathering children outside of his marriage, establishing and maintaining connections with the Mafia, being possessed with an evil spirit and, by virtue of that possession, possessing others through whom he made threats against his fellow Christians.

Because we admitted Gorman was a public figure, we also had to prove that these statements were not only false, but also that they were made by the defendants in the full and complete knowledge that they were false or in reckless disregard for the truth. In short, our job was to show that the defendants knowingly made false statements with the intent to inflict damage on the character and reputation of Marvin Gorman and that they acted in concert with one another, thereby engaging in a conspiracy against Gorman. By establishing this proof, we had also to demonstrate what possible motives might have existed to prompt the defendants to take such defamatory action.

After a delay of nearly a year, our work began in earnest. Because of the exceptions filed by defense counsel in the spring of 1987, we had been prohibited from taking sworn depositions of the various witnesses and named defendants. Now, the process of discovery commenced. We began by deposing witnesses who were ministers of the Assemblies of God or who were business acquaintances of Marvin Gorman. We took hours of depositions, sometimes days of depositions; in all, it would take us nearly three years to assemble and digest it all.

Because no witness can be compelled by subpoena to testify at a trial unless he or she is a resident of Louisiana, our work took us well away from New Orleans and racked up miles of travel, days of fast food and motel rest. But it was all, we agreed, necessary to build our argument. Our intent, of course, was to eke a little evidence out of each witness in order to prove what would be a very difficult case.

As time passed, our stack of deposition tapes and transcripts mounted. In the meanwhile, defense counsel were by no means idle. A continuing series of motions and exceptions were being prepared and filed in Judge Ganucheau's court, requiring us to prepare arguments and counter-arguments and to deal with tactics designed to delay if not once again to quash the suit entirely.

One of the more serious motions filed by defense counsel in this period was a motion for Summary Judgment filed on November 3, 1989. Already, we had been at work for months, had conducted dozens of interviews, prepared dozens of affidavits for various witnesses to sign. Now, we were once again faced with a delaying tactic.

Before we could begin arguing the motion for Summary Judgement, Judge Ganucheau surprised us. On November 6, 1989, he granted the defense counsel's motion for a Protective Order and closed proceedings on the Motions for Summary Judgment. His Honor announced that he wanted to hear arguments concerning the question of following defense counsel's motion that we use fictitious names for the women: "Jane Doe" for Lynda Savage, "Jane Poe" for Lynette Goux, and "Mrs. X, Mrs. Y and Mrs. Z" for the three other named women allegedly involved with Marvin Gorman.

Because the only women whose names were mentioned in the case were those who voluntarily gave their names and wished to be known, or women whose names had been tossed around in public by the defendants in an order to smear Gorman, such a Protective Order was ridiculous and completely unnecessary. Judge Ganucheau was playing right into the hands of the defendants by honoring their motion. Ultimately, it was designed to give Gorman a black eye he didn't deserve.

Frasier pointed out to the judge that such secrecy imposed a clumsy and unnecessary requirement on all parties. Lynda Savage had made her "great confession" to Michael Indest about her affairs, not only with Gorman, but also with her brother-in-law and other men. Lynette Goux had confessed to Frances Swaggart about her indiscretions with Gorman. Jane Talbot, with whom Gorman vehemently denied ever having had any sexual contact, gave her well-coached statement to the First Assembly of God's business manager, Eddie Trammel. An attempt to protect these or any other accusing women after Gorman's name had been defamed was absurd.

The point of the defendants' move, of course, was to place in the court's—and the public's—mind the notion that there were hundreds of women who were willing to come forth and testify against Gorman, but only if their names were kept anonymous. This move especially incensed Frasier, who once more saw it as a method of suggesting that Gorman's sexual peccadillos were of a greater number than even Swaggart and his minions had suggested.

Because of his pique over this obvious attempt to use the trial as a medium to ruin Gorman's name more than it already had been, Frasier did something that gravely worried me, Milo, and Hickman. After Judge Ganucheau heard arguments on the secrecy motions and took the matter under advisement, we left the courthouse, where we were immediately surrounded by the press. As usual, Frasier rolled forward to take questions. When a reporter asked him what he thought about these women's names not being exposed and having to use obviously fictitious names, Frasier whipped out a list. Steve Hickman, Milo and I immediately retreated out of view of the cameras, across the street; we feared what he was going to say.

"Well," Frasier began, "I don't know who Jane Doe and Jane Roe and Mrs. XYZ are, but I do know Lynda Savage, Lynette Goux, Jane Talbot, Cheryl McConnel, and others whose names were tossed around by Jimmy Swaggart. Now, they want to protect them."

I whispered to Hickman, "Oh shit! We're in contempt of court!"

At this point, Denise Pilié and other defense lawyers heard Frasier giving this interview to the media. They were already at odds with Frasier because of frictions that had developed during several of the depositions, and now they were severely distressed, to say the least.

This may well have been the first meaningful shot in the exchange of hostilities between counsel which would escalate during the discovery process into a full-scale war by the time the trial began.

Within a few days, Phil Wittmann wrote Judge Ganucheau a letter informing him of what Frasier said to the press. In effect, of course, Frasier had obviated the need for the secrecy order or the fictitious names, if, actually, it had any need of more obviation than had already been applied through the statements of Swaggart, Indest, and other Assembly of God officials. Obviously, Judge Ganucheau was displeased with Frasier's brashness, but he did not cite us for contempt, as I feared. Instead, we received an order from the court closing the Summary Judgment hearings and requiring us to use fictitious names in all proceedings.

After receiving the court's ruling, I became indignant and instructed my associate, Milo Nickel, who was working on Gorman's brief in opposition to Swaggart's motions for summary judgment, to disregard the suggestion of "Jane Doe" or "Jane Poe" or "X, Y, Z" and instead substitute biblical names such as Delilah, Bathsheba, Jezebel, etc., in the brief we were preparing for defense counsel. Fortunately, on November

13, the Fourth Circuit Court of Appeals overturned Judge Ganucheau's ruling and opened the Summary Judgment hearing to the public; this permitted us to use the women's actual names in all proceedings.

*Un*fortunately, defense counsel had by this time received our brief using the names of the Delilah, Bathsheba, and Jezebel which further outraged them. A second shot in our battle of lawyers was fired. The war between opposing counsel was on.

Quickly, defense counsel appealed to the Louisiana Supreme Court on the matter of the Secrecy Order and Protective Order, but on November 17, the high court denied writs and refused to hear the matter. Hence, the hearing on the motion for Summary Judgment commenced on December 20, 1989; Judge Ganucheau ruled subsequently against the defense, denying Summary Judgment for the time being. Needless to say, I had a smirk on my face thinking about the use of Delilah, Bathsheba, and Jezebel when making the oral argument.

In the months and years to come, further motions for Summary Judgment would be filed by different members of the defense team. For the longest time, it appeared that we would be beating a regular path to Judge Ganucheau's court to argue against the ploys and tactics designed to thwart the suit and protect the reputation and fortune of Jimmy Swaggart.

It was all to no avail. Marvin Gorman would have his day in court, and so, as it turned out, would the arrogant and self-confident Jimmy Swaggart.

There was no question that the deposition we all looked most forward to taking was that of Jimmy Swaggart himself. The day finally arrived in December 1988. Swaggart's deposition was to be held in the luxurious conference room of the Stone, Pigman office on Carondelet Street in New Orleans. Upon arrival, though, we were told that the deposition had been moved to the Chaffé, McCall offices in the Energy Center, so we hurried in that direction.

Our assumption was that the change of location was to avoid television cameras and reporters who followed Swaggart's every move. Frasier had already embarrassed some of the defendants by allowing a reporter from *Inside Edition* to follow us into Stone, Pigman's conference room for Cecil Janway's deposition. Denise Pilié grew angry and shouted at the reporter and cameraman to leave. Frasier feigned indignance at her reaction. Hickman and I enjoyed the theatrics, although they were harbingers of even more serious breaches between Frasier and Pilié and the rest of defense counsel to come.

As expected, Swaggart entered the room with a display of nonchalance and unconcern, apart from a slight annoyance at having his busy schedule interrupted with such tedious nonsense. Although his credentials had been canceled eight months before, he was still very much the preacher, very much the "Grand Poobah of Gospel," as one pundit called him. He was overtly amiable and vocally friendly to everyone present, even the plaintiff counsel and Gorman himself.

One of the cardinal rules for any lawyer is to coach a client and/or witness not to enter into friendly conversation with the counsel on the opposite side. Obviously, defense counsel was unable to control Swaggart or to suppress his unbridled self-confidence and personal arrogance.

No sooner had Swaggart made his gestures of greeting to all present, than Tomy Frasier approached him and struck up a conversation about mutual friends. Frasier's goal was to ingratiate himself with Swaggart and invoke a sense of fraternity and trust before the trial. For this reason, Frasier insisted that I take Swaggart's deposition and pose the questions to him; that way, he could appear to be a "fifth wheel," merely "along for the ride" and offer sympathetic and conciliatory overtures to Swaggart should matters heat up. It was, in other words, a classic case of "good cop-bad cop" strategy. And, to my surprise, it worked.

Swaggart, like a chump, accepted Frasier's offer of friendly banter and conversation with genuine affability. What he didn't know was that Frasier had a collection of magazines with Swaggart's face on them; he often produced these photographs as graphic evidence that Swaggart stood more for hatred than love. Swaggart, of course, was also ignorant that Frasier had vowed that this would be his last big case. The Tulsa attorney planned to end a highly successful legal career by taking down the great Jimmy Swaggart. For Tomy Frasier, this case had become a personal mission.

During his deposition, Jimmy Swaggart held onto a book he was reading, once again signifying his lack of concern as to why he was there in the first place. The impression he wanted to give was that of a busy and important man who was interrupted unexpectedly, but who was giving impatient but full cooperation, not as the primary defendant in a multi-million dollar lawsuit.

Frances Swaggart accompanied her husband; she sat on the other end of the room, and at Jimmy's request brought him a Coke. He made a great show of thanking her for the chore, then loudly declared how much he loved her in front of the entire crowd. It was an embarrassing display, and I wondered how Denise Pilié could keep a straight face.

During breaks in the deposition process, Frasier continued his strategy of endearment. He wheeled himself next to Swaggart and talked about horse racing and other matters. Frasier said he was bored listening to all this, and he could not wait to get to the renowned Louisiana racetracks so he could compare their facilities to those in Arkansas. Personally, I couldn't believe Swaggart would carry on these conversations with Frasier or place any faith in Frasier's apparent sincerity. It was even more incredible that the Stone, Pigman firm could not prevent Swaggart from conversing with the one man in the room who more than anyone was dedicated to Swaggart's ruination.

This became more obvious when defense counsel objected to certain questions and instructed Swaggart not to respond. He did so anyway. True to the role he was playing, Frasier took the opportunity each time to note for the record that Swaggart had overruled his attorneys' objections, thereby firmly cementing a bond between him and Swaggart and implying that the two of them stood together against all the legal machinations going on around them. It was a masterful performance, and an effective one.

In spite of some legal improprieties and confusion concerning the "bate stamping" of documents and their unorthodox withdrawal after being placed before us, the deposition went well. But my biggest personal revelation was the discovery that Swaggart was not as intelligent as I had imagined. I could hardly believe that a man who had amassed an empire worth hundreds of millions of dollars, who controlled the spiritual guidance of millions of people, could be so naive, so unwise in his choice of words and manner of behavior. The charisma he demonstrated on television and the fact that he was well read though he had only completed the eighth grade had led me to believe that he was an extremely bright individual. It was now apparent to me that Jimmy Swaggart was nothing more than an arrogant, conceited, and self-centered performer, a buffoon, talented in voice, gifted with charismatic charm, but sorely lacking in common sense and innate intelligence.

One of the biggest mistakes an individual facing a court session can make is to assume his intellectual superiority is great enough for him to match wits with a competent and experienced trial lawyer, even a small-town redneck from Lake Charles, Louisiana. It may be that the individual is smarter, more erudite, even better educated and more experienced in the methodologies of rhetorical argument; but a trial is a different setting from a college classroom, public forum, or pulpit. In a court of law, an experienced attorney is on his own turf, can control what is said and, more importantly, what is not said aloud within a judge's or jury's hearing. That advantage will generally outweigh any edge anyone untrained in the law and court procedures can bring to a trial.

Swaggart was neither as well educated, nor as experienced in legal arguments as the newest paralegal in the room. Indeed, the average law office receptionist had more background than he in all those categories. Yet, his outward display of egocentric superiority even to his own attorneys and their assistants was obvious. He was an experienced orator, to be sure, but his arguments were one-sided, backed not by logic, law, precedent, or any evidential or syllogistic system of proof. They were only backed by his personal interpretation of scripture and by what he claimed to be personal and vocal revelations from the Almighty Himself.

I quickly developed a strong sense that this arrogant man could be had on cross-examination during a trial, that he would stumble over his reliance on his own ethos, over his devotion to emotional appeal, and over his dependency on personal point of view. Tomy Frasier, on the other hand, was just the opposite sort of person, the opposite sort of advocate.

• CHAPTER FOURTEEN •
OTHER WOMEN, OTHER MEN, OTHER AFFAIRS

"And the Lord God said unto the woman, What *is* this *that* thou hast done? And the woman said, The serpent beguiled me, and I did eat."
—*The First Book of Moses, Called Genesis, 3:13*

If one looked at a photograph of Marvin Gorman taken in the early 1970s, one would discover the picture of a handsome man with a winning smile, open countenance, and genuine, piercing eyes. He exuded success, confidence, even compassion. There was no doubt that he was a physically attractive man. Given the human propensity for being drawn to individual power, it also was not hard to believe that numerous women—and men as well—felt his passion, even felt sexual desire forming beneath their open admiration for him. Such is the nature of human psychology; such is the nature of human sexuality.

There was never any question that Marvin Gorman had both the means and the opportunity to engage in virtually limitless sexual affairs perhaps from the beginnings of his ministry. The question, one only Gorman himself can answer, was whether or not he found the motive, the desire, the compulsion to avail himself of the proffered favors of beautiful and increasingly younger women who found in him the symbol of sexual apotheosis.

Gorman claimed that, save twice prior to his marriage, and one time since, he had never found within himself even so much as the momentary motive to commit adultery. And we, his legal team, believed he was telling the truth. It bespoke a strength of character that most of us could not necessarily claim for ourselves, perhaps, if we were presented with similar means and opportunities; but such thinking fails to take into account Gorman's personal commitment to his faith, to his calling, and his intense awareness of his responsibilities to both God and man.

From the outset, Gorman had been accused through rumor and direct report of having slept with many women, but it took the defense counsel nearly four years of discovery, litigation, and argument to consistently find any way to support the allegation that Gorman had had a sexual affair with more than one: Lynda Savage. This was confusing, at first, for we were steadfastly maintaining all along that Jimmy Swaggart and his minions had characterized Gorman as something of a sexual athlete, a libertine, regularly misusing his power and position to seduce innocent women, primarily admiring parishioners, including an eighty-year-old woman.

By late 1990, while the discovery process was still ongoing, it was becoming obvious that the defendants were not going to be able to produce any other concrete witnesses to any adultery apart from Gorman and Lynda Savage, and we were growing more confident with our corroboration of Gorman's version of events touching on the Savage affair.

Savage's version of events did not worry us because her credibility was increasingly questionable; also, she was the only woman who seemed willing to come forth and admit under oath to committing adultery with Gorman. On the face of it, this seemed reasonable, as we had maintained all along that the other allegations were pure fabrications born in the imagination of Jimmy Swaggart and his associates or that they had been coerced from the other women by Swaggart and his minions.

It was apparent that they had made such outlandish charges as a "scare tactic," designed to frighten Gorman into resigning and to convince any lingering supporters of the minister's moral corruption. Once this was accomplished, the false rumors took on a life of their own, and the perpetrators were forced to defend them by claiming they were true, even expanding them to absurd proportions.

A single act of adultery, even a prolonged affair, between consenting adults, even between a minister and a parishioner should not, probably could not, be sufficient cause to destroy a man's life and career, particularly if the affair was over and the minister had confessed it to his wife and family and close friends. What Swaggart and his cronies knew they needed to establish was a pattern of immoral behavior, of adulterous relationships, all of which were tied directly to Gorman's misuse of his power and authority as a coercive device to force otherwise unwilling women to have sex with him. This had been Swaggart's primary aim in defaming Gorman in word and print; now, it had become the only viable weapon available to the defense counsel to defend their clients from the law.

Our supposition that providing sworn testimony to support this position would be difficult if not impossible seemed to become more solid as more and more depositions and investigation continued. Similarly, it was increasingly obvious that everything Swaggart had said about Marvin Gorman was part of a carefully orchestrated conspiracy.

One of our best witnesses on this point was Eddie Trammel, a business manager for the First Assembly of God of New Orleans. On July 19, 1986, Trammel, along with other board members from the First Assembly of God, particularly Carl Miller, Trammel's predecessor as business manager of the New Orleans church, visited Swaggart at his home in Baton Rouge. In his deposition, and subsequently from the witness stand, Trammel stated that during this visit, Swaggart indicated that he had a list of "fifteen or sixteen women" with whom Gorman had had affairs. He did not reveal this list, but this was apparently the genesis of the rumors that would soon grow in both proportion and scope as time went on.

Trammel also testified that he was ordered by the Board of Directors of First Assembly of God to retrieve Gorman's files from his office, and to burn them, although for what purpose, he never understood.

We additionally deposed Miller. He testified that during this same meeting, Swaggart accused Gorman of misappropriating funds at the First Assembly of God as well as Marvin Gorman Ministries. Miller knew this was untrue, since he was the business manager and controlled all the disbursements of money. Indeed, if it was true, it could only have been done with Miller's knowledge and consent. But he went along with the charges anyway. Both of these men would prove to be excellent witnesses against Swaggart, although they were enlisted on the side of the defendants.

We also called several former ministers of the church to demonstrate how from July 16 to July 19, 1986 a spirit of forgiveness toward Gorman existed throughout the congregation and staff of the First Assembly of God; there were numerous expressions of willingness to help Gorman, also. Furthermore, according to these witnesses, the board expressed a profound interest to continue Gorman on salary until some unspecified future date.

Following the July 19 meeting at Swaggart's mansion, though, the generosity and forgiving spirit in the church changed to a mean-spirited desire for vengeance. The Board of Directors met immediately following that Saturday session in Baton Rouge and decided to terminate Gorman's salary forthwith, thereby rendering him without income and sealing the fate on his attempt to purchase Channel 29 in Lake Charles. It was during the July 19 meeting at Swaggart's mansion, of course, that the infamous July 20 statement was drafted by the conspirators Allan McDonnel, Jim Rentz, Bill Treeby, Carl Miller, and, of course, Michael Indest and Jimmy Swaggart himself.

In my view, the Lake Charles television station deal may well have been the precipitating cause behind Swaggart's entire attack on Gorman. It was an attempt to nip in the bud Gorman's bid to expand his ministry and challenge Swaggart's position in Louisiana and the greater South. To that extent, it worked, of course.

But in spite of all these accusations, statements, and binding decisions, there still was no specific evidence that Gorman had indulged himself in numerous or even one prolonged illicit sexual affair with any member of his congregation or anyone else. Michael Indest claimed that he was in possession of motel receipts proving that Gorman and Lynda Savage had met often over a period of years, but these were never produced either.

In late 1990 or early 1991, with less than six months remaining before trial, the defendants apparently began to feel the pressure of the lack of evidence or concrete testimony against Gorman. They finally put forth the name of a second woman who was willing to swear under oath to having had a sexual affair with Gorman.

Her name was Gail McDaniel, a resident of Shreveport, Louisiana. She claimed she had had sexual intercourse with Gorman in the early 1970s while attending First Assembly of God in New Orleans at its old address on Elysian Fields Street.

This news was most distressing to me. I had hoped we would go to trial with the defendants only having one woman claiming adultery with Marvin Gorman. I called Gorman to discuss the matter; he could not believe it. He stated that Gail McDaniel was the daughter of a woman who had been a church officer. Gail's father died of kidney disease, and for reasons Gorman didn't immediately explain, her mother left the church feeling very bitter toward Gorman.

I talked to Frasier and Hickman, then we all met with Gorman and asked him to reconfirm his story that he had committed adultery with only one woman, Lynda Savage. Gorman assured us again that was the truth;

167

he had no explanation for Gail McDaniel's accusation, except that she was possibly carrying out a vendetta for her mother.

Within weeks, I received a notice that a video deposition of Gail McDaniel was to be taken at the Remington Hotel in Shreveport. This was odd because McDaniel was a resident of Louisiana, she could legally be subpoenaed for trial testimony, so no deposition was necessary. I met with Gorman again, now trying to obtain all available information on McDaniel.

Gorman finally told me there had been another problem besides the death of Gail McDaniel's father involved in her mother's leaving the church. When Gail was very young, she was confronted by Gorman about allegations that she had made homosexual advances toward another, younger girl in the church.

Ronnie Goux, another church officer, was involved when Gorman confronted Gail. This was because the complaining girl was none other than Gaylette Richardson, Ronnie's sister-in-law. This news put a new and somewhat bizarre cast on things, particularly because Ronnie's wife, Lynette, would later confess some sort of sexual encounter with Marvin Gorman to Frances Swaggart. Or such was the rumor. We also believed that Lynette Goux, who had moved into the Swaggart mansion temporarily, may well have been the "other woman" Swaggart mentioned in connection to Frances when he told Catherine Kampen that his wife preferred the love of women to men.

It was possible, even likely, that McDaniel now was seeking revenge against Gorman because he accused her of being homosexual, whether it was true or not. The general line of the Assemblies of God faith is that homosexuality is unnatural and perverted and is always a matter of choice of lifestyle. Hence, a homosexual or lesbian has deliberately and sinfully chosen this "perverted" path of life in direct contradiction of scriptural prohibition. A charge of homosexuality is far more serious, even, than a charge of adultery within the Assemblies of God. This also made Swaggart's supposed allegations about Frances to Kampen remarkable.

When I arrived for the deposition, it was obvious within the first few minutes that Denise Pilié and Gary Zwain, attorney for Allan McDonnel, had previously met with Gail McDaniel and had prepared her well for the questioning. Furthermore, Allan McDonnel was present and in a nervous state, walking around the room and making protective comments and gestures as though McDaniel was his own daughter.

Gail McDaniel was presently attending a church in Shreveport pastored by Reverend Rodney Duron, whose wife, Frances, was, by happenstance, a close personal friend of Frances Swaggart's. Frances Duron also wrote for *The Evangelist,* which further indicated that a close relationship existed between the families. It was apparent, in other words, that the connection between Gail McDaniel and Marvin Gorman came through the two Franceses, and, hence, through Swaggart himself.

McDaniel's story was that when she was a young and innocent child attending the First Assembly of God of New Orleans, she was suddenly and wrongfully accused by Gorman and Ronnie Goux of inappropriate sexual conduct with a minor teenager of the same gender four years younger than she. According to McDaniel, Gorman and Goux threatened to turn her over to the police and drive her out of the church; but, Gorman told her, there was an alternative: If she would have sex with him, the entire matter would be forgotten.

McDaniel went on to state that she was a virgin at the time—most definitely heterosexual—and that Gorman knew this when he coerced her into having intercourse with him on the floor of his office at the church on Elysian Fields Street.

The story was so incredible that it was dangerous. But I immediately perceived a problem.

During cross-examination, McDaniel could not recall her age at the time of the alleged sexual congress with Gorman. She initially stated that she was eighteen or nineteen years old, but she gave the year of the incident as 1972 or 1973. This didn't jibe, as it would have made her twenty-one or twenty-two years old, still young, perhaps, but hardly an "innocent child." I knew a jury would have a hard time believing she did not know how old she was or the date—at least the year—in which she lost her virginity in such a traumatic manner.

Other points of inconsistency arose as well. Although the experience was horrifying enough to burn itself into her memory and compelled her to come forward at this late date, she could not remember whether Gorman wore boxer shorts or briefs, what the furnishings were in the office, or any other pertinent details of the alleged incident. Anytime I attempted to pin her down on a specific detail, she waffled or neatly sidestepped it.

Another interesting point was that McDaniel had never married or had an open relationship with a man or any close male friendships; she had always lived alone. She had other problems throughout her life, as well.

During the deposition, I repeatedly fired questions at her, deliberately covering the same ground and points again and again, hoping to undermine her credibility or, at the best, catch her in an outright lie. Unfortunately, she was an attractive and highly articulate woman, well coached, intelligent, and sure of herself. It would be hard to believe that any man wouldn't be sexually drawn to her, particularly one who held her in his power, as it were. She obviously had an ulterior motive such as hatred or money for giving the deposition, but discovering what it was would be tricky unless I could cross-examine her on the witness stand.

When the deposition was over, I knew we had to conduct further investigation on this witness, and I could only hope that the video of her deposition would never be played to a jury. If Gail McDaniel was going to testify, it needed to be live.

Apart from McDaniel and Lynda Savage, the other women whose names continued to surface through the Assembly of God's rumor mill were Jane Talbot, Cheryl McConnel, and, of course, Lynette Goux. Goux's role in the case, actually, provided another interesting twist in the trial.

Lynette and Ronnie Goux had been members of the Gorman church for many years. Lynette was also a very good friend of Frances Swaggart's. According to Lynette—or possibly according to Frances—in 1980, Lynette was having marital problems with Ronnie; she went to a motel room where Gorman was staying, ostensibly seeking counseling for her troubled marriage. Where this was supposed to have taken place is not entirely clear. During the course of her visit, Gorman allegedly got fresh with her, but she left the room short of any sexual misconduct. Lynette told Frances about this, and Frances, of course, told her husband; Swaggart filed it away for future use.

Gorman and Swaggart had a conversation about the incident while waiting for a plane in the Dallas Airport in 1980. On a later date, Gorman was summoned to Swaggart's ministerial office to talk it over, as well. Gorman maintained that there was a little truth to the story, but Gorman was the one that left the room, not Goux. Swaggart allowed the matter to drop. In 1986, however, this alleged incident with Lynette Goux was brought up again, now in the context of Gorman's alleged pattern of immoral behavior.

Virginia Gorman had always held the opinion that Lynette Goux was sexually interested in her husband, and she seemed to have a much more hostile attitude toward her than even toward Lynda Savage. Although there never was any evidence to link Gorman and Goux, Virginia intuited that Goux had designs on her husband and actively pursued him.

From a legal position, it would have been most damaging to Gorman's case had Goux come forward and been able to prove, or even testified in a convincing fashion, that her version of events in a motel room with Gorman was true. The parallels to the Lynda Savage incident were just too strong for a jury to ignore and might have undermined Gorman's version of his single encounter with Savage.

Even so, during the entire litigation no one ever took the deposition of Lynette Goux. Allegedly, Goux locked herself indoors so she could not be subpoenaed to testify at the trial; or that was, at least, Phil Wittmann's explanation for her absence.

Our theory was a little different. We were highly suspicious of Goux's motives for coming forward in the first place, particularly since Gorman's description of the incident was different from what Goux supposedly told Jimmy and Frances Swaggart. The similarities of particulars between Goux's story and Savage's story of her and Gorman's initial meeting were too starkly parallel to overlook. Further, Goux's closeness to Frances Swaggart—and to Jimmy—was highly suspect. In the course of events, she actually moved into the Swaggart mansion in Baton Rouge.

Of course, what we more specifically suspected was that Goux and Frances were extremely close friends. Knowing what we did about Catherine Kampen's story of Swaggart's confession, and knowing what we did about his alleged proclivity for watching two women make love, the pieces of the sexual puzzle surrounding Swaggart began to fall into place. Whether it was an exact fit or not, that is, whether we were correct or not, would never be known, as we were prohibited from using either Murphree's or Kampen's statements as a basis for inquiry.

At the same time, the issue of homosexual behavior continued to emanate from the case, almost like a dark aura that could never be clearly seen or defined. The obvious scenario with regard to McDaniel, for instance, was that she and Frances Duron were connected, and that Frances Duron and Frances Swaggart were connected, and that Frances Swaggart and Lynette Goux were connected. If these connections were sexually based, then what we were viewing was a secret ring of lovers in the very heart of Swaggart's ministerial family. Further, if McDaniel, as we suspected, was either homosexual or at least bisexual, then it was not beyond the realm of possibility that her experience of being deflowered by a minister might well have come at the behest, not of Marvin Gorman, but of Jimmy Swaggart; we knew from Murphree and Kampen, that Swaggart was at least a marginal pedophile, and by her testimony, McDaniel had been both a child and a virgin at the time of the alleged incident. Was it possible that the Swaggarts had somehow persuaded her to come forward and tell of a true incident but to alter the name of the minister in question from Swaggart to Gorman?

Of course it was possible, but it was not provable, not without McDaniel's cooperation, which we never had. Indeed, she insisted that she was presently and always had been completely heterosexual, and at the trial, she would produce a fiancé to prove it.

Even more strangely, Lynette Goux's husband, Ronnie, who had since divorced her and remarried, did testify for the Swaggart defense. Supposedly, Ronnie had listened to taped conversations between Gorman and Lynette, but the tapes supposedly had been destroyed before trial and could not be produced. Ronnie also claimed to have seen copies of revealing letters that Gorman wrote Lynette, but none of this correspondence was ever provided. (As it turned out, most of Swaggart's defense was based on tapes and letters that people supposedly read and heard, although they were never produced, just as Michael Indest's motel receipts were never entered into evidence.)

Thus, for four years we kept hearing about Lynette Goux, but we never saw her. It was soon apparent that her name had been included in the legendary list of women in Swaggart's possession along with the names of a half a dozen other women, none of whom was willing to come forward and testify that the rumored allegations against Gorman were true. They were merely pawns in Swaggart's game, devices used to destroy the reputation and career of Marvin Gorman.

We were now at full circle, back to the problem of Lynda Savage. The question that plagued us more than any other was what motive she would have first for confessing her "sin" with Gorman to Michael Indest, and secondly for lying about the affair being one of long duration and sustaining endurance. A third question had to do with why—even if she was telling the truth about the length of the affair—and we were convinced she wasn't—did she wait so long to come forward? The answer came in the form of a gentleman by the name of Paul Dunn.

Although reared a Baptist, Paul Dunn had in the late 1970s taken a job with the Assembly of God Church in Kenner, Louisiana where David Savage was pastor and where Michael Indest had been a member years earlier. The Kenner congregation was in need of a Minister of Music, and Dunn had a fine voice and was in need of steady employment. At the time, Dunn was in his late twenties, married, but had no children. But most significantly, Dunn claimed that during his tenure in Kenner, he had a longstanding sexual affair with Lynda Savage.

Dunn gave us a statement in which he acknowledged that his work with the Assembly of God Church in Kenner was amazing to him. He had never been around Pentecostalist-based fundamentalists of any stripe, and his techniques, learned in the Southern Baptist tradition, did not sit well with his new employers. In his experience, as is the case in most churches, the Minister of Music stands on a podium and leads the congregation in hymns. He also directs the choir or orchestra, should there be one. But in the Assembly of God, Paul was instructed to involve the congregation more directly, to go out among them, encouraging them to join in the singing.

Accordingly, he not only led the music, he also paraded up and down the aisles, encouraging people to rise and follow him in a march around the sanctuary, working them up to a frenzied display of hugging and kissing which often became passionate, uncontrolled, ecstatic almost sexual displays. He described the experience as "one giant orgy."

Paul Dunn was a handsome man. When I met him in July 1991, he was living in California. Long since departed from the Assemblies of God denomination, he was now divorced. He stood only five feet nine inches tall, and weighed about one hundred sixty-five pounds. He had curly brown hair and a deep, California tan. He was also very well-spoken and articulate. My secretary, Laura, confirmed that he had a strong sex appeal, one that would easily attract women.

Dunn's voluntary statements to us were extremely revealing of the character and nature of Lynda Savage. He described her as an extremely attractive and sexually active woman. He said once it was clear that they were drawn to each other, they began meeting on a regular basis over a long period of time. She was, he said, demanding and insistent. She developed the habit of telephoning him at his church office after David Savage left for the day; Paul would go to her house, and they would have sex in her bedroom. At other times, they had sex in the church itself, once in Dunn's office while David Savage was down the hall in his own office. They copulated everywhere, he said: in one of the pews of the sanctuary, on his office desk, up against the wall, on the floor, and in a variety of beds. Dunn said it was sex with no holds barred.

Eventually, she revealed to him that she had had a one-time sexual

173

affair with Marvin Gorman, and that she had also slept with her brother-in-law.

In any event, Dunn's testimony would provide important corroboration to Gorman's claim that his affair with Lynda Savage had been but one time, seven years before, if, of course, we could place Dunn's account in the record without any hearsay objections.

Yet, there was more. By May 1986, Dunn's marriage was troubled, and his adventures with Lynda Savage continued. At that time, Dunn's wife, Susan, came to Marvin Gorman seeking counseling because she was certain that her husband was having an affair, although she had no idea who the other woman might be. She feared the marriage was breaking up, which, as it turned out, it was. Ironically, Susan Dunn was brought to Gorman's office by none other than Lynda Savage herself.

Gorman instantly perceived what the situation was. He excused Dunn from his office and called in Savage. He openly accused her of trying to wreck the Dunns' marriage and asked her what she thought she was doing. Her response was, "Well, Marvin, if you would just get with me, I wouldn't have to be having a relationship with any other minister."

According to Gorman, he rebuked her, instructed her to straighten out her life and to leave Paul Dunn alone. Enraged, Savage stormed out of his office. She apparently believed that by revealing her affair with Dunn, she would entice Gorman's interest in her. Having failed, she apparently sought revenge by confessing her affair with Gorman to Michael Indest; and within sixty days, Gorman was finished as a minister in the Assemblies of God.

Dunn turned out to be an unschooled but excellent witness when he appeared in court. During his testimony, he was harshly cross-examined by Phil Wittmann, who did an excellent job of trying to paint Dunn as a sexual deviant and libertine. Wittmann produced affidavits of five other women from the Kenner church with whom Dunn had had affairs, and Dunn admitted that these were all true. But he stuck to his testimony about Lynda Savage's sexual appetites and her statement that she and Gorman had met for sexual purposes only once.

Dunn's descriptions of Savage's no holds barred demands for physical satisfaction were eloquent evidence that he was hiding nothing. Moreover, he was a volunteer witness, appearing without benefit of subpoena, which gave him a great deal of credibility with the jury. Finally, Dunn's testimony persuaded the jury that if anyone, apart from Dunn, was the libertine, it was Lynda Savage, not Marvin Gorman. Also, if they could produce five women against Dunn, why couldn't they produce any more against Gorman?

More to the point, however, was the suggestion that Savage had a motive for confessing her one-time affair with Gorman to Michael Indest and for going further and confessing her sexual affair with her brother-in-law. Her desire to lure Gorman back to her bed—or wherever—and her anger at her failure to do so was the seed from which Swaggart's conspiracy against Gorman grew.

• CHAPTER FIFTEEN •
THE ROAD TO JUSTICE

"Oh, that I were made judge in the land, that every man
which hath any suit or cause might come unto me, and I
would do him justice!"
—The Second Book of Samuel, 15:4

In the four years of preparing for the trial, our legal team had stayed
at almost every motel and hotel in Orleans and Jefferson Parish; however,
Frasier's needs were different from an ordinary person's. He required a
comfortable room with a bathroom equipped for a handicapped
individual in a wheelchair. Thus, we all agreed to defer to Frasier on his
choice of hotels for our stay during the trial. We were anticipating a six-
to eight-week ordeal, and we all wanted to be able to move freely
between our quarters and the courthouse. We also wanted privacy and
sufficient space in which to work.

Frasier decided that the hotel in the New Orleans area with the best
"cripple room," as he called it, was the Sheraton on the Lake in Metairie.
It was also referred to as the Sheraton on the Causeway because it was
located adjacent to Lake Ponchartrain where the Causeway Bridge begins
at the south shore of the lake. It was a lovely setting, one conducive to
contemplation but sufficiently isolated from the bustle of downtown New
Orleans.

We reserved rooms for Frasier and his wife, Julia; Steve Hickman;
my associate, Milo Nickel; Frasier's paralegal, Laurie Phillips; my
paralegal, Kristie Plumb; my secretary, Laura Beatrice; and, of course,
me. Additionally, we blocked rooms for witnesses who would be coming
in and out during the course of the trial. We negotiated a rate of fifty-nine
dollars per room a night, which was probably the cost of an expensive
apartment in New Orleans. Because of Frasier's limitations, he wanted to
eat his meals in the hotel and entertain the staff in the restaurant and bar

176

at the Sheraton. We all got to know everyone at the hotel on a first-name basis.

I had chosen Milo Nickel to assist me in this case because my brother, Matt, whom I trusted most, had taken over my admiralty cases, one of which was going to trial at the same time as Gorman versus Swaggart.

Regardless of how long the trial took, the accommodations and requirements of our legal team—which was modest in size—would be considerable. The wisdom, however, of filing suit against a number of individuals rather than merely focusing on Swaggart was now proved out, however.

In May and June 1991, a final bid to delay or quash the suit before it came to trial was made by William Treeby, the General Council of Assemblies of God, and the Jimmy Swaggart defendants. The court dismissed the General Council of Assemblies of God but denied all other motions. The court felt the actions taken by the General Council of Assemblies of God and its superintendent were in good faith based on the actions of others, so they were dismissed. However, the jury was going to decide the guilt or innocence of the other parties.

Less than a month later, the First Assembly of God of New Orleans, Waldo Risner, Allen McDonnel, the Louisiana District Council, Cecil Janway, and Michael Indest, and the Lakeview Christian Center also settled out of the case; they were dismissed as defendants on June 8. They were, however, still key witnesses for the defense.

These settlements provided the financial wherewithal for our legal team to focus our efforts on the individual we saw as the true villain of the piece: Jimmy Swaggart.

I arrived in New Orleans to stay almost three weeks before the trial and set up shop in the law office of Jesse Stone and Curklin Atkins on the twenty first floor of the Energy Center on Poydras Street in New Orleans, right across the street from the courthouse. I had met Jesse Stone in March 1991, at a political function. About two months before the trial date, Frasier and I decided to bring Jesse and his law partner, Curklin Atkins, onto our team as associates. Atkins was an experienced criminal lawyer and had been handling defense work for the state as well.

Atkins had taken his degree at Texas Southern University in Houston, then came back to practice with a big silk-stocking firm in New Orleans. Ultimately he left that firm and sued them for racial discrimination. He later joined with Jesse Stone, a past president of

Southern University and dean of the Law School at Southern University, to form a practice. He was generous with his time and the sharing of his facilities with us, and he was also an entertaining character.

Apart from the convenience provided by the use of the Stone & Atkins' offices, both these attorneys were familiar with New Orleans politics and could be immeasurably useful in helping us select a jury. They also were African-American, which would broaden our image in a multicultural sense and would appeal to the local press.

I believed that being ready physically was as important as any other preparation an attorney can make for a long trial. I guess I still had a lot of jock in me. Prior to leaving Lake Charles, I had gone on a rigorous exercise and diet regimen, and I had dropped about fifteen pounds. I was able to continue vigorous exercise after relocating to New Orleans. Alongside the levee adjacent to Lake Ponchartrain that ran on the north side of the Sheraton was a jogging trail several miles in length. Every morning before going to the office, I would jog two or two-and-a-half miles, then do about one hundred push-ups. I continued this exercise program, switching to running in the evenings on days off for the next three months. I discovered that jogging provided me with a therapeutic exercise that would ease my frustrations while improving my cardiovascular and muscular condition.

My dedication to fitness did not rub off on my lead counsel, Tomy Frasier. Despite his health problems, Frasier continued to smoke like a locomotive and drink like a fish. Many an afternoon we sat in the lounge at the Sheraton to have cocktails, often several. I can remember one evening watching Frasier down seventeen Crown Royal and Diet Cokes and entertain the entire hotel staff with stories and jokes. Afterward, we wheeled him up to his room and helped Julia put him in his bed.

This was a very trying time for all of us. Julia Frasier had been diagnosed with cancer and Frasier was emotionally overwrought because of her declining health, which became gradually more obvious. Nevertheless, she was by his side during the entire trial with the exception of a couple of days.

Originally, my role was more or less to provide a legal anchor in the State of Louisiana and, naturally, to be the resident expert on Louisiana law. But in the course of the four years we spent readying ourselves for trial and after Tomy's heart attack, I had been graduated to a position of far greater importance. Sometimes, it seemed that I was running the whole show and Frasier was only there as a kind of spiritual guide and moral support.

But there was never any doubt that Frasier was standing right behind me if not at my side, shouldering his share of the work and lending the expertise of his experience. There were many days when I was concerned about a witness's testimony or how I was performing before the court, and he always assured me that everything was going well and to guide my course of actions.

My involvement in the case became a process of gradual immersion which soon engulfed me entirely. Nowhere was this more evident than in my prolonged absences from my family and in the lack of concrete income being generated by my still fledgling legal practice. Around Christmas in 1988 when we were just beginning to take depositions, I realized how much time and energy I had already devoted to this case. I had spent hundreds of hours merely driving back and forth between Lake Charles and New Orleans, and we had only begun to scratch the surface. At that point, my practice was barely making it; I was spending almost all my energy preparing to defend a client who was bankrupt.

This case represented a huge gamble, and my weariness and doubt had to be showing. Furthermore, I had to work day and night on maritime defense files to create billings that would support my law practice and family during the Gorman crusade.

We had just concluded deposing Cecil Janway in the Stone Pigman Office. We came outside into the December chill of Carondolet Street; I was headed back to Lake Charles to be with my family, and was eager to be off. Frasier delayed me, though, and pulled out his Crown Royal pouch which he kept with him in his wheelchair. He extracted four one-hundred dollar bills and gave them to me and said, "Merry Christmas."

He then told me he was proud of the way I was handling this case. Such words were a mark of his esteem for me, and they meant more to me than the cash. Still, the money came in handy at that particular time.

Prior to meeting Tomy Frasier, I suppose the most important influence in my life was my father, T. E. Lundy. He taught me that my gut reaction was generally the correct reaction. With that in mind, I often quoted the cliché, "If you think long, you think wrong."

Frasier, though, taught me how to be patient and to think things through. Anytime there was a crisis in the case, Frasier refused to react hastily; he insisted on taking as long as he could, sometimes requiring several days to think on it, then he would make a decision that, as it turned out, was almost always right.

I also observed his technique with people, his ability to talk to almost anyone on almost any subject. Even if he knew nothing of a person's background, he would discover some topic that would draw him out, make him feel that this man in the wheelchair was genuinely interested in what he had to say. More often than not, he was.

Tomy Frasier possessed a unique personality, one I admired, one I sought to emulate in my work and in my private life as well. Unlike our adversary at the moment, Jimmy Swaggart, there was nothing about Frasier that suggested arrogance or braggadocio, no affectation of manner. One left his presence with the impression that he was the same way with everyone, that he never altered his outward personality to fit either the moment or the person.

Although he was not without a capacity for cunning, he softened his antics with a deep sense of humor. One of his tricks, for example, was to make use of his handicap in subtle but telling ways. Whenever things seemed to be going against our client and the jury seemed to be taking too much interest in defense counsel's presentation, Frasier sought a quiet means of distraction.

There was a nerve in his hand which, if pressed with his knuckle, could cause one of his paralyzed legs to begin to quiver violently. Invariably, when he used this device, the jury's eyes drifted surreptitiously toward the disabled veteran in the wheelchair. They tried not to stare, not to gawk, but they couldn't help but notice what was apparently a pitifully involuntary physical reminder of Frasier's sacrifice for his country. In the meantime, their minds were off what was taking place right in front of them. Without saying a word, Frasier could virtually sustain an unsustainable objection to almost anything defense counsel might try to accomplish.

Such antics were always staged with a profound sense of humor and irony. They served to endear me even more to this strange, exciting man. I don't think I ever met anyone as genuinely honest and likable as he; I can think of almost no one, except perhaps my father, whose approval and respect I wanted more.

The weeks I spent at the Sheraton before the rest of the legal team arrived enabled me to meet a number of the hotel's staff, particularly the maids, all of whom were well aware of Jimmy Swaggart and Marvin Gorman and were eager to share their opinions about the case. These New Orleans natives—most all of whom were African-American—gave me a good sense of direction with respect to how to approach a jury from The

Big Easy.

It became obvious to me that Marvin Gorman was well thought of and respected in the area; and from the stories that I heard at the hotel, most people were willing to overlook his single indiscretion in light of his other good works. As one hotel maid put it: "A preacher from New Orleans who has only had one affair is a pretty good fellow." I wondered what she would have said had she known what we knew about Jimmy Swaggart.

Our rooms were on the sixteenth floor of the hotel, where the executive rooms were also housed. In each room was a mini-bar with snack trays of chips and candy, which we depleted on a daily basis. Such amenities may seem frivolous, but in time we came to appreciate them as part of our home away from home.

A few days prior to trial, the team arrived to work on strategy and preparation of trial. The first night we were together, the ladies from Lake Charles had a chance to meet Curklin Atkins.

Atkins was fascinated by the workings of Swaggart's mind. Each letter written to another minister or an official within the Assemblies of God would begin with "Choice Christian Greetings" and end with "Your Brother in Christ." However, the paragraphs in between were filled with condescending and patronizing nonsense.

Milo Nickel and I frequently walked the halls at the Sheraton wondering if Bill Treeby had the rooms bugged. He was a senior partner in the Stone, Pigman firm, and he remained loyal to Swaggart. Although extremely intelligent and a bright attorney, he acted, in my opinion, in the same way as maverick cops do: that is to say the hell with legal niceties and moral means if it justifies the end.

Outlandish as it may seem for us to worry about spies and bugs, there was a healthy case of paranoia on both sides of the lawsuit. After it became public knowledge that we had photographs of Jimmy Swaggart meeting Debra Murphree on Airline Highway, the Swaggart defense counsel sent investigators out to try to discredit all the evidence that had become public about Swaggart's escapades. This included, or so we were given to understand, observation and monitoring of the members of Gorman's defense team.

My wife, Beth, learned through a friend who was a colleague of the Calcasieu Parish Sheriff's Department that Swaggart's investigator contacted a private investigator in Lake Charles about conducting surveillance on me. One night while I was attending a client function in

New Orleans, Beth called to tell me that someone was watching me. I put nothing past Bill Treeby or Swaggart. Our investigator, Scott Bailey, was also followed frequently by people we traced back to the Swaggart defense team. Naturally, when we got into the course of the trial, we assumed that we were being watched or trailed right up to the minute we walked into the courtroom.

It was not so unreasonable, therefore, to presume that our rooms were bugged and our telephones tapped. We learned to be careful about everything we said or did. We knew we were being observed, if not by our opposing counsel and their clients, then certainly by the press.

There were also suspicious disruptions in our schedules and in our sleep. About 3:00 A.M. on the day before we were to begin Swaggart's cross-examination in court, the Sheraton's fire alarm went off. My first thought was, "That son of a bitch Bill Treeby!" However, I just rolled back over, while Laura Beatrice and Kristie Plumb beat on my door, thinking that I was going to burn to death. As expected, it was a false alarm. During the course of the ten-week trial, we probably experienced at least three or four false fire alarms at two o'clock or three o'clock in the morning, always on the day a very important witness was to take the stand. At the very least, it was an amazing coincidence.

One of our concerns from the time we first filed the lawsuit against Jimmy Swaggart and his minions and associates in 1987 was precisely which side Judge Richard Ganucheau would take in the matter. He was closely aligned by society if not by business and politics to many of the high-dollar silk-stocking law firms of the Crescent City; and while he had a reputation for fair-minded adjudication, there was no doubt that he cast a narrow eye on a "redneck" and an "Okie" legal team taking on the best and brightest among New Orleans' mouthpieces.

In a manner of speaking, trial judges function much in the same way as umpires in baseball. Often a batter will assume a pitch is ball four, drop his bat, and start trotting down the first-base line, only to hear the umpire call "strike" before he's taken two steps. The ball might have been a foot outside or over his head or a dirt-ball bouncer that slid by the catcher; but the umpire wants to let the batter know that he, not the player, calls the balls and strikes, he is in charge of the game. He doesn't like being shown up.

Judge Ganucheau may well have felt that we out of town lawyers were attempting to call the balls and strikes in his court, that the appeals and subsequent overturning of his rulings might have "shown him up."

However, there was no way to know for sure, not until we walked in to begin the actual trial.

Fortunately, though, we never had to find out. In late 1990 or possibly early 1991, the State Supreme Court reassigned the case to an ad-hoc judge, His Honor, Julian Bailes. Judge Bailes was from the middle Louisiana city of Natchitoches, one of the oldest and most graceful Old South communities in the state. He was by no means connected either to the New Orleans or to the Baton Rouge legal establishment. And he was not susceptible to political pressure from anyone.

At age seventy-six, Bailes was a lanky, silver-haired gentleman who disdained the frippery and flamboyance of the Yuppie attorney; he wore modest but tasteful clothing and drove a Ford pickup truck. Retired from the bench, he was a veteran of World War II, an outspoken, God-fearing, Anglo-Saxon conservative. He was never shy with his opinions and openly clung to old fashioned values; it was rumored that he left the Episcopal Church because they had allowed homosexuals in the ministry. Bailes was father to five children, nine grandchildren, and five great-grandchildren. During the course of the trial, he often invited members of his family to attend.

It was apparent that Judge Bailes was not a publicity seeker. He was appointed by the Louisiana Supreme Court to preside over this controversial suit; it may well be that he was appointed *because* he was not a publicity seeker. Since his retirement in 1972, Bailes had been appointed by the Louisiana Supreme Court in several cases. He had served as Natchitoches City Court Judge for twenty-three years and had been a District Court Judge for Red River and Natchitoches parishes in Louisiana.

• PART FOUR •
ARMAGEDDON

"Are ye not then partial in yourselves, and are become judges of evil thoughts?"

—The General Epistle of James, 2:4

• CHAPTER SIXTEEN •
OPENING PRAYERS

"For this *is* a heinous crime; yea, it *is* an iniquity *to be punished by* the judges."
—*The Book of Job, 31:11*

After nearly four years of preparation, legal wrangling, study, investigation, and interrogation of witnesses and defendants, the trial date, July 8, 1991, finally arrived. The legal team for Marvin Gorman had worked hard and we believed that we were as well-prepared as we could be. We held slight hope that Swaggart would realize that he had no solid grounds for defense and would offer a settlement, but we grossly underestimated the man's capacity for self-delusion, for profound arrogance. Defense counsel also seemed confident and wanted to take us to task, sometimes, it seemed, merely for bothering them with such niggling matters.

Because of their attitude throughout the course of preparation for trial, I had strong doubts that either Jimmy or Frances Swaggart would appear on the first day of trial. I suspected their strategy would be to display Swaggart as a man too busy, too otherwise occupied, to be troubled with a court appearance until he absolutely had to. I was wrong.

Later, it would occur to me that Swaggart's monstrous ego would feed hungrily on the notion of sitting in a room jammed with people and the press, all devoted to discussing what he said and what he meant by what he said. He wouldn't have missed it for anything.

Thus, while we watched from our twentieth-floor office of the Energy Center, the Swaggart entourage arrived and made a great show of entering the courthouse. Unfortunately, the media had not yet appeared. We timed our entrance better.

Marvin Gorman led our group into the building pushing Tomy Frasier in his wheelchair just ahead of the media. I walked a flank

187

position at Frasier's side; and we both fired remarks and fielded questions from the press, hoping to start something in advance of the formal proceedings. Virginia Gorman stayed close to her husband, holding his hand. As per Frasier's instructions, neither spoke to reporters or answered any questions. Our party was completed by Steve Hickman, Milo Nickel, Stone and Atkins, and our paralegals and secretaries. Compared to the army of attorneys in the Swaggart party, we presented a compact, efficient-looking group.

Swaggart, in the meantime, stopped outside the courtroom and allowed the cameras and microphones to find him; he had already given a speech and was inside by the time we arrived at the courtroom's doors.

In some cases, the presiding judge designates on which side of the courtroom the parties should sit, but in this case, Judge Bailes did not do so. Thus, Atkins sent his associate, Bruce Harris, to the courthouse at 6:30 A.M. to hold five seats closest to the jury box. For the next ten weeks, we continued to occupy the best seats in the courtroom. We all came in and waited until the curtain rose on Act One of The Only Show in Town.

The consensus among our legal team was that I would be the primary spokesperson for the plaintiff. I would handle opening and closing statements and almost all of the direct examination of witnesses. Nickel agreed to handle our two damage experts, Hickman would conduct the cross-examination of the defense's expert witnesses, and I would cross-examine all other defense witnesses.

We wanted Stone and Atkins to have a significant and visible role in the case, so the jury would not have the impression that they were merely present as token minorities. Thus, Atkins was assigned to examine David Adler, trustee for Gorman's bankrupt estate, who was technically the party plaintiff to the suit, but whose testimony would turn out to be of little significance. Stone, on the other hand, would question Mrs. Gorman, whose testimony we believed would be most vital to our case. By choosing Atkins to handle Adler, he would not need to review all of the depositions taken in the last four years before his association in the case. As for Stone, we planned on preparing a script for Virginia Gorman to closely control her testimony. If things went awry in cross-examination, I or Frasier or even Hickman could handle the re-direct. About three weeks into the trial, though, Stone decided to run for a State Senate position in Baton Rouge. He felt that he needed to keep a lower profile during the trial; therefore, Frasier agreed to question Mrs. Gorman on direct examination.

Known as *voir dire* in legal parlance, jury selection in a civil suit can often be the most tedious and frustrating part of the entire trial. Inasmuch as this case had been highly publicized and enjoyed sensationalist tabloid-style publicity, we anticipated a lively process. The sensational and sexual nature of the charges laid against Gorman by Swaggart's attacks, plus the anticipated revelation of Swaggart's consorting with a prostitute promised an entertaining sequence of questions and answers between opposing counsel and prospective jurors.

Unfortunately, Swaggart's lawyers successfully obtained a ruling from Judge Bailes that Swaggart's escapades with prostitutes on Airline Highway or anywhere else were not relevant to the case; hence, we couldn't inquire into his sexual improprieties when we called him as a witness.

We, of course, argued that Jimmy Swaggart's peccadillos were directly relevant to his veracity and credibility, that the primary issue in the case was not Marvin Gorman's alleged pattern of immorality, but rather was the question of Swaggart's motive in defaming him. In short, Swaggart was alleging that Gorman was engaging in sexual activity that was, on the face of it, far less provocative and outrageous than Swaggart's own activities.

Unfortunately there is a Rule of Evidence that excludes any testimony or evidence that alludes to a compromise. The Swaggart defendants argued that the meetings between the Gorman family and the Swaggart family, as well as Gorman and Swaggart's conversation on Airline Highway following their encounter at the Travel Inn, contained evidence of compromise. We understood the court's reasoning (although disagreed) as to why Swaggart's sexual activity was not relevant to Gorman's case of defamation; however, we had a problem with the court's rationale on excluding conversations between Gorman and Swaggart on Airline Highway and the Swaggart mansion.

We lost the argument, nevertheless. The facts of Swaggart's proclivity for prostitutes, vulnerable housewives, young girls, and other bizarre sexual deviation would not become part of the court record, and we would not even be permitted to subtly remind the jury of those facts by addressing the Gorman-Swaggart conversations on Airline Highway or later in Baton Rouge.

Even so, Swaggart was being tried for alleging without foundation or truth that Gorman enjoyed immoral and untoward sexual activities, and every potential juror—indeed almost every person in the country—had in fact watched television and read about Swaggart's dalliances. This meant that during *voir dire,* defense counsel had to address Swaggart's reputation, both in the long term as well as his more recent history in order to determine a potential juror's potential prejudices about matters religious versus matters sexual.

Thus, Phil Wittmann, lead counsel for Jimmy Swaggart, asked one prospective juror after another if he or she had seen the CNN specials or television news programs about Swaggart, read newspaper articles about Swaggart, or whether they read *Playboy* or *Penthouse* magazines or any other magazine interviewing "the woman" (Debra Murphree) with whom Swaggart had allegedly consorted on Airline Highway. Wittmann and his colleagues, Wayne Lee and Denise Pilié, also asked each juror, one by one, about their religious beliefs and whether those beliefs would have a bearing on their position on the case.

We also were concerned with jurors' religious beliefs, but when I leaned over to Frasier during his *voir dire* of one prospective juror and suggested that he ask about the person's personal faith, he responded loud enough for the juror and half the courtroom to hear, "Let those sons of bitches insult her."

One thing we noted early was that most of those empaneled for jury selection were enthusiastic, even eager to serve on this case. When asked if they could put aside any material they had read or seen on television about Jimmy Swaggart and judge this case solely upon the facts presented at trial and the law as instructed by the judge, all but a few said yes. In ninety-nine percent of all jury trials, this is an "easy out" for any potential juror who does not want to serve. In this case, though, those who did not want to serve on the jury sent a clear message to the lawyers, forcing us to be more concerned over those who did.

One lady, for example, when asked about Gorman and Jimmy Swaggart, made the statement that she had formed preconceived opinions; when asked what those might be, she said she thought that Gorman and Swaggart were nothing more than "two rattlesnakes in a box fighting it out." As it happened, such opinions tended to be more widespread than not among the jurors as well as abroad in the general public. Although we on the legal team were convinced of Gorman's innocence, his veracity, and his personal integrity, there were hundreds of thousands, possibly millions who saw him as being no different from or better than Swaggart: charlatans and mountebanks both, men with huge appetites for riches, power, and money—and sex.

One of the strategical moves we made early in the process was hiring Allan Campo, a litigation consultant from Lafayette, Louisiana. Campo had assisted me in picking a jury in Opelousas, Louisiana, in early 1991 in a case where liability was tenuous; but my client still received a verdict for $750,000. I credited Campo's exceptional skills in linguistics and perception of character with playing a large part in that trial; in fact, I often referred to him as "the guru." We hoped that Campo's unique abilities would give us something of an edge.

Campo spent days with our clients. Particularly, he visited extensively with Marvin and Virginia Gorman. Campo believed that the key to a victory would be Virginia's testimony, as she would serve as a human polygraph for Marvin. If she took the stand and said Marvin had been a loving, compassionate man all those years, and that she understood that he had made a mistake, but that she believed God had forgiven him and knew she had forgiven him, then Campo believed that the jury was also going to forgive Gorman and focus on the meanness of Jimmy Swaggart.

Naturally, Campo's input on jury selection was an important factor as we winnowed our choices from the overall panel. After six days of questioning, we had compiled an extensive list of jurors with a personal biographical sketch for each. We had a weekend to study the data and created a priority list: jurors who were "primary strikes," "secondary strikes," and a list of those we would like to have in the jury box under any circumstances.

One of the jurors who was an absolute necessity was Renita Scott, a young black female who worked at the jewelry counter at Macy's Department Store. Married to a Postal Service employee, Scott was an attractive and well-spoken candidate. But our principal reason for favoring her was that she held a bachelor's degree in Psychology. Swaggart had repeatedly opined over the years that psychologists were "of the devil" and unscriptural. We knew that educated jurors would be offended by this attitude; having a juror with a degree in psychology would be a blessing.

During *voir dire*, Swaggart's counsel asked Scott if she would be offended by the fact that evidence would show that Marvin Gorman had an extramarital affair. She responded by saying it would not, that she would judge the case based upon the facts and the merits of the evidence. As a jewelry salesperson at Macy's, she added, she knew that many of her customers were married men and that the jewelry they purchased was going to persons other than their wives. She "had to be discreet."

The minute Scott made that statement, I didn't care what any of my associates said. I wanted Scott on that jury at all costs. She had *damages* written across her forehead.

Because of the size of the case and the number of parties involved, the court had awarded each side ten juror challenges. Defense counsel had to share theirs among almost twenty lawyers. We, on the other hand, were in a much better position with our single client. Generally, we sought to empanel a predominantly African-American, Roman Catholic, female jury. We succeeded better than we ever hoped.

The seated jury consisted of ten women, two men; nine were black, and five were practicing Roman Catholics. The majority held college degrees. There was no question that it was a plaintiff's jury, particularly for this type of case.

The only juror Campo and I disagreed about was Juror 12, Brian Niehart. He was a single, white male who worked as a staff writer for the president of Tulane University and had been a member of the Church of Christ until he was sixteen. I feared that his Campbellite background might unduly sway him away from Gorman's position, particularly because adultery, even one instance, was an anathema to most members of the Church of Christ. Niehart also appeared completely disinterested in the case and seemed willing to serve because he had nothing better to do.

Another appealing juror, because of her outward display of liveliness, was Kimberly Veal, a twenty-year-old Wal-Mart employee. A single and remarkably vivacious young adult, her enthusiasm was often pronounced. After the trial, we discovered that her extroverted personality was enhanced by a remarkable intelligence and a certain sly ability; she emerged as the jury's leader during deliberations.

The jury was seated on Tuesday, July 16; the plaintiff's attorneys were to begin their opening statements on Wednesday morning. My wife, Beth, drove to New Orleans to be with me over the weekend and stayed until I completed opening statements. That I was nervous to the point of distraction was plain. I was about to make the boldest opening statement of my career. It had to catch hold of that jury and keep their attention for the next six weeks or more; and I had to convince them that Marvin Gorman was a man who had been viciously and deliberately wronged by one of the most powerful conspiracies ever to emerge in modern organized religion. I could hardly sleep the night before I was to open the trial.

I knew I should have felt more confident than I did. I had come a long way in my profession during the past four years. My practice with David Dwight had grown, and I had tried and won several important cases. I had turned much of my work recently over to my brother, Matt, focusing completely on this sensational case. I was never sure whether my labor on Gorman's behalf was a distraction from or an inspiration for my other work, but the important point was that I had a fine track record in court, and I was no stranger to serious litigation.

Moreover, I knew this case better than I knew any I had ever tried. I had taken most of the depositions over the years, had written the majority of the briefs; and except for help I received from my brother Matt while he was in law school, and Nickel after he became associated with my firm, I was more responsible than anyone for the preparation and gathering of documentation and evidence. I cannot think of any trial in my career for which I had been better prepared.

On Wednesday morning, dressed in my good-luck suit, I took a deep breath and readied myself. We left the Energy Center and proceeded to the courthouse across the street; Beth held my hand. I had been in court before, many times, I had made many opening statements; but somehow I could not shake the feeling that I was about to cross a significant professional line. In another way, I felt like a child being taken to his first day of school.

The courtroom was jammed, and all involved parties were present. Observers had to take a ticket to be admitted into the courtroom. The only people who had guaranteed admissions were those suing and being sued, their attorneys, and their staffs; Beth had a staff ticket, so she would be assured a seat.

Early on in the case, Frasier and I found ourselves discussing the short story, "The Devil and Daniel Webster" by Stephen Vincent Benét, a piece commonly anthologized in grammar school readers. We discovered that we both identified with Daniel Webster, for he had one of the most difficult cases to ever to go trial. We saw ourselves as facing similarly long odds, and we gave ourselves a one in three chance of winning. Fortunately, unlike Webster in the story, we did not have a bunch of demons sitting on the jury; rather, we were to present our arguments before a well-chosen group of attentive, educated individuals from the community of Orleans Parish. We hoped the demons, in their eyes, would be at the defendant's table. At the same time, we kept the legendary lawyer Webster in mind as we approached the bar to try Jimmy Swaggart and the Assembly of God establishment that stood, at least officially, behind him.

Without a note, I walked in front of the jury box and began outlining what we intended to prove. I began with an account of Gorman's professional life as a minister. I pointed out the success he had had, not only since arriving in New Orleans, but beforehand, when he began working in a small, rural church in Arkansas. I then noted his more recent expansions and successes while minister of the First Assembly of God in New Orleans, mentioned his television ministry, his support of missionary work, and then illustrated the respect he enjoyed within the greater body of his denomination by his nomination as General Superintendent of the Assemblies of God, the highest office in the church's national organization.

That nomination, I argued, was the beginning in what would become a turbulent series of ritualistic and carefully planned attacks on Marvin Gorman. In August 1985, I pointed out, Gorman stood before hundreds of fellow ministers at the General Council meeting in San Antonio. He was about to enter the highest tier of offices in his denomination as a most favorite son of the elders of his church. Then, suddenly and inexplicably, after the first round of balloting, he withdrew his name from the ballot sheet. Gossip about his supposed affairs was being actively circulated from the Swaggart camp, and Gorman, to avoid the embarrassment of defeat in the election, decided to withdraw until things could be straightened out.

I then turned to the case at hand. I admitted that Gorman had committed an act of adultery in 1978 and had never publicly disclosed it. It was Gorman's view, I asserted, that God had forgiven him and the sin was "under the blood of Jesus," in accordance with his faith and with the doctrine of his church. Be that as it may, I continued, Jimmy Swaggart—and for reasons that were not entirely clear, Michael Indest—learned of this singular indiscretion and turned it into an opportunity to destroy Marvin Gorman and his nonprofit corporation and charitable organization, Marvin Gorman Ministries.

I told the jury that we would prove that Swaggart had accused Gorman of having not merely one but hundreds of affairs, of misappropriating monies from his church, of transforming himself into an evil spirit, of fathering an illegitimate child, even of being connected to the Mafia and sleeping with Mafia boss Carlos Marcello's wife. I then began to explore damages, arguing that defendants' unfounded

194

accusations forced Gorman and Marvin Gorman Ministries into bankruptcy. I asserted that they should be required to pay dearly in hopes that Gorman and his bankrupt enterprise's creditors could be satisfied.

When I began speaking, I had the jitters and tremors in my voice, but as I warmed to my subject, my nerves calmed and my tone became more confident. I spoke for a full sixty minutes, then sat down, feeling I had been at least thorough if not effective.

Milo Nickel, who had tried several other cases with me, looked up and told me that was the best statement he had ever heard me make. I felt more confident.

Actually, there were two complaints about my opening statement. One came from Beth, who was seated at the back of the courtroom and was unable to hear me clearly because of noise coming from other people. This led me to speak louder and more articulately when addressing the court; I wanted to make certain that the press could understand every word of the trial.

Beth was also bothered by a comment she overheard from one of Wittmann's female acquaintances in the corridor. The gist of the comment was that she could not understand why a man like Marvin Gorman would hire a young "country" lawyer from Lake Charles to represent him.

Rather than upsetting me, this comment became a standing joke among our legal team over the next nine weeks. It actually fired me up, and it confirmed our notion that our silk-stocking opponents had seriously underestimated us. Underestimating the quality and preparation of opposing counsel can be a fatal mistake in any trial; when combined with Swaggart's innate arrogance and demonstrated feelings of superiority, it could spell disaster for the entire defense counsel.

The second complaint was actually more interesting and not without a certain implied threat to me and the rest of our legal team. This had to do with my emphasis of the name *Carlos Marcello* and use of the word *Mafia*, when I outlined the numerous nefarious rumors spread by Swaggart about Gorman's alleged sexual escapades.

Marcello was a New Orleans character of long standing criminal reputation and was well-known to law enforcement agencies throughout the country. It was widely assumed, if not known, that he was a part of organized crime in New Orleans and was well connected throughout the United States. He had been subject of many books, including theories that he was involved in the John F. Kennedy assassination.

In the late 1970s, Carlos Marcello had been convicted of tax evasion and sentenced to the federal penitentiary in Fort Worth, Texas. Prior to Marcello's conviction, Gorman ministered to and counseled with Marcello's daughter, daughter-in-law, and members of his family who attended his church. As a gesture of gratitude, Marcello gave Gorman an option on a large tract of property located on the West Bank in Orleans Parish, which Gorman valued in excess of four hundred thousand dollars on his financial statement. It was Gorman's plan to build a school, drug rehabilitation center, nursing home, and other facilities to further his ministry at this location. Following Marcello's conviction, though, Gorman decided not to pursue financing to exercise the option and allowed it to expire.

At the request of Marcello's daughter, Gorman traveled to Fort Worth to visit and counsel with the Mafia boss on several occasions. As I had learned from experience during our previous association, Gorman was no stranger to penitentiaries, or to visiting supposedly prominent individuals incarcerated in them. Marvin witnessed to Marcello, prayed for him, corresponded with him, and offered him spiritual support. Further, the Gorman family and the congregation of the church treated Marcello's daughter and grandchildren as part of the church family.

Gorman's direct connection to Marcello was common knowledge among the leaders, as well as the parishioners of the First Assembly of God and Marvin Gorman Ministries. But when the gossipmongers cut loose and more or less went public with the rumors of Gorman's supposed sexual activities, in the summer and fall of 1986, they included members of Marcello's family among Gorman's supposed partners in embezzlement and sexual activity. This added a unique twist to Gorman's purported misbehavior. Specifically, the rumors accused Gorman of having Mafia connections, and, ludicrous as it may seem, of sleeping with Carlos Marcello's wife, a lady who was more than eighty years of age.

It was absurd to believe that if Gorman had mob connections he would allow himself to be so publicly embarrassed and financially ruined by any individual not so aligned, especially one of Swaggart's nature. In other words, if Gorman *did* have a pipeline to the Mafia, Swaggart could have been fairly easily silenced by Marcello's and the mob's obvious means at hand. But it was patently ridiculous to suggest that Gorman, a man of early middle-age, could find sexual attraction in an octogenarian whose husband was serving time.

Lynda Savage, Lynette Goux, and the other women associated with Gorman by Swaggart's rumors were, at least, young, attractive women

196

with a certain appeal to any adult male. The suggestion that Gorman was courting lonely old women and seeking their sexual favors spun the entire Swaggart rumor mill into a vortex of farce. My purpose in mentioning it in the opening statement was to illustrate just how far Swaggart and his minions were prepared to go to defame Gorman's character. No story seemed too outlandish, no lie too far from reasonableness, for them to invent and repeat.

The next day at the office, however, I had a phone message from an attorney who indicated that he represented Carlos Marcello. Marcello, as it happens, had been released from the penitentiary just prior to the trial and had returned to reside with his family in New Orleans. He obviously learned through the press or by word of mouth that his name was being bandied about by this "country lawyer," and he was less than pleased.

I did not return the call, but instead discussed it with Nickel and Curklin; we agreed Frasier should handle this matter. Frasier had defended criminals, had been indicted and tried himself, and was very much a politician. He would know how to handle the situation.

For the first time in the case, I had a queasy feeling in my stomach. In short, I was afraid. It was one thing to take on Swaggart and his faux religious position, to deal with the likes of Bill Treeby and false fire alarms and possible listening devices. I could even handle being followed around by a private eye. But the Mafia was a whole different matter. I had a wife and three children at home, and I was starting to wonder why the hell I wasn't there with them.

The next afternoon, the man called again and asked to speak to someone from the plaintiff's legal team. Atkins received the message from his secretary, then passed it to me, and I handed it over to Frasier. He never thought twice about it. He returned the call immediately. The attorney on the other end asked Frasier if it was at all possible for us to keep the Marcello family's name out of court. Frasier replied that Marvin Gorman loved and respected the Marcello family, but that the rumors touching on Mrs. Marcello and Gorman were started by Phil Wittmann's clients; if Mr. Marcello or anyone else had a complaint about the family's name being trotted out in court, he should take it up with them.

As legal counsel for Gorman, he went on, we were doing nothing more than prosecuting our client's case, which, of course, we would be more than happy to cease doing—if the defendants would admit that what they had said was a lie and offer a reasonable and generous settlement. Otherwise, Frasier noted, there was nothing he could do to prevent the mentioning of the Marcello family name in court.

Marcello's attorney seemed to accept Frasier's position, but the next day in court, Wittmann requested a bench conference with Judge Bailes. Wittmann stated that he had received a call from Marcello's lawyer about the use of the family's name in court, particularly with reference to the word *Mafia*; he did not indicate whether or not he knew that we had received a call. But it was obvious that Wittmann was concerned.

Judge Bailes also seemed disturbed; he instructed me not to mention the word *Mafia* or the name *Marcello* any further during the course of the proceedings. He added that this was a reasonable directive, since "we all knew that the '*Mafioso*' or Mafia was fiction."

I immediately took issue with the judge. I told him that the allegations linking Gorman to the Marcello family had been made by the defendants and were an important part of our case of defamation; we had originally pled it, and we intended to prove at trial that Swaggart and his associates had said it. I argued that we were entitled to use both the word and the names, since Swaggart and his friends had used them to smear Gorman.

I also advised the court to take judicial notice of the fact that the Mafia was a name commonly denoted to mean organized crime both in the United States and abroad; at the same time, the name *Marcello* had been connected, not only in the press but also in a court of law, with organized crime; in fact, Carlos Marcello was a convicted felon.

Judge Bailes informed me that I was at least partly wrong, that the Mafia was fiction, a product of novels, films, and television. I then decided that it would be Noah, not Daniel Webster who would prove inspirational to our case. I went to the attorneys' table, and pulled out *Webster's Dictionary*. I turned to the word *Mafia* and read the second acceptable definition to the court:

> Mafia . . . 2. An international criminal organization active, especially in Italy and the United States, since the late nineteenth century.

Judge Bailes listened, then looked at all counsel and said, "Well, if *Webster's* has defined the word *Mafia*, then obviously it is not a fiction." He instructed us to proceed accordingly. However, he asked us to use *X* and *Y* in place of Carlos Marcello's name.

Although I felt we had won something of a victory in this episode, I scrupulously avoided the name *Marcello* from that point on. I did not want to stir up a problem for Gorman outside of the courtroom, more than what he had already experienced. And, to be honest, and speaking as one who most definitely does *not* believe the Mafia is a fiction—*Webster's* definition or no *Webster's* definition—I saw no reason to invite trouble for any of us, then or later.

Still, I received a lot of pleasure in watching Wittmann's nervous reaction to the call from Marcello's attorney. Quite obviously, defense counsel was also of the opinion that the Mafia was no fiction; nor was it to be trifled with by the likes of Jimmy Swaggart or his distinguished attorneys.

In any event, the preliminaries were over, the ground rules established. We were ready at last to expose Jimmy Swaggart for what he was.

• CHAPTER SEVENTEEN •
GIVE ME A WITNESS

"I have no greater joy than to hear that my children walk
in truth."
—The Third Epistle of John, 3:4

We decided to call to the stand all the individual defendants and co-
conspirators in our portion of the case including Jimmy Swaggart,
Frances Swaggart, Bill Treeby, Michael Indest, Cecil Janway, Allan
McDonnel and Tom Miller. In all, plaintiff's counsel would consume
eight of the ten weeks of the trial in presenting our case. Of the forty-two
witnesses called, indeed, we would summon more than thirty of them,
approximately ten of whom appeared by deposition. Deposition
testimony is offered by someone merely sitting on the stand and reading
the testimony given by the witness outside the courtroom. Two of the key
witnesses, David and Lynda Savage, testified by video tape.

Prior to going to trial, Judge Bailes had ordered us to provide the
names of witnesses to defense counsel the day before each was called.
Thus, for several days before the trial, we had sorted through stack after
stack of videotaped interviews and depositions, trying to decide who
would be the first witness we would call. It was by no means an automatic
decision. We wanted to present our witnesses in an order that would allow
us to build to something of a climax for the jury; in other words, what we
hoped to do was establish a slow but developing pattern of deceit, moving
from the minor functionaries in the conspiracy we perceived, to the head
of the "snake" himself: Jimmy Swaggart.

I had always anticipated calling Michael Indest as our first witness,
since it seemed that Indest was not only the conduit through which the
majority of Swaggart-generated lies and rumors about Gorman passed, he
was also a principal player in the events of July 1986 as they unfolded.

Additionally, the deeper we delved into the workings of Swaggart's
movement against Gorman, the more obvious it became that Swaggart's
modus operandi was seldom to expose himself as a direct source of

200

rumors or lies; rather, he preferred to appear as one who had merely heard such things and was reacting to them. Clearly, his method was to make use of such minions as Indest as "stalking horses," individuals who actually started and spread the rumors until they were so widely disseminated that Swaggart could safely latch onto them and make use of them in a direct and damaging way.

Further, it was obvious to us that Indest was something of a Swaggart operative in New Orleans, connecting Swaggart to such men as Tom Miller and working with Bill Treeby and to connect Swaggart to Alan McDonnel and other powerful members of the Assembly of God community.

If we were going to "seek out the Devil," as Frasier put it on the day we filed suit back in 1987, then we would be wise to first expose his chief proxy, his Mephistopheles, as it were, Michael Indest. It thus made sense from both a logical and a chronological standpoint to begin our dismantlement of the conspiracy with him.

But even so, I wasn't entirely certain that this was the wisest move, at least from a legal standpoint. During the two weeks of preparation immediately before the trial, the entire legal team reviewed Indest's depositions, trying to evaluate his worth as a lead-off witness. There was no clear consensus.

Indest was now, and had been throughout this ordeal, the pastor of the Lakeview Christian Center in New Orleans. He had followed Swaggart out of the Assemblies of God in 1988, but he had maintained his pastorate by virtue of his connections with Swaggart Ministries. The Lakeview Christian Center was a small church, attended by Bill Treeby and others who had close Swaggart associations. Treeby also sat on the Board of Directors there and was responsible for hiring Indest to pastor the church in the first place. Their friendship and professional connection was one of long duration.

Although Indest's insurance company, USF&G, had settled with Gorman in May, 1986, he was still a principal witness in the case. It was also our contention that he was at the heart of the conspiracy to destroy Gorman's reputation, just as it was a growing belief among our team that he had a personal motivation as well as a professional one.

Prior to the trial, Indest frequented the halls of the courthouse, button-holing reporters and bragging that we had backed off of suing him and had agreed to settle. He noted that he had signed a release and that he and several others had been dismissed from the suit, implying that we admitted that there was no liability. Of course he failed to mention that USF&G had paid us a substantial sum of money just short of seven figures to release the company and their insureds.

There was no question in our minds that Indest was one of the most vocal enemies Gorman had. He had not only spread the rumors about Gorman, we knew from our investigation that he had authored chronologies about Gorman and Lynda Savage as well as Gorman and other women. Indest also implied in his writings that Gorman had fathered Lynda Savage's third child. In order to prove his role as co-conspirator, we needed to establish his motive for harming Gorman. The most obvious impetus was jealousy.

After Indest finished high school, he became a wine salesman; he subsequently converted to the Assembly of God faith and attended the Kenner Assembly of God, where David Savage was pastor. At some point in these years, Indest decided to go to Bible College, very possibly with the encouragement of David and Lynda Savage. Indest, his wife Christy and their children were close friends of the Savages.

Exactly what relationship, apart from the obvious platonic friendship, that may have existed between Michael Indest and Lynda Savage remains speculative; however, given the statements and subsequent testimony we had from Paul Dunn about Savage's sexual appetites, it seems reasonable to assume that at the very least, Indest was aware of her potential for indiscretion with other men.

In any event, it was doubtless "strange" that in the summer of 1986 Savage allegedly chose to stop by Indest's house and make to him her elaborate confession of all her extramarital affairs, including and especially the one with Marvin Gorman. Savage contended that she had stopped by Indest's house to return a borrowed guitar, and that the confession was more or less spontaneous. It struck us that since the other two confessions she made about her marital infidelities were to two men with whom she was sexually involved—Marvin Gorman and Paul Dunn—it seemed logical to assume that Indest's interest might have been of the same ilk. Regardless, it was hard for us to imagine her going to Indest's home and telling him the details of her sexual activities while Indest's wife and children were in the other room.

Nevertheless, our argument of jealousy as a motive could only suggest a relationship may have existed between Savage and Indest, and that when he discovered her continuing crush on Gorman, he could not abide it and took action to eliminate his competition for Savage's affections.

Reasonable argument for this could also be made when we considered that, apart from the damage done to Marvin Gorman by Indest's revelation of Savage's confessions, it had also harmed her and her husband, supposedly Indest's close friends. Even if Savage had felt sufficiently spurned by Gorman to sacrifice her reputation in an effort to harm him, it would seem that, as a minister and counsellor, Indest's more compassionate and considerate position would have been to urge silence on her, to try to handle the matter personally and confidentially without harming anyone's public image.

Although no specific motive was obvious enough to pin down in a concrete way, there was little question that Indest's actions against Gorman from the summer of 1986 on had been both vindictive and vitriolic; it was also obvious that Lynda and David Savage had paid a high price themselves. We had trouble accepting the idea that such vituperation as Indest exhibited was spurred on by nothing more than religious zeal. It seemed obvious to us that he had a personal axe to grind with Gorman, and we believed the wheel that sharpened the axe was none other than Lynda Savage herself.

A far more demonstrable possibility, though, was the question of Indest's jealousy of Gorman as a rival minister in his own New Orleans backyard. Indest was a "little duck on a little pond" and with Gorman "swimming around" nearby, there seemed to be no possibility for Indest to grow, at least by honest means. As a result, we believed, Indest endeared himself to the biggest duck of all, Jimmy Swaggart, and began running with his Baton Rouge-based crowd. By delivering Gorman's head, as it were, to Swaggart, Indest eliminated his chief rival in religion, if nothing else, and was now the "only duck" of any size on the New Orleans water, next to his mentor and sponsor, Swaggart.

Three days before trial, we still had not decided who would be our first witness–the others still weren't comfortable with my idea of leading off with Indest. Atkins, Campo, and Nickel and I went over and over Indest's deposition tapes, trying to make up our minds. Although Indest would obviously be a difficult witness to approach, particularly at the outset, I argued that he could be made effective. At that point, Frasier wheeled into the room, took one look at the video, and told the bunch of us watching, not to worry so much about the order of witnesses or how they might come off before the jury. "No matter how long you polish a turd," he said, "it will never shine."

This broke us up, but it also put things into perspective. Our first witness would be the Reverend Michael Indest.

It is common within the Assembly of God for members to use the terms "brother" and "sister" as honorifics of direct and indirect address. With this in mind, and given the layered texture of all these alleged and supposed sexual relationships between ministers and other ministers' wives—affairs that crossed individual church boundaries and parish lines, but remaining within what might be termed the "church family"—the notion of incest often came up, at least in a metaphoric sense. This was enhanced during the weeks of trial preparation by Frasier's insistence on referring to Michael Indest as "Michael Incest." I never knew if this was an accidental or deliberate slip of the tongue, but knowing how much of the trial I would be personally conducting, I asked him to stop it. I feared that I or someone else might inadvertently transpose the two names either in the courtroom or while speaking to the press. In spite of my requests, Frasier continued calling Indest, "Incest" until we went to trial.

Sure enough, during my examination of Indest while he was on the stand, I inadvertently called him "Reverend Incest." He caught the reference, may possibly have seen the smirk on Frasier's face behind me, and immediately stood up on the witness stand and shouted, "Judge, did you hear what he called me? Did you hear what he called me?" Judge Bailes told him to sit down and answer the question.

Obviously, Judge Bailes did not hear the slip of the tongue—or perhaps he did. In any case, the court reporter did not hear it, as it did not appear in the trial transcript. (It did, however, appear in the *Times Picayune* the next morning.) The fallout of the incident was actually in our favor. Bailes noted Indest's reaction and ruled that he was a hostile witness and gave me permission to "lead"—that is, to suggest the answers I wanted in the phrasing of my questions—from that point on. Whether Frasier suspected that Indest would have such a explosive and costly reaction to an inadvertent slip of the tongue or not, I never knew. But it worked out handily for us.

I was growing more and more satisfied with the decision to lead off with Indest. My confidence was affirmed to some extent, when about five minutes before giving my opening statement, an attorney with Jack Martzell's law firm handed me a letter, indicating that they now represented Michael Indest and that if I said anything in the course of the trial that in anyway maligned their client, I would be sued personally.

This came as no particular surprise. One of the Swaggart groupies was a lawyer who went by the sobriquet of Colonel Weber. Before the trial, but after we settled with Alan McDonnel and his underwriters and some of the others, McDonnel hired Weber to sue us for malicious prosecution. I referred the case to a friend of mine, John Litchfield, who removed the suit to Federal Court, where it was subsequently dismissed.

Nevertheless, the Colonel made repeated appearances in the courtroom in an effort to intervene and have a voice in the trial on the merits of the case at hand. It was only after Judge Bailes threatened to hold him in contempt that he quit coming to the courtroom.

Thus, the threat by Martzell's partner caused Frasier and me little worry. I figured there would be a lot of lawsuits flying around once this case was decided.

Michael Indest

Many of our trial exhibits were offered through the testimony of Michael Indest. It seemed that he had not only taken pleasure in summarizing the events leading up to the resignation and dismissal of

Marvin Gorman but chose to argue with the Assembly of God officials over what he believed to be inadequate punishment of Marvin Gorman. We offered most of our documents into evidence and we certainly laid the foundation to prove a conspiracy.

Indest was adamant that Lynda Savage did not tell him that she had an affair with Gorman, but rather God did. Furthermore, he reiterated that all of his actions were taken in furtherance of Scripture and it was his duty to tell the entire church, i.e. the Christian world, of Marvin Gorman's sin.

After the trial, I learned that the majority of the jury made up their minds on liability after hearing Indest's testimony. The panel took an instantaneous dislike to him and mistrusted everything he said. There was no question that we had made the right decision by calling Indest first. He possibly damaged Swaggart's position more than any other single witness, apart from Swaggart himself.

Andy Harris

Following Indest's testimony, our strategy was to lay the groundwork for demonstrating that the defamation of Gorman's character was the culmination of a well-orchestrated conspiracy that had been going on for quite a while. The conspiracy theory, which I had suggested early on, as far back as 1985, was now becoming central to our whole case, particularly in light of the settlements with the individually named defendants. The problem, once again, was motive.

We needed to establish a reason why Swaggart and his crowd would benefit from the destruction of Marvin Gorman's character and reputation; at the same time, we needed to illustrate that the conspiracy reached well beyond any merely personal pique or dispute between two rival ministers. We had to show, in other words, that Swaggart planned Gorman's downfall early on, and that he systematically organized and enlisted the support of others in his campaign to ruin Gorman's career in order to achieve some concrete, personal advantage.

Accordingly, one of our early witnesses was the Reverend Andy Harris, a twenty-nine-year-old Assembly of God minister and former administrative assistant to Jimmy Swaggart. Harris worked for Swaggart from early in 1986 until early in 1988; he had ghostwritten several of Swaggart's books and had an intimate knowledge of many of the inner workings of Jimmy Swaggart Ministries. He also proved to be an excellent mole inside the Swaggart organization, given his propensity for overhearing conversations relevant to our case.

Harris testified that Swaggart openly longed for national office in the Assemblies of God, and that he was nearly obsessive in his worry about the doings of other ministers, particularly successful televangelists. He said that Swaggart monitored their broadcasts and Arbitron ratings and kept an eye on all their activities.

Harris testified that at one point Swaggart was number one, Robert Schuller was number two, and Oral Roberts was number three on the television scoreboard. It was at this point that Swaggart began speaking out on television and in the press against Roberts and Schuller. Swaggart also worried about Jim Bakker, whose star was rapidly on the rise, particularly because of the growing political activity of Pat Robertson and Jerry Falwell, who were both associated with Bakker's geographical region.

Indeed, Harris's most interesting testimony concerned his overhearing Swaggart calling the Assemblies of God headquarters in Springfield, Missouri, about the Bakker-Hahn affair long before *The Charlotte Observer* broke the story. Harris testified that when the Assistant Superintendent, the Reverend Everett Stenhouse, told Swaggart that they knew about the Bakker matter and did not need Swaggart's help, Swaggart's reply was "Look, Brother Stenhouse, if I hadn't done what I did at General Council for you, Marvin Gorman would be sitting behind your desk right now."

Harris's assertion was that Swaggart begun spreading gossip about Gorman during the 1985 General Council election and forced Gorman to withdraw his name from the ballot. Everett Stenhouse got the job instead. A number of people had been perplexed by Gorman's sudden withdrawal from that election. Without question, Gorman was well-qualified and had more or less been groomed for high office in the Assemblies of God. His education, background, comparative youth, and popularity—particularly among the young—suggested that he was a natural for national administration, unless, of course, something untoward happened to prevent his continued rise in the church. That "something untoward" did happen; and Harris alleged that it was made to happen by Jimmy Swaggart.

According to Harris, Gorman would have been elected to the national office had Swaggart not spread the word Gorman was guilty of a moral failure. Harris stated that Swaggart was overtly ambitious for an office himself; he overheard Donnie Swaggart say that Jimmy also wanted Marvin Gorman's seat as Executive Presbyter. That was the reason for spreading the rumors in San Antonio. Harris added that Donnie Swaggart asked for a list of requirements for the post and sent a letter to members of Swaggart's congregation asking them to attend a meeting to vote for Jimmy Swaggart.

As it turned out, the Reverend Harris offered some of the most enlightening testimony of all the witnesses at trial. He went on to say that he often heard the Swaggarts discussing Gorman, saying that he had slept with hundreds of women. But the most significant point in his testimony was that he was aware of Swaggart's intense jealousy of Gorman's popularity, not only among the rank and file of the Assemblies of God, but also among the executive officers. It was now apparent—and on the record for the jury's consideration—that Swaggart considered Gorman to be his chief rival in the church and an impediment to his further advancement; in other words, we had established motive.

In concluding his testimony, Harris repeated that it was general knowledge among the employees of Jimmy Swaggart Ministries from January 1986 through February 1988 that Jimmy Swaggart had evidence that Marvin Gorman had been involved with hundreds of women, although none ever saw any such evidence in any demonstrable form.

During cross-examination, Harris was forced to admit that he had mistakenly stated that Jimmy Swaggart was the source of the rumor that Gorman had hundreds of affairs while in fact it was Donnie Swaggart that had made the statement. Wayne Lee was very effective in pointing out inconsistencies between Harris' testimony in court from that provided in his earlier deposition. Although hesitant, Harris's admitted that most of what he heard at Jimmy Swaggart Ministries about Marvin Gorman was watercooler conversation.

Donald Brankel

When we originally filed our lawsuit in 1987, we named the Reverend Donald Brankel as a defendant. Brankel was an evangelist who had gone to work for Jimmy Swaggart Ministries in February 1986. Shortly after we filed suit, John Hainkel, Brankel's lawyer, contacted us to request a deal that would get Brankel off the hook. We agreed that we would dismiss the Reverend Brankel without prejudice in consideration for his sworn statement. Thus, one afternoon in a New Orleans hotel room, I met with Hainkel and Brankel to take the statement.

Brankel was about five feet eight inches tall, weighed about 250 pounds, and had bright red hair. When he smiled, he looked like a playful gnome or child's doll, but that was deceiving. He had a very strong voice and sweated profusely, and when he spoke, he showed he was the sort of a dynamic Pentecostal preacher who could rattle the rafters, not only in sermon. As it turned out, Brankel was privy to much of the gossip and rumors touching on Gorman. In his statement, Brankel recalled many a conversation with Swaggart and Treeby about Gorman at Ruth Chris's Steakhouse in Baton Rouge, El Chico's Mexican Cafe, or some other restaurant. Why Swaggart and Treeby were so eager to enlist Brankel's support was not clear, but it was immediately apparent to me that Brankel could provide even further evidence to support our claim of conspiracy; we were excited that we could call him as a witness.

Unfortunately, Don Brankel proved as reluctant to testify as he was reluctant to be sued. He spent the next two-and-a-half to three years dodging subpoenas. Ultimately, he was located and served by the defendants' counsel in Arkansas, where they took his deposition.

In that deposition, Brankel substantiated almost all of the allegations that we made in our complaint, including the allegation that Swaggart stated Gorman was connected with the Mafia and had had sex with many women. He also named names of many of the women that were suggested to him by Swaggart, including Vicki Jamison and Beverly Hudson.

Brankel also testified that he heard Treeby state that Gorman had misused funds belonging to the church. He said that he heard Swaggart and Gorman discuss Gorman's having fathered children outside of his marriage, and he remembered that Swaggart told him about the exorcism at Tom Miller's church, where the devil was supposed to have spoken in Gorman's voice.

It seemed that every question the defense attorneys asked Brankel pushed them into a deeper hole. It was difficult for us to believe that they worked so hard to serve him with a subpoena. When Brankel's deposition was read at the trial, it turned out to be some of the most powerful and damaging testimony against Swaggart. And ironically, most of it was gathered by our opponents.

Jonas Robertson

In sharp contrast to the smooth, professional ministers we called to the witness stand—many of whom were the very picture of outward perfection and decorum—one particular witness stood out: Jonas Robertson.

Robertson's story was remarkable. He grew up in New Orleans, the rebellious son of a law enforcement officer. At age sixteen, he lied about his age, joined the Merchant Marine, and went to Vietnam. In the course of that adventure, he became addicted to drugs and returned to New Orleans where he became a "pusher." He was soon arrested and charged with the distribution of cocaine; at that point, for some reason, he elected to attend a church service.

The service Robertson attended happened to be one held at First Assembly of God where Marvin Gorman was preaching. During the service, according to Robertson, he was converted by the Holy Spirit and became a born-again Christian. He also met one of the deacons of First Assembly of God. This individual, as it happened, was also a local assistant district attorney. He saw to it that Robertson's charges were reduced to a misdemeanor.

Within a few years, Robertson committed his life to the ministry and went off to Bible College in Texas. While there, he met the daughter of an Assembly of God minister, and they were soon married. At the time of the trial in 1991, Robertson had three children of his own and had adopted a fourth. He was thirty-five years old, six feet tall, and presented to the jury the picture of good looks and perfect health, with 220 pounds of muscle and a booming voice. In part because of his physical appearance, and in part because of his candid revelation of his background, he exuded integrity from the witness stand.

Robertson testified that he had been an employee of Marvin Gorman Ministries. and worked with the First Assembly of God. He had a French Quarter mission that he called the Granola ministry: he took fruits, nuts, and flakes and combined them to make granola. Jonas was outspoken and convincing. He had a purpose in his life, and he didn't mind sharing it every time he had the chance. He also called Gorman his "Spiritual Daddy" and had great admiration for him.

After Gorman confessed to an act of adultery, Robertson began hearing the many other rumors, which he had trouble believing. This led him to go see Michael Indest. During that meeting, Robertson testified, he came to believe that Gorman had affairs with as many as twenty women. Indest also convinced Robertson that sexual escapades had become a lifestyle for Gorman. The young minister suddenly turned off Gorman, and, in effect, he became an unwitting co-conspirator to defame his Spiritual Daddy.

Robertson stated that he and some friends started their own church on the West Bank in Orleans Parish and disassociated themselves completely from Gorman and his family. This attitude continued until one day in February 1988, when he saw a television program with Jimmy Swaggart weeping and confessing to an unspecified sin and begging for his church's and family's forgiveness.

Taken aback by Swaggart's confession, Robertson made inquiries among friends he had in law enforcement in Orleans Parish and discovered the details of Swaggart's being caught in the motel on Airline Highway. This was obviously a more serious matter than Swaggart's sensational confession led viewers to believe.

Robertson stated that he immediately called Indest and asked, "What's going on with Jimmy?" Michael replied, "Oh, it's nothing. Jimmy's repented and been forgiven, and I know this is no problem because I just went fishing with him."

Robertson was, of course, aware that Gorman had filed suit and accused Indest, Swaggart, and others of defamation and of conspiring to ruin his ministry. He initially believed this was nothing more than a futile gesture on Gorman's part, pitiful really, a kind of sour grapes parting shot at those who had discovered Gorman's secret lifestyle. Now he wasn't so sure. When Indest said Swaggart had been forgiven, something went off in Robertson's head.

He asked Indest, "Well what about Brother Gorman?"

Indest said, "Well, Gorman didn't repent."

Robertson responded, "Gorman didn't repent? You got Jimmy

Swaggart on Airline Highway, not two blocks from Marvin Gorman's church, coming out of a motel room with a two-dollar whore with hair under her armpits and tattoos on her butt, and you're telling me that Jimmy has repented and been forgiven and Marvin hasn't?"

Indest became angry with Robertson, and closed the conversation; but now Robertson was convinced that there was a conspiracy against Gorman. He called Gorman, and asked for a meeting, and Gorman agreed. Robertson begged for his forgiveness and, predictably, if one knew Gorman, he received it.

Robertson told Gorman that he met with Indest in the fall of 1987 and was told that Gorman had had affairs with over twenty women. He also told Gorman about the telephone conversation with Indest. Robertson said he was convinced at that point that the entire matter was about money and nothing else. The lies told about Gorman were designed to do nothing more than bring him and his family into financial ruin and, he believed, to enhance the personal fortune and fame of Jimmy Swaggart.

We knew from our first interview with him that Jonas Robertson would be a prize witness. Unlike some of the other ministers in this case, men who often equivocated, waffled, sidestepped, and generally did everything they could to avoid answering a direct question or volunteering a direct truth, Robertson took a hard-line position on what he believed. There was nothing slick or unnatural about him, nothing affected or put-on. His sincerity came through with every word he spoke.

In his view, Gorman had been defamed, and Indest and Swaggart and others had conspired to ruin him. He had told us he would take the witness stand but would not lie for anybody. He would tell the truth. That was fine with us.

Although Indest was no longer a defendant, we still wanted to prove that he was a deliberate co-conspirator with Swaggart against Gorman. We also were eager for the jury to hear Robertson's testimony about his conversations with Indest. No one outside the legal team was more convinced than Robertson that there had been a conspiracy against Gorman all along; we were content to allow this notion to come directly from a witness—particularly one as impressive as Jonas Robertson—rather than from our own mouths.

The day finally came when Jonas was sworn in and every face was turned toward this handsome young man with light blue eyes. As expected, he was superior on the stand. Unfortunately, much of his testimony was disallowed because it fell under the heading of *hearsay*, and until we established a prima facie case (a presumption that we would prevail) of conspiracy, it could not be used against Swaggart. Additionally, because the judge had disallowed testimony about the

Swaggart-Murphree tryst on Airline Highway, a good deal of what Robertson had to say never came out in court. Thus, Robertson's testimony was limited at this point, but his obvious belief that there was a conspiracy was a valuable tool for us, one we could use to our advantage very soon.

Robertson's testimony concluded on a Thursday. Each Friday, the jury was excused and the judge worked with opposing counsel to prepare for testimony for the following week. On the Friday following Robertson's testimony, I was in our Energy Center offices waiting on portions of the transcript to be delivered by the deputy courtroom clerk, Shaneta. She worked for the ad hoc judge's committee and had been working with Judge Bailes during the trial. We had been asking for daily transcripts from the court reporter in order to oppose the defendants' numerous and constant motions that would be filed in the course of the trial.

That afternoon, when Shaneta arrived with the transcripts, she looked at me and said, "Boy, Jonas was something special! The entire jury was fascinated and most of all the women were attracted." She indicated to me that if there was any way Robertson could be recalled as a witness, it would probably be a smart move. This caused us to redouble our efforts to compel the judge to find a prima facie case of conspiracy in order to recall him.

At last, on August 15, the court did just that. That morning, Judge Bailes excluded all press from the courtroom and sealed the record in order to rule on the question of whether or not we had established a prima facie case of conspiracy. Bailes's preliminary opinion was that he found that we had indeed proved a prima facie case of conspiracy involving a number of parties, including Jimmy Swaggart, Jimmy Swaggart Ministries, Frances Swaggart, Michael Indest, Bill Treeby, and others.

This finding allowed us to recall numerous witnesses to the stand, including Marvin Gorman and Jonas Robertson, who this time was allowed to give details of his conversation with Michael Indest.

Bill Elder

Back in 1987, a local television news personality named Bill Elder had worked hard to secure an interview with Gorman. A reporter for WWL-TV in New Orleans, Elder was in the process of launching his own locally produced news and editorial program, *The Bill Elder Journal*. He was most interested in using Gorman's story as a high-profile promotional device for his new show.

Elder accordingly contacted Gorman and said he was working on a story connected with Gorman's resignation from First Assembly of God; he said he wanted Gorman's input. He had heard the rumors of Gorman's many love affairs and obviously smelled a scandal in the making. At the time, we were rushing to file our petition in the District Court; our original timetable had been moved up because of the revelations of the Jim Bakker scandal and the implied connections between that situation and the Swaggart-Gorman conflict.

Elder was persistent, but we forbade Gorman to speak to him, and later Frasier handled him in the press conference following the filing of our suit. Frazier gave him absolutely nothing he could use either to corroborate or comment on Swaggart's rumored allegations.

Elder decided to proceed with the story anyway and aired it as one of his program's premiere episodes; he secured the most willing assistance of Bill Treeby, Michael Indest, Allan McDonnel and Forrest Hall, Assistant District Superintendent of the Louisiana District of the Assemblies of God in Alexandria, Louisiana. (Hall was also named in the lawsuit, but because he proved marvelously adroit at dodging subpoenas, we never could serve him, and we ultimately dismissed him from the suit because we did not need him as a witness.)

Gorman continued to refuse to participate in Elder's program, but Elder played excerpts from Gorman's television appearance on August 29, 1986, entitled *My Greatest Storm,* wherein Gorman admitted on the air that he had failed. This was also the sermon in which he stated that ninety-five percent of what had been said about him was untrue.

With the help of the Treeby-Miller-McDonnel-Hall cabal, Elder's program finally aired on April 5, 1987. We were told that the program had been substantially edited as a result of the lawsuit, but it was hard to tell what Elder might have left out. Gorman was depicted as a complete charlatan. McDonnel was quoted as saying, "Gorman could sell snowballs to Eskimos in Alaska." Another interviewee was quoted as saying Marvin Gorman was a "Jim Jones, a fake." Virtually no one spoke on Gorman's behalf.

Naturally, then, we were compelled to call Bill Elder as a trial witness. We had already offered as exhibits of evidence an exchange of letters between Treeby and Elder's superior, Joe Duke. This correspondence provided the foundation for questions that were to be asked of the individuals on the television program. We also knew that Elder and Duke had met with Treeby on occasion and that the filming of the interviews took place in the Stone, Pigman law offices. To underscore the connection and the bias, I repeatedly referred to *The Bill Elder Journal* as the "Bill Treeby Journal" during our examination of Elder on the stand.

Under oath, Elder admitted that he was led to believe Gorman had misused funds from church, but he could produce no evidence to support the contention. He also believed that Gorman had preyed on women who came to him for counseling, and that Gorman had had several affairs, through, again, he had no evidence to support such a story. Additionally, Elder admitted that he had learned about Tom Miller conducting an exorcism and casting out a demon that identified itself as Marvin Gorman. Elder said he wanted to get that on his program but could not get anyone to talk about it on camera.

He did interview Forrest Hall on the air, and in that interview Hall stated, "Women should be warned about counseling with Gorman." The overall message of the television broadcast was that Gorman was a sexual predator, taking advantage of women who came to him for counseling, and that the public should be warned. *The Bill Elder Journal* played to approximately 100,000 viewers in more than 39,000 homes from New Orleans to Biloxi, Mississippi.

This program probably had a more harmful effect on Marvin Gorman than anything else that was said about him or done to him. It not only cemented the defamatory remarks generated by Swaggart and Indest in the minds of Gorman's followers and parishioners, it also sent the word abroad to thousands of viewers that there was a man who had been leading a double life: outwardly a minister and a philanthropic do-gooder; inwardly a perverted scoundrel and a mountebank.

We had to wonder what Hall and Elder would have made of Catherine Kampen's story about her "counseling" sessions with Jimmy Swaggart.

One of the saddest parts of the story is that Elder had solid evidence that Lynda Savage was a sexual libertine and had had numerous affairs with other men, including another minister; but he chose not to divulge this information on his show. It apparently was much more sensational— "newsworthy" in Elder's parlance—to portray Gorman as an evil minister preying on innocent counselees than it was to portray him as a fallible human being who yielded once to temptation and fell into sin with a woman who came looking for trouble.

Elder's single regret, it seems, was that he could not locate Rosary Ortego, the mysterious "Theresa," or anyone else who would go on camera and relate the highly attractive—from tabloid television's point of view—events that took place at Canal Street Assembly of God on a foggy Sunday night in September of 1986.

Gail McDaniel

One of my concerns all along had been the role that Gail McDaniel would play in the courtroom. I was not surprised to see that defense counsel had designated McDaniel's video deposition for trial, something I desperately wanted to avoid. I wanted this witness, the only "other woman" willing to testify that she had had sexual intercourse with Gorman, to appear live and subject herself to cross-examination. By offering only her videotaped deposition, defense counsel confirmed my original notion that her testimony was a sham, that she never intended to be available for testimony at trial. I was now convinced that she was coached, scripted and paid off in exchange for her deposed testimony.

I believed the only way a jury would sense McDaniel's lack of credibility was to see her in person. Accordingly, as soon as I became aware that defense counsel planned to use only her deposition and not to call her, I fired off a subpoena. Unless I compelled her appearance in court, she could arrange to be out of the state, could even relocate conveniently without severing personal or vocational ties in Louisiana. Shreveport is immediately across the state line from Texas and isn't far at all from Arkansas; she could even commute back and forth to work, if she so chose.

In response to this preemptive action, an attorney from Shreveport who had not been previously involved in the case appeared and filed a Motion to Quash the subpoena on the grounds that McDaniel would be going into the hospital for back surgery and would not be available for the trial. A hearing was postponed on that issue, but we immediately sent our man Scott Bailey to Shreveport to put her under surveillance. He learned that she had indeed checked into the hospital there; however, she was released during the trial. We also had an attorney friend of Gorman's, Carl Rice, go to the little restaurant owned by the Assembly of God church Gail attended; he found her waiting tables in the restaurant, work that would not be routinely recommended for a person recovering from back surgery.

We also learned that after giving her deposition, McDaniel acquired a 300ZX which was originally registered to her good friend, Frances Duron, who was also a close friend of the Swaggarts as well. The car was ostensibly a gift, but it was evident to us that Gail McDaniel had been bought and paid for.

Based on this information, we objected to the defendants' use of the McDaniel video, and the court ordered her to appear. Her attorney returned from Shreveport and again argued that she had had back surgery, but we produced the medical records showing she had long since been released from the hospital and that we had evidence she had been doing work that would require her to put her back under greater strain than appearing in court possibly could. We, of course, were doubtful that she had ever had back surgery. Even if she had, we thought this was a somewhat extreme length to go to merely to avoid having to repeat her deposition lies in open court.

Bailes denied her attorney's pleas and ordered her to be in court to give her testimony in person, and she ultimately did appear, though not until the next-to-last week of the litigation.

When she did appear, McDaniel paraded into the courtroom with an all-male entourage, including a man who appeared to be her bodyguard. She took the stand and represented that another man in her company was her fiancé. We knew this was a lie, since by now we believed that she was a lesbian, had never been married, and never intended to be married, at least not in a heterosexual sense. She stated under oath that her back surgery required this "fiancé" to carry her up the stairs to the courtroom. (It was not until after the trial that we learned that she walked up the stairs under her own steam, immediately in front of four of the jurors.)

On cross-examination, I was easily able to impeach her on times and dates and the fact that she could not remember anything about the details of the purported coerced sexual encounter with Gorman. Again, she testified that she was a virgin at the time this took place and that it had created a rage that stayed inside of her all of these years and that she had just waited until recently to disclose it to Frances Duron who subsequently disclosed it to Frances Swaggart.

I asked for information concerning the gift of the 300ZX from Frances Duron, which also produced responses that were vague and evasive. I was itching to establish a sexual connection between her and one of the key players in Swaggart's circle, even to Swaggart himself, but I was unable to find a way to lay the proper foundation in order to make such testimony relevant. Although I did argue in closing arguments that the car and the job in the church cafeteria were payoffs for Gail's perjured testimony.

In the first analysis, though, McDaniel's story of blackmail and coerced sex was so incredible on its face that it may, in the long run, have helped Gorman more than it harmed him. No one seemed to believe it— not even apparently defense counsel. It was merely further evidence of the maliciousness of which the Swaggarts were capable.

In spite of my fears to the contrary, and owing in large part to Judge Bailes' ruling that a *prima facia* case of conspiracy existed, Gail McDaniel proved to be a costly witness to Swaggart's case. Ironically, they and the Durons paid a great deal merely to harm themselves.

Jonas Robertson—Redux

The key to proving that a conspiracy existed, though, rested almost completely on the large shoulders of Jonas Robertson. During his recall testimony, he was allowed to give hearsay testimony about conversations he had with Indest, as well as with Alan McDonnel, Carl Miller, and other persons who were no longer party defendants to the suit but who were now named as co-conspirators.

During his recall testimony, Robertson testified for thirty minutes about the lengthy conversation he'd had with Michael Indest in September and October 1986. He gave it word for word and it was convincing. He proved to be an excellent witness for Gorman.

215

On cross-examination, Wittmann, taking a page perhaps from my examination of Gail McDaniel, brought out the fact that Robertson was mistaken or confused about a few of his dates. Wittmann noted that Robertson had at one time in his life abused cocaine, heroin, amphetamines, and other mind-altering drugs, which might well have affected his memory. But true to form, Robertson handled this line of questioning very well. He admitted without shame or apology that every word of it "was absolutely true," but he stood firm on his testimony. Prior to the trial, Robertson testified, he conferred with Peter McMahan, an insurance agent and personal friend from Baton Rouge, who was present during the conversation with Indest in October, 1987. Robertson said that prior to his court appearance he called McMahan and went over his recollection of the meeting and that McMahan confirmed that Robertson's version of events and account of the words spoken were accurate.

During one of the many pretrial interviews I conducted with another witness, Eddie Trammel, I learned that even though he had initially gone along with Swaggart's attack on Gorman, he now felt that Gorman's removal from the church had been poorly handled. Further, he continued to admire Gorman as a man and as a minister. He understood that no minister could conduct himself in a way that brought shame and scandal to his church and expect to continue to hold a powerful position in the church, but he also understood that a continuing campaign of defamation, which amounted to a death sentence for that man's reputation, was clearly not right.

Trammel's comment to me was, "There's nothing wrong with stepping on a man's shoes, but you should never try to mess up his shine," he said.

Wittmann's attempt to mess up Robertson's shine by bringing up his criminal past and history of drug addiction backfired. Robertson was living testimony to Gorman's good work in the New Orleans community. The former pastor of the First Assembly of God was widely known as a man who had helped to rehabilitate those with chemical dependencies, feed the hungry and clothe the needy. Robertson was concrete evidence of the power of the Gospel that Marvin Gorman preached and of the results he could achieve. Robertson had been delivered from the "belly of the beast" of sin and personal degradation as the direct result of Gorman's efforts on God's behalf. It was not too much to infer from Robertson's testimony that Gorman had unselfishly saved his life, and that, in spite of the fact that Robertson had been temporarily turned against him by lies and rumors, Gorman was willing to forgive him unconditionally for having done so.

Wittmann's attack on Robertson's character angered the jury and pushed their inclination a great distance toward the side of Robertson's "Spiritual Daddy."

• CHAPTER EIGHTEEN •
THE MEDIA AND THE MESSAGE

"Mischief shall come upon mischief, and rumor shall be upon rumor; then shall they seek a vision of the prophet; but the law shall perish from the priest, and counsel from the ancients."

—The Book of the Prophet Ezekiel, 7:26

The drama in the courtroom was exciting, but what was going on around the trial and as an insular part of it was sometimes even more fascinating. Very soon, the entertainment aspect of what we were involved in threatened to overwhelm the more serious purpose at hand.

Every morning Swaggart's followers would come in and sit on one side of the courtroom and Gorman's followers would sit on the other. Swaggart's defense team invariably put on a theatrical production, which included Phil Wittmann, on the first day of trial, asking Jimmy and Frances Swaggart to stand up in the middle of the courtroom and introduce themselves to the jury and spectators. This ritual continued every morning. Loud and dramatic prayer sessions were staged in the back of the courtroom as well as in the hallways during the course of the trial by both camps. I was fairly disgusted, personally, for I knew how much these people hated one another.

During breaks and recesses, Swaggart's followers would gather in the rear of the seating area and sing hymns, quote scripture, and address members of the opposing party as "brother" and "sister." In-between time, they sniped at each other and shot heated, hateful looks in our direction. The hypocrisy was too much to take for very long without laughing out loud.

Every morning, Swaggart arrived with his entourage and tried to monopolize the press's attention. Frasier and I always waited until Swaggart finished and had entered the courtroom before we came through the milling reporters. Thus we could respond to rather than initiate comments and questions. Frasier's philosophy with regard to the media seemed to be that our position should be one of reaction to newsmakers instead of trying to make news ourselves. It was far better, he believed, to allow Swaggart to seize center stage, the better to make a bigger fool of himself.

Throughout the entire process of preparation and the trial itself, we were successful in keeping a muzzle on Gorman. He was forbidden to answer questions from the press or to make unscripted statements. We also made sure Marvin and Virginia presented themselves in a modest, wholesome manner in dress and decorum, which contrasted sharply with the flashy and sometimes tacky appearance of the Swaggarts. Lawyers from all over the state as well as Oklahoma, Texas, and Florida dropped by during the course of the trial just to watch the spectacle.

There was a profound sense of "center stage" every morning when proceedings began, and we were intensely aware that the eyes of the media and the general public were on our every move. Regardless of how the trial came out, we knew we would be judged outside the courtroom according to our behavior far more than according to our legal success.

A full complement of national print and broadcast media were on hand every day, and they were all looking for headlines, sound bites, a scoop. This created a roller-coaster effect for us, and we were never sure what to expect when we opened the morning paper or tuned in to a news broadcast.

Initially, when we first filed our suit, the press was very much against us. The prospect of a well-known minister being caught having affairs with a variety of women was just too juicy a story to pass up. Indeed, on July 17, 1986, Gorman went out to pick up his morning newspaper and was accosted by reporters demanding a statement about his resignation from his church. Gorman, somewhat befuddled and caught off guard, stated that he was quitting the local church to promote his evangelistic ministry. Throughout the trial, defense counsel would present this "interview" to the jury as evidence that Gorman was a liar.

But after Swaggart was caught on Airline Highway, the press's mood shifted, and they became more favorably disposed toward Gorman, who was increasingly being seen as a victim of a vendetta launched by Swaggart. Still, there were problems with both image and accuracy in the New Orleans press, which unfortunately functioned as both touchstone and conduit for the national media.

It was obvious, because of their direct connections with the newspaper, that the Stone, Pigman firm could influence the New Orleans *Times Picayune,* not only in its editorial stance, but also its daily coverage of the trial. Susan Finch, who was the *Times Picayune* reporter assigned to cover the trial, was a Millsaps graduate like myself, but she did not seem to offer any favoritism toward me or my client. It seemed, in fact, that the contrary was the case.

Each day, as we called our witnesses, the paper would report the cross-examination rather than the direct; then, when the defense put on their case, the reporters cited nothing but their direct testimony. Unfortunately, most of what was printed in other media sources, including my hometown paper, the Lake Charles *American Press,* was taken from the Associated Press wire service, which was, in turn, directly lifted from either the *Times Picayune*'s or the other New Orleans paper, the *Morning Advocate*'s articles. As a result, my friends and colleagues in Lake Charles drew the impression that we were losing badly in court, when in actuality the opposite was taking place.

Fortunately, a more neutral and unbiased series of articles was coming from such reporters as Art Harris, who was working as a freelance stringer for *The Washington Post*. Also, *The New York Times* consistently carried accurate and highly detailed stories.

But locally and regionally, readers of the *Times Picayune* were receiving a version of events that was heavily slanted toward the defendants. It occurred to us that one reason for Swaggart's continuing and even expanding confidence in what was a rapidly deteriorating position was the result of his believing what he read in the newspapers and saw on local television news rather than what he witnessed taking place directly in front of him in court.

• CHAPTER NINETEEN •
THE EXORCISM

"O full of all subtlety and all mischief, thou child of the devil, thou enemy of all righteousness, wilt thou not cease to pervert the right ways of the Lord?"
—*The Acts of the Apostles, 13:10*

Of all the accusations, rumors, innuendoes, and suggestions about the personal and moral failings of Marvin Gorman disseminated by Jimmy Swaggart and his minions, none incensed Gorman more than the allegation that he had taken the form of an evil spirit, a demon, a devil, and invaded the body and soul of an innocent girl. Gorman could grow excited, agitated, indignant, even angry when closely questioned about his associations, real or imagined, with women or about his use of church funds, but he became enraged whenever the subject of the Canal Street exorcism came up.

In a way, this made sense, when one understands the mystical nature and spiritual commitment of Assembly of God devotees. Glossalia, or speaking in tongues, is a central activity at many if not most worship services. During this process an individual becomes possessed of the Holy Spirit and is capable of rendering wisdom, prophecy, prayer, or other holy words in a language that individual is incapable of speaking or even understanding in ordinary circumstances.

To the uninitiated, it can be a startling experience to be seated quietly in a church when a person in the next pew suddenly rises to his or her feet and begins speaking in a loud voice, mouthing what to most ears sounds like gibberish and babble, often accompanied with copious effusions of saliva and mucus.

Ordinarily when this occurs the service grinds to a halt and everyone reverently listens while the "speech" winds to a conclusion. Usually at that point, some other individual, sometimes the minister, sometimes merely another worshipper, will fall into what appears to be a trance and will render a translation of what has just been said.

In spite of its obvious trappings of apparent hokum and bunk, this ritual is one of the most time-honored in the Christian Church. It's mentioned in the New Testament, and is the principal gift of the Holy Spirit to the Apostles on the Day of Pentecost. It is acknowledged as being possible even by faiths and denominations which do not practice it or welcome its evidence in their own services—the Anglicans and Episcopalians, for example. Not even Roman Catholics deny its possibility.

At the root of this phenomenon, of course, is the acknowledged possibility that a living human being can be so utterly possessed of a supernatural power that he or she will say and do things that would otherwise be impossible or, at the least, unthinkable. And as an obverse to being possessed of the Holy Spirit, the possibility also exists that an individual can be utterly and completely possessed by a demonic spirit, a minion of Satan or Satan himself, who can invade the body and soul of some innocent and compel his or her voice and actions to behave according to the spirit's dictates.

Although to a nonbeliever this might seem to be the stuff of ghost stories and sensational motion pictures, there is strong Biblical precedent for it. It is mentioned throughout Scripture, particularly and especially in the Gospels. It is also the holy mission of all Christians to endeavor to cast out these evil spirits, thereby curing the spirit of the possessed and banishing at the same time any attendant diseases, ailments, disfigurements, or handicaps that might have been related to or caused by the possession.

The prospect of finding someone to go on television and discuss this phenomenon must have had Bill Elder's mouth watering; unfortunately, no one would. Yet after Michael Indest induced Tom Miller to relate Rosary Ortego's experience to a restaurant filled with Assembly of God ministers and leading church members, it was common knowledge in New Orleans that Marvin Gorman had taken the form of the devil, had possessed a fourteen-year-old deaf-mute, and had threatened the lives of "all you Christians" in the midst of a cloud of smoke and pungent odors.

Though many, including Gorman's successor at First Assembly of God, James Brown, dismissed Miller's story as "malarkey," some undoubtedly believed it. In the more ill-educated and naive congregations of New Orleans, many undoubtedly accepted it as truth—after all, a minister had given testimony about it to his brethren. It was one of the most damaging rumors launched against Gorman's ministerial career. Being called a thief, a liar, and a philanderer—even a sexual pervert— was one thing, but for a minister to be accused of being the Devil incarnate was an altogether more serious proposition.

The point for us was that although we had trouble taking Gorman's

222

anger at the charge entirely seriously—at first, anyway—it finally became clear to us that this issue had to be pursued vigorously; for it did not matter whether or not we, as plaintiff counsel, believed in the reality of possession and the possibility of glossalia or exorcism; what mattered was that Gorman and his fellow Assembly of God members did. So the allegations took on merit in their minds that was far more significant than it might have been in the minds of the general public.

On a more practical and down-to-earth note, though, it wasn't just a coincidence that the parties involved, particularly Indest, were also included among the co-conspirators. This was the connection we sought.

One of the doubts we had about the sincerity of the Reverend Tom Miller and his account of the exorcism concerned his motivation for notifying Michael Indest of the exorcism almost immediately after it was concluded. And Indest's response—including holding an immediate prayer service to "cleanse" the Canal Street Church—also seemed too carefully orchestrated to have been an impromptu reaction to this unusual—even within the Assembly of God—event.

Ruth Turner, one of the witnesses to the exorcism, told us that she later learned from Michael Indest that Rosary Ortego had attended Indest's church and pretended to be a deaf-mute West Indies woman for some time prior to visiting Tom Miller's Canal Street mission. And we learned that Ortego's real name was Troy Lynn McGee, who held a music degree from Loyola University. It made no sense that she, if she genuinely believed herself to be possessed, would seek Miller and not Indest for spiritual relief.

But Turner was a woman of strong convictions and despite these revelations she was utterly convinced that on the night of September 7, 1986, Troy Lynn McGee, alias Rosary Ortego, was possessed, and that Rev. Tom Miller exorcised the evil spirits.

It was Turner, however, who told us that she was aware that after the exorcism Miller called First Assembly of God to discuss the matter and that the Reverend Brown refused to discuss it. Turner said that Tom Miller told her that he then called Jimmy Swaggart Ministries about the exorcism. Turner also said that the Reverend Miller's wife, who died prior to the trial and was never deposed, believed they all had been tricked.

Curiously, Ruth Turner was willing to be a witness for us because she believed that Miller should never have told anyone about what transpired that night. On the stand, she testified that she believed what she had witnessed was genuine, but that all ministers know that anything that the devil says is a lie, so those things should never be repeated.

After my first meeting with Turner in New Orleans, I returned to Lake Charles and told Matt and Milo about the exorcism. Like me, they were both astonished. In order to make use of Miller's testimony, we knew we would need more information and details, and that we would have to draft an affidavit. So Matt and Milo called Turner and talked to her over the phone and taped the conversation. During the call, Turner chose to mimic the devil speaking in Gorman's voice; we had it all on tape. We laughed so hard, and spent the next three or four weeks repeating Ruth Turner's mimic of the devil so much, that it turned into a comedy at our office.

However, I knew that Turner was serious and that she would be taken seriously by many devout Assembly of God members or, for that matter, by any devout Christians who subscribed to the belief that possession was a possibility. That meant we needed to treat her with "kid gloves."

Actually, we eventually discovered, the entire matter needed to be handled with more seriousness than we originally thought it deserved. The story about the exorcism was bizarre enough to provide an entertaining dimension to the case, not only for our legal team but for all counsel involved in the lawsuit. This was best evidenced at Tom Miller's deposition.

On any single deposition taken in preparation for this case, there could be as few as six or seven lawyers or as many as thirty present. Naturally, Gorman's and Swaggart's depositions were well attended. But apart from these two principals in the suit, the only other deposition that proved to be a big draw was Tom Miller's.

During the deposition questioning, which I again conducted, Miller was perpetually incensed that so many of those present had to put their heads down beneath the table to hide their laughter while he gave his account of the ordeal with the devil and Rosary Ortego. Much of what he said was ludicrous, and much of it was simply unbelievable—not so much because of the story's incredibility, but more because even a man of Miller's limited education and experience would believe it was real.

In order to establish the depths of Miller's naiveté, I asked him if he could perform an exorcism on anyone. He replied that he could. I pointed out a heavy-set, bald-headed fellow across the table from me, Peter Feringa, counsel for Michael Indest, and asked the Reverend Miller whether if Feringa were possessed, he could deliver him from the spirit. Miller displayed a look of disgust and appeared insulted, probably because he felt that I was making fun of him, which I was. The comment, however, triggered laughter among all the lawyers (and it finally eased the somewhat hostile relationship between me and Peter Feringa).

We were not eager to bring up the exorcism at the trial, for we believed that the elements of the case were already sensational enough and were attracting enough stories in the press (too many of them misleading) without adding this apparently absurd dimension to the whole thing. Further, the allegations and statements made against Gorman had centered on fairly concrete and serious matters—sexual misconduct and misappropriation of church funds. These were matters easy for a jury—or for the public—to judge. Venturing into spiritual matters could lead us into dangerous territory, and such a move could backfire.

But the matter had come up in our examination of Bill Elder, and it appeared to be unavoidable. Further, Gorman was sure that in a public forum we could dispel any believability in this story. Additionally, we were interested in linking Miller to Indest, thence to Swaggart, to support our conspiracy theory, so we were left with little choice but to call Miller as a witness.

The Reverend Tom Miller came across as a very nice individual, a simple but plain man with a clear sense of who he was and what he was about. Fortunately, the way things turned out he did not appear to the jury to be a wild-eyed mystic with an easy disposition toward zany supernatural stories. He also did not appear to be a man who could be easily fooled. This set him up as a more or less deliberate co-conspirator or, at the very least, an unwitting tool of Indest and Swaggart.

The first question we needed to dispose of, then, was whether or not he and Ruth Turner had been duped. Who duped them? Was Troy Lynn McGee paid to deceive them with theatrics—and, if so, by whom—or did she believe herself truly to be possessed by the spirit of Marvin Gorman and/or Satan?

Miller's account of the ritual was stunning, but we could not locate either the mysterious "Theresa," or McGee. It wasn't until shortly before trial that we learned that McGee was living in St. Louis, Missouri, and by then it was too late to depose her. And because she was no longer a resident of Louisiana, she could not be compelled to appear by subpoena.

Despite the revelations about McGee, Miller was unshaken in his belief that what he had experienced on that September Sunday was genuine. He testified that regardless of what her real name might have been, at the time of the exorcism she was a deaf-mute because she was possessed by the devil. He speculated that the deliverance brought her back to her "normal self."

We could never get Miller to say when he learned that Rosary Ortego was in fact Troy Lynn McGee and not a deaf mute. He testified that following the exorcism he was invited to an opera staged in New Orleans in which McGee was performing. That the girl was a professional actor as well as a trained vocalist in no way shook his belief that she had been in the grip of the devil and Marvin Gorman.

What was clear, however, was that he reported the incident to

Michael Indest and also to Jimmy Swaggart, although his motives for doing so were never clear. Also, on September 16, 1986, in a restaurant in New Orleans, Miller testified that Indest prompted him to repeat the details of the exorcism before a sectional meeting of the Assembly of God Ministers.

This established for the jury a connection between the chief co-conspirators and the naive and somewhat befuddled Tom Miller, and it circumvented the question of whether or not Rosary Ortego/Troy Lynn McGee believed herself to be possessed, then exorcised (or "delivered") by Miller or not. Thus, it put the whole matter back on firm legal ground, and then placed the burden of disputing the implied claim that she was possessed squarely on the shoulders of the defense.

Their response spoke eloquently to the matter and put it to rest: they never attempted to depose Troy Lynn McGee or call her as a witness.

• CHAPTER TWENTY •
PLAINTIFF'S TRUTH; DEFENDANT'S TRUTH

"The wicked is snared by the transgression of *his* lips: but
the just shall come out of trouble."
—*The Proverbs, 12:13*

Perhaps the most significant difficulty we faced in asserting our
client's case was that his infidelity to his wife had occurred once and only
once. In the greater but more philosophical scheme of things, it really
shouldn't matter. If a sin is a sin, whether it takes place once or many
times shouldn't make any difference either to the sinner or to those asked
to forgive it. Jesus, after all, didn't count the whiplashes of those who
scourged him, nor did he interrogate the thief he forgave from the cross
as to how many times he might have stolen or from whom.

But if I learned one truth more than any other during this case, it was
that organized religion, particularly fundamentalist religion, rarely
concerns itself with the meaning of the Scripture it so exalts. It is the
application of the interpretation of that meaning that's important. If the
interpretation is contradicted by the actual words of the Bible, then the
words themselves may be passed over or even ignored. To such people, a
preacher is both the conduit and the filter of God's Word; what is actually
said or meant by Holy Writ is of secondary importance to what believers
are told to believe about it.

Hence, what was important to the case of *Marvin Gorman vs Jimmy
Swaggart et al* was not whether Gorman was a tempted and sinful man,
but how often he was tempted, how often he sinned.

To aid us in demonstrating the frequency of Gorman's transgression,
we found help in a defense witness named Robin Martin. She had worked
in the vault at the First Assembly of God with Lynda Savage, and she was
called by defense counsel to testify as to how often she heard Lynda
Savage paged by Gorman to come visit with him in his office. This was
often.

On cross-examination, however, we were able to persuade Martin to

227

testify that after the Savages left the church on July 15, 1986, and that following the subsequent resignation and confession of Gorman, she had a conversation with Lynda Savage wherein Lynda indicated that her "affair" with Gorman actually involved only one act, many years before. This doubtless struck a sour note in defense counsel's plan for a series of harmonious witnesses who would come to the stand to destroy Gorman's claims to what came to be known as the "one time seven years ago" theory.

We also called Richard Dobbins, Ph.D., a licensed Assembly of God minister and psychologist from Akron, Ohio, who was well respected among the Assemblies of God (in spite of Swaggart's pronounced mistrust and condemnation of psychology). After Gorman resigned from his church, he and Virginia were counseled by Dobbins. During the course of the counseling Dobbins administered the Minnesota Multiphasic Personality Inventory (M.M.P.I) exam as well as some other tests to both of the Gormans. Dobbins also did some in-depth probing of Marvin's background, particularly his counseling with women over the years. This was based on a list of names of counselees provided by the church staff of First Assembly of God.

After several weeks of counseling and testing, Dobbins wrote a letter to the Assemblies of God stating that, "It appeared that in years past after Gorman had become overworked and stressed out that he had fallen into sin, which included an act of adultery and some acts of becoming overly affectionate with other counselees." Of course, Gorman used this letter to demonstrate that he had told the truth and that he had committed only the one act of adultery to which he had confessed. Swaggart, who had stated from the pulpit that psychologists were "of the devil," immediately attacked Dobbins and wrote a letter chastising him.

To us, the danger of Dobbins's testimony was that he held the opinion that Gorman had become overly affectionate with women because he had kissed them either before, during, or after counseling. But as others, particularly Paul Dunn, had testified, hugging and kissing was almost an anticipated and ritualistic practice within the Assemblies of God. Further, it only took a little personal exposure to Gorman to learn that he was an overtly affectionate and compassionate person and that he routinely greeted many women by kissing them either hello or good-bye. And even further, Southerners generally tend to be more affectionate in greetings; a hug or light bussing is a common display whenever people who know one another meet.

Dobbins, on the other hand, believed such greetings constituted inappropriate conduct—that was part of what he was referring to when he indicated that Gorman had become "overly affectionate." He attributed sexual overtones to this practice, when to Southern jurors it was more

228

likely to appear as platonic and devoid of sexual intent.

Dobbins's testimony presented a dilemma for both sides, and each wanted part but not all of Dobbins's deposition read to the jury. We particularly wanted the portion of his testimony touching on the MMPI and Dobbins's assessment of Gorman's one-time indiscretion entered into evidence; the defense was more interested in the jury's learning of Dobbins's opinion with regard to Gorman's inappropriate displays of affection with counselees.

As it turned out, and thanks to legal maneuvering by Steve Hickman, Dobbins' entire testimony was read to the jury, both the parts we wanted and the parts defense counsel wanted. As an unexpected bonus, a portion of Dobbins' deposition touching on his opinion that Swaggart and Gorman were competitors was also read to the jury, thereby furthering our assertion of motive for Swaggart's conspiracy.

We had always known that our most central witness in corroborating Gorman's testimony would be his wife, Virginia. Alan Campo had always insisted that Virginia would be viewed by the jury as "Marvin's polygraph." If the jury decided that Virginia believed that he was telling the truth, then the jury would also believe him. Frasier, who would conduct her examination, worked with her for weeks, scripting her and coaching her for her ordeal on the witness stand. If ever there was a prepared witness for trial, it was Virginia Gorman.

In spite of her husband's celebrity, Virginia Gorman was a very private person, very quiet in her manner. She was very much a homemaker, the supportive wife of a famous and powerful husband. After Gorman's ministry grew within the Assemblies of God, the family moved from Gentilly to a lakefront house on North Cullen Drive in Metairie; they lost this house in the 1987 bankruptcy, but throughout the entire ordeal, Virginia was never anything less than supportive of her husband in both their public and their private lives.

On the stand, Virginia appeared at ease. She wore a modest and well-tailored blue dress. Still an attractive woman, she was obviously concerned for her husband of thirty-seven years, despite anything he might have done. In a manner of speaking, she offered the image of the perfect wife: loyal, loving, desirable, and steadfast.

She testified that she was long past the shock of revelation of Gorman's infidelity. She indicated that she was angry at first but that she did in fact believe that it was a single incident years ago. She said she was convinced that Marvin Gorman had loved but one woman his entire life: her.

For cross-examination, defense counsel sent up their third string attorney, Denise Pilié. Perhaps they thought using a female attorney would be more effective; it wasn't. Despite the fact that Virginia was being questioned about her husband's alleged sexual indiscretion with Lynette Goux, a personal friend of the Gorman family, and other women, Virginia held her own. Pilié's questions elicited a number of replies the defense counsel neither liked nor expected.

Virginia Gorman then surprised everyone by saying that she was not only convinced that Gorman's temptation was only a one-time incident with Lynda Savage, but that she also believed that her husband was overcome by guilt and left the room without completing the sexual act .

Pilié was not so sure. She responded, "Well, you weren't in the room with him—"

But before she could finish the question Virginia cut her off: "Neither were you."

Virginia went on to say that she more than anyone was the victim of all that had happened. It was she who stood back while mistakes were made. She repeated over and over that if we could all see inside her, we would understand that she loved Marvin and that she forgave him. She concluded by saying she thought everyone should forgive him and that they should quit calling him a liar.

Virginia Gorman sent a strong multiple message to the jury: that she wanted people to know she loved her husband and that he was worth defending; that she knew him better than anyone, and in her mind he was not guilty; that he had never loved any woman but her; and that she was his wife, then, now, forever, amen.

Following Virginia Gorman's stunning defense of her husband's honor and character, it was absolutely vital that the defense put on a good show with their display of the testimony of Lynda Savage, the only other person besides Marvin Gorman who knew for sure what happened in that motel room in 1978.

Lynda Savage was deposed on March 28, 1990, in Edmond, a suburb of Oklahoma City, where she then resided; her story, of course, was that she had an affair with Marvin Gorman over a period of three years. Her video was played to the jury in its entirety.

In the spring of 1978, she said, she began counseling with Gorman because of marital problems between her and her husband David. She said that during the counseling sessions there never was any physical contact between her and Gorman. In the course of the counseling, she testified, she confessed to Gorman that she had had an adulterous relationship with her brother-in-law, Mike Wall.

According to Savage, Gorman invited her and her husband to attend a church camp meeting in Indiana in July 1978. While there, around 11:35 P.M., Savage went to Gorman's hotel room, pursuant to her husband's instructions, for a regular counseling session. At that time, Gorman hugged her and kissed her very affectionately in what she described "a sexual nature." She claimed she was so devastated that she returned to her hotel room and stood in the shower in her black pants, vest, and printed blouse, to cleanse herself. Upon returning to New Orleans, she said she saw Marvin Gorman next on July 24, 1978, at the Travel Lodge Motel on Veteran's Highway in Metairie. She had gone there, she said, because she was depressed and wanted to be alone. She remembered that she had called Gorman's residence looking for him and had left a message with his wife as to where she was. According to Savage, she had decided that day that it might be best for everybody if she just died but she could not remember whether or not she had made that statement to Gorman over the telephone before he came to the motel room.

When Gorman arrived at the room, she was wearing a peach-colored robe with only her panties on underneath. She said Gorman stayed in the room approximately forty-five minutes and that they had intercourse. She stated that Gorman remained partially dressed in his undershirt, socks, and underwear and, to the best of her recollection, he apologized and showed remorse for what had happened before he left the room.

Savage then testified that from July 24, 1978, until January 20, 1981, she and Gorman had intercourse several times. Although she could not remember all of the locations, she did remember the Fountain Bay Hotel on December 28, 1978, her husband's birthday.

Interestingly enough, Lynda Savage also testified that she had been blackmailed by Paul Dunn when Dunn approached her indicating he knew of her affair with Gorman and wanted her to sleep with him. If she wouldn't, she claimed, he threatened to expose the affair. She testified that she had sex with Paul Dunn six times from March until May 1986.

In response to the question of why she confessed her alleged affair with Gorman to Michael Indest, she stated that she went to the Indests' home because her son and Indest's son were playing in a band together; when Indest noticed that she was depressed and he asked, "What's the matter? Have you committed multi-adultery?" She then opened up and told him everything. She denied having a sexual relationship with Indest.

She further testified that she told Indest about her affairs with her brother-in-law, Dunn, and Gorman, mentioning dates, times and places. She also confessed her affair with Dunn to the congregation at her husband's church in Kenner. Jim Rentz, Jimmy Swaggart's cohort, began attending the Savages' church in the first part of December, 1986, and was present during the service wherein she admitted her affair with Dunn. At this point, she began seeing Glen Miller, a counselor at Jimmy Swaggart Ministries.

On March 1, 1987, the Savages took a sabbatical from the Assembly of God Church in Kenner, and they ultimately resigned in August of 1987 to take a position at the Philadelphia Assembly of God Church in

Edmond, Oklahoma. By the time we deposed Lynda, David had been forced to leave the church in Edmond because Lynda had developed a close relationship with another minister there; the Reverend Savage was now associated with another church in Lubbock, Texas. Lynda admitted that her so-called "friendship" with this other minister caused David to leave.

I had not met Lynda Savage prior to her deposition, but she was everything that I expected her to be. Attractive, blonde, intelligent; she exuded sex appeal and an uncommon self-confidence. She also communicated strong, personal power. I never did develop any respect for her, but I did understand how Gorman could fall into sin with her. She was a compelling personality, one who had "danger" written all over her–a true *femme fatale*.

Savage employed her own counsel for the deposition and refused to answer certain questions asked by the defendants, something I'm sure made them less than happy. She did her best to cooperate with the defendants' theme of the case and to make it appear that Gorman took advantage of her, but it was clear in the deposition that she probably did have deep feelings for Gorman; it was also clear that Gorman probably tried to help her.

Additionally, it was undisputed that she had had numerous affairs, including liaisons with men who might have been relevant to the litigation; but this was never admitted. My suspicion that one of those men might have been Indest was somewhat bolstered by the fact that Indest brought his wife Christie to Oklahoma and made sure she was present for Savage's deposition. There might have been another perfectly good reason for this, but Indest never brought his wife to any of the other depositions, and there were many opportunities for him to do so. The question in my mind was why would a man, much less a minister, want to subject his wife to the sordid details of sexual contact that could come out in Savage's trial deposition, unless it was to use her presence from discouraging Savage from saying anything about him—or them.

David Savage's trial deposition was taken in Lubbock, Texas, in the fall of 1990. After meeting him and hearing what he had to say, I developed a better understanding of how Lynda came to be the way she was.

The male half of the Savage couple appeared to be an unemotional person, one I thought of as first cousin to Howdy Doody. He had been forced to leave Kenner Assembly of God because of his wife's affairs and moved on to Edmond, Oklahoma, where he once again had to move on as the result of Lynda's "unhealthy relationship" with a minister there. Savage's career meant more to him than his wife, because he obviously did nothing to save his marriage other than picking up and moving on when his wife's behavior presented a problem for his ministry.

Under cross-examination, I asked Savage about his reactions to learning of Lynda having sex with Marvin Gorman, Paul Dunn, his brother-in-law, and others; Savage's answer was strange. He simply said he forgave her and asked if it was over then told her "Let's go home"— certainly not the reaction one would expect from a man who has just learned that his wife had committed "multi-adultery."

I was so shocked and disappointed by his responses, that I became somewhat cruel during my cross-examination. I had always assumed Savage would probably be on our side, since it was Swaggart, Indest, and others who exposed his wife's private life and caused him such great embarrassment. To my surprise, Savage played right along with the defense's strategy in the case, a company man right to the end.

I asked Savage on cross-examination, what did he say after his wife made this admission to the entire church.

He responded, " 'Are you through, honey?' " I asked him what she said, and he replied, "She said, 'Yeah.' And I said, 'Well, let's go home.'"

I said, "Well, Reverend Savage, what did you say to her when you went home?" and he said he couldn't remember because he said he "wasn't functioning very well" at that time. Disgusted, I asked, rhetorically, "Well, you hadn't been functioning very well for a long time, had you?"

Naturally, this portion of the deposition was played to the jury by the defendants to try to demonstrate that I was excessively mean to Savage during his trial deposition. However, I learned after the trial the jurors sized up the Savages the same as we did: as a pair of dysfunctional, pathetic individuals, each feeding off the other's weaknesses.

At the trial, many of the lawyers who had not attended the deposition were seeing David Savage's testimony for the first time. Among these was my associate, Milo Nickel.

I was trying to ignore the testimony and instead watch the jury's reaction to some of my cross-examination to try to assess if they thought I was being cruel to this sad and pitiful man. When the tape reached the point where I asked the rhetorical question about Savage's not having functioned for a long time, some of the jurors got tickled; Nickel started laughing so hard he had to get up and leave the courtroom. That offered some measure of relief; I had not to that point considered my remark as potentially funny.

The Savage testimony made great sleazy news stories during the trial, but because of the spin local reporters put on it, Gorman was once more tarnished in the public eye. However, the jury had seen the entire testimony, and they concluded that this was a woman who came after Gorman and was successful on only one occasion, and not completely successful even then. Because of my rhetorical remark, the jury also inferred that this woman was probably deprived of sexual gratification by her husband and went out on the prowl, or maybe that she was just a sport, seeking sexual satisfaction wherever she found it.

• CHAPTER TWENTY-ONE •
THE DEVIL AND DANIEL WEBSTER

"Judge not, that ye be not judged."
            —*The Gospel According to St. Matthew, 7:1*

It is amazing how much psychology is involved in the trial of a lawsuit. When I was preparing my opening statement, for example, Alan Campo told me that I needed to give the jury a choice of ways to view Jimmy Swaggart. In other words, I needed to paint several pictures depicting a man with two or possibly three personalities and a chameleon's ability to shift his outward appearance depending on circumstances and surroundings. If I was successful, the jury could choose which personality they wanted to believe, which one they wanted to punish.

The idea was that Swaggart's charisma might, on the one hand, win the jury's personal favor; but, on the other hand, we hoped that the evil that lurked beneath the surface might draw their ire when they understood Swaggart for what he truly was. As it turned out, Campo was right.

Because of his suggestion, I told the jury about the Reverend Jimmy Lee Swaggart, the man with the eighth-grade education, the preacher with charisma and a fabulous voice, the virtual poet who had an instinctive knack for using sound, rhythm, metaphor, and figurative language with persuasive power to move people to religious commitment. I also told them about Jimmy Swaggart, the entertainer, the dancer who could do the Tennessee Trot, a kind of high-kicking strut across the platform, a Bible in his hand, while he preached and exhorted the faithful to join him in a virtual orgy of spiritual excess. I also described another facet: the Honorable Jimmy L. Swaggart, Chairman of the Board of a $150,000,000 enterprise, who would do anything to preserve his empire or increase his personal and corporate power.

My only regret was that I could not display a picture of Jimmy Swaggart, aka Billy, who donned the jogging suit and headband and frequently piloted his Lincoln Town Car to New Orleans, where he

235

indulged himself in the illegal and immoral blandishments proffered by the likes of Debra Murphree at the Travel Inn Motel on Airline Highway, the Swaggart who preyed on emotionally overwrought housewives in Shell station parking lots. That, alas, was prohibited by the courts.

But everybody in South Louisiana–in fact most people in the United States–by now knew this third Jimmy Swaggart, and all of these were the Jimmy Swaggarts who were on trial in the courtroom. All were culpable, and all were capable of going to any length to preserve the empire of the man in the mansion behind the brick wall in Baton Rouge.

We knew from the beginning that we would have to call Swaggart to the stand not only in order to offer *prima facia* evidence of a conspiracy but also to prove the fundamental elements of malicious defamation of Gorman's character. However, we wanted to wait until the latter part of the trial to call him; that way, we knew we could milk the attention from the media and marshal our forces in such a way so as to swing public opinion—and, of course, the jury's opinion—completely in Gorman's favor. We had represented to the court that we would advise defense counsel in a timely manner so they could prepare Swaggart to take the witness stand. But for six weeks, we kept everyone guessing as to precisely when we would issue the call.

At last, the day came–August 6, 1991. We called Swaggart to the stand at 8:30 A.M. The mood in the courtroom was tense. I was a bag of nerves, but I had built up a high measure of confidence over the past weeks. We had laid sufficient foundation and now planned to primarily use Swaggart to corroborate testimony that was already given, or to have him deny it in a way that would convince the jury he was lying. It was possible things could backfire, that Swaggart could come off as the injured party himself; but that is always a calculated risk in a lawsuit.

As it happened, if there was ever a day that we had everything go our way and nothing go the defense's way, it was that day. Swaggart turned out to be the most telling witness for the entire case.

When I called Swaggart to the witness stand, I had a volume of documents that he had authored which I would have to put into evidence through his testimony. One by one I went through these, most of which were letters written to other ministers, asking him to identify his signature and confirm that he had indeed written them. Each, in one way or another and in varying degrees, accused Gorman of lying.

Swaggart admitted to authoring each, although he almost never acknowledged what he meant by what he'd written. Often, it was obvious that the letters had been dictated and that he had signed them or had them signed for him without bothering to read over what was being sent. Nevertheless, they all were posted over his signature, and he was liable for their entire contents, right down to the last mark of punctuation.

One document in particular was the famous August 29, 1986, letter that he wrote to Gorman and blind carbon-copied all the Executive Presbyters as well as others. This was the letter that accused Gorman of being a liar and informed Gorman that Swaggart knew that there were other affairs, other women. This was the same document that made its way into the *Washington Post* and was published following the Jim Bakker-PTL scandal.

Although the transcript of Swaggart's testimony does not reveal it, Swaggart's presence on the stand was symptomatic of his entire attitude toward the trial and, in a broad sense, toward everyone he encountered. He was wearing a gray suit, a navy patterned tie, and his hair, as usual, was carefully styled. He appeared confident and self-assured, but he was perspiring a little and kept running his eyes over the spectators. He rarely looked directly at the jury.

He needed no microphone or amplifier to be heard in the courtroom but always spoke in a resonant tone, prefacing many responses to my questions with "Mr. Lundy, to be totally honest with you. . ." This, of course, gave the impression that without such a qualifier, he was being something less than total in his honesty. Many of his answers revealed through their inflection or through his body language a contempt for me and plaintiff's counsel in general, as well as for Marvin Gorman.

That Swaggart felt superior to everyone in the court was also made plain by the fact that he repeatedly attempted to amend his answers with small speeches, statements, and declarations, many of which were offered over the objections of his own counsel. His single-word responses— "Okay," being the most prevalent—to admonitions from Judge Bailes or even from Phil Wittmann, Swaggart's own attorney, were also tinged with a note of sarcasm, implying that this was all some elaborate game, that he was being remarkably patient in condescending to participate.

From time to time he would continue to answer a question to which defense counsel had objected, even though the judge had not yet ruled on the objection and it might have been that he wouldn't have to answer. Several times, I found myself pointing out to the court in response to defense counsel's shouted objections, "He's already agreed," or "He's already answered that," with a metaphoric shrug of my shoulders. It was obvious that he was not going to be coached or controlled by his highly paid attorneys.

At the same time, he equivocated whenever he could, a technique I surmised he might have picked up from watching too many legal programs on television. For example, when I asked him if he made a telephone call to Michael Indest from Costa Rica, he denied it. When I rephrased the question to ask if he had had a telephone conversation with Indest while he was in Costa Rica, he admitted he had; Bill Treeby placed the call, apparently. To the annoyance of his own attorney—as well as the court—he used this level of specificity even during defense counsel's direct examination, when the inquisitors were tactically on his side.

This mode of response soon became tedious, both for opposing counsel and the court as well as for the jury. On the surface, it appeared that he was being precisely truthful; but beneath that thin veneer, it was obvious that he was attempting to conceal the truth, and only if the question went to the heart of the matter would it receive a credible response.

Swaggart seemed blithely unaware of, or at least indifferent to, the seriousness of the questions being put to him throughout his examination. He took every opportunity to draw attention to what he imagined to be his superior intelligence and his superior moral character. In short, Swaggart patronized the entire court, and everyone from judge to jury to spectator was aware of it.

Swaggart also wanted everyone to be aware of his high moral position, presumably because of his ministerial identity. At one point, for example, I asked him if he remembered being placed under oath before giving a particular deposition. His reply: "I'm always under oath, counsel."

At another point, he drew the ire of both defense counsel and Judge Bailes. The exchange took place during Wittmann's examination on the second day of Swaggart's testimony. Wittmann had already admonished Swaggart—on the record—not to elaborate in his answers nor to answer a question before plaintiff counsel had had a chance to object. This hardly slowed him down. At this point, the issue was what took place at the conclusion of the meeting of July 15 at his home:

> *Wittmann:* What happened as the meeting ended, what if anything did you do?
>
> *Swaggart:* Well, I saw that Marvin Gorman was in a very distraught—
>
> *Wittmann:* I think we're going to be better off today, Reverend .Swaggart, in view of the nature of the testimony and the objections and the Court is correct in sustaining them, please answer my question and tell me what did you do so we don't get into that kind of difficulty. I just want to know if you can tell the ladies and gentlemen of the jury what you did, and I'll ask you more questions, so Mr. Lundy will have a chance to object.
>
> *Swaggart:* Okay.
>
> *Wittmann:* Please tell us what you did.
>
> *Swaggart:* I drove Marvin Gorman to New Orleans.

> *Wittmann:* Why did you drive Marvin Gorman to New
> Orleans? And now you may answer the question for us.
> *Swaggart:* I'm a preacher, and I have a tendency to want
> to build a sermon.
> *The court:* You're not going to have a sermon here.
> *Swaggart:* Yes, I understand. I know that, sir.

This interruption by Judge Bailes was timely, for Swaggart was "winding up" and about to come "uncorked," as Frasier put it. But now he had been put in his place, and he became somewhat subdued from his former excited state, at least for a while.

Such admonitions from the court and his own attorneys never calmed Swaggart for long though. At another point, he turned to Gorman in the courtroom, with wall-to-wall people and members of the press, and told Gorman that he had not repented. This led me to explore during my cross-examination one of our principal themes: that Swaggart had set himself up as judge over Gorman's immortal soul.

Swaggart was operating to the extent he was against Gorman without having, by his sworn testimony, ever having spoken personally to Lynda Savage or Gail McDaniel or, really, anyone other than his wife and Lynette Goux about any purported immoral acts Gorman might have committed. The point I wanted to make was that Swaggart had not only passed temporal judgment on Gorman's professional role in the Assemblies of God without benefit of authority or official office—which he admitted he did not hold, had never held—but that he also was judging the disposition of Gorman's immortal soul without any scriptural authority whatsoever. My hope was to hang him with his own words.

> *Lundy:* Now, I heard you say a minute ago that you have
> never spoken to Lynda Savage about her alleged affair
> with Marvin Gorman; is that correct?
> *Swaggart:* I have no recollection of ever having ever
> mentioned Marvin Gorman to Lynda Savage.
> *Lundy:* But, yet, you can say in this paragraph to a
> clinical psychologist [Dr. Dobbins] who's counseling the
> Gorman family that she has totally repented, but Marvin
> Gorman hasn't?
> *Swaggart:* That was my belief at that time.
> *Lundy:* Do you think you have the right to decide who's
> repented and who hasn't?
> *Swaggart:* Most definitely—
> *Wittmann:* Objection; argumentative.
> *Swaggart:* —most definitely.
> *Lundy:* Haven't you said on television programs, on *A*

Study in the Word that any time a man makes a decision whether or not someone has repented, he's becoming a judge and playing God? Aren't those your words?

Swaggart: I don't recall that I made that statement, but if I made it on television, I made it, and that's exactly what I meant.

This was followed by the introduction into evidence of Swaggart's letter to Dobbins, which brought relevance objections from defense counsel. The letter was, however, admitted, and I was allowed to continue my cross-examination on the same theme.

I first re-established *Study in the Word* as a regular broadcast of Swaggart's, then went on:

Lundy: What kind of program is that?

Swaggart: It's a daily teaching program that is aired Monday through Friday on a daily basis, as I mentioned. It's thirty minutes in length.

Lundy: What kind of viewing audience do you have?

Swaggart: I really don't know at this particular time.

Lundy: You taught out of Romans on many occasions—

Swaggart: Oh, about, I would say, roughly two years ago, we taught over *Study in the Word* the entire book of Romans, beginning at the first verse down to the last chapter.

Lundy: And, as a matter of fact, on November 15, 1989, you were teaching from Romans 2. And, isn't it a fact that you quoted—You stated, "And, it is so, so wicked when we judge another. We're guilty of the sin of self-righteousness, and whenever we do it." He uses the word *despisest.*—"'despisest thou the riches of His goodness and forbearance and long-suffering'—it's like we take our hand and slap the face of God. It's like we spit in the face of Jesus Christ when we do it."

Wittmann: I object to counsel taking these long statements and asking him if he made the statement without—

Lundy: He agrees with it—

Swaggart: It seems to me to be a correct statement, but I don't know what the word *despisest* is. That loses me. I never heard of that word.

Lundy: So, when you judge another, it's like spitting in the face of Jesus Christ?

Swaggart: That is exactly right.

Thus, in this series of questions, I was able to establish through Swaggart's own testimony several telling points: that he had never met or counseled Lynda Savage and had no firsthand knowledge of her supposed confession to Michael Indest; that Swaggart had passed judgment on Marvin Gorman in spite of his own professed belief that such judgments were an anathema in the sight of God; and that even though he had no faith in psychological therapy he had gone out of his way to write to Gorman's psychological counselor and inform him of his judgment of Marvin Gorman. In all, it was a most productive exchange.

But Swaggart's arrogance continued to show in almost every response he made. At another point, I asked him what he meant in the August 29 letter when he told Marvin that there had been other women and other affairs as well? Did he mean one woman, two? Swaggart answered "No." I asked, "Did you mean twenty women?" Swaggart answered "No." I continued, "Do you mean one hundred women?" Swaggart answered in the negative again.

I finally asked, "Well, how many do you mean, Reverend Swaggart?"

Swaggart said, "You would be shocked if you knew, Mr. Lundy." Clearly, Swaggart himself didn't know, because there was nothing to know. This response angered the jury and, I think, the judge as well.

Swaggart was apparently unaware of the gravity of having revealed a primary contradiction between his pronounced philosophy and his behavior. Even after the exchange on the question of judgment, he stated directly to Gorman, "Marvin, let me tell you something, partner. If you don't straighten this thing out with God, when you die you are going to hell."

Such condemnation in the presence of the jurors was perhaps Swaggart's greatest gaffe on the stand. I wondered how defense counsel could sit still while he opened his mouth and systematically dismantled their entire case for them.

Two points we desperately wanted to make in front of the jury had been forbidden to us by Judge Bailes. These were, of course, the revelation of Swaggart's condemnation of Roman Catholics—his professed position that Catholics were not Christians—and the escapade at the Travel Inn on Airline Highway. In spite of the judge's prohibition of questions on these two points, I was determined to put them into the jury's mind one way or another. Ironically, my efforts almost cost us the case.

On the question of Swaggart's position on Roman Catholicism, I didn't get very far at the outset, but the results were telling. We knew there were five Roman Catholics on the jury, so the question was extremely relevant to the point of proving Swaggart's propensity for seeing himself and his faith as the only "true faith," himself as the judge of all men. I had offered a document into evidence that would have shown Swaggart condemning numerous religions, including Roman Catholicism. I asked him to examine the document:

> *Lundy:* I see on the second page, the fourth paragraph, you state, "I've done my best to tell the eight hundred million Catholics around the world what I believe the Lord spoken unto them. I've done my best to speak to the denominational world about their denial of the Holy Spirit"?
>
> *Swaggart:* Yes, I wrote that.
>
> *Lundy:* You don't believe Catholics are Christians, do you?

At this point, a woman somewhere in the courtroom stood up and screamed, "Oh, my God!"

Wittmann leaped to his feet with an objection, which Judge Bailes automatically sustained. I was admonished that the question was "inflammatory and very objectionable" by the judge, and he immediately ordered the jury to disregard the letter. But they had already seen it; the damage was done, as Wittmann and his co-counsel were keenly aware.

Even though Judge Bailes's immediately declared a recess, I was allowed to proffer after lunch. A proffer is an exercise wherein counsel can read into the record evidence or argument outside the hearing of the jury which can be considered by an appeals court. In my proffer I pointed out that Swaggart's tendency to exaggerate had led him to call the Catholic Church as well as the Assembly of God cults, and that such exaggeration was indicative of precisely what he was doing from 1984 on concerning Marvin Gorman's supposed immorality.

My proffer was interrupted several times with objections, until finally Wittmann called my introduction of the document, my question to Swaggart, and my proffer a "cheap shot." He moved immediately for a mistrial on the grounds that I was attempting to prejudice the Catholics on the jury. This, of course, was precisely what I was trying to do.

Other defense counsel joined in Wittmann's motion, accusing me of violating the Legal Canon of Ethics, and as Ross Buckley, attorney for Treeby, put it, "Mr. Lundy has demonstrated miserable and miscreant behavior in attempting to inflame the jury." Charles Boggs, counsel for St. Paul Fire and Marine Insurance Company, added that I had "poisoned" the minds of the jurors.

Judge Bailes noted that he had instructed the jury to disregard the letter and denied the motions. Boggs asked him to instruct the jury in addition to disregard my last question, but Bailes wisely pointed out that to do so would only serve to call their attention to it once again, which would be counter to the defense counsel's entire point.

Although I had been admonished by the court, I said to Frasier privately, "Yeah, get that skunk back in his cage, but they'll play hell trying to clean up the stink."

Outside the courtroom, of course, during the recess and later on, the defendants rushed to the press to claim that what I had done was exactly what Wittmann called it, "a cheap shot" designed to inflame the jury. But in doing so, they were presented with a dilemma. If they claimed that my implied charge—that Swaggart denied the Christianity of Catholics—was a lie, then the obvious question was why had they not remained silent and allowed him to deny it under oath. If, on the other hand, they admitted that it was true, they risked alienating a good number of New Orleans (to say nothing of Louisiana and Southern and general American) Roman Catholics, who already saw Swaggart as a Catholic-bashing charlatan.

It was a delicious victory, one that inspired me to go immediately to the bench and demand, that because Swaggart's testimony was in direct contradiction on several points to the sworn testimony he had given during his depositions, that his entire deposition be read to the jury. Defense counsel objected strenuously, and not without a couple of snide remarks about my educational background and experience, but Judge Bailes put an end to their personal remarks and denied my request.

Undaunted, I moved to our second determination, which was to bring before the jury the question of Swaggart's own morality. I believed I had laid some groundwork for this early on in my examination by establishing two points. One was that Swaggart held no official office in the Assembly of God—that he had no authority to impose sanctions on anyone—and secondly that his only source of authority was in his own personality and ministerial success. Secondly, I wanted to establish his pronounced position toward any attempt to cover up a minister's sin, rather than reveal it so that he might make the proper atonement to both God and man.

The key to this point, of course, was Swaggart's tearful televised confession of an undetermined sin, a confession which he believed would somehow be sufficient to keep him from serious punishment by his own superiors in the church. By voluntarily stepping down from the pulpit for a very short time, Swaggart hoped to slap himself on the wrist (and avoid professional counseling), even though the precise nature of his transgression was never revealed to his parishioners until they saw it on national television and read about it in the national press.

This didn't work exactly as planned, of course, but Swaggart more or less landed on his feet anyway. I wanted to establish his exact position on the matter of sin and atonement within the church itself.

Accordingly, I asked him early in his testimony if he had ever said,

"Somebody said that the church is the only institute in the world that shoots its wounded, and that's true." He admitted that it was his statement, and I pressed him to explain it by referring to a December 1984 letter in which he had used the story of Ham's attempt to expose the nakedness of his father, Noah, in order to justify the need for the church to cover up its own transgressions.

Swaggart attempted to sidestep the question by complaining that the context of that document and that statement were completely different from the Gorman situation, but the point was made that Swaggart applied a double standard: one set of rules for situations that benefitted him, another set for situations that did not.

Late in my cross-examination, I turned to the question of a conversation he purportedly had with Gorman on Airline Highway on October 17, 1987. The date itself was hot enough to be inflammatory; predictably, defense attorneys were immediately on their feet with objections. Buckley requested that the judge should castigate me for asking such a question, particularly since Bailes had ruled that Swaggart's sexual escapades were inadmissible.

I pointed out in a conference outside the jury's hearing that our intention was not to discuss Swaggart's sexual escapade on October 17, but to bring out the point that he had admitted to Gorman in a supermarket parking lot on October 17 that he had written the letters spreading the rumors, that he had lied, and that he was sorry for having done so. We wanted to go on and pursue the matter of the meeting between Gorman and the Swaggarts at the Sheraton Hotel, wherein Frances Swaggart urged Gorman to drop the lawsuit, and the subsequent dinner at the Baton Rouge Country Club, where the matter was discussed again.

None of this was allowed, and once more I offered a proffer for the record, detailing these events and incidents; and once again, defense counsel, this time led by Boggs, moved for a mistrial. The judge found that no specific violation of his prohibition had occurred, though, and denied the motion once more.

When court resumed for the final session of the afternoon, I turned to Swaggart's attacks on other ministers: Glen Cole, Robert Schuller, and others, and I explored his increasingly hostile relationship with the PTL Network. We offered documentation that reflected Swaggart's condemning comments about Robert Schuller regarding his association with Jim Nabors, whom Swaggart believed to be homosexual, and with Sammy Davis, Jr., who was Jewish, and not incidentally, African-American.

In light of statements made by previous witnesses, Swaggart came off once more as a man who was either lying outright or was dangerously self-deceived. Contradictions in his own statements caught him constantly, and his only defense against such revelations was that when he said one thing at one time, he meant it, but when he said a different thing at a different time, he meant that as well.

The many different Jimmy Swaggarts were emerging in fine form. There was no clear definition of what Swaggart believed on any significant point at the moment he was speaking, except that he was consistently determined that Marvin Gorman was guilty of adultery and was damned to hell.

Our greatest fear in calling Swaggart had been that he would woo the jury with his famous charm and charisma. But after admonitions from Judge Bailes and from his own counsel and after he continually exceeded the boundaries of solid, conservative testimony and attempted with a poor show of wits to do battle on minor points of word meanings and details, our worries subsided. After more than six hours of testimony, his open contempt for Gorman and his utter lack of respect for his own legal team made his entire testimony favorable to our side. Ironically, he was one of the best plaintiff witnesses I called.

As Swaggart's testimony concluded that afternoon, Frasier and I, Gorman, Virginia, Hickman, and Nickel were on the elevator together. Frasier said, "Son, this is the day that *you'll* have to make an important statement to the media, and they're going to all be waiting to hear from you."

We all agreed that Swaggart's testimony had gone extremely well for our side, but Frasier pointed out, "Well this is America and people have the right to believe lies if they want to." That gave me the sound bite I wanted.

When the elevator opened on the bottom floor of the courthouse, camera strobes blinded us, and bright lights of mini-cams filled the hallway. The entire mob bristled with microphones, all of which pointed at me, and reporters were shouting questions one on top of the other.

I took a breath and said that I thought Jimmy Swaggart's testimony had gone extremely well for us and we had proved what we said we were going to prove. Then, I gave them Frasier's sound bite:

> This is America, and you can believe lies when you want to. But when you start spreading them, someone's got to stop it. I think the jury will put a stop to it.

Sure enough, the words were printed in the local paper, picked up by the wire services and reprinted all over the world. Matt and his wife, Marti, had the quote blown up and framed for my office.

I felt we had passed a significant milestone in the case that afternoon. Although logic dictated that it had to happen, I had never let myself entirely believe that we could put Jimmy Swaggart on the witness stand, get control of him, make our points and have him make an ass of himself all in the same day.

Furthermore, I never dreamed that a focal point of the case would be made that distinctly and that we would be able to use the press as a vehicle. The mouthpiece that spread the lies had clearly done it outside the courtroom, but with only a little prodding, he had continued to do it inside the courtroom as well, under oath, on the stand, in the middle of a cross-examination.

Because of the defense team's apparent inability to control their own client, to keep him quiet when he should be quiet, and to urge him to respond when he preferred to split hairs and debate minor points of diction and syntax, we felt certain that when he got off of the stand that day he would not be recalled by the defense in the presentation of their evidence.

• CHAPTER TWENTY-TWO •
MONEY

"For the love of money is the root of all evil; which while some coveted after, they have erred from the faith, and pierced themselves through with many sorrows."
—The First Epistle of Paul the Apostle to Timothy, 6:10

Every Friday afternoon, Steve Hickman had the lead role of working on the deposition testimony on behalf of the plaintiffs. Possibly because in his career he had so often stood alone against larger and more powerful forces himself, Judge Bailes found Hickman to be extremely entertaining, and he admired the way he handled all the defense lawyers single-handed.

I would often be back at the office working on the testimony of witnesses for the following week while Hickman was fighting all the defendants over the testimony that would be read to the jury the following week.

The Swaggart defendants had hired Ernst & Young, one of the largest CPA firms in the country, in their damage defense, and we were told that they had as many as fourteen people working on the case at one time. This was a clear indication that they anticipated a verdict for Gorman and that damage control had become the order of the day.

Barry Mabry, a CPA and a very well-schooled witness, testified that the records reflected that Marvin Gorman was going into bankruptcy before the allegations were made by Jimmy Swaggart; thus, Marvin Gorman Ministries was not a viable nonprofit corporation long before Gorman fell into personal difficulties.

Additionally, the defendants called R. Michael Ellison, whose specialty was as a religious media broker and who supposedly supported the premise that Marvin Gorman Ministries was on a downhill slide and would have been in bankruptcy regardless of Swaggart's slander. Both allegations by both witnesses were supported by a raft of statistics and formulaic numerical breakdowns.

Steve Hickman was, in my view, by far the smartest lawyer in the

247

courtroom. He knew the Rules of Evidence better than anyone, and he had a profound sense of how to keep a jury's attention during boring examination of expert witnesses. He was also a technically minded individual who did an excellent job on cross-examination.

One of the most entertaining moments of the trial was Hickman's cross-examination of the media expert, Ellison. The direct examination put on by the defense counsel listed on a blackboard all these statistics and documents supporting the premise for a zero-damage award. And it looked like a cut-and-dried case of a "dry win."

On cross-examination, Hickman went to the blackboard and wrote the word *lies* and turned to the Ellison and asked, "You've heard the statement, 'There are lies' before?" Ellison replied, "Yes."

Hickman then asked, "And you have heard the statement, 'There are damned lies'?" Again, the witness answered, "Yes."

Then Hickman asked, "And you've heard of the statement 'There are statistics'?"

The entire defense counsel objected in unison, but the jury rolled with laughter, while the judge sustained the objection.

Hickman was persistent. He came back immediately and asked the witness to discuss the meaning of "lies, damn lies and statistics" whereon the defendants objected once again.

Judge Bailes instructed Hickman not to mention those three words again.

Shortly, we broke for lunch, and when we came back, Hickman began his questioning once again by saying, "You know those three words that the Judge asked me not to mention?" Again, the jury roared with laughter, the defendants objected, and the Judge sustained the objection and asked Hickman to move on to another subject. In any event, Hickman had the jury's full attention and respect after that, and he did a good job of discrediting the two expert witnesses by showing that their figures were really nothing more than carefully calculated speculations.

We later learned after the trial that the jury had nicknamed Steve Hickman "Pooh Bear." Whatever his nickname, he was effective. Judge Bailes had open admiration for him, as well, and I had gained an immense respect for him during the course of the litigation.

As the verdict revealed, the damage defense by the Swaggarts was both theatrical and costly, and most ineffective. In my opinion, the extravagant cost incurred in hiring witnesses and presenting their damage defense did more to demonstrate to the jury the kind of money the defendants possessed rather than achieve any reduction in a final award based on damages.

Although we pled ninety million dollars in damages in our petition, proving the same was a little more difficult. Marvin Gorman Ministries,

Inc., had basically been a non-profit corporation and was spending more money than it generated. Gorman had been a talented pastor, who made about one hundred thousand dollars a year, including salary and benefits. Somehow, we had to come up with an argument that would support damages somewhere close to what we had alleged in the petition.

The CPA Firm of Gragson, Casiday and Guillory had been accountants for KVHP Channel 29, the station that Marvin Gorman Ministries tried to buy in 1986. I had known Ray Guillory for several years and had encouraged Gorman at one point to retain him as the accountant for the station once the deal was transacted. Of course, it never was.

Guillory and I were neighbors and close friends. George Gragson, senior partner in the firm, had a reputation for being creative, exceptionally bright, and he was an attorney as well as an accountant. When Milo Nickel finished at Tulane Law and joined our firm, he moved into the house across the street from Gragson and they became close friends as well.

Gragson also had an accounting partner named Daphne Clark, who had testified in several trials and had proved to be very effective. Therefore, we allocated the damage portion of our case to Gragson and Clark, with Gragson taking the lead on Gorman's personal damages and Clark taking the lead on Marvin Gorman Ministries' damages.

Gragson, who was slender and of average height, sometimes came across as too self-assured. However, his experience in litigation proved to be valuable inasmuch as he was always anticipating the follow-up questions and the directions opposing counsel might take. Clark, on the other hand, is the mother of four children, and came across as a dutiful, wholesome individual who could be nothing more than an extremely credible witness. Together, they presented a sound team.

It was toward the end of our presentation of evidence that we called our damage witnesses. Nickel had been assigned the task of putting on that portion of our case, and he called Clark first. Clark gave extensive testimony regarding Marvin Gorman Ministries' damages, knowing that she was going to have to defend the premise that the corporation spent more money than it made; therefore, it was on its way to going broke, as the defense experts alleged.

I had opened the trial with the theme that Marvin Gorman had fed the needy, clothed the naked, and had helped those who were chemically dependent and homeless. Marvin Gorman Ministries, Inc. had pumped a million dollars into a program called Teen Challenge, which was under the umbrella of the Assemblies of God, but in this case solely financed by Marvin Gorman Ministries. I argued that he did not show a profit under Marvin Gorman Ministries because all of his discretionary income was spent on Teen Challenge.

The core of Clark's appeal to the jury, therefore, was that the underwriting by the corporation of the Teen Challenge Program had proved to be a worthwhile but excessively expensive enterprise. Nevertheless, Marvin Gorman Ministries would have been showing a net profit year in and year out, had they not taken all their discretionary income and spent it on the program. Clark then summarized her testimony by displaying a chart to the jury that Marvin Gorman Ministries had experienced in excess of $52,000,000 in damages as a result of slanderous statements by Jimmy Swaggart and others. Clark indicated that had Gorman closed on his purchase of the television stations and satellite uplink, the "sky would have been the limit" for fund-raising.

For his portion of the testimony, Gragson had to be a little more creative. We knew Gorman's salary, but we also knew that Gorman resigned without duress; we were going to walk into a strong defense position because he had voluntarily given up his job. Thus, Gragson had to demonstrate through a survey that Gorman was still a marketable personality and but for the rumors spread that he could have taken a job at another church—be it Assemblies of God or some other denomination—for a lucrative salary.

Furthermore, Gragson calculated the royalties that Marvin would be earning on the sale of his books and tapes but for the slanderous conduct of Jimmy Swaggart and the removal of Marvin Gorman Ministries and Marvin Gorman himself from the airways.

There were only a couple of instances during this case that really made us nervous. One of them was when Gragson was on the stand. The morning that Nickel called Gragson as a witness, he took the stand with a file in hand. Another of those cardinal rules in practicing law is that unless it is desirable for the jury to see everything in the file it does not go to the stand with a witness. Otherwise, opposing counsel had the right to go through whatever is in that file, including personal notes, marginal reminders, everything.

When we broke for lunch at noon that day, Frasier and I both chastised Nickel and Gragson about taking that file to the witness stand. Gragson was using his notes to testify from, and we told Nickel to make sure that he did not get back on the stand with the file, because there was no way of knowing what might come up during cross-examination.

No sooner had we started the completion of Gragson's testimony after lunch, than I saw Gragson moving back toward the stand with his file in hand. As expected, when Wittmann took Gragson on cross-examination, the first thing he did was to pick up Gragson's file. Inside the folder file were several handwritten notes; we had no idea what they said.

Wittmann asked a few general questions about the notes, but then proceeded directly to one that was in a different handwriting. Wittmann asked him if I had written this note, and Gragson responded no.

Wittmann then asked, "Well, whose handwriting is it?"

Gragson replied, "It's my wife's handwriting. She's sitting over there." Sure enough, Terri Gragson was in the courtroom and had been sitting through the trial for the last three or four days. An expert witness is not sequestered from the courtroom when other witnesses are testifying, so both Gragson and his wife had been present for many days during the course of the trial.

Another one of the cardinal rules of trial law is that an attorney should never ask a question when he doesn't know what the answer will be. Phil Wittmann apparently forgot that rule.

He asked Gragson, "So this is your wife's handwriting?"

Gragson said, "Yes."

Wittmann said, "So would you read it to the jury?"

Frasier and I were about to throw up from sheer anxiety because of what was happening. We figured whatever was on the note would be seriously harmful to us.

Gragson cleared his throat and read the following:

It is obvious that one act of adultery seven years ago is not enough to destroy Marvin Gorman, so the defendants had to spread lies about him.

The entire courtroom was stunned into silence. I could not believe what I was hearing. Moreover, I could not believe that Wittmann had demanded that it be read aloud.

After all our worries over the jury's response to our arguments, after all the uncertainty about how things were going, here was a woman who had no direct involvement in the case, sitting in the courtroom, listening to all the evidence; she drew the conclusion that one act of adultery seven years ago was not enough to destroy Marvin Gorman, so that the defendants had to go spread lies about him to accomplish their goals. It was a stroke of luck that was almost too good to be true.

And it was. Gragson had orchestrated the entire episode, and Wittmann played right into his hands. One evening, during the course of trial preparation, Gragson was sitting in the bathtub in his hotel room at the Sheraton on the Lake. He was reading his file and thinking through the entire matter, when he had an idea. Terri was in the bedroom, and Gragson called to her and asked her to write down what he dictated. She did so on a piece of Sheraton Hotel stationary.

Thus, the jury did see a document that was in Terri's handwriting, and an attorney for the defense had it admitted as an exhibit, but he never

251

thought to have Gragson explain it or discuss its genesis.

I had the quote blown up and was able to use it as an important point during final arguments. Once again, it seemed that if not God, at least one of His angels was constantly on our shoulder. It would never have occurred to me to see Gragson as such a being, but that afternoon, he proved to be.

• CHAPTER TWENTY-THREE •
CLOSINGS

"I would order *my* cause before him, and fill my mouth with arguments."
—The Book of Job, 23:4

Every lawyer hopes that once in his life, he or she will try one big case, and usually he or she imagines it will come late in life, toward the end of a long career that has built a history of success and experience from which wisdom can be drawn.

When I contemplated Tomy Frasier's commitment to the Gorman case, that was the way I saw it. It was to be his crowning achievement. When he called me and asked me effectively to be a consultant and expert in Louisiana law for *Marvin Gorman vs. Jimmy Swaggart et al.*, I presumed my role would be a minor one. To quote T. S. Eliot, I assumed my part in the Marvin Gorman drama would be to "swell a progress, start a scene or two." It was Frasier who would take center stage, I thought; it was he who would be the hero in the "Only Show in Town."

After Tomy's heart attack and as the case developed, though, it became increasingly clear that this was to be the biggest case of *my* career. I was interviewing and deposing the main witnesses, gathering the evidence, lining up the expert testimony. And I was the one who interrogated Jimmy Swaggart himself, made him look foolish in front of the press and even his own attorneys. Perhaps more than anyone on our legal team, I also believed Marvin Gorman was telling the truth.

Moreover, I had opened the case, handled 95 percent of the witnesses and it would fall to me to close it. As I looked at the man in the wheelchair from time to time, saw his bright eyes dance with every victory—however small—we achieved, I came to understand that he was pushing me forward, thrusting me out front, not to take the blame if we failed, but to take the credit for the achievement if we won. In another sense, he was gambling with my life, my career, risking my future as a viable and credible trial lawyer on what was, on the face of it, a one-in-three chance of even a partial victory.

But in a third sense, Frasier was playing knight to my squire. His long and successful career was pockmarked with victories, with challenges that he met with courage and determination. He had no use for another personal laurel. What he sought, I came to understand, was the satisfaction of taking a "small town lawyer," a "redneck attorney" and helping him mold and direct the prosecution of a highly visible, sensational, and emotionally charged lawsuit.

These were valuable lessons, and I had tried to learn them. One cannot learn such things in law school.

What one does learn in law school is how to prepare a closing argument. In many ways, it is the most important part of an attorney's trial presentation. Whereas the opening argument must attract a jury's attention, then hold it for weeks and weeks of testimony and presentation of evidence, a closing argument must summarize, encapsulate, epitomize everything that has been said. It must reassert an attorney's position and points of argument, refute opposing counsel's position and points of argument, and it must bring home to the jury in a climactic, concluding manner the just and right cause as it has been revealed and interpreted through testimony and evidence.

At the same time, it must be as concise and intelligent as possible. The one mistake many attorneys make is to patronize a jury, to belabor the obvious, to insult the jury's intelligence, their capacity to remember, their ability to weigh and decide for themselves which side of a case is correct based on a preponderance of the evidence. In this case, much more than money was at stake—although there was a great deal of money at stake, too—in this case, the national reputations of celebrity-level men were at stake.

I worked and waited for over four years for this day. At last, it came.

On the weekend before closing arguments, I went back to Lake Charles that Saturday, I sat down with my law partners in the conference room and kicked around ideas for closing. As any well-schooled lawyer will, I had generally prepared my closing remarks before the trial began, but now was the time for me to decide the precise nature they would take, the tone, the organization, the point.

I consulted with my parents, also, and late on Saturday night, Mrs. Daughenbaugh, Milo Nickel's mother-in-law, telephoned me; she and her husband had sat through most of the trial and were very interested in the outcome. She wanted to share her ideas of what should be said in closing. Although some lawyers might be insulted by unsolicited advice at this juncture, I was pleased that everyone had ideas, wanted to help.

Fortunately, Judge Bailes did not limit our time for closing arguments. The jury had heard ten weeks of evidence, and it was going to be impossible for me to summarize it and make points if I had a strict time limit. It was hard enough to do with an open-ended clock.

On Monday, we went to work on the final draft of the jury instructions. On Tuesday, September 10, I was to give the final words the jury would hear from me on behalf of Marvin Gorman. The jury had been released until Tuesday.

I wanted Beth to come back to New Orleans with me, to lend moral support to my preparation, but she was unable to make it until Tuesday, so I went back to New Orleans Sunday night and put my finishing touches on the argument. I consulted with Frasier and Hickman on Monday afternoon and night. I had by this time discarded much of my preliminary preparation, but I had notes of how I wanted to conclude. Specific documents, such as the damages chart and Terri Gragson's note, were enlarged. I also had blown up much of Swaggart's correspondence with many sentences highlighted. I dressed in my lucky gray suit and tie that I'd worn for my opening argument, and I felt as confident as I could under the circumstances.

I agreed that Frasier could conduct the rebuttal after the defendants concluded their arguments. This actually presented us with some concern. Frasier continually harped on Swaggart's peccadillos on Airline Highway. He'd mentioned them whenever he could, both privately and in public, for over four years. His personal sense of justice was outraged by the notion that Swaggart could set himself up as judge over Marvin Gorman when he himself was guilty of far more grievous and deliberate sins than a mere dalliance with a lying woman we now believed to exhibit symptoms of nymphomania.

Judge Bailes had given us strict instructions—as had the Fourth Circuit Court of Appeals—that Swaggart's affair with Debra Murphree or anyone else was not relevant; we were prohibited from discussing it. Indeed, merely mentioning Airline Highway in my cross-examination of Jimmy Swaggart had prompted defense counsel to move for a mistrial. This subject had to be avoided at all costs.

My greatest fear in the last few minutes of this four-year crusade, ten-week trial, and expenses in excess of two hundred and fifty thousand dollars was that Tomy Frasier would ruin it all with an idle comment to the jury about Swaggart's sexual perversions. (Tomy insisted on delivering part of the closing.) I was never sure, though, whether he was merely teasing us or whether he was seriously considering addressing Swaggart's sex life in closing argument and violating the judicial order. That kept me on edge as I prepared to make the longest and most important closing argument of my career and hopefully keeping Tomy's time to a minimum.

I rose and started speaking at 8:30 A.M.; except for one ten-minute break, I spoke without stopping until noon.

It's always difficult to try to see ourselves as others see us; and when we are told about how we appear, even by those who like and love us, we tend not to believe them—unless, of course, it's negative. Alan Campo, my guru, whose perceptions I almost always trusted, said that when I addressed the court my demeanor was that of a Walter Brennan or maybe a short Jimmy Stewart. He noted that I had a somewhat disorganized, sometimes daffy approach, but that I also exuded a likeable, affable nature that suggested an underlying confidence unencumbered by egocentricity. In part, I think, this might have been part of my country lawyer background, unaffected by the champagne and caviar of the silk-stocking set.

Campo had also once told me that because of my projected personality, I had a better chance of success in longer trials, for such cases gave me time to ingratiate myself with a jury who rarely were people of means and high social standing, but rather were "folksy"–in a sense, capable of detecting through tone of voice and gesture when they were being talked down to. Such an assessment bolstered my confidence that morning, and it was a good thing. I knew I would be on my feet in front of those twelve vitally important people for a long time.

I used very few notes. I summarized the evidence of a ten week trial. I suggested numbers for damages to the jury without being pushy, but I pleaded with them to make history in this case. I asked them to send a message to the world that regardless of what they might think of Gorman or his religious preferences or his behavior as a minister, his rights were as important as anyone else's. I asked them to consider and decide that the good people who had helped Gorman needed to be reimbursed. I wanted them to see that this case was not about adultery, not about whether or not Gorman had sinned or repented. What this case was about was the dissemination of lies and falsehoods with the intent to destroy a man's name, his reputation, and this all in the name of greed and power.

I felt I did as well as I could, and I was confident that the jury listened carefully to everything I had to say. We broke for lunch, and at 1:00 P.M. the defendants began their closing arguments.

As Phil Wittmann rose to begin, Frasier and Hickman looked at me and said, "Well, we got the Frasier Rule in effect."

I asked what that was, and Frasier responded, "If they call you by name more than seven times in their closing argument, then we're going to win this case."

Wittmann made an impressive closing argument. Then came Lee Butler of Adam & Reese, who limited his points primarily to the question of damages. Butler became bold in his comments about Gorman, called him a liar, cheat, and a fraud, which in my view, invaded the province of the jury; but emotions had run high throughout the case, and there was no reason for excessive tact at this point.

Ross Buckley, attorney for Bill Treeby, had been the most vocal against me personally throughout the trial. He stood up next, then walked behind me and positioned himself in a manner that allowed him to speak over the top of my head. I suppose he hoped I would lose my cool and blow the whole case while he spoke.

He informed the jury that I was mistaken in my assessment of what this case was about. It was not, he said, about a list of lies that Jimmy Swaggart told about Gorman but rather was about a "litany" of lies that Hunter Lundy had made up in the course of the trial. Buckley told the jury there should be a *D* on my chest for "deception."

Once more, though, defense counsel were disadvantaged in their presentation. Unlike our legal team, they had to divide their time, meaning that none of the speakers could really build to a rhetorical point or emotional climax. Each was followed by another, who might be more or possibly less likeable from the jury's standpoint.

Charles Boggs closed for St. Paul Fire and Marine Insurance Company, then Frank Beahm, spoke on behalf of Travelers, arguing that all the jury had to do was answer No to "numbers. 1, 4 and 5" of the Verdict Sheet, and we could all go home. Beahm concluded by saying, "one plus four equals five, and we will all be out of here in five minutes."

By the time defense counsel concluded, their combined speakers had called me by name fifty-two times.

The rebuttal argument traditionally follows immediately after defense counsel concludes. Our strategy to turn this over to Tomy Frasier paid off, because all of the defendants were under the assumption that I was going to do it. Their attacks on me personally, they hoped, would lead me into putting aside the issues of the case while I tried to respond to their comments and defend myself as an attorney.

It was 6:00 P.M. when defense counsel concluded their arguments; they had taken nearly five hours, and it was assumed by many that Judge Bailes would call a recess until the following morning. The courthouse's air conditioning shut down automatically at 4:30 P.M. every day, and the room was packed with spectators, press, and involved parties and their families. Everyone was sweating, and there was hardly a breath of air in the courtroom. Everyone, of course, had been present all day.

But outside the courtroom, the halls and anterooms were jammed with reporters and television crews, all awaiting the end of the trial. To borrow a phrase, "the whole world was watching," and Judge Bailes wasn't about to call an intermission at this point. "The Only Show in Town" would go on.

When Frasier rolled his wheelchair up next to the jury box, complete

257

silence fell in the room. The jury had only heard from Frasier once during direct examination of Virginia Gorman, and, of course, during some of the *voir dire*; during most of the ten weeks, though, Frasier had been quiet. He had rolled into and out of the courtroom, consulted with me, Nickel, and Hickman, occasionally smiled or smirked over a point, shook his head or exhibited his famous leg-shaking technique to distract everyone from a point defense counsel was trying to make. But in no way had he appeared to be a major part of the defense team. In many ways, he appeared more in the role of press secretary than lead counsel for the plaintiff.

Now, however, these twelve citizens of Orleans Parish would find out who the brains in our outfit was. After ten weeks of patience, lecturing, hectoring, and presentation, they at last would hear from the man in the wheelchair, who, the undeniable impression was, would give them the true truth.

"If it please the court," Frasier began, "I came down here with my remarks, two-thirds of a yellow pad. I can't promise you anything and I don't. I've accumulated a lot of stuff here, because I was told by my friend, Hunter—whose name you have now heard fifty-two times in this closing argument—that I am to rebut. Well, I have a little different idea from some people.

"You know I want to tell you at the outset that I have never—and, I've been on this earth almost seven decades, and I've been doing this for four decades—I've never spoken to a jury when I wasn't frightened to death, and I'm frightened now. This government of mine and yours is run by the people, and you know who the ultimate authority of this government is? You twelve sitting in that jury box. And, that makes me emotional, and I could easily cry because of the awesome power that you have. It is your sworn duty to use it.

"I love everybody in this room, everybody." Frasier turned and waved to Jimmy Swaggart, gave him a broad smile. "I will admit that insurance lawyers test me a little bit when they do this to you—'One plus four equals five.' Come on: Forget your duty. Forget all about your duty. Or, one plus four equals five. They probably don't know it, but four plus one also equals five. And, they come in here with fifty questions and say to you, 'Listen to us, you're not going to have to answer these fifty questions, if you will do one plus four equals five.'"

Frasier frowned, shook his head. "You can shirk your duty and all of the blood and all of the God-awful things that happened to maintain this jury system will go right along with it. But the insurance companies will be well served. Will they reduce your premiums? No." He gave a slight, sly smile, then sobered and continued.

"If those lawyers are so unhappy about this law suit, why don't they take their hourly charges and give it to a worthy cause?" he asked. "I'll hold my breath if Mr. Ross Buckley does that. When they send his hourly fee for sitting here taking up your time for ten weeks, he'll probably go to that pub that this other gentleman was talking to you about.

"Don't belong—don't believe that malarkey, please, don't.

"I'm going to leave here happy. Because I'm leaving you. But, I'm going to tell you a little bit later on why I believe in my case and I'm proud to be here. I shall never, never, forget this judge." Frasier gestured slightly toward Judge Bailes. "He has been most fair, and these ladies," pointing to the court reporter and Shaneta, "have been most courteous, and you have been attentive.

"Don't let a bunch of lawyers, including me, put a bunch of hogwash on you and keep you from doing your duty. Don't let them come in here with fifty questions and say, 'Take the easy way out.'

"Yeah, I probably would have been a pretty good preacher. I would have whipped *with* everyone of them. I could! I can do it. I promise you I can do it.

"Hunter Lundy—now, you got fifty-three," Frasier said, looking at me, then back to the jury. "Hunter challenged them to show him in the bylaws or in the Constitution of the Assemblies of God where it was called for that they got the July 20 or September 2 statements for him after he resigned. And I—I tell you, this is America, and you can resign from the Assemblies of God Church, and you can resign from the Ku Klux Klan, and there's a lot of other things you can resign from.

"That's part of our freedom. They talk about church and state and the First Amendment. First Amendment, the last few words in it—this will make Hickman mad at me—I carry this thing around with me and he gets angry, it's called The Constitution, 'Congress shall make no law respecting an establishment of religion, or prohibiting the free exercise thereof.' And, getting out of it, my friends, is exercising your religious right, too, if you so choose. And nowhere does it say that in this constitution or in the Assembly of God's church constitution or even in the Bible, that it is necessary that you got to have your sins forgiven in Baton Rouge by Jimmy Swaggart."

For the first time since Frasier took the mike, the silence in the room was broken by snickering from the spectators.

Frasier turned his chair slightly to face Swaggart. "No, no, no, no, no. God has many spokesmen, not just one, not just one, not just one, Brother Swaggart." Then he looked again at the jury. "And, I quote it—I checked it—I wrote it down, and then I checked it—'Marvin, let me tell you something, pardner, if you don't straighten this thing out with God, you're going to lose your soul, die and go to hell.' That's Jimmy Swaggart. He doesn't even bother to say that God told him that.

"Then, he comes along, and this quote, this question by Hunter Lundy—fifty-four—'Do you think you have the right to decide who has repented and who hasn't?,' Lundy demanded. That's me. This is coming out of the newspaper. You can check it with the transcript.

"Swaggart's answer, 'Most definitely.' " Frasier put his hands over his face and dipped his head toward his lap in total disgust.

"This is the man who tells the whole Pentecostal world, the whole Catholic world, and other denominations, 'Come unto to me. Come unto me. I'll deliver him.'

"One man. One man has that awesome power?"

"Another quote: 'He hardly knew what I was talking about, and that's the way I intended it.' Is that the truth? He hardly knew what you were talking about, and that's the way I intended it.

"Said that words are wonderful. Said that all those conspirators—and, each and every one of them are here right now, every single, solitary one of them." The jury's faces, almost as a single face, swept the courtroom, and there they sat: Indest, Swaggart, Treeby, Jim Rentz; the whole bunch of them, seated together, where they had been for the whole ten weeks of the trial. "They're still gathered together in a cluster," Frasier went on, "All of them. Every one of them is here.

"They said Marvin Gorman never wrote anything. However, he got on that witness stand with thirteen volumes, each volume representing one day of testimony, thirteen volumes of them, thirteen days that they took his depositions, and three days he was on the witness stand in this courtroom. And, they say he didn't have any paper?

"What else came from that witness stand? They burned his files. That's uncontradicted. They burned his files. Who told us that? Eddie Tramell, as well as Marvin Gorman. It was uncontradicted. Now, how is it he was going to produce correspondence, if after they persuade him not to come back to the church, they burn his files?"

Frasier then rolled his wheelchair back toward the counsel table, looked at me, shuffled his notes and rolled back in front of the jury box. "I've got to get this rebutting on so you can go home. I'm using up all that 'one plus four' business.

"They talked about Hunter's fairy tales. I don't think they're any worse than the Aesop's Fables I heard from these gentlemen around here, I'll tell you that.

"The *Times Picayune* article. I don't have these big blown-up things, but y'all saw it. And, you're the trier of the facts. I'm not. They're not.

"The *Times Picayune* article. It's true that Marvin Gorman did not say that, 'I fell with Lynda Savage.' That's true, but it's also true that Carl Miller, who was the head of the First Assembly of God Church, who was in the rest of the article, never said it either. Now what does that tell you as a reasonable inference question: That they didn't want Gorman to go to the church? That they were going to keep it quiet—'they' the church?

"And why? Because, they had to finish their building program. They wanted it, Marvin Gorman wanted it, and they all went along with it. So the *Times Picayune* article has got two sides to it, not just one."

At this point, Frasier went to the heart of the first confrontation at Swaggart's house. "And it's true," Frasier said, "as Phil Wittmann said that Marvin Gorman didn't say blah, blah, blah, in five words. But Indest, Jimmy Swaggart, and David Savage all said that Marvin Gorman said, 'It's not like you're saying. It's not like you're telling it.'

"Now, why didn't he go ahead and elaborate? Because the person he had hurt was sitting six feet from him, David Savage. They had driven to Jimmy Swaggart's house together, and, incidentally, Savage had forgiven him and they wanted him to say, of course, Indest was there, and he was—I'm amazed they didn't get into what Indest called 'kinky sex.' I don't know.

"All this hogwash of it being—please I don't want to waste your time with it. Marvin Gorman never wrote down about his sex affairs. I'm getting to be an old man, but I never wrote mine down either. I want to tell you that. As a matter of fact, they," he gestured toward the defendants, "had to go back to 1978. Man, if he had made peace with his God and lived a pure life that long, he's my hero. And that's what I told Bill Elder. Of course, it wasn't on that program.

"And, he says that he fell. You don't have to prove that. He says, 'Because I fell, I had to resign my church,' and he did.

"Man, I love Jimmy Swaggart! And I'm going to tell you something: It is '*Reverend* Jimmy Swaggart.' It is 'Reverend Jimmy Swaggart.' It is '*Reverend* Miller.' And I've heard my colleagues talk about cheap shots in this courtroom. '*Mister* Gorman, *Mister* Gorman, *Mister* Gorman, *Mister* Gorman', but '*Reverend*' the rest of them. Now, you talk about cheap! And y'all caught that. You're so much smarter than us lawyers. You ought not allow us to talk to you.

"I hate to use the term, but I will use it anyway. The other Freudian slip was from you, Phil," Frasier gestured toward Wittmann, "when you said, 'The final nail in the coffin.' That's right, that's what they're trying to do, put the pastor in the coffin and seal it and put it away forever and ever.

"Can I quit this rebutting business? I'll do Boggs, and then I'll quit rebutting. 'Brother' Boggs, a colleague of mine, even though I'm a stranger in this land. He's the one that first came up about this fraud on the jury system that makes me angry and emotional about that. He says— also the other business about why we didn't sue WWL. Well hey, they were duped. They were duped. Treeby went to them, screened, edited, put

261

on the program for them, and had the veto power. They were just duped.

"Mr. Boggs—I like Mr. Boggs. You know he represents the insurance companies. I understand they get paid so much an hour to represent them. You know their client. You can cut their arms, and they don't bleed. You can't take their pulse or heart beat, and they don't have to worry about going to heaven or hell. Insurance companies. They collect premiums and do everything on earth to keep from paying the claims and leave the people, the insured, like Swaggart hanging out to dry.

"I'm going to quit rebutting. You folks are better judges of the facts than me. History has proven that ever since it was started, this world. I feel so proud to be able to talk from time to time to a jury because that's what my country is about. For you are the ruler. You know, the only difference between us and Russia and other totalitarian governments is the jury system. And you've got to take it seriously or else the blood and the guts that's been spilled for this country was for nothing.

"This, right inside this box is even more sacred than your vote. (Frasier was, of course, referring to the jury box.) So please take it seriously. Don't let somebody do that to you. Ten weeks of your time and they would have you get out of here in five minutes.

"Believe me, this case wouldn't have taken five years if there wasn't substance to it. So I'm going to call your attention to what I started out to. Plaintiff's exhibit number twenty-five. In the seventh paragraph it says—and this is a letter from Jimmy Swaggart to Richard Dortch dated December 28, 1984—'You see in Genesis 9, we're told the story of Noah's drunkenness. Ham sought to expose the nakedness of his father. Shem and Jeb had sought to cover him. I believe this is the correct position for anyone to take concerning their brother with a problem. Instead of exposing it, we endeavor to cover so as not to hurt or hinder the work of God.'

"Well, if they thought to cover the confession of Reverend Gorman, they failed miserably. But that's not what this lawsuit is about. This lawsuit is not about religion, this lawsuit is about the law. And despite all the talented lawyers and attorneys for insurance companies they put together, Gorman looked you right in the eye and he said 'Yes, I did. I asked my God to forgive me, and I asked my God and my wife to forgive me. Ronnie Goux forgave me, and David Savage forgave me.' Everyone forgave him except who? The conspirators.

"Let me tell you this: I am proud to represent this man. Not the man who ministers via Palm Springs, California," he again shot Swaggart a look, reminding the jury that he kept a home out there which he frequently visited. Then he nodded toward Gorman. "But the man who ministers in Orleans parish and in New Orleans, Louisiana. The man who,

262

a Protestant minister, Pentecostal minister, who I believe the testimony is, was on the board of the Mercy Hospital. The man who believed in taking his efforts to do good for people into the street. I think Mrs. Gorman testified that if he had fifty dollars and you needed it, you got it. As a man who went out and sought those in trouble to help them.

"Yes, they made much fun of Jonas Robertson, he's one of six— Hunter was right—who stood up or sat on the stand and said, 'I was saved because of Marvin Gorman, I was saved because of Marvin Gorman,' and one of them was Jonas Robertson.

"And sure I don't know why my colleague Phil Wittmann sought to drag up the fact that he smoked crack cocaine, heroin, Big *H*, or whatever the stuff is, marijuana and all that business. I don't know what that had to do with this lawsuit, but I know how it affected me. I thought, 'My Lord, what a change Marvin Gorman has had in the life of that man.' And, he gave Marvin Gorman credit for it."

Frasier went on and on and had the jury in laughter and in tears, but he made excellent points. He had spoken for twenty-five minutes and rebutted the statements made by the defendants. He did slide a little when he got into the facts. For example, he started to review the chronology and placed Indest on the plane to Costa Rico with Treeby and Swaggart. That was totally wrong and likely to confuse the issue, so I quietly leaned over and said, "Wrap it up." I had already reviewed all these facts for the jury. He nodded.

"I'm going to quit," he said, "And I'll tell you why in case you're curious. I just consulted with my co-counsel, and you know what he told me to do?" He pointed to me. " 'Wrap it up.' So, I'm going to wrap it up with this remark.

"Phil Wittmann said that Reverend Jimmy Swaggart had very strict standards, religious standards about sex, but Wittmann never told you what those standards were."

At this point, Nickel and I almost came out of our seats because we thought Frasier was about to "turn the goose loose" by mentioning the Airline Highway incident. But Frasier was smarter than that, and in looking back on it, we should have known better than to worry.

He continued, "Well, I submit to you that Reverend Gorman is the one who has standards. When they said 'you have fallen,' he said, 'yes.' And they took that and they stomped it and stomped it. And if you're at my house and you step on a bug on my carpet, I appreciate it. But if you stomp till you wear out my carpet, I'm going to get mad as hell.

"Please don't let them hurry you at all. Take all the time you want, but you return a just verdict. God speaks through more mouths than just one, believe me.

"Thank you, Your Honor, and I appreciate the courtesy of being here

263

and you all allowing me to be here."

It was worth it. The four years and ten weeks that I waited were worth it to hear this man talk to a jury. Frasier spoke to the jury as if he were one of them, a man who was put up with all the legal rigmarole that had taken ten weeks to unfold. He spoke in a folksy way, suggesting that the machinations and maneuverings of opposing counsel really meant nothing in the greater scheme of things. He asked them to be themselves, to set themselves above these well-dressed men and women of the law, to rely on their own, innate sense of justice, and to respond to their sworn duty from the facts as they perceived them.

It was a masterful performance, one worthy of the best silk-stocking lawyer in any firm in any city; but it was also one that none of those high-dollar lawyers could have pulled off.

At 6:30 P.M. the court instructed the jury on the law, and they went out. Five minutes went by, and there was no verdict. Thus, the jury had ignored the defense's "one plus four equals five" formula. They came back shortly thereafter and wanted the court to reinstruct them on the definition of "defamation." By this time, it was eight o'clock, and the Judge ordered that the jury be sequestered for the first time. They were taken to hotel rooms, and we were instructed to reconvene 9:00 the next morning.

The outcome was now in their hands, and, as Gorman doubtless believed, in the hands of God.

264

• PART FIVE •
JUDGMENT DAY

"Pilate saith unto him, What is truth?"
—The Gospel According to Saint John, 18:38

•CHAPTER TWENTY-FOUR •
THE JURY'S TRUTH

"To do justice and judgment *is* more acceptable to the Lord than sacrifice."

—The Proverbs, 21:3

The next morning, Wednesday, September 11, we returned to the courthouse to wait for the notices—the verdict—to be published. The jury filed in to be reinstructed by Judge Bailes on the question of defamation once more, then they went out again. We believed that a quick verdict would go against us, so after ninety minutes ticked off and the jury was still out, we began to relax.

In the court house lobby downstairs, a regular circus was going on. Lawyers, spectators, involved parties, media people, and reporters milled around expressing concern, curiosity, cautious optimism first for one side, then the other. Ross Buckley assured reporters that the jury would be back in thirty minutes, a statement that spread throughout the building and kept everyone inside and kept reporters standing near telephones, all expecting to hear the verdict very soon. Frank Beahm was walking around holding a T-shirt that said, "One plus four equals five and we're all out of here in five minutes." Chaos vied with anxiety everywhere we looked.

I personally avoided as many questions as possible. I clung to Frasier's original projection that we had but a one-in-three chance of winning, although every minute that ticked by seemed to increase the odds in our favor. At noon, I finally agreed to give a television interview. I didn't want to appear either overly confident or overly cautious; therefore, I merely said that it appeared obvious that the jury had taken this case seriously since they didn't come back in thirty minutes, and I felt confident that whatever their decision would be, it would be the right one. I left it at that. I later learned that the noon interview was viewed by several judges who had been following the case. One in particular was Justice Jack Watson, a Louisiana Supreme Court Justice, who later commended me for the humility of my statement.

267

If I appeared humble, it was because I was truly uncertain of the verdict. All I knew for sure was what I said: based on the amount of time they were taking, the jury was obviously considering our case closely.

Later that morning a letter came back from the jury to the judge asking that they be given all exhibits authored by Jimmy Swaggart. Frasier couldn't pass up the opportunity to comment to the press that the jury had asked to read "Jimmy Swaggart's mail."

The day dragged by, and we sought any distraction to keep our minds off the sweeping second hands on the clock. Mark Gorman, whom I didn't really know as well as I did the rest of the family, sat with us in the courtroom while we waited, entertaining us by telling one joke after another. I gained a much better appreciation for Marvin's character simply by listening to Mark. It was clear that a lot of Gorman's talent had been passed on to Mark, a twenty-nine-year-old minister who could sing and preach with the best of them. We spent all day Wednesday in the courtroom sharing stories.

Late Wednesday afternoon the jury had another legal question that required the judge to bring all the attorneys into chambers in order to agree on a response to the jury.

By late afternoon on the eleventh there was still no verdict. Judge Bailes sent the jury back to the hotel for the night. We all went out to eat, we were feeling much better about our chances. A second night's wait could only mean that there was a sharp division among the jurors— indicating that at least a healthy minority were on our side—or that they were past the verdict and were now trying to decide damages. Either proposition cheered us, but the second one kept our hopes high.

By mid-morning on September 12 our hopes were confirmed. We learned that the jury was now on page seven of the special verdict sheet. That meant they were indeed past liability and were now most certainly arguing over damages.

That understanding lifted us to a new level of anxiety.

We had taken bets among ourselves as to what the jury would find in the way of damages and compensation. I felt that two to three million dollars would be a reasonable expectation. Kristie Plumb guessed a figure of ten million dollars. The Gormans and Frasier and the rest would never name a specific figure, the former because they never really expected to receive any money, and the latter because he hoped for a high dollar figure as a symbol of Swaggart's punishment. It was a tricky guessing game, even so; we had absolutely no clue what the jury was thinking.

Milo Nickel wouldn't admit it openly, but he later told me he always thought we were going to lose. The Sunday following the verdict I learned that Milo had taken a job with another law firm just prior to the commencement of this case, obviously never thinking that we would win the lawsuit.

As the day plodded on, we continued to sit around and listen to Mark's stories and jokes. Once or twice during the day, the jury came back with questions requiring all counsel to meet in chambers with the judge in order to compose answers. One of these chambers conferences was called after Phil Wittmann had returned to his office. Denise Pilié, acting for him but unwilling to offer input on his behalf, handed Judge Bailes her cellular phone so he could call Wittmann to discuss the question with him directly. The crusty old jurist just looked at her, laughed, and ignored the suggestion. I think His Honor had the same impression that we did on the self-importance of some of these silk-stocking defense lawyers.

While the jury was out, the tension among the spectators was no less than it had been during the entire ten weeks. "Gormanites" were in one area praying for Marvin; "Swaggarites" were someplace else, singing and praying for Jimmy. Swaggart himself roamed the halls, pressing the flesh and offering words of comfort to all he imagined might want them.

Beth and I were sitting on the bench in the hall when Jimmy Swaggart walked up and said, "Who is this lovely lady?" Of course, Beth introduced herself, and he replied with a somewhat half-hearted compliment about me. In spite of the obvious tact and diplomacy he was showing in the matter, I was uncomfortable during the exchange. I don't think Jimmy Swaggart ever really held any animosity toward me personally, although Frances and Bill Treeby certainly did. They despised me.

I also don't think Swaggart ever truly understood the gravity of the issue being tried. He never quite grasped that what was really being judged in that court was not the question of who said what about whom, when and why, but rather Swaggart's entire character, his veracity, his credibility, his very integrity, not merely as a man, but as a leader in his faith. He always saw his position as a matter of point of view, not as a matter of morality; he never seemed to acknowledge that it was he who was on trial.

Up to that point, I had assumed that Swaggart's innate arrogance, his egocentric nature, his unshakable belief in his personal infallibility had carried him high above the issues of the lawsuit. But in that moment, while he held Beth's hand and mouthed a platitude or two about me, I understood something else: Jimmy Swaggart was basically a naive and ignorant man, an ill-educated bumpkin who had somehow stumbled into greatness—into celebrity—by virtue of God-given talents and an imperfect understanding of human nature. He had instinctively mastered the powers that came from combining spectacular showmanship with faux eloquence to exploit the masses, to move millions to emotional expression to enrich himself and enhance his personal status. This was a sufficient measure of success for him, a sufficient sign of God's blessing on him.

Perhaps, I thought, Frasier was wrong. Perhaps Swaggart wasn't evil. Perhaps he was nothing more than pitifully myopic, blinded by the bright lights of his own accidental success and by his unshakable belief in his own divine anointment.

Regardless, the pressure of waiting was finally penetrating Swaggart's outward display of self-confidence. By Thursday morning, he was walking up and down the halls, clapping his hands and chanting, "Ring the bell, someone just needs to ring the bell, it needs to be over."

Although I had counted on Frasier's presence right up to the bitter end, he and Julia had to fly back to Tulsa at noon on Thursday because she had a doctor's appointment regarding her cancer diagnosis. The jury stayed out through the afternoon. That evening we dined out again, as did the jury; we returned to the courthouse afterwards to sit around and wait some more. By now, they had been in deliberation since 6:30 p.m. on Tuesday the tenth. At 9:30 P.M., on Thursday, September 12, we finally received the message that the verdict was in. The moment we had been waiting and working for had arrived.

The courtroom was jammed once more. Reporters, television personalities, attorneys, and their staffs, family members, and, of course, the plaintiff and defendants and their families and friends crowded in, all jockeying for positions from where they could see both Gorman and Swaggart. Television reporters had advised their local stations to stand by; they were prepared to read the verdict as soon as it was rendered. The beeps of cellular telephones were constant as order was called for. The atmosphere was electric with nervous anticipation. Like so many other experiences in this case, this was a first for me.

Angie Hanes, a very pleasant young black woman who sat on the front row in the jury box, had been named foreperson. The court clerk read the verdict:

The jury found that Jimmy Swaggart, Jimmy Swaggart Ministries, and Michael Indest had defamed Marvin Gorman and Marvin Gorman Ministries. The jury found no invasion of privacy, but they did find that Jimmy Swaggart, Jimmy Swaggart Ministries, Michael Indest, the First Assembly of God, and Bill Treeby had committed intentional infliction of emotional distress against Marvin Gorman. Then, the jury also found that a conspiracy existed among Jimmy Swaggart, Jimmy Swaggart Ministries and Michael Indest to defame Marvin Gorman and Marvin Gorman Ministries; they also found that there was a conspiracy among the First Assembly of God, Jimmy Swaggart, Jimmy Swaggart Ministries, Michael Indest, and Bill Treeby to intentionally inflict emotional distress on Marvin Gorman.

We received everything we asked for. Jimmy Swaggart's "bell" had rung. He and his minions had been judged by "twelve people, good and true," and their verdict was guilty.

A major surprise was the inclusion of Jimmy Swaggart Ministries in both the conspiracy findings. It was apparent to me that the jury believed that Donnie Swaggart, head of Jimmy Swaggart Ministries, was as much a part of both conspiratorial moves against Gorman as anyone else and that he and Swaggart were mainly responsible for Jimmy Swaggart Ministries' liability.

I had made the point vehemently during my the closing argument that the one person the defense didn't call to testify was Donnie Swaggart. My assertion was that the reason they didn't call him was because they feared he would tell the truth, and I let the jury draw and hold the same conclusion.

Later, I would learn that the question of conspiracy, an idea born in the parking lot of Marvin Gorman Ministries back in 1987, really a kind of fall back position to protect all of us financially, had become a kind of buzzword among the jury. In their minds, Gorman's ruination had taken place not at the hands of a single individual, but rather at his behest. It was a deliberate program of character assassination and defamation orchestrated and performed by the entire Swaggart establishment.

In any event, the conspiracy was now revealed and on the record, and it was possibly the most professionally satisfying portion of the verdict for me.

Once the hubbub in the courtroom subsided, the jury moved on to the question of damages.

On the issue of defamation of Marvin Gorman personally, the jury concluded that the damages to Marvin Gorman were six hundred thousand dollars plus four hundred thousand dollars for intentional infliction of emotional distress; as to the question of damages to Marvin Gorman Ministries, they found that the conspirators were liable for nine million. Kristie Plumb was correct. The jury came back with a ten million verdict.

Behind me, to the right, Ross Buckley and Bill Treeby sat in stony silence. Treeby slumped in his chair, looking completely deflated, shriveled. For his part, Swaggart just sat in stunned amazement, looking as though he could not believe he had been plucked. The only gentleman on the defense team was Phil Wittmann, who walked over and congratulated me. The rest of the silk-stocking attorneys went into a deep sulk.

It was ten o'clock, time for the *Nightly News* on most TV stations. Reporters rushed out of the courtroom and downstairs where their microphones were arranged on a platform. Live feeds were quickly established. We let the Swaggarts and the defendants clear the courtroom first and then we followed.

It was hard not to react to such unexpected success. When the elevator doors opened on the first floor of the courthouse, more than fifty microphones were pushed in our direction, and lights from the cameras flashed in our faces. Gorman and I made our way side by side to the platform and faced the press. We were both elated, but both of us were trying to appear professional, when inside we were jumping up and down and howling at the moon. My only regret was that Frasier wasn't present to bask in the glow of success.

Gorman said that he was happy with the verdict, happy that the jury believed him, and most happy that his good name was restored and that the decision was fair. He then turned to me, and I was "on."

I was physically and emotionally drained as I listened to the many questions being asked, seemingly all at once. I thanked God for helping us through this victory; then I lost composure. Tears rolled down my cheeks as I told them that it took five long years of hard work, but the system was a true system. The jury heard the evidence, applied the law, and returned a just verdict.

I looked out into the mob and waving cameras and microphones and tape recorders, but I saw no one I knew. The lobby was so jammed that I couldn't tell if of any my friends were there. It was strange to suddenly feel so alone while surrounded by so many jostling, shouting people, all focusing their attention on my face. I turned and found Beth's hand.

CNN and other networks interrupted their programming to read the verdict, which is the way Frasier heard it. The Associated Press put the news on the wire, and every television station in the State of Louisiana interrupted programs to announce it. The "jury's truth" was revealed, and it was just. Back in Lake Charles, my friends and colleagues were stunned. The tainted press coverage of the trial had led them to believe we didn't stand a chance of even the smallest victory. They expected I would return from the Big Easy with my tail between my legs, a hard lesson learned at the hands of the big city, silk-stocking lawyers and their courts. Plans for gatherings to extend consolation were hurriedly altered to celebrations of victory in anticipation of my homecoming.

Following the press conference, Gorman asked the entire plaintiff team to walk across the street and into the lobby at the Energy Center. There, Gorman asked everyone to join hands in a circle as he gave thanks to God for giving the jury the wisdom and the patience to come to a just decision.

Homecoming was delayed, though. Nickel, Hickman and I were back in court Friday morning, the 13th, to submit another set of

272

interrogatories to the jury. Through these, the jurors would answer questions to determine which insurance coverages would apply to their verdict. Though the process was tedious, the atmosphere in the courtroom was relaxed; it was a pleasure to be there. Gorman seemed particularly at ease, bereft of the tension and worry that had burdened him for four long years, truly longer than that. Now, he felt, God had seen us through this ordeal and lifted the weight of doubt from his shoulders.

The jury answered the questions involving insurance coverage in about an hour and came back in before noon. That verdict sheet was read, and we made an oral motion that the two verdict sheets be made the Judgment of the Court; Judge Bailes said that we could address the judgment at a later time, but that he was going to let the jury go home.

During the ten weeks of the trial, our legal team had scrupulously followed the rules of jurisprudence governing contact with the jury. With the exception of a few instances of Tomy rolling down to the jury room and eyeballing them, offering newspapers and an occasional smoke, I neither visited with nor spoke to any juror throughout the trial; I tried not to persuade them in any form or fashion except in closing argument. I did see Audrey Sams leaving the courthouse in her vehicle one afternoon; she turned and gave me and Nickel a thumbs-up. That was the only signal—positive or negative—we received from any juror until the return of the verdict.

However, that Friday after the jury was excused but before court was dismissed, the bailiff said something to Judge Bailes, who then asked me to approach the bench and told me the jury wanted to see me and Marvin Gorman outside the courtroom. When we came out of the doors of the room, there they were, waiting for us. Three young women came up and hugged me, saying, "God bless you." Several of them also hugged Gorman, and they all had pens and paper and wanted our autographs. Again, the analogy between court and theater seemed to hold true, only now, our most feared critics were our biggest fans.

Still, I would have thought these people were being silly; but in their eyes, perhaps, we *were* celebrities, and, not to belabor the point, this verdict made history. Of course, that was their doing, not mine, not Gorman's. This jury had taken Swaggart down a notch—a big notch. He was the most charismatic, powerful televangelist in the world, but these twelve people had shown him that no man, no matter how self-proclaimed of godly virtues, is above the law.

Gorman and I stood around and visited with the now former jurors and asked them several questions, revealing why certain things had gone our way, and how particular points of the trial had persuaded them that the evidence we presented was preponderant.

Eventually, Gorman and I left to meet with several newspaper

273

reporters beneath a large oak tree in front of the court house on Loyola Avenue. Marvin led off. He spoke of continuing his ministry and said he had no intention of leaving New Orleans. Despite the efforts of these defendants, he said, he would not "be run out of town." He said his intention was no different now from what it had ever been: He was going to serve God.

The reporters then turned to the question of money. Gorman stated that he had no idea if he, personally, would ever receive any money from the trial. It was his goal, he said, to see his creditors paid. That was all. He let them know he didn't enter into litigation for money, wasn't seeking financial gain for himself, truly not even for his ministry. What he wanted was the satisfaction of justice, of revealing the truth.

During the course of the interview, a car drove by with the window down, and the driver yelled, "God bless you, Marvin." A few moments later, another car drove by with the window open and somebody screamed, "You're wasting the taxpayers' money!" The contrast was funny, because both sides of the story were still on the street, but Gorman answered both with nothing more than a slight smile.

He then expressed gratitude to his legal team, naming me and Frasier in particular, but including Nickel, Hickman, Atkins, and Stone as well. I never ceased to be amazed at the completeness of his mind or his capacity to remember faces, names, and to be able to include everyone whenever he mentioned anyone. His humility before these reporters—barracudas, some attorneys call them—was total; there never was a sense that but for their repetition of so many rumors and lies spread by Swaggart and his minions, he would never have been harmed so seriously. Instead, he greeted them as friends, almost as supplicants, and used the occasion not to make a sermon, as Swaggart might have done, but rather to demonstrate through his quiet responses and generous sincerity that what was past was past. It was time now to look ahead.

I decided that I could not be so generous or forgiving when my time came to be interviewed. These same reporters, or the papers they worked for, had consistently made fun of me, ridiculed me, teased me and called me "the country lawyer from Lake Charles" for four years. I had been denigrated and derided by the silk-stocking attorneys, who had questioned my ability, my education, my competence and who had marshalled the forces of the New Orleans press to depict me as a redneck who was in way over his head in the deep legal waters of the Crescent City.

It came as a welcome opportunity for me, then, when one reporter blithely asked, "Well, Mr. Lundy, just why did Marvin Gorman hire a 'country lawyer from Lake Charles?'" I looked at him and I said, "There's eight reasons." The reporter gave me a dismayed look, thinking doubtless that he was going to hear a long dissertation. But I shocked him with brevity: "And the eight reasons are, one plus seven zeros." That was the end of my interview, and I walked off with a smile, leaving the reporters standing agape behind me.

The newspaper articles on the morning of September 13 were fascinating. The article in the Mobile, Alabama, newspaper was entitled "Judgment Day;" the articles in New Orleans papers were very strong in favor of Gorman; the article in the Lake Charles paper also came out strongly in Gorman's behalf. Many newspapers ran a photograph they picked up off the Associated Press wire. It showed Gorman, Virginia, and me walking together down the sidewalk after the trial, and it was probably the picture I will remember most from the entire ordeal.

Following the interview, I went back to the hotel, packed up the Suburban and a trailer to carry all the equipment and documents back to Lake Charles.

As I made my way around the rooms of the Sheraton by the Lake, I could see stacks of files and videotapes and boxes of documents and notes jammed against walls and piled behind furniture. I saw in my mind the detritus of pizza boxes and Chinese food containers and barbecue cartons, napkins, plastic utensils, candy wrappers, and wadded napkins, crushed beer and soda cans, empty coffee cups and half-filled glasses, ashtrays filled with Frasier's smoldering butts, and the occasional empty Crown Royal bottle tossed idly aside. I could smell the women's perfume, the men's aftershave, and, of course, the stale odors of sweat and fatigue following days of testimony, weeks of study, worry and work. I could still hear the hum of VCRs rewinding, the blare of television news, the shouts of arguments for or against this point or that witness, the tragic wrangles and agonizing frustration of what we were not allowed to do, the shouted triumphs and comedic celebration of what we were.

It was all there, echoing through those rooms, that in a very short time would be cleaned, sterilized, made the same as any other rooms in any other Sheraton hotel. But a drama had been played there, and relationships and emotional highs and lows had been felt as truly as they are felt in real life.

Now, it was over. And I couldn't help but feel that my euphoria from victory was tainted by a profound sense of loss of comrades, of friends, of people who had become as close to me as my own family as I shut the door on those suites for the last time and made my way back to southwest Louisiana to a simple practice which would never again be simple.

275

• CHAPTER TWENTY-FIVE •
THE AFTERMATH

"It ain't over till it's over."

—The Gospel According to Yogi

On the nights of September 12 and 13, the dates the verdict and damage assignments came in, the legal team had calls from *Nightline* and Larry King to appear on their shows. I personally favored appearing with Larry King, as many of Swaggart's more inflammatory statements about other ministers had been broadcast on that program. Frasier, though, asked me to afford him the courtesy of controlling the television appearances. Inasmuch as handling the media had been, up until the trial began at least, Frasier's special area of interest, I agreed. He wanted us to appear on *The Donahue Show*; he had been on Donahue back when he tried the *Marianne Guinne vs The Collinsville Church of Christ* case, and he maintained that *Donahue* was the '*créme de la créme*' of talk shows.

Unfortunately, the Swaggarts and their codefendants refused to appear on *The Donahue Show*, and he would only have us if both sides of the dispute agreed to appear. This resulted in their backing out. By the time *Donahue* decided not to use us, *Nightline* and CNN were no longer interested. I did give some personal interviews for *Inside Edition, Hard Copy,* and some other syndicated and cable network programs, and I appeared on a local television program in Lake Charles. Additionally, I was interviewed for the *American Bar Association Journal*, a particularly satisfying experience.

By the time I returned home, unpacked and realized that I no longer had to make an immediate turnaround for New Orleans, I had to go back to work. My family needed attention and I was exhausted emotionally and physically, but I also was far behind on all my other work. Moreover, I had just spent six months on a case that brought no financial return to the firm except a minimal amount from the settlement with USF&G.

We prepared a judgment and sent it to the court for signature, and we waited for the aftermath to conclude. Defense counsel naturally filed their

276

motions for new trial, motions to amend the judgment, and motions to set the verdict aside. We traveled to New Orleans twice to argue those motions, resulting in the court denying all of them.

The court reduced the verdict on defamation of Marvin Gorman and Marvin Gorman Ministries by one-third because of our pre-trial settlement with Michael Indest. Since Indest was an *insolido obligor* (joint tortfeasor) under Louisiana law, there was a pro-rata reduction of the verdict because of the settlement. The same thing applied with intentional infliction of emotional distress as far as Indest and the First Assembly of God were concerned. There was a two-fifths reduction in the intentional infliction of emotional distress because of these settlements.

In December, we asked Curklin Atkins to contact all the jurors and arrange for a small social at the Sheraton on the Lake. The jurors and their spouses or dates were invited to meet and visit with us, so we could do a post-mortem on the case. The gathering turned out to be better than we expected. We learned many things from the jury, some of which surprised us.

Some of the now former jurors revealed that they saw Ross Buckley as something of a villain. They thought he displayed the most anger towards me personally and that it was unwarranted by the events of the trial alone. Others, though, thought that Buckley and I were really friends and that this was merely theatrics. I explained that I had no idea what Buckley thought of me personally, but I acknowledged that I was more than a little perturbed by his comments and antics at my expense.

I also noted that I understood that Buckley was under a lot of pressure having to represent Bill Treeby; I knew there were several occasions during the course of the trial when he wanted to withdraw from Treeby's defense. I suspected that Treeby was trying to be his own lawyer, telling Ross how to defend the case, which caused a breakdown in the attorney-client relationship. The old adage about a man who defends himself having "a fool for an attorney" was actually borne out in Treeby's case, I believed.

It seemed that the jury had taken notice of absolutely everything that took place in the courtroom. They observed the gaudy apparel worn by Frances Swaggart and they noted apparent discord between her and Swaggart. They believed Marvin and Virginia Gorman, by contrast, had a close, loving relationship and made a modest, self-effacing appearance.

Many of the jurors asserted that they didn't care how many women Gorman had slept with. Their verdict was strictly based on the fact that it was "none of Jimmy Swaggart's damned business what Marvin Gorman was doing." Again, it was Swaggart's arrogant display of self-righteousness that angered them.

That night we learned we had been correct in selecting our

absolutely-must-have-no-matter-what jurors and also in seeking a predominantly African-American panel. Frasier and I had observed for four years Gorman's relationship with blacks in the Orleans Parish community and were aware of his professed love for everyone of all colors and races. The young black women at our social hugged Gorman and declared that they "just loved him to death." Gorman ultimately picked up two of the jurors as visitors to his church; late in the spring of 1994, Tammie Ange, converted and was baptized in Marvin's new church on Elysian Fields Avenue.

I cannot speak for Gorman any longer, but I feel certain that that moment when he baptized this woman who had played such a significant role in his temporal salvation had to be one of the most profoundly moving experiences of his life.

We learned that four jurors had wanted to give us as much as sixty million and two jurors wanted to give us ninety million. Eight jurors agreed to award twenty million, with the exception of Michael Hyde.

In the State of Louisiana, it takes nine out of twelve to reach a correct verdict in a civil case. According to "Little Bit," (the nickname Atkins had given to the diminutive but vivacious Kimberly Veal), she had to use her feminine wiles to persuade Hyde to obtain his concurrence on a monetary amount. Apparently, nine panelists agreed on liability, but Hyde just wouldn't agree on the amount of damages. They ultimately compromised on the ten-million-dollar figure.

Our decision, then, on "Little Bit" was right on the money in more ways than one; so was my feeling about Reneta Scott, the Macy's jewelry counter salesperson who I believed had "damages" written across her forehead. Both these women wanted to give us the full ninety million dollars; Little Bit also wanted to "tag" Frances Swaggart as well as the others.

In all, that evening proved more valuable to me as a trial lawyer than a standard postmortem with a bunch of attorneys and paralegals sitting around and poring over transcripts ever could have been. I learned that I should never underestimate a jury's capacity for finding the truth, no matter how well it's disguised by either a defendant or a plaintiff. As a body, a jury seems to develop a built-in "bullshit detector," and they become highly sensitive to the smallest gestures, details of dress and decorum, even unconscious signals of nerves and anxiety projected by those moving on the stage before them.

This jury had every reason to be persuaded by defense counsel's arguments just as they had every reason to be persuaded by our own legal team's arguments. In the end, though, they were persuaded by the evidence; that, more than anything else, is what makes the law work, that, more than anything else, is what justice is all about.

By December 1991, all the post-trial motions were disposed of and Judge Bailes had entered a final judgment. Jimmy Swaggart and his insurance companies were scrambling around trying to suspend the judgment in order to appeal. Even though the verdict had been reduced, with interest, it still exceeded ten million dollars. Thus, Jimmy Swaggart Ministries had to put up real estate as collateral before the bonding companies would suspend the judgment to appeal the case.

Much later, I learned of the difficulties between Federal Insurance Company and Jimmy Swaggart Ministries in agreeing to collateral for the bonds. Swaggart was in serious financial trouble at this point, it seems, and the judgment against him was just one more crushing blow to the economic base that had made him an international religious presence.

Before the briefing schedule is established by the court in any appeal, the record or transcript of the trial with all testimony and exhibits, must be lodged in the Court of Appeals. Given the length and complexity of this case, it took some time to complete the transcript. Unfortunately, it took until late 1992 before the record was lodged.

As soon as the record was lodged, briefing schedules were published by the Fourth Circuit Court of Appeals, and the defendants, who were, of course, now the appellants, immediately moved for an extension of an additional sixty days to file their briefs. Stone, Pigman took the lead in writing the appeal brief on the issues of liability. Adams & Reese took the lead in writing the issues of coverage as to Federal Insurance Company and addressing the primary issue of damages. Since Adams & Reese was representing Federal Insurance Company, which had the largest policy involved in the case, they had the most to address. Aetna, Jimmy Swaggart's homeowner's carrier, as well as St. Paul, Jimmy Swaggart Ministries' general liability carrier, were also involved. State Farm satisfied Treeby's judgment and did not appeal.

When Milo Nickel left our firm in September 1991 right after the trial, I was the only one who had the background to write the brief—unless, of course, we wanted someone to go over a cold record and write it. Some lawyers think that's the best way to handle an appeal. In April of 1993, a friend of mine from Mississippi, former United States District Judge Walter L. Nixon, called and asked if he could come work for us in Lake Charles and possibly help write the brief.

Nixon was convicted of perjury in 1988. He was only the second United States District Judge in the history of the country to be impeached. I had followed Nixon's problems closely and had always been his close supporter and friend. In a few words, I felt that he had gotten a raw deal.

Regardless, Nixon was neither eligible for reinstatement to the Mississippi Bar before the end of 1993 nor was he eligible to be reinstated to the Louisiana Bar. However, the State of Louisiana's policy differs from Mississippi's in that it allows former members of the bar who have been suspended or disbarred to work as paralegals under licensed attorneys. Given the ongoing demands of my practice, I felt that the Swaggart brief might be a good project for Nixon to undertake. I knew he was a brilliant lawyer and, prior to his troubles, was a well-respected jurist. Nixon came on board with our firm in April 1993.

Nixon, Kristie Plumb, and I flew to Tulsa to brainstorm with Frasier and Hickman about issues that should be addressed in the brief. Upon returning to Lake Charles, Nixon and I agreed to split the responsibility of the appeal. I would take all liability issues, and he would address damages. Hickman and I always thought the issue of damages would be the problem to address in the appeals court. We were wrong.

Nixon spent weeks going through the record. We had received the briefs of the defendants, knew the issues, and had sought our own extensions to give ourselves plenty of time to respond. But it did not take Nixon long after reviewing the record to tell me that if there was a way to settle this case I should attempt to do so. He said that there were so many issues, many of which were volatile, that this case could go anywhere on appeal.

Louisiana is a very political state and politics do not stop at the court house door. We knew that Stone, Pigman as well as the other involved firms would attempt to exercise influence on every aspect of the appeal procedure. We had some very heated discussions among ourselves as to whether separate counsel or additional counsel should be hired for the purposes of arguing the appeal. My friend John Litchfield, a very capable lawyer who had defended us in the frivolous action filed by Allan McDonnel, suggested that we hire his law partner, Joe Berrigan, to assist us. Berrigan, incidentally, was married to the former law partner of Camille Gravel, a well respected lawyer who had successfully defended Governor Edwin Edwards, so he was not without some valuable political connections and insights.

I discussed the matter with Frasier and Hickman and recommended that we engage Berrigan. Principally, this meant that we would pay him to sit with us and maybe argue part of the case, but that we would still do all the work. I was chiefly interested in using his name. For reasons I never completely understood, Frasier vehemently opposed the idea. He said we had made it this far with "just us," and that we should see it through with the same team that won the verdict.

Frasier had made very few mistakes in the four years that I had known him, and despite the fact that I probably could have overruled him on the matter of Berrigan, I remained silent out of respect for his experience and knowledge. As it turned out, this was one of the few times Frasier was wrong.

During 1993, I had casual conversations with some of the parties as to possible settlement; however, I had little success. Federal Insurance Company's in-house claims manager, who had followed the trial, did call me about possibly setting up a meeting to discuss settlement, but we both postured on the telephone, and my figures were apparently out of their reach.

The day the jury went out, September 10, 1991, the Federal Insurance Company's claims manager handling this case indicated that he had a package of nine hundred thousand dollars to one million dollars available to settle the case. We refused the offer. Our bottom line before trial was two million dollars.

We were finally given an oral argument date in November, 1993. Additionally, I received a motion in the mail to permit the procedure to be televised. Louisiana is one of the few states that does not automatically allow television cameras in court without a special order from the court granting permission. This was rarely done. In fact, to my knowledge, this court of appeals argument would be the first case in the history of Louisiana in which such a proceeding was filmed. We had no objections and neither did the defendants. Now, all there was to do was to wait to hear the names of the judges who would sit on the panel.

The judges selected for an appeals court panel serve on a regular rotation. None of the attorneys have any direct input as to their selection. We finally learned that Judge Patrick Schott, the Chief Judge of the Fourth Circuit Court and a conservative Roman Catholic, would sit on the panel. He also would probably emerge as the most influential member of the court. We next heard that Judge Charles Jones, a newly elected judge, was on the panel; the trio of jurists would be completed by Judge Robert Klees, another newly elected judge from St. Charles Parish. Jones was an African-American, but the other two judges were white.

With two new judges and a staunchly conservative jurist who would most likely run the show, it was a difficult panel for us to assess. The defendants felt otherwise, and for good reason. By unfortunate—for us—coincidence, every powerful law firm in the City of New Orleans had been involved one way or another with one of these defendants. The influence, once again, of the silk-stocking firms would most definitely be a factor during the appeal.

It would have been pleasant for us to have had the original three judges—particularly Judge Plotkin—on the panel that reversed the case and remanded it for trial, but the same panel could not be reappointed to hear the case after a trial on the merits. We knew we faced large problems.

Approximately two weeks before the oral arguments, we learned our fears were justified. We received a questionnaire from the court, in which we were asked to designate all points of defamation in the record. There

281

had been more than two or three hundred pages of briefs already written and filed with the court arguing what was defamatory and what was not, so to receive a questionnaire like this was not only puzzling, it was also frightening.

Plumb and I went back to the Fourth Circuit and went through the record in its entirety, extracting each quote and citing each volume number and page number of the transcript. We then sent a brief statement to the court listing everything that we believed to be defamatory and the location of the defamation in the record.

The day of the oral arguments was a Friday. We all gathered at the courthouse once again—Frasier, Hickman, Atkins, Stone, the Gormans, and me—but this time we had Nixon sitting in the courtroom observing as well. Nixon had moved back to Biloxi about a week before the oral argument, and he and his wife, Barbara, came over to watch.

Phil Wittmann again led off. He argued the issues of liability for the defendants; Lee Butler argued the principal damage questions for Federal Insurance, and Denise Pilié argued the coverage issues of Jimmy Swaggart Ministries. Renee Pastorich argued on Aetna's homeowners appeal, and Charles Boggs argued St. Paul's coverage appeal. I argued all issues for the plaintiffs.

It was more than a little ironic that in more than four years, Pilié and I had not agreed on anything, but now, we were agreeing on the point of Jimmy Swaggarts Ministries coverage. It was a pleasure having her agree with me on one issue. She and I had been combative during the entire case. She always had a snide remark to make about me and was usually condescending. Frasier often said she had a "thing" for me, and that was why she was being ugly: to cover it up.

We had given her a hard time whenever we could too. Once, I caught her in the lobby of the hotel in Chicago with her hand on her boyfriend's thigh. Another time, during the trial, she came out of the restroom with toilet paper stuck in her panty hose, dragging it behind her into the courtroom. We teased her about both incidents; she didn't seem to have much sense of humor around me, though.

Still, she was a fine lawyer, and she did an excellent job during the trial; it was often apparent that she was better prepared than most of her colleagues.

Wittmann was also a good lawyer, and he did a good job of presenting the appeal. But it seemed that most of the questions directed from the bench were directed toward me by Judge Schott.

It finally dawned on us, and shocked us as well, that Schott was again dancing around the question of subject matter jurisdiction. We thought this had been previously resolved by the Fourth Circuit in our 1988 appeal. Schott also had a problem with the fact that Cecil Janway had testified that the September 2 statement was performed in accordance with Scripture, and that we had not seemed to do much to impeach him as a witness.

This line of questioning was directed toward retrying the facts of the case, even though none of the panel had been present during the trial and were not witnesses to the demeanor and manner of those who testified. In our view, Janway belied his own credibility in the way he testified, not so much in the words he used but in his tone of voice and body language. He effectively impeached himself. We also knew this was true from our post-mortem conversations with the jury. Further, to attack Janway and reduce him verbally might well have made us look mean, and heartless, for Janway was obviously a sincere but seriously confused man, trying to be loyal to what he had been told was right.

None of this, of course, appeared in the transcript, and it wasn't possible to testify to it or even, really to argue it. In my opinion, Schott was clearly out of line in this line of inquiry. Nevertheless, he was following it, and he had license to do so.

In Louisiana, unlike most states, the courts possess a *de novo* right to review the evidence on appeal. But when politics are involved, it gives judges a chance to review the facts that have already been tried and adjudicated. In the context of a civil trial, this constitutes the equivalency of double jeopardy, wherein a jury can decide a case on the preponderance of the evidence, but then have their decision rescinded strictly by virtue of a reexamination of the evidence by a judicial panel. This panel might simply change the verdict out of whim, even though they have nothing to go on but the transcript and the exhibits. It was unfair, but there it was, and there was no way around it.

Judge Jones' line of questions concerned the issues of damages and were directed more towards Lee Butler and others. It became apparent to me from the nature of his queries that Jones was on our side, while Schott was on the other side. We couldn't get a reading on the third judge. But we all knew that Schott was the big kahuna in this court and that his influence would be profound on two freshman judges.

After oral arguments, we were once again faced with the press. This time, we remained businesslike, conducted our interviews and started to leave. Wittmann, though, claimed victory, so I had to speak up and do the same. The truth was, I had no idea how things were going. I had no sense of the panel or what it might do. Everyone speculated that things would go in our favor, but for some reason I couldn't define, I was uneasy about the entire process. Over the next thirty to sixty days, settlement discussions continued; I was becoming more and more interested in hearing the defendants' postures.

We anticipated an opinion by Christmas, but we were disappointed.

The court remained quiet. I talked to the clerk of the court, who incidentally was Judge Schott's daughter, and she assured me we would have an opinion by the first of the year. We didn't. Finally, in the second week of January, we received a notice from the court. The judges were split on the issue of liability. We figured that Judge Jones was for us, and Judges Schott and Klees were against us. It was not a healthy split. This meant that the entire case would have to be re-argued before a five-judge panel.

The reargument was set in February. Somehow we would have to convince the two new judges assigned to the panel, Judge Moon Landrieu, former Director of Housing and Urban Development under the Jimmy Carter Administration, as well as former Mayor of New Orleans, and Judge Byrnes; or we would have to convert the two judges who were already against us. I knew we would never change Judge Schott's mind; this left us with the thankless task of having to convince two judges completely new to the case that the verdict, as rendered, was both correct and fair.

Given Judge Schott's attitude, this meant only one thing, we effectively would have to present our case all over again. It was a proposition that almost made me sick to contemplate, but there was no way to avoid it: We were back to square one.

• CHAPTER TWENTY-SIX •
THE SETTLEMENT

"Wherefore, gird up the loins of your mind, be sober, and hope to the end for the grace that is to be brought unto you at the revelation of Jesus Christ."
—*The First Epistle General of Peter, 1:13*

Personal experience dictated that our chances of winning the appeal and breaking the stalemate by changing Judge Schott's mind were thin. That meant we would have to focus on the two new judges, try to convince them that the jury's verdict had been both correct and fair.

I was not without some political influence myself; by comparison, though, it was minuscule. I had given our State Treasurer, Mary Landrieu, Judge Moon's daughter, a contribution toward her unannounced gubernatorial campaign. I also had previously arranged a dinner party for Mary Landrieu at my house the night following the date scheduled for the rehearing. That was a pure coincidence, but I was now hopeful that Landrieu would put in a good word for me with her father, although I would never be so bold as to ask her to do so.

Meanwhile, both sides were still talking about the possibility of settlement, and we agreed to a conference on the afternoon before the oral argument was scheduled for rehearing.

In February 1994, David Adler, the Trustee in Chief for Marvin Gorman and Marvin Gorman Ministries, Inc., Tomy Frasier, and I met in Adams & Reese's office. We knew if the Fourth Circuit on rehearing overturned the verdict, our only recourse would be to take the case to the Louisiana Supreme Court. That would be an uphill battle all the way, with a major struggle waiting for us once we arrived. *If* we arrived.

However, we did believe that the Supreme Court would grant a writ and hear the case. It was too politically charged and newsworthy to ignore. We also thought the defendants believed that as well. I was almost certain that the defendants had some type of inside information on this Fourth Circuit panel and felt much better about their position than we did.

285

They were more concerned with what the Supreme Court might do than what the Fourth Circuit was going to do on rehearing.

Charles Boggs had run a computer search on every opinion that Judge Schott had written in his career as a presiding judge on the Fourth Circuit. His statistics demonstrated that Schott had been reversed in only fifteen percent of his cases. Additionally, Judge Schott had been the author of a couple of other cases involving the First Amendment and had taken a very conservative approach to protect the church from interference by any state entity. It didn't seem to matter to him that his church was one which Jimmy Swaggart had condemned as being non-Christian. Schott was a strict reader of the Constitution, and in his mind, the church was the church, whether it was Roman Catholic, Assembly of God, or some cultist gathering on the fringe of a golf green in Baton Rouge.

Hickman and I spoke by telephone before the day of the settlement conference, since he couldn't be present. He said that if we could get two million dollars, we should get out of the case. Frasier, on the other hand, was adamant about demanding a great deal more money. I knew that he wasn't prompted by greed. He had plenty of money and was a gambler by habit. The issue for him never did concern money; it concerned principle.

Gorman's point of view was that we needed to maintain the upper hand. He had won the verdict and restored his good name; he had never thought he would make any money out of this case, but he did not want to lose what he had gained through the verdict's victory.

Frasier and I had taken this case on a fifty percent contingency fee with the Bankruptcy Trustee. The court approved that contract because the case was risky for us. We had the same fifty-fifty agreement with Gorman. However, the court had made us finance the case ourselves, and we were doing so from that contingency fee. We had received a large sum in settlement from the insurance company before trial and had used it to pay part of our expenses, hoping to recoup our other costs and pay ourselves on the appeal.

It was apparent, though, when the Fourth Circuit split and we went for rehearing that we had lost some of our leverage. Nevertheless, we spent hours shouting at one another in the settlement conference. The defendants dug in and refused to budge from a $1.5 million offer. That was not nearly what we had wanted in the case, but it was the most that ever had been offered since the suit was filed in 1987.

About two o'clock that afternoon, Frasier seemed to tire. He told me to keep him posted and went back to his hotel. He didn't want to take the $1.5 million, but he would defer to whatever decision I made. Adler was antsy and would have taken one million dollars, maybe less, out of a fear that in the rehearing, he could lose it all. I suggested that we go back one more time and make another stab with a bottom line of two million dollars.

The defendants refused to agree, but they did come up to a higher figure. As that meeting commenced, I casually mentioned that I had to leave early and return to Lake Charles, where I was hosting a dinner party for Mary Landrieu. I sensed that their sudden willingness to move upwards from $1.5 million might have been stimulated by that news.

David Adler, the Trustee, and I left the room to allow them privacy to reconsider, and after a bit, Butler found us and suggested a new figure. Adler indicated that he wanted to take it; since it was his case—that is, since he was our client—he had the authority to do so. I telephoned Gorman and talked to him on the phone and he agreed. He said he wanted this matter over with, done, out of his life. And he wanted to go out a victor. This settlement would allow him to do that.

I called Frasier at the hotel, but he said for me to do nothing until he called me back. Five minutes later, he rang and said "Fine, do it." From his tone of voice, I knew that he was not at all happy about the settlement; it was probably the first time in all these years Tomy was truly disappointed in me.

I didn't feel, though, that we had a clear choice. The odds were well stacked against us at the Fourth Circuit Court, and both Adler and Gorman wanted to put an end to the case. My duty, I felt, was to listen to my clients' wishes and do as they instructed me. I agreed with Frasier that the principle here was important, but it was foolhardy to jeopardize what we had won simply to make a philosophical point.

And there was another consideration as well. In the past few years, Gorman had built up momentum in his ministry again; any negative publicity now would certainly have been a setback.

We went back into the room and shook hands with all the lawyers and agreed to the settlement with the understanding that it would have to be drafted and approved by the bankruptcy court. The parties immediately roughed out a draft of a settlement which was circulated inside. Approximately a month later I went to bankruptcy court and made a statement to the court why this settlement was in the best interest of the creditors. There were no objections, and the court approved it. We received the funds in May and disbursed them. This brought an end to the litigation.

True to his instincts, Marvin Gorman did not make a dime.

After more than five years of work, sacrifice, pain, embarrassment, anxiety, and worry, it was finally over: the gavel had fallen the last time on the question of *Marvin Gorman vs Jimmy Swaggart, et al.* I know Frasier was disgusted that it ended the way it did and I have to confess to something of a letdown myself; but it was hardly a question of ending with a whimper rather than a bang. We proved what we set out to prove, that Jimmy Swaggart was a liar and a self-righteous hypocrite; we proved that Marvin Gorman, a human being, was capable of recognizing the wrong in his life and correcting it to his and his family's and followers' satisfaction; we proved that it doesn't take a fancy legal office and political connections to win a case in a big-city court; and we proved that wit, determination, hard work, and a dedication, when combined with a commitment to the truth as we believed it, can prevail over anything.

In that sense, and in every other sense that mattered—except money, perhaps—justice was served. And money, the central, driving force behind this entire case, the cause of the whole thing, was never, in my mind, an issue.

• EPILOGUE •
REVIVAL AND BENEDICTION

"They that dwell under his shadow shall return; they shall revive *as* the corn, and grow as the vine . . ."
—*Hosea, 14:7*

No one but Marvin Gorman and Lynda Savage knows what happened in that motel room that fateful night in 1978. Was she distraught, suicidal, desperate for any male's attention, especially Gorman's? Was she naked? Did she surprise him with her sexuality, her sensuality? Did he succumb? Did he stop himself before the act was completed, chastise his wicked sister in Christ, then flee the room, still faithful to his mission, his faith? Did they then renew their sexual adventures? Did they see each other regularly, copulate in the pews and choir lofts of the church? Did they find secret motels to hide their sinful lust? Or did Gorman tell her continually to straighten out her life, to leave other men alone, to find solace in her marriage, to seek forgiveness of God?

No one knows. It is possible that neither Gorman nor Savage knows either. It is possible that the version of events they give is actual in their minds. Although, in reality, neither is precisely accurate.

The point is that only Marvin Gorman knows what is in his heart. And no lawyer, judge, or jury can sit in judgment over that. That will always remain between Gorman and God.

Throughout the trial of Marvin Gorman, I chose to believe his version of events. I believe them to this day. Almost nothing short of Gorman's confession that he deliberately deceived me could sway me from that commitment, that belief. But at the same time, I am aware that Gorman may not be completely level with himself, and it is that doubt that keeps me waking up in the middle of the night from time to time, wondering if my commitment to him, to his truth, falls somehow short of what God and only God knows is the true truth.

In any event, I take solace in the notion that I did what I was called

289

to do and did it as well as I was able. I stepped between a man and his accusers and demanded justice before the bar. As a lawyer, this was my job, my commitment, both ethically and practically. And I was successful. Questions of whether what I did was right in a moral or spiritual sense will have to wait for another day, a day when we all will be called before a higher and more profound bar of justice, a day when we are all called to answer for all our sins.

Following the settlement, Jimmy Swaggart returned to his ministry on a full-time basis. Although diminished in the national eye and no longer the television power that he once was, he continues to purchase airtime through his corporation and to conduct his affairs from his palatial mansion and offices near the Baton Rouge Country Club. He also continues to preach from his "naked platform" in the Family Worship Center, and continues, doubtless, to do the Tennessee Trot.

He is not frequently sought by talk show hosts and reporters from the national media, but his following continues to be strong, and his corporation continues to be profitable. The "nickels and dimes" of the faithful continue to come in, though not to the degree they once did. The Jimmy Swaggart Ministries sign that has been on Interstate 10 for many years has been removed, and many of the buildings in the Swaggart complex have been leased to agencies of the State of Louisiana. In the fall of 1997, John Camp, a long time nemesis of Jimmy Swaggart, with CNN Impact reported that Jimmy Swaggart Ministries was still worth over one hundred million dollars and that the ministry had just purchased five new Mercedes-Benz automobiles.

He still lashes out at other ministers from time to time, but he more or less confines his comments to matters of doctrine, not personalities, and he is careful never to attack the personal behavior of his rivals for religious supremacy.

The revelation of Swaggart's sin on Airline Highway had little long-lasting impact on the minister's outward personality or conduct. Insofar as anyone outside his inner circle knows, he has never sought counseling for his weakness for prostitutes or for his alleged sexual deviancies. Indeed, within two weeks of the trial's conclusion, he was stopped in Southern California for solicitation. In 1997, he was seen at the Red Light District of Port Allen, Louisiana. Nevertheless, he maintains his close ties to his former associates and allies within the Assembly of God.

Tomy Frasier remains in Tulsa, Oklahoma, where he is the leading spokesperson for the Oklahoma Trial Lawyers and one of the strongest lobbyists for Oklahoma Bar Association. However, Tomy has had repeated bouts of ill health and hospitalizations which have disabled him even more. His spine has continued to degenerate, affecting his ability to sit up straight in the wheelchair. This also has affected his ability to speak clearly. Since the trial, he has had heart surgery and a recommendation for a second operation.

But he is still the same Tomy Dee. He goes into the office on a regular basis, drives his own vehicle, takes phone calls and brings in business for the Frasier firm. Tomy's days as a trial lawyer, however, ended the Summer of 1991 in New Orleans, Louisiana. *Marvin Gorman vs. Jimmy Swaggart, et al.* marked his last court appearance. I think now that he knew it would.

Since our disagreement over whether or not to accept the settlement, Frasier and I were never quite as close as we were during the four years of the trial and preparation. It was an "all or nothing" program for him, and I am certain that he was disappointed in my acceptance of the defenses offer. As a result, I believe, we can never have the same close relationship that we shared at one time. But I still love him, admire him above any other attorney I've ever met. He was—and remains—my mentor; he taught me how to advocate.

Steve Hickman is still Frasier's partner and is now one of the leading principals in the firm Frasier & Frasier & Hickman.

Milo Nickel is a partner in another Lake Charles firm and seems to be doing well for himself, his wife and three children.

My brother, Matt Lundy, the brief writer, has become an excellent trial lawyer in his own right and is now running our Houston law office.

During the course of the trial, Denise Pilié became a partner in the Stone, Pigman firm. I run into her from time to time, and our meetings are always cordial. Wayne Lee has continued to receive honors as one of the most outstanding black graduates of Tulane University Law School, and he and I frequently meet at political fundraisers.

Phil Wittmann is still considered one of the best trial lawyers in the Southeast. After finishing the Swaggart trial in September 1991, he went into a trial in Baton Rouge, Louisiana, representing International Paper Company and remained on that case until January 1992. My opinion of Phil Wittmann rose tremendously after realizing that he was able to come out of one ten-week trial and go immediately into another marathon legal battle. Phil and I see each other often in New Orleans; he referred a couple of cases to me in southwest Louisiana that had come to him for representation, and each time made very flattering comments that made me believe that despite the emotional rollercoaster, I did succeed in gaining the respect of a very talented and well-schooled lawyer and a major representative of the Crescent City's silk-stocking firms.

Bill Treeby is still practicing law with Phil Wittmann but is no longer representing Jimmy Swaggart Ministries. I am told that Treeby bites his tongue and turns shades of red when he hears my name in public places.

The last we heard, Lynda Savage was living in Lubbock, Texas, with

David.

As for me, my professional practice has prospered. The case provided me millions of dollars of free advertisement and was a great stimulant for my career. I have been sought out all over the South to provide legal advice in First Amendment cases. The Lundy & Dwight firm became the Lundy & Davis law firm in 1993 and has now become a regional law firm with offices in Lake Charles, Louisiana, Houston, Texas and Jackson, Mississippi. We have gone from two attorneys in 1987 to fifteen in 1996. My practice still consists of personal injury work with an occasional defamation or First Amendment case on referral. In 1996, I left the practice of law for a brief stint in politics. I ran for Congress and out of a field of eight, made the runoff by the second closest margin in Congressional history. Although, I lost the runoff to Chris John, the experience was positive and has resulted in blessings to me and my family. I am back in the law practice, enjoying it more than ever.

I never know how to react, though, when I am introduced in Louisiana or elsewhere as "the lawyer who brought down Jimmy Swaggart." I'm never certain if the speaker is paying me a compliment, or about to curse me for harming "God's Evangelist."

Twelve years after his resignation as pastor of the First Assembly of God of New Orleans, his confession of adultery, his loss of credentials from the Assemblies of God and ultimate bankruptcy, Marvin Gorman has returned to the basics of his original ministerial calling. He now pastors a church called the Temple of Praise. It is housed in the same building on Elysian Fields Avenue where Gorman first preached when he moved to New Orleans in 1965.

Gorman has also returned to the old-fashioned tent revivals, acknowledging that his sin of temptation was not so much the temptation of the flesh, but in fact was the temptation of power and greed associated with his desire to become a high-ranking church official. Today he seems content to drive a Toyota Camry instead of his big Buick, and he has no desire to own a Lincoln or Cadillac. He and Virginia live in a more modest home, enjoy a less lavish lifestyle from that they had before.

But he is no less charismatic, no less effective in the pulpit. He is still devoted to his calling and has as much altar appeal as he had ten years ago when he was in the prime of his career. Thus, the services on Elysian Fields are as emotionally enhanced as they were a decade ago. The singing, the swaying, the tears, the chorus of individuals speaking in tongues, and the altar calls are as powerful now as ever.

At the Temple of Praise, Marvin preaches to a congregation of all colors and nationalities. He has also begun a special Hispanic ministry by hiring a pastor who is affluent in Spanish to hold special services.

Outwardly, it would seem that Gorman and his family are up and rolling once again. On November 20, 1994, the *Times Picayune* published an extensive story on him and the chronology of events surrounding his ordeal. It turned out to be a most positive front-page story for the Sunday Metro Section. Entitled, "Survival and Revival," the reporter states, "Marvin Gorman says his troubles with temptation put his head straight." In more than a manner of speaking, that is accurate.

Gorman extends his ministry beyond the boundaries of The Temple of Praise. He goes out into the street, seeking people in need of help, both spiritual and otherwise. Although Gorman has a radio program once again and frequently purchases television air time, his focus today is directed to his church's immediate ministry in Orleans Parish. There is no talk of satellite dishes or international church politics, no private jet, no deals with convicted criminals for millions of sequestered dollars.

However, there are still ambitions in Gorman's plans for the future, modest though they are. He hopes to find a way to purchase the building on Airline Highway where the First Assembly of God was located for twenty years, where he realized the height of his former earthly glory. He hopes to repay his community for supporting him, to justify their faith in him.

Gorman's present ministry is joined by his son, Randy; his daughter, Beverly; son-in-law, Garland; and many of other people who have been with him over the years, who stood by him in his hour of crisis. His other, younger son, Mark, has become a popular evangelist in his own right and has his own worldwide ministry. Mark Gorman preaches primarily in independent Full Gospel churches around the world and has no apparent ambitions to "pander" to the Assemblies of God.

In the *Times Picayune* article, Gorman was quoted as saying, "There's nothing motivating me today except the call of God to reach out to hurting, and I'm not angry at anybody or mad at anybody." He also acknowledged that at one time he was a renowned personality in the great city of New Orleans. If he weren't, the *Times Picayune* wouldn't have been at his doorstep trying to get a front page story. Marvin also points out, ironically, that when he dies, the obituary in the paper probably will not read that a man devoted to God and the children of God died, but that a man who fell from grace and was at the center of a religious scandal had finally passed on. However, I don't believe that is the way things will turn out.

I personally believe God used Marvin Gorman's sin to bring a man of the cloth who had been blinded by ego and ambition face to face with his own human frailty. I also am convinced that Gorman's witness may have been harmed by his acknowledged sin, but that his character and faith prevailed. I believe that he found his lesson in the lessons of Scripture, in the lessons of Moses, King David, Solomon, St. Peter, St.

Paul, and of all those biblical figures who sinned, who asked forgiveness, and who were blessed by the love and "peace that passeth understanding."

Today, Marvin Gorman has been humbled before God. He still makes a decent living from his ministry, can still be found in an airport, traveling to some distant church where a handsome honorarium will be paid for his wisdom, his deliverance of the message. He still seeks the nickels and dimes of the faithful to finance his work. But he can also be found elsewhere. He might well be spied in a shabby "no-tell motel" lobby, at the counter of a greasy Canal Street diner, or even the back booth of some French Quarter bar, sharing his testimony of the Gospel, holding the hand of some repentant sinner, praying for the salvation of some wayward soul, and beseeching God to forgive and bless us all.

If there is one single lesson in the Gospel for everyone, then that, perhaps, is it.